CANDLELIGHT
Ecstasy Supreme

"THIS IS IT! THE LAST STRAW! THE DEALS ARE OVER AND DONE WITH. I COULD KILL YOU!"

"You're my responsibility," Dan said in return, "and that makes it my business. You're not going to make a fool out of yourself on my time!"

Alex stood dead still, feeling her fury run through her bloodstream. "Like I said, D'Alesio, the deal is off. I'm walking. And then it will be my time."

"And what about your father?"

Her head was spinning. Suddenly, as angry as she was, she was ready to cry. "I can raise an expedition on my own," she said coolly. "I'll send for my things."

"You're not walking," he promised in a quiet but heated tone. "We went through all this at Ali's. The deal was that we see it through together. Just consider it a deal you really made with the devil, Doctor. No backing out once the papers are signed."

CANDLELIGHT ECSTASY SUPREMES

ARABIAN NIGHTS

Heather Graham

A CANDLELIGHT ECSTASY SUPREME

Published by
Dell Publishing Co., Inc.
1 Dag Hammarskjold Plaza
New York, New York 10017

For my cousin JC and Gail Spence

Dell ® TM 681510, Dell Publishing Co., Inc.

Candlelight Ecstasy Supreme is a trademark of Dell
Publishing Co., Inc.

Candlelight Ecstasy Romance®, 1,203,540, is a registered
trademark of Dell Publishing Co., Inc.

ISBN: 0-440-10214-6

Printed in the United States of America
First printing—August 1984

To Our Readers:

Candlelight Ecstasy is delighted to announce the start of a brand-new series—Ecstasy Supremes! Now you can enjoy a romance series unlike all the others—longer and more exciting, filled with more passion, adventure, and intrigue—the stories you've been waiting for.

In months to come we look forward to presenting books by many of your favorite authors and the very finest work from new authors of romantic fiction as well. As always, we are striving to present the unique, absorbing love stories that you enjoy most—the very best love has to offer.

Breathtaking and unforgettable, Ecstasy Supremes will follow in the great romantic tradition you've come to expect *only* from Candlelight Ecstasy.

Your suggestions and comments are always welcome. Please let us hear from you.

Sincerely,

The Editors
Candlelight Ecstasy Romances
1 Dag Hammarskjold Plaza
New York, New York 10017

PROLOGUE

UPI—July 5

WORLD RENOWNED EGYPTOLOGIST PLANS EXPEDITION

The eminent Egyptologist Dr. James Crosby recently announced plans for an expedition into the Valley of the Kings. The dig will be financed by the affluent Sheikh Ali Sur Sheriff of the United Arab Emirates. The expedition will be filmed by broadcast journalist Daniel D'Alesio, who recently brought to television audiences around the world the news documentaries "The Middle East. Past and Present Crisis," "Is the Cold War Growing Hot?" and "Central and South America: What Should the American Role Be?"

D'Alesio has had a continuing interest in filming a documentary on ancient Egypt, but until now, Dr. Crosby has refused to allow his expeditions to be filmed.

D'Alesio, owner and operator of his production company, writes, directs and narrates his films. Scholars and political scientists worldwide consider his total commitment to excellence the key factor in his outstanding indepth news reporting.

Dr. Crosby will have an assistant for his search for the tomb of Anelokep.

When asked about the "death curse" associated with the tomb of the Eighteenth Dynasty king, Crosby said, "I wouldn't be searching for a respectable burial chamber if there was not a death curse associated with it!" He insisted that the deaths associated with the discovery of Tutankhamen's tomb in the 1920s were merely coincidental.

Crosby stated that he is more concerned with the twentieth-century curse of greed. "There is a fierce black market in the field of Egyptian antiquities," Crosby stated. "A single relic from a tomb is priceless—but there are private collectors willing to pay any price for select pieces. This type of avarice, in which obsession often overrules the value of human life, is far more frightening than the thought of ancient curses."

The slim blond man reading the paper as he walked through the Abu Dhabi airport was both very handsome and very out of place among the dark Arab businessmen bustling through the terminal. But that was in appearance only. James Crosby loved his travel through the Arab nations, spoke the language and knew the culture well. Usually he loved the hubbub that so often surrounded him; but today he barely noticed it.

It wasn't the newspaper article that bothered him but what had been happening that made him uneasy. He had been followed in Egypt; he was being followed here. And he was being followed by more than one person.

He stopped suddenly and stared across the small lobby at a public phone. He shrugged and thought that he would never get a call out in the time he had, and he would be seeing her tomorrow night . . . just a little more than twenty-four hours from now.

But he wanted to talk to Alex. He suddenly felt it urgent that he let her know she had the same information he did.

He walked determinedly to the phone. To his amazement, he was able to put his call through. But even as he waited to be connected across the miles, the feeling of uneasiness started sweeping through him.

He heard her voice across the miles, startled, but sweet, so very sweet to his ears. At least he would be able to say what was necessary. . . .

CHAPTER ONE

Tomorrow, Alex thought, a sweep of excitement seeming to swell within her like an ocean tide, I will be in Paris. And then I will be in Cairo, and I will see Dad, and we'll start searching . . . living out a dream.

And I can talk to Dad about another dream. Wayne. Maybe now is the time for all dreams to come true.

Stop it! she railed at herself. Wayne was nothing but a dream, and her divorce from him had been a nightmare.

That thought reminded her that she was sitting at her desk, staring at a half-finished page that had to be completed if she was ever going to leave the museum.

There was nothing, she told herself dryly, quite like thinking about Wayne to bring her back to reality. The cold, hard facts about Wayne brought her crashing back down to earth so that she could forget her fingers were quivering with excitement and get back to the tedious paperwork. She placed her fingers on the typewriter keys and picked up with her next paragraph.

"Only the pharaohs were entitled to life after death in the Old Kingdom, as exemplified by the three Great Pyramids at Giza, the Step Pyramid and other grand structures built during this era. By the dawning of the New Kingdom, after Egypt had broken into various sections and been restored to glory by the kings of Thebes, it was accepted that all men might seek an afterlife. Still, it was the rich and powerful who went to their final resting places with the greatest display of grandeur. The more a man had, the more he *would* have for his rebirth after the judgment of Osiris. It was from these dynasties, beginning with the eighteenth (1570–1300 B.C.), that we are bequeathed the

'Valley of the Kings,' and hence the forever famed discovery of Tutankhamen's tomb by the determined archeologist Howard Carter in 1922.

"Many believe that the treasures of 'Tut' were the last that remained to be discovered by contemporary man. Still, there remains documentation of eighteenth-dynasty kings who remain mysteries. One of these is Anelokep, a man who reigned for approximately a decade. He was terrified of grave robbers and left this threat: 'He who enters here shall be avenged by the gods, and by myself. My *ka* [soul] and my *ba* [physical vitality, believed to flee at the moment of death] shall remain to protect that which goes with me, which assures my comforts through eternity!'"

Alex finished typing and pulled the sheet from her typewriter to add to the papers in the folder on her desk. She glanced up to see that the offices were empty. She smiled as she remembered that several of her co-workers had stopped to tell her good-bye and wish her good luck.

After gathering her things, she left her office and listened to the eerie echo of her heels in the empty hallways. The guards were still on duty, of course, and they nodded to her as she passed out of the building and hurried to her car.

The summer heat was so intense that the asphalt on Michigan Avenue shimmered. To the east, Lake Michigan itself appeared to be an eternity of indigo crystal; the air was heavy and humid.

But as she left the museum parking lot and battled her way through the hectic late-afternoon traffic, Alex gave no thought to her present environment. Her mind was on a different heat— that of the desert. As she waited at red lights, vaguely hearing the impatient honks of numerous horns, she made a mental checklist. Yes, she was ready to leave. She was packed, she had copies of all the documents Jim had requested, and she had her passport and tickets in order.

She sighed softly as a red light turned green and she shifted her small Datsun from neutral to first, then back to neutral as the traffic again snagged. She started her checklist all over again. She had a very meticulous mind, so there was no reason to make a checklist, but reviewing her plans kept her from thinking about

Wayne, and she didn't want to think about Wayne again. A year ago the divorce had been final. She had learned to live without him, and now, suddenly, she had heard from him again. "Perhaps we can talk, Alex. Negotiate our problems. Learn to compromise. . . ."

How she would love that to be possible! She had handled the divorce with quiet dignity; few knew how deeply it had wounded her.

But she had loved Wayne, and even when she discovered he hadn't loved her enough to be either faithful or encouraging of her career, she had missed him with an excruciating pain that seemed to eat at her physically. She had managed to be strong and realistic, fully aware that a relationship could not be full—or even decent—with one partner giving up everything.

But if he wanted to come back, would she still be strong enough to resist him? There had been times when it had been so incredibly beautiful between them, times when she knew that he did love her, and appreciate her, and find her irresistible.

Don't be an ass! she warned herself. If he was reaching out to "negotiate" now, it was only because Jim was on to a find that might rock the world beyond the discovery of Tutankhamen's tomb decades ago.

"Back to the checklist, girl," she whispered softly.

But thinking of the checklist meant thinking about Egypt again; and thoughts of Egypt made her remember how Wayne had hated her enthusiasm in his field of expertise—a field that had been her own since she had been a little girl.

Wayne wanted fame—and a wife who would sit in the background. He had never wanted her to use her degrees; they should merely have left her competent to join in his conversations when he entertained others in the academic world.

But maybe I'm wrong, she told herself. Maybe he understands now. Maybe he really wishes to remarry, to make our marriage a partnership, to believe that I will not tolerate his casual infidelities.

He had been shocked when she actually filed divorce papers. He knew that she loved him. He had signed the papers but had not contacted her at all in the past year. There had not even been the recriminations she had expected.

Nothing, Alex thought bitterly. Nothing at all. Because of Wayne, she had been unable to date, unable even to enjoy a cup of coffee with another man other than a colleague.

Logically she tried to tell herself that Wayne hadn't changed, but as little strings seemed to pull at her heart, she also argued that she was being illogical and closed-minded not to give him the benefit of the doubt. And she still loved him. That was actually the deciding factor. If he wanted to talk, she would be willing to listen.

Finally she reached her apartment building. When she opened her mailbox there were two letters. The first, with its Egyptian stamps—a row of sleek portraits of a bust of Queen Nefertiti—caught her attention immediately. She hurried into her apartment and ripped open the envelope as she entered the living room, plopped down her shoulder bag and research folders and sank into the caramel-colored sofa.

Dear Alex,

I am riding on a cloud of exhilaration so incredibly high that sometimes I am afraid I shall explode with it. I read over a papyrus in the Cairo museum that I had read a dozen times—and there it was! The final proof! The burial chamber of Anelokep, eighteenth-dynasty Theban king, *is* in the Valley of Kings! I am no longer going on conjecture, Alex, but on documented proof. All the little clues tied together— I had just stared at them so long that I was blind to the piece in the puzzle that made it a whole! Between the hieroglyphics you deciphered in the Field museum and the papyrus here, the story is told.

I can hardly wait for you to get here. It is really more your victory than mine. After all, it was you who first insisted against all expert opinion that another unplundered tomb could exist—did, in fact, exist—and that the mystery of Anelokep could be solved in the Valley of the Kings.

Alex, the characters with whom I've become involved are right out of Arabian nights! Ali Sur Sheriff is as extraordi-

14

nary as any movie sheikh racing across the desert upon his black stallion. He has a running feud with another nearby sheikh of the same emirate—Omar Khi Haman—and he too is out of a fantasy. Potbellied and jowled, he sits upon his satin pillows while his harem girls pare his fingernails all day! (Here, dear Alex, I realize you are gritting your teeth and huffing away in your mind about the ill use of the female gender! But we are talking about a different world, as well you know.)

Anyway, this Sheikh Haman has become interested in me because Sheikh Sheriff is financing my "mysterious" project! Mysterious? For the moment, I suppose so. I fear what could happen if those of—what shall I say?—crasser values? —should discover exactly where I am going until I am ready to be there. The wealth, both material and historical, that we will find will be beyond the imagination!

As for Dan D'Alesio, he is nothing less than pure energy, Alex. Intense, striking, brilliant—not even his fantastic programs can give you a true picture of the man himself. But then I've mentioned before how I admire him. I guess I'm still attempting to find a way to describe him on paper. He's mercurial, magnetic, hypnotic! (Of course, I suppose he could also be described as quicksand—he suckered me into agreeing that he could join me with his film crew!)

Ah . . . the desert! And the Arab world and the history of the ancients unfolding. The sky at night is indigo velvet, littered with stars seemingly so close you could reach out and touch them. Enigma and mystery . . . and ever-elusive danger!

I hear via the grapevine that your ex-husband has been snooping around. You're an adult, Alex, so I won't give you a lecture. I'll just remind you that you're a beautiful and bright young woman, and your life stretches before you. You deserve nothing less than the best.

Since I shall see you soon, I will end here. Oh—if anything should go wrong, get hold of Sheikh Sheriff. I am on my way to the UAE now to see him. A few things are making me a little nervous. Our compelling Mr. Dan D'Alesio is the link to the sheikh.

See you at the Cairo airport, July 6, ten P.M. Don't be late!

Love,
James

Alex smiled as she refolded the letter and carefully replaced it in the envelope. Tingles of excitement raced furiously up and down her spine. She didn't doubt Jim for a second—he knew where he would discover the tomb of Anelokep. And she would be there.

It was the ultimate fantasy. Since she had been a child and first heard Jim weave tales of the mystical and awesome wonders of ancient Egypt, she had dreamed of just such a discovery. Since she had first seen the Pyramids of Giza and the Sphinx standing a silent, ageless sentinel, she had known her life would be dedicated to the quest of new understanding of the people who had created such indestructible magic.

"I'll be there right on time, Jim," she whispered tenderly to the letter as she stuffed it into her bag. I wouldn't miss it for the world. She leaned her head back against the sofa and closed her eyes to dream again for a minute. A frown suddenly puckered her brow, and she pulled the letter out again.

"If anything should go wrong, get hold of Sheikh Sheriff . . . A few things are making me a little nervous. . . ."

Thanks, Jim, she thought. Now you're making me nervous. You can sure explain that paragraph to me when I get there!

Thoughtfully she refolded the letter a second time.

Only then did her eyes fall upon the second envelope she had drawn from her mailbox. Her heart seemed to leap and squeeze. It was from Wayne. She would recognize his chicken scrawl anywhere.

Slowly, hesitantly, almost as if it were a snake and would bite, she opened it.

Alex, Not Dear Alex, she thought dryly, just Alex:
Understand Jim is in Cairo and that you are going to

meet him. Happen to be in Luxor myself. Meet me in Cairo at
the Hilton on the seventeenth. I believe we can get it together.

Love you,
Wayne

Love you, love you, love you, love you. . . .

The words rang in her mind until she felt dizzy. Then she
twisted the envelope around. Yes, it too had Egyptian stamps;
she hadn't noticed them because she had seen Wayne's writing.

She swallowed and took a deep breath. I won't be in Cairo on
the seventeenth, she thought sickly, I'll be somewhere in the
Valley of the Kings.

She bit her lip and stood, stretching to shake off the painful
dizziness and churning in her stomach. Maybe I can get back to
Cairo for the day, she thought. Travel by the Nile was slow, but
now there were plenty of flights from Luxor.

"Don't let him ruin your life," Jim had warned.

She bit her lip again, then hurried to the cherrywood secretary
where she kept her correspondence. You are right, Jim; I am an
adult and I have spent my life studying and researching and
dreaming of just such a venture as ours.

She drew out a sheet of her monogrammed paper with the tiny
etched oasis scene in the far right corner.

Wayne [No Dear Wayne, just Wayne. Anyway, how had he
known she was going to be in Egypt? A lucky guess? He
knew her father, he knew her own expertise. If he had read
that James was bringing an assistant, wouldn't he expect it
to be her? It didn't really matter. When she saw him, she
could ask him. Right now she had to write a brief, noncom-
mittal note],

I'm sorry, I cannot make Cairo on the seventeenth. If you
wish, I will meet you in the dining room of the Luxor
Egyptian on same date.

*   *   *

17

She hesitated a long time before signing the short note. And then she brought her pen back to the paper.

Love,
Alex

Feeling satisfied with her solution—one that proclaimed her her own person and yet stated she would be willing to see him, Alex copied off the Luxor address on Wayne's envelope and applied postage to her letter. She would have to mail it first thing in the morning. She strode with light steps into her kitchen.

Life suddenly seemed incredibly beautiful—a dream in process of fulfillment, a chance to begin again.

Fifteen minutes later Alex brought a small broiled steak and a large salad with all the trimmings into the living room. For company she turned the TV on, not bothering to check the program listings.

It seemed strange that one of the men Jim had mentioned in his letter suddenly came to life before her.

Dan D'Alesio.

It was a rerun, the special on the different hotbeds of unrest in the Middle East, delving into the turmoils of centuries past which, never resolved, now exploded again and again.

It was an excellent documentary, and D'Alesio was good. He was a striking man, dark, well built and apparently agile. He climbed the cliffs of Afghanistan as well as the soldiers he accompanied. His report was intelligent and articulate and more. He gave it something—a rare insight.

Alex could understand why Jim had agreed to let him film the expedition.

She had never met D'Alesio, but Jim had been impressed by him at their first meeting. And she would be meeting him soon. For a totally inexplicable reason, she felt a tiny trail of chills shoot down her spine as D'Alesio's dark eyes seemed to meet hers across the barrier of the color screen.

They were powerful eyes, she thought, chuckling and giving herself a little shake. So dark, brooding, yet sharply alert. They

18

were jet; they were the intensity of slow-burning fire. They were cool, and yet they were a tempest.

Alex finished her steak and rose to carry her dishes into the kitchen. Meticulously she washed and dried them and tidied the kitchen. She wanted the apartment in perfect order before she left.

She showered and carried a few of her books into the bedroom, hoping to make it a very early night. She was susceptible to jet lag and therefore liked to fly across the Atlantic with an abundance of sleep behind her.

With a glass of wine at her side, she went over various notes, then idly thumbed the pages of a large pictorial book on ancient Egypt. But it was hard to concentrate on either her notes or the pictures. Her mind kept leaping from Jim to Wayne, from hieroglyphics to Wayne, from the Sphinx to Wayne. She even began to wonder if she should back out of the expedition. This was her chance to reconcile her personal life.

Don't be more of a fool than you've already been! she warned herself harshly, and as if in emphasis to the warning, the phone at her bedside began to ring stridently.

She answered it hastily. "Hello?"

"You were supposed to call!"

"Oh, Kelly! I'm sorry, I—"

"No excuses," Kelly said and chuckled, and as the soft, husky sound reached her, Alex shook her head slightly. Kelly's natural voice was incredibly sexy. She should have been doing voiceovers for escort services rather than compiling dinosaur bones all day.

"I am sorry. I forgot," Alex admitted ruefully.

"That's okay. I know your mind must be working overtime. I just wanted to wish you a great trip! And I wanted to warn you to look out for those desert sheikhs."

"Kelly," Alex said with a sigh, "I'll be in Cairo and Luxor. Believe it or not, there aren't a lot of sheikhs running around the Valley of the Kings!"

"What about Sheriff?"

"He lives in the United Arab Emirates, not Egypt."

"He lives where?"

Alex shook her head again with a small smile. Kelly could

probably rattle off full volumes on the subject of anthropology, but as to current affairs, she was woefully remiss.

"He lives on the Arabian Peninsula, Kelly, miles and miles from Cairo! He's financing Jim; he's not going on the expedition."

"Oh." Kelly sounded a little disappointed. "Actually I think it would be the best thing in the world for you if this sheikh were to gallop across the desert and sweep you onto his Arabian charger—"

"Kelly," Alex interrupted with a soft sigh. Her closest friend was a brunet beauty who loved men only next to dinosaur bones. They flocked to her by the score, and Kelly accepted and went through them as casually as she might a roll of paper towels. It was unthinkable to her that Alex, as a divorcée, could refuse even to date for a year.

"I've heard from Wayne," Alex said softly.

Her remark was greeted by silence, and then an explosion. "Alex, you're incredible. Most of the time, you are the strongest lady I know. You've got a smile cool enough to freeze a whole football team; half the men I know would give up ten years of their lives for a single date—yet you handle them like steel and turn to putty in the hands of Dr. Wayne Randall! Listen to me, kid. I'm not going to try to tell you that Wayne isn't dynamite-looking, or that he isn't personable. But Alex, you're even more dynamite-looking, and more personable. And smarter, which I think is what has always bothered Wayne!"

"Oh, come on, Kelly—"

"It's true, Alex. He's jealous of you."

"Don't you think he might have changed?"

Again Kelly hesitated. "It's possible. Are you going to see him?"

"Yes. Just to listen."

"There is no fool worse than a woman in love!" Kelly said with a snort.

"I'm not going to be a fool, Kelly. It half killed me to file for that divorce, but I did it."

"True. I think I'm still going to go light a few candles and pray that the desert sheikh carries you off! If you'd let yourself go a

20

little . . . I mean, honey, the only man you've ever known is Wayne. Give another man a chance and you might discover there are more fish in the sea."

Alex grimaced and asked dryly, "So you suggest an Arabian sheikh, huh? They're all Muslims, Kelly. I don't think I'd be happy as a fourth wife or as a harem girl!"

"Maybe not," Kelly mused with a solemnity that made Alex bite back her laughter. "Hey—what about D'Alesio?"

"What about him?"

"Well, he'll be filming the expedition. And I tell you, *that* is one hunk of a man. He makes me pant just watching him on TV. Dark, rough, rugged—he is raw sexuality, honey, he's—"

"He's married."

"D'Alesio? Uh-uh. He announced once on an interview show that his life was too hectic for a family." Kelly giggled. "What he meant was that he wasn't about to have any strings attached to slow him down. Ummm. Have an affair, Alex, a wild fling. Just don't lose your heart."

Alex sighed. "Kelly, it's already lost. And I'm certainly not in the mood for an affair."

"I'll bet D'Alesio could put you in the right mood."

An affair. Alex blinked, barely listening as Kelly droned on. She bolted upright in the bed and holding the phone between her ear and shoulder and jerked open her bedside drawer and begin delving with one hand through a pile of lingerie. On the bottom she finally found what she sought—the pills she had long ago stopped taking. As Kelly continued about D'Alesio, Alex engaged in a mental dilemma over another man.

She would be a fool to hop into bed with Wayne. It would be easy to do so . . . too easy. But it wouldn't solve the problems between them. But she loved him so much. Missed him so much. What if she couldn't resist temptation? She would be more of a fool if she took a chance on a pregnancy at this stage of the game.

She popped a tiny pill into her mouth and juggled the phone to wash it down with a sip of wine.

"Alex?" Kelly queried.

"I—I'm listening!" Alex lied quickly. "Umm . . . how do you know so much about D'Alesio and the expedition and all?"

21

"Don't you ever read the paper?"

"Yes, I usually do—and you usually don't!" Alex laughed. "Did you read the article?"

"You bet. Mike—you remember Mike, don't you, the race car driver?—called me up to point it out because he knows you're my friend. It gave me quite a thrill! You're the unnamed assistant! I know something UPI doesn't!" Kelly chuckled softly, then asked, "How come Jim didn't announce your name?"

"I'm really not sure, Kelly. He's been very secretive about a lot of things. There's bound to be some competition. He probably doesn't want much known about anything until we're halfway into the tomb."

"Umm . . . probably," Kelly said. "Oh, well, I'll let you get some sleep. Watch out for curses. And if a sheikh should come riding along, trip him, will ya? You need a little experience!"

"Very cute, Kelly. But thanks a lot. And I'll call you as soon as I get back!"

Alex had barely hung up the phone before it started ringing again. She picked up the receiver with a smile, certain Kelly had a few more last words of wisdom she had forgotten to give her.

"Okay, Kelly," Alex answered dryly, "What is it? Am I supposed to trip D'Alesio, too?"

There was a pause on the other end. "I certainly don't suggest it, honey. He's kind of a tough individual to trip!"

"Jim!" Alex exclaimed joyfully at the sound of the gentle and beloved voice. The line suddenly filled with static, and she closed her eyes as if somehow she might hear better. "Where are you, Jim? This is a terrible connection!"

"Abu Dhabi. United Arab Emirates," he responded a little impatiently. "Did you get my letter?"

"Yes—"

"Is your flight all set?"

"Yes, I'll be there."

"Good. I've heard via the professional grapevine that your ex has been getting in touch with you. You're an adult, honey, and I can't tell you what to do. I can only remind you that you're a stunning and bright woman and you've got an entire lifetime

22

ahead of you. Don't accept anything less than what you deserve —which is the best."

"You're sweet, Jim, but—"

"I've seen him, Alex. He's been in Egypt a couple of months, exploring something or other."

"Yes, I—"

"Don't miss out on the expedition, honey. If a man loved you, he'd want this opportunity for you."

"I'm not going to miss—"

"Good. Now listen to me, Alex. I want you to know that you have all the puzzle pieces. Do you understand me?"

"I what? The puzzle pieces? Jim, there's a lot of static on the line. Jim?"

The static suddenly stopped, shut off by a sharp click. "Jim?" Alex repeated. She was answered by a monotonous buzzing. The connection had been severed.

"Damnit!" she hissed, tapping furiously upon the phone with her fingers. The buzzing continued. Sighing with frustration, she stared at the phone, then tried the international operator. The call couldn't be traced any farther than the province of Abu Dhabi. Exasperated, Alex hung up the phone. How many people could have been calling Chicago from Abu Dhabi at that particular time? Not many, she would warrant.

For a while she tried to stare at the pictures again, hoping Jim would call back. But as the time passed, she grew drowsy and accepted the fact that the phone systems in the UAE must not be among the best. He had probably decided not to call back since he would be seeing her tomorrow night.

She finished her wine and plumped her pillow a little vengefully to take out her frustration, then closed her eyes and prayed for a decent night's sleep. She didn't want to dream about Wayne. A long time ago she had schooled herself not to think about him or her broken marriage, and she didn't want to start spending sleepless nights again because he had written. And she didn't want to worry about Jim. Little tingles of fear had touched along her spine when the connection had been broken, but she was sure she was being ridiculous. Nevertheless, it seemed to take her forever to doze off again.

23

When she did sleep she didn't dream of Wayne once. The visions that spun in her mind were of colossal statues, endless sand dunes and golden idols. She dreamed of massive puzzle pieces floating in space. And when she did dream of a man's face, it wasn't her ex-husband's. It was a deeply tanned face with piercing dark eyes, eyes that could impale one, eyes that could reach across space and touch someone. Stern, remote, yet vital and electric. The face and eyes would merge with visions of Bedouins racing across desert sands on Arabian stallions with majestic tails flying high. Sabers slashed the air as they rode, their Arabic chants riding high to the skies. . . .

None of the hodgepodge of dreaming mattered. Alex didn't remember it in the morning. She overslept and had to rush to dress and race against time to make her initial flight to Paris.

Once airborne, she was both too tired and too excited to dwell on either worries or dreams. Her real-life fantasy was just coming true, and she wouldn't worry about anything again until she reached the airport in Cairo.

Then she would worry herself sick. Because Jim would never show up.

CHAPTER TWO

The setting of the sun created a strange orange and golden glow in the western sky, a haze of color that seemed to shimmer with the cooling remnants of a shattering heat. The everlasting sand of the desert, which permeated even Cairo's central streets, seemed to combine with that strange color and shimmer. It was the twenty-third of July, and hot as could be in Cairo. The workday was ending; buses with passengers hanging precariously to windows and doors honked their way through the melee of traffic, humanity, chickens and occasional other animal life.

A taxi stopped in front of the Hotel Victoria, an establishment owned by British interests but operated by a pleasant crew of Egyptians. The man who exited the vehicle might have been Arabian himself, except perhaps for his height. In stocking feet he stood a few millimeters over six foot three. He was dark, and his hair went beyond jet. The mahogany of his eyes was so deep it too might be mistaken for black.

He was a man who was seldom at a standstill. A vital and passionate interest in life sizzled from those deep jet eyes, and even when he sat quietly, he seemed to emanate explosive energy. Those jet eyes were always alert. When seemingly half closed with laziness beneath jet lashes and thick arched brows, they were still assessing, probing, searing.

His features, taken separately, were not particularly handsome. His nose was long and a shade crooked due to a break in a college boxing match years before; his cheekbones were high but a shade too gaunt. His jaw was decidedly stubborn—square, determined and strong. His mouth was a curiosity; the full lips

25

were well shaped, but when he became angry, they could draw to a grim line as white as his eyes were black.

Yet whatever analysis could be made of his individual features, they somehow combined to make him a devastating man. Or perhaps the uniquely arresting quality had nothing to do with looks; it might have been that sheer, radiating vitality, creating an aura about the man that was so rugged and earthy, it was shattering.

He wouldn't have thought himself particularly vital as he alighted from the taxi that evening. Having just wrapped up background filming in the Valley of the Kings, he had returned to Cairo by way of the Nile on a barge and stopped briefly at Giza to oversee a few brief shots of the Great Pyramids. He felt as if he hadn't slept in a week, and he would have sworn under oath that he was wearing half the Sahara.

Hoisting his duffel bag, which now contained nothing but dirty clothing, over a khaki-clad shoulder, he overtipped the driver and stepped to the sidewalk in front of the Victoria. The hectic pace of the streets suddenly came to a lull as chanting voices rose from the minarets of the city's mosques. The cryers, or muezzins, were calling the Islams to evening prayer. All across the city, the followers of Muhammad would be turning to face Mecca.

Dan D'Alesio stopped himself for a minute, feeling the pulse of Cairo. He glanced toward the shimmering orange sky and grinned slightly, then strode on into the Victoria lobby.

She was a quaint old hotel, Victorian in fixture as in name, with an Old World graciousness Dan found charming. She hadn't the elegance of the Cairo Hilton, but she far surpassed it in character. Ceiling fans helped along the laboring air-conditioners and created the pleasant feeling of a breeze. An abundance of lovingly tended greenery fringed about carved wood railings and lattice-work and added to an atmosphere of gracious hospitality.

He hadn't planned to stop at the desk. He was dead tired and plagued by a curious problem. But Rajman was there and eagerly hailed him. "How was the filming, Mr. D'Alesio? Did you find Dr. Crosby?"

26

Dan grimaced and shook his head as he turned toward the curious Egyptian. Rajman's family owned the Victoria, and Raj usually acted as host for his father and helped manage the hotel. But when Dan came to town, Raj became his unofficial personal manager in Cairo with the full blessing of his father, who was proud to see his son beneath the wing of the respected journalist.

"The filming went as well as could be expected without the principal player. And I couldn't find out a damn thing about Crosby."

Rajman shook his head mournfully in return. "What do you think happened? I thought he was supposed to have met his assistant here two weeks ago and then called you—"

"He was. I don't know what happened, Raj," Dan interrupted tiredly. His lips compressed into a white line and he added softly, "But I am going to find out."

"I hope so," Rajman said fervently. "May Allah be merciful, I certainly hope so."

"Yeah. Well, listen, Raj, it's been a rough week. I'm going to head up and soak in a tub and get some sleep. Don't put any calls through, huh?"

Rajman, his huge dark eyes soulful, half nodded and half bowed several times. "I'll make sure nothing gets through, Mr. D'Alesio. But I guess I should warn you, I have a basket full of messages from that Dr. Randall who keeps writing and I've had a dozen calls from a woman—"

"Toss those messages from Dr. Alex Randall in the garbage," Dan said impatiently. "The man has been plaguing me with wires from West Thebes to Memphis to Cairo! I don't know if he thinks he has some big discovery and is a publicity hound or if he's trying to cash in on Crosby. I wrote the man a note to tell him I was sorry—I just don't have time right now for anyone. Feel free to toss anything that comes from Randall."

"What about this woman who keeps calling?"

"Who is she?"

"She won't say—"

"Then hang up on her! No, I guess she'd just keep calling you back and harass you. If she calls again, tell her I'm leaving the country. I am, by the way—I'm going to head for the United Arab Emirates tomorrow."

"To see Ali Sur Sheriff?"

"Umm." Dan liked Rajman. He was a bright twenty-year-old with a quick and engaging wit, and a curiosity and penchant for life not unlike his own. Rajman worked for him every time he came into Egypt. Dan appreciated the young man's exuberant help, and Rajman loved the excitement of Dan's life. The relationship had grown to a bond of special friendship.

"Ali was—or still is—planning on financing Jim's expedition. And I know Jim met with Ali two weeks or so ago, so if anyone knows anything about what Jim is up to or where he might be, it's Ali. So get me a flight out, will you?"

"Of course. For just you? Or are you taking a film crew?"

"Just me."

Dan drummed his fingers lightly on the counter and grimaced. "See you in the morning, Raj. I'm beat."

Raj nodded. "Don't worry about your flight," he called after Dan as the older man headed toward the gilded-cage elevator. "I'll take care of everything."

"Thanks," Dan answered as the doors clanged open for him. "One more thing, Raj—send me up something to eat, will you? Whatever you've got that looks good. Just tell the boy to set the tray in the parlor."

Raj nodded again, and the doors clanged shut on Dan. Dan grinned slightly as the little cage began to grind its way up to the third floor. There was one good thing about the situation—he was going to be glad to see Ali Sur Sheriff.

The Arab was one of the wealthiest sheikhs within the incredibly wealthy emirate of Abu Dhabi. His father had become extremely affluent when vast oil resources had been discovered in his sheikhdom in the fifties. Ali had been sent to school in the United States, and there he and Dan had become fast friends.

Now Ali was second only to the emir himself in power. He was a man of strange contradictions. He traveled frequently, had homes in Paris, London, New York and Cairo and could meet with the best of company in the best of places with suave sophistication. He was a brilliant man with an astounding perception of the world around him.

But he was also an Arab sheikh and a Muslim, a man dedicated to his people and his culture. He preferred his desert tents to all the luxuries of the so-called more civilized world. He followed devoutly the teachings of his religion, and very much a family man. As a husband, he was touchingly faithful—to all four of his wives.

The elevator groaned and clanged as it halted at the third floor. Dan left the small cage with his smile fading, his worry about James Crosby returning as he automatically moved down the hall with long strides.

Dan's room was actually a suite consisting of a bright parlor that overlooked the street, a nice-size bedroom and a gargantuan bathroom with a massive claw-foot tub. Dan dropped his duffel bag on the love seat in the parlor and headed straight for the bathroom.

He grimaced at his reflection in the silvering mirror over the sink. He needed a shave badly, and he looked as dusty as he felt. Anyone who met me in a dark alley would probably scream, he thought dryly, rubbing his scratchy chin. It was hard to believe that his was a face millions of Americans tuned in to see three or four times a year when he presented his documentaries. Shaking his head at the sorry reflection, he considered shaving first, then decided the hell with the idea and turned to grasp the ancient faucets for the bath and began to run a stream of steaming hot water. As the water ran, he stripped off his boots, grimacing again as a little molehill comprised of sands of the Sahara formed on the floor. He tossed his boots into the bedroom, shed his shirt and trousers and briefs and sank gratefully into the tub, leaning his head against the rim and closing his eyes. The hot water felt wonderful, permeating his worn muscles and creating a spell of comfort. He leaned up for a moment to douse his face and hair strenuously, then reflected that he could really go for a drink. He jumped out of the tub, dripping over the white and black tiles, raced through the parlor like a streaker, and dug through the small mahogany bar for a bottle of Scotch. He reached for a glass, then shrugged and decided he was all alone,

29

then returned to the tub, taking a swig of the Scotch and setting it on the ledge beside him.

Ahhh . . . comfort!

He took another long swig and settled back against the tub, closing his eyes as the steamy mist rose around him.

As the heat relaxed him, the Scotch somewhat revived him, or at least revived his mind. He had been thinking about Dr. Jim Crosby, probably the most respected Egyptologist in the contemporary world, for the last two weeks, worrying about the man so much that it had actually hurt, his mind protesting with throbbing headaches.

He had tried to sound low key when he spoke about Crosby to Raj, but in reality he was as anxious as could be. He had met Crosby several times during his journalistic-broadcast career—in Cairo at a big demonstration to preserve antiquities, twice in London when Crosby spoke at exhibitions at the Victoria and Albert Museum and just last year in New York. He was an affable man, just forty-four, very good-looking in a beach-boy sort of way, which hardly seemed to fit a specialized archaeologist who spent his days studying the lives of pharaohs and digging up sand in the desert. Yet despite his easygoing ways and pleasant appeal, Crosby had a mind that went beyond the genius level, if eccentric, and a sense of honor and responsibility.

Dan couldn't believe Jim Crosby would simply walk out on his commitment to him—or that he would give up an expedition in the planning stages simply to disappear on some lark.

Granted, he and Crosby had agreed to do the special on Crosby's new dig when they had both been half lit in Crosby's New York hotel room, but they had spoken since then. And besides, that had been a good night. They had left the stuffy conference room of the Belmont behind them, agreed to talk and discovered they had a lot in common—mainly dislike for armchair world-authorities and critics, champagne and caviar and being choked to death by black ties while attempting to converse cordially with the fluff of "concerned" society. In Crosby's room they had discarded jackets and ties, and Crosby, with a grin on his face like that of a wayward kid, had pulled out of ice a few six-packs of beer. By the time Dan left, he had agreed to arrange a meeting for Crosby with Ali to obtain financing for the proposed expedition, and Crosby had agreed to allow Dan to film the entire proceedings.

Dan had begun to worry when Crosby hadn't contacted him in Cairo when he first arrived, but he hadn't felt panicky. They had already set up their filming dates; Crosby would show in the Valley of the Kings. But on July 10, the day they had agreed to meet, Dan had found no Jim Crosby in the Valley of Kings; merely a number of lost and confused workers.

Something was wrong. He didn't know Crosby's life history, but he knew the man. And he knew—

His thoughts suddenly froze as his body tensed. He couldn't put his finger on exactly what had alerted him to another presence, but he knew he wasn't alone. Years spent filming in the world's hot spots had left him with a keen awareness not unlike that of a guerrilla fighter.

Who would be sneaking in on him? It wasn't the hotel boy. He had vaguely registered minutes before that someone had quietly entered, lightly clicked a tray upon the parlor table and just as quietly left.

Without moving, he lifted his eyelids just a shade, in a manner that left his thick, dark lashes still shielding his eyes. He was ready to whip into split-second action if he discovered danger, his muscles tensed to catapult him into a fighting stance, his fingers ready to grab the liquor bottle, the only available weapon.

His tensed muscles seemed to freeze and heat at the same time as his covert glance fell upon the intruder. He was swamped by both incredulity and outrage and was—possibly for the first time in his life—momentarily speechless.

The intruder was a woman.

She might just have stepped off the veranda of a Paris café. His first surreptitious assessment was of a very cool, very sophisticated woman. Her elegant skirt suit was both tailored and ultrafeminine, in a crisp and clean cream color that seemed incongruous when compared to the heat. And the low-brimmed suede hat she wore at an intriguing and fashionable angle over one eye made her look as if she had walked out of a fashion magazine. She was about five foot six, and as fashionably sleek as her outfit. Her eyes, he noted, were an extraordinary shade, neither green nor hazel but a unique blending of amber and lime that was shockingly arresting and bizarrely intriguing. Besides the paralyzing effects of simply seeing a woman—any woman—suddenly appear in his bathroom, he was annoyed to realize that he was further immobilized by the enticing mystique of those eyes. He gave himself a mental shake and continued his secret scrutiny, registering that her hair, pulled into a chignon and neatly secured—not one strand out of place—beneath that chic hat, could no more be called blond than her eyes could be called hazel.

It was pale gold. Not platinum, because it had deep, rich color. Spun gold, filigree. . . .

He broke his thoughts off furiously. What was she doing invading a man's privacy as if she were the Queen of Sheba herself?

And she was just the type of woman he disliked: no broken nails because she never lifted a finger.

She stood in the threshold of the doorway, looking upon the clothing-littered bathroom with great distaste but also with annoying resignation, like royalty stooping to visit the poor.

The outrage of this unknown woman snooping around his bathroom and looking down her nose while she did so suddenly made his temper snap. His eyes flew wide open, and his voice was a thundering whip crack.

"What in damned hell are you doing here!"

She jumped, and a flush seeped into her cheeks. He noticed that for a moment she looked very uncomfortable—and that she was very carefully keeping her eyes upon his face. But she recovered her composure very quickly. He could literally see the stiffening of her spine as she stepped into the bathroom and gingerly took a seat on the commode, crossing one elegant, nylon-clad leg over the other.

Dan did a double take. The strange woman had the uncanny ability to sit on a toilet seat as if it were the throne of England. But she sat with determination, apparently ignoring the fact that a man's bathroom was not the place to have a discussion.

"I'm sorry, Mr. D'Alesio," she began smoothly but quickly. "I've been trying to get hold of you for the last two weeks and—"

32

"Who the hell are you?" he lashed out again.

"Dr. Randall, Mr. D'Alesio; Dr. Alex Randall. I kept writing after you responded because you obviously didn't understand that it was imperative that I see you—"

"You're Dr. *Alex* Randall?"

She completely ignored the obvious insinuation behind his question and continued to speak, still keeping her eyes carefully level with his. "Yes, I'm Alex Randall, and I wrote, I wired and I called, and I'm sorry to burst in on you like this, but it seemed to be the only way to get to see—"

"Had it occurred to you, *Dr.* Randall, that I might be busy, as my letter suggested?" Sitting like a little queen upon her porcelain throne, she was really irritating him. He felt like a fool, trapped naked in a bathtub. And after his long day, she was the wrong side of too much. So cool, so sophisticated, with that delicate femininity, aggressively—but with the best of drawing-room manners—accosting him.

She was so perfectly put together, from dress to hair to face. Her skin was as flawless as marble, her lipstick a perfect coral gloss upon a perfectly shaped mouth, and it even appeared as if she was wearing false eyelashes. No amount of mascara should rightfully give such a golden blond woman such incredibly dark, thick lashes.

Irritation and aggravation flashed through her provocative amber and green eyes at his question. "Mr. D'Alesio, I must get through to see Ali Sur Sheriff. And I understand that you're one of the few people—"

"Why?"

"Pardon?"

Pardon? She issued "pardon" so politely while she interrupted his bath . . .

"Why do you want to see Sheriff?"

"Because of Dr. Crosby. You see, Ali Sur Sheriff was, I believe, the last known contact with Jim Crosby and—"

Dan's eyes narrowed as he surveyed the woman. Crosby, he knew, wasn't married; he was widowed or divorced or some such. Who was she? No one too close; Jim had mentioned in his hotel room that although he was as fond as any man of the fairer

33

sex, he liked being free as a bird and had no intention of making any commitments. The marble-perfect little doll reigning over the toilet seat had mentioned that she was a doctor. A Ph.D.? An Egyptologist? A beautiful parasite trying to hone in on Jim's successes?

"Listen, Miss—" Dan interrupted, closing his eyes and leaning his head against the rim of the tub.

"*Doctor*," she interrupted in turn, with a core of steel in the cool tone of her voice. "Dr. Randall."

His eyes flew open again. "Miss—Mrs.—*Doctor*—it doesn't make a damn bit of difference to me. I wouldn't take a simpering rose like you out into the desert to meet Ali if I thought you had a legitimate reason—which I don't. Now get the hell out of my bathroom."

It appeared the simpering rose had a bit of a temper. He saw her eyes narrow sharply, her slim gamine chin protrude at a strong angle as her head tilted. She stood, long fingers curling into fists at her sides as she lashed back at him. "You listen to me, D'Alesio! I am not any simpering rose, I'm a damned good Egyptologist and I'd weigh my desert knowledge against yours any day. And I'll tell you another thing, Mr. World Famous Journalist—I know Jim Crosby a hell of a lot better than you do and I don't care if you're Walter Cronkite and Henry Kissinger rolled into one, I can guarantee you will *never* get an interview with Crosby when he's found if you don't—"

His eyes had slowly become dangerous, obsidian slits as she spoke, and he broke into her speech with a soft, cutting disdain that seemed to fill the room. "Sorry, Dr. Randall, but I believe Jim Crosby is a man of his word. I think you should reassess the situation. I just don't see Jim Crosby breaking his word over any bedroom antics."

"Bedroom antics . . . ?" She echoed his words with confusion; then comprehension filtered into her flashing eyes, to be followed by indignant outrage. "How dare you—"

Suddenly he'd had enough. He was dead tired and worried half sick. All he'd wanted out of the night was a bath and some sleep—and relief from the anxiety caused him by the puzzle of Jim Crosby.

And instead he'd gotten this—this powder puff barging into his bathroom and issuing threats. And making him feel uncomfortably like some nude centerfold in a woman's magazine.

His irritation and wrath reaching a breaking point, he suddenly stood up. He noted with perverse pleasure that she blanched slightly and took a step backward, her eyes involuntarily taking in his body before latching on to his eyes again.

"Mr. D'Alesio," she snapped. "Your sense of decency is about on a par with that of a desert goat!"

"Mine!"

It was absolutely the last straw. He stepped out of the tub, no longer aware of his nudity, and moved menacingly toward her, the water sluicing from his body. His temper had simply snapped, and before either of them could say more, he grasped her cream-sleeved arms, lifted her bodily a foot off the floor and started striding through the bedroom to the parlor—and the door.

She gasped with outrage at his forceful touch, the amber streaking through her eyes until they blazed gold as they met his while she jounced along, her body leaning against his. "I promise you, D'Alesio, you will definitely live to regret this—"

He smiled pleasantly despite the sizzling black jet that sparked from his eyes. "Will I? We'll see."

The door was still slightly ajar, probably from her unsolicited entry, he thought grimly. He edged it farther open with his foot and set her down on the outside. As she gasped again for breath and struggled to regain her composure, he noted that he had thoroughly soaked her perfect cream suit. It clung to the curves of her figure, and he was annoyed that he noticed their fullness and firmness and that her clothes outlined her angles so deeply and provocatively.

"It's been a pleasure, Dr. Randall," he said quickly, suddenly realizing again that he was nude and now standing in an open doorway. "Let's not do it again, though, huh?"

He closed the door in her face with a firm click.

He heard her fist immediately slam against it. "We certainly won't, D'Alesio. I'll find Sheriff on my own, Mr. D'Alesio—and

35

I'll also find Jim Crosby." Her haunting voice became very sweet. "And I sincerely doubt you'll be doing any documentaries on the great discoveries of the twentieth century—not in this field, at any rate."

He heard the perfect staccato click of her heels as she started down the hallway.

Who in the world was she, and what in the world did she want?

He leaned against the door and crossed his arms over his chest, then realized that the parlor windows were open to the street and a couple of kids were pointing upward and laughing.

"Damn!" he muttered, automatically doubling over and trotting back toward his bedroom.

If she hadn't burst in on him, if she hadn't irritated him so, if it hadn't felt quite so absurd sitting in the tub while the "queen" swept in . . . he might have found out who she was. Was she Jim's mistress? Lucky guy. She might look like a rose petal, but she was also stunning. Thinking of her now made him wonder what it would feel like to pull the pins out of that rich gold-filigree hair . . . see the lime and amber eyes smolder to gold with passion . . . touch that alabaster skin. . . .

Actually, he thought dryly, he was wondering what it would be like to go to bed with her. She was delicate, she was elegant, she was fastidious, cool, regal . . . And she'd probably do very well in a wet-T-shirt contest, too!

He laughed aloud at the incongruity of his thoughts, then sobered. She had threatened him! She had barged into his bathroom, made him feel like a fool. His jaw took on a slow twist, and he sauntered to the bed to sit and pick up the phone.

"Raj? There's a woman heading downstairs. You'll notice her, believe me. She's not the type of female a man would miss. I want you to get someone to follow her. See where she heads next."

He had fallen asleep when Raj called him back. The Arab had had no difficulty discovering what the woman was up to.

"She called the airport from the desk, Mr. D'Alesio. She's got a flight into Abu Dhabi just a few hours after yours. And then

36

she called one of the guide agencies and requested a man familiar with all the Arab countries who was willing to travel for at least a week."

"Thanks, Raj," Dan murmured speculatively. He hung up his phone and stared at the ceiling. The little witch! She was going to go straight after Sheriff!

Who was Dr. Alex Randall, and just what was she after?

If he had her in front of him he'd be tempted to throttle her.

He mused for several minutes longer, aggravated with himself for the impatience that had cost him that knowledge; aggravated with her for breaking in on him and issuing threats like the Queen of Sheba.

So her desert knowledge far surpassed his, did it? She looked too fragile to withstand one sandstorm. But she was an Egyptologist, he reminded himself. She had to have learned something to earn that degree.

Or was she really a Ph.D.? She might have made up her title; he had no proof of anything about her. Only her say-so.

Besides which, he thought with a little grin, Egyptian antiquities had become tourist attractions and perhaps she had come to add them to a private collection. And even if she was an Egyptologist, she probably knew nothing of the Arab world she was about to enter. In the actual desert, life was not so civilized, according to Western standards.

He was suddenly wondering just how much she actually knew about the Middle East—about the emirs and sheikhs who ruled their tribes in the United Arab Emirates today almost as they had through the centuries.

She must know something, he thought. She had had the sense to hire a guide to enter a world where women were still treated as property rather than as individuals. Yet even with a guide, a woman—especially a blonde—might find certain places, ruled by tribal law for centuries, dangerous.

He began to worry a little. What if she was someone special to Crosby? He really couldn't allow the man's fragile mistress to go traipsing alone into a desert where just the shade of her hair would make her worth countless camels and goats, a land of

Islam where slavery was permitted in the Koran, the holy book of those who "submitted to God."

A slow grin worked its way along his mouth as he thought of a way both to teach her a lesson and to protect her.

Ali would probably find the plan amusing and lend his full support. And, Dan decided, mentally doing a bit of arithmetic, he should have plenty of time to set his little scheme into action.

He rolled over on the bed, suddenly awake and alert. First he called Raj. "Can you get a few days off from the hotel?"

"For you, Mr. D'Alesio? Certainly. My father will be most happy to replace me in order to accommodate you!"

"Wonderful," Dan said shortly. "What I want you to do is this: First, get me a private plane out of here tonight. Second, call that guide agency and cancel Dr. Randall's request. I want you to appear tomorrow morning at her hotel as her guide."

Raj started chuckling. "I will be the best guide in the world, Mr. D'Alesio! But won't we wind up in trouble?"

"Trust me, Raj; I'll handle anything that comes up. All you have to do is go along with the lady. . . ."

He detailed his plan for Raj and hung up the phone to start packing the few things he would need for the trip. Raj called him back to tell him his plane would be leaving in an hour.

Dan had one more phone call to make.

Jesse Coffee, Dan's makeup man, thought his request a bit strange, but when Dan was on a streak, it was best not to question him. Dan was a great employer, confident in himself, confident in those who worked for him. He never questioned his employees' abilities once he had hired them, but he was also a private man, working his ideas out in his own mind before bringing the others in and asking their opinions. D'Alesio was charismatic, adventurous, fascinating. Life with him was never dull.

Jesse Coffee enjoyed his job too much ever to rock any boats. He agreed to have everything Dan wanted in fifteen minutes. When Dan was ready, he would let the film crew in on whatever story he was off chasing now.

Dan knew this was one adventure the film crew would never be in on.

He was out of his hotel room in another five minutes. His taxi stopped at the Cairo Hilton, where Coffee gave Dan the paraphernalia.

And then, with plenty of time to spare, Dan headed for the airfield and the small private plane he had hired.

CHAPTER THREE

As the small plane soared over eastern Egypt, the Red Sea and Saudi Arabia toward the United Arab Emirates, Alex reviewed the time spent—or wasted—that had brought her to this rattling flight across endless deserts. She had tried not to panic when Jim hadn't been at the airport when she had arrived two weeks ago. She had taken a taxi straight to the Hilton and had inquired studiously at the desk. But Jim had not checked out of his room when he had left for the UAE, and none of the desk clerks could remember exactly when they had seen him last.

She had tried to reach D'Alesio. And tried, and tried and tried, inquiring at the Cairo museum and the antique shops and anywhere else she could think of while she awaited a response that never came. When she heard that D'Alesio had traveled on down the Nile, she had followed, but when she reached Luxor, he was touring the Valley of the Kings, and when she reached the Valley of the Kings, he had gone back to Luxor. He had managed to elude her all the way up and down the Nile, the son of a—

Calm down, she warned herself. You are now taking positive action.

Alex held her father's letter, her long fingers uncreasing the worn folds that were becoming fragile. Her eyes became like uniquely colored crystals as the turmoil of her mind shone through them in the privacy of her seat. She read Jim's words again. " . . . If anything should go wrong, get hold of Sheikh Sheriff . . . A few things are making me a little nervous. . . ."

A few things are making me a little nervous, she thought.

40

What had Jim known when he wròte the letter? She had to believe that he knew something, that he was missing because he was in hiding.

He isn't—dead, he isn't dead, he isn't dead. She hadn't even realized she recognized that possibility until she started repeating the rebuttal in her mind. But he wasn't dead! He couldn't be!

Tears began to form in her eyes, and she quickly blinked them away. Get mad, she told herself. If you get mad, you won't cry.

It would be easy to get mad, she told herself. All she had to do was think of that man D'Alesio again.

D'Alesio. How had her father ever gotten involved with such a man? Jim had never craved publicity. He loved discovery for discovery's sake; his thirst for knowledge was unslakable. He had never before consented to an interview, much less the filming of an expedition!

Maybe Jim hadn't realized just what an insolent, arrogant, insufferable bastard D'Alesio was. Alex had seen a number of the man's documentaries over the years, as had most people. D'Alesio owned his own production company and chose his own work. But whether he filmed in the Middle East or the Antarctic, about historical treasures or contemporary hot spots, he could sell his films to any major network. Because he was good. He had the ability to get to the crux of a matter and present it in a smooth, objective, comprehensible light. And on television, Alex thought bitterly, he appeared civil, intelligent and reasonable.

The anger she needed to take away her anxiety suddenly ripped through her like a bolt of lightning. She could almost feel her blood begin to boil, and she wondered if she had turned a steamy red from head to toe.

"Insufferable bastard!" and a few other even less complimentary descriptions filtered in a flash fire through her mind when she remembered how he had thrown her out of his room bodily without even listening to her. She was red, she knew it; she could feel the color fill her face. She squirmed slightly, remembering his nude form, rising like Atlas from the water, the water running over his firm and agile muscles.

She hadn't realized that he was so tall. Or dangerous-looking. In the bathtub he had looked a bit like a cave man with his shadowed cheeks, dripping black hair and menacingly masculine form.

The man was a menace—to society. Totally deceptive. He had the manners of a barbarian, a chauvinistic monster. He was the type of man who thought he was a law unto himself simply because he had biceps the size of bowling balls and a sinewed physique that allowed him to brutalize those weaker than himself.

Well, Mr. Dan D'Alesio, she thought with bitter vengeance, you are not dealing with a simpering rose! And you are not a law unto yourself. By the time this is over, you are going to learn a few lessons in common courtesy.

She closed her eyes tightly as she bit down on her lip, annoyed with herself again. Now she couldn't shake the image of the man's lean physique. Whether she despised him or not, she had to admit that he was in very good shape. She doubted that there was a single spot on him from which a half-inch of flesh could be pulled. He was ruggedly, rakishly toned, from his broad shoulders and his chest, with its thick spattering of coarse dark curls, to his handsomely narrow waistline, to . . .

Oh, Alex, how long did you stare at him to picture him so clearly? To his well-corded thighs, she finished firmly. She was, she told herself, proving herself objective by giving the man his due, as an applaudable physical specimen.

And she could still feel the touch of heat and vitality and concrete that had held her so powerfully as he manhandled her, she reminded herself firmly.

Oh, Dad, how *did* you get involved with him?

She reflected suddenly that part of what had happened had been her father's fault. If he had been planning on her joining him, why hadn't D'Alesio recognized her name on the first note? Obviously her father had never mentioned her.

No, she couldn't blame her father, not when she was so terribly worried about him. If she wanted to blame someone, she could blame herself. Why hadn't she merely used her father's name? Because it isn't my name anymore. And because I like to use my own name when I work so that people won't think I want to cash in on my father's reputation. And she had tried to explain

42

to D'Alesio who she was in her second note after his first refusal to see her. He had obviously ripped up the note, since he had accused her of bedroom antics with her own father.

It shouldn't have mattered what my name was! Any civil human being should at least have given me the courtesy of listening, she argued silently. But she couldn't help the intrusion of the facts filtering through her arguments.

She *had* wandered into his bathroom only to make sure he was there. She had been desperate, but she reluctantly realized that she shouldn't have allowed him to make her temper flare.

Alex temporarily forgot the dilemmas plaguing her as the plane shuddered and convulsed like a shaking tin can as it dipped low to make its final descent to the small airfield at Abu Zaby, the island town in the Persian Gulf that was one of the few major towns in the emirate of Abu Dhabi.

The gulf itself appeared like a panel of aqua velvet, studded with a million tiny diamonds. And as the plane came closer and closer to sea level, she could begin to make out all manner of ships and boats, from tiny fishing vessels to massive oil tankers. Fishing, Alex knew, was one of the mainstays of the coastal people. Oil was the mainstay of the country.

The per capita income of the United Arab Emirates was staggering—hundreds of millions of dollars per merely a couple of hundred thousand people. But it was a land still grappling with its sudden catapulting into wealth, and backward in comparison with the Western world. The riches were held by the powerful emirs and sheikhs, and though they cared for their tribal domains like loving parents, the wealth was still theirs.

Biting her lip, Alex begin to wish she knew a little more about the country. Or a little more of the language. But in school she had spent so much time studying the ancient language and hieroglyphics that she had had little time for Arabic—and besides, she had learned early that the natives who made their living by working for the Egyptologists and archaeologists spoke English quite competently. She had never thought she would be chasing down an Arabian sheikh in the desert of a little-known and tiny oil power.

43

The plane came to an abrasive landing. Cheer up, Alex tried to tell herself. Perhaps the wealthy sheikh will be in the city.

She turned to the young Egyptian she had hired to guide her into the masculine realm of the emirs and sheikhs. If nothing else, Raj at least was proving to be a blessing. He was younger—much younger than she had expected from the reputable agency. But what he lacked in age he made up for in charm. She had told him only that she needed to reach an Arabian sheikh; he had assured her he was a Bedouin by ancestry himself, and a devout Muslim. If anyone could guide her through the male-dominated society of Muslims, it was he. "Well, Raj," she said softly, "we're here."

Raj gave the woman a wide smile. His teeth were beautiful and perfect against his bronze complexion. "Yes, miss, we're here."

Alex sighed as she gathered her bag, a simple and large goat-skin satchel, in her arms. "Raj," she said with soft determination. "I appreciate your respectful manners, but I am not a miss. If you must address me formally, I'm a doctor. A Ph.D. I spent eight years of my life studying to achieve that title!"

She smiled softly as she finished the little speech, and young Rajman felt his heart take on a little flutter. She was surely one of the most beautiful creatures Allah had ever deigned to put on earth. But there was something more about her, something that had swept away his heart since he had first appeared at her hotel room door that morning.

Her determination was like steel, and yet she was not a hard woman. There was a gentleness about her that was a cloak over the steel, tempering it, guiding it. She was firm yet quiet, and her voice was soft thunder. Her smile was like the dazzling stars in a desert night sky.

And she certainly was bright, Raj added to himself dryly. He remembered her expensively tailored suit of the previous day; but now, to wander into a world more alien to Westerners than even Cairo, she was clad in the simple robes of the Arab fellahins, or peasants. She wore a veil respectably drawn over the lower portion of her face. Her hair, a color too soft to be that of the sun, too golden to be the color of the moon, was discreetly covered with a hooded shawl.

Raj realized suddenly that he was staring at her as stupidly as a lovesick goat. He snapped himself out of his paralysis, reminding himself that he was on a mission—a very important mission —for the man he adulated almost as much as Allah.

"Yes, indeed, we are here!" he said quickly, the tassel of his fez bouncing about his face. "First we must inquire about the sheikh through the authorities. It is possible we may find him in his city palace."

With a premonition of impending difficulty, Alex doubted that as she and Raj threaded their way through the tiny—but growing—bustling airport to a small center cubicle that offered information in English. Alex breathed a thankful sigh for American oil interests as she questioned a handsome young man about getting around and finding Ali Sur Sheriff.

"A bus will take you over the highway bridge to the mainland," the Arab man in a neat European suit told her. "Sheikh Sheriff has a palace in town, but I do not believe he is in residence now. His tribe is largely Bedouin, and the sheikh spends a great deal of time with his people." The man hesitated a moment, then added softly, "He seldom consents to meet with outsiders."

I already know that, Alex thought silently, but I must see him. She realized suddenly that the man was staring curiously at both her and Raj. She had dressed out of respect for Arab custom and to blend with the mainstream of Arab life as much as possible, but she realized that she must appear strange. She was so very fair.

As they left the information clerk behind, Raj lowered his mouth close to her ear and whispered, "You'd best let me do the speaking from now on. They are not accustomed to meeting many American women. It is seldom that even the oil workers bring their wives here, and when they do, they remain within their own communities."

Alex nodded mutely. She was paying him a small fortune to join her on this odyssey, but it was precisely for the reasons he had just mentioned. As long as they both knew she was the boss.

Outside the tiny terminal a bus did indeed arrive. She and Raj were forced to split up to find seats. She found herself situated between an old veiled woman with a chicken on her lap and a

45

youth of about ten, who smelled worse than the chickens. Gritting her teeth, she sank against the seat.

The trip to the mainland was mercifully brief. With a few short questions to the driver, Raj learned where to find the government offices and the sheikh's residence. It was strange to enter the modern buildings with their wooden ceiling fans and encounter the Arab officials working in their desert robes. Alex hovered nervously in a corner while Raj and an official spoke rapidly in Arabic; then she came forward as Raj addressed her in English with a polite, "Dr. Randall? The sergeant would speak with you."

It was stranger still to hear the young official speak in perfectly enunciated King's English while he stared at her in her alien dress.

It was not alien dress here. The Western world was alien in this land, she reminded herself. Throughout Cairo many wore the costume of their ancestry, but just as many had adopted Western customs and wore Western dress.

But here it was different. The sudden onslaught of riches had forced these people into awareness of other customs, and they had made certain concessions to the foreign interests that worked the oil fields. But they had chosen to retain some of their old life-styles.

The young man who spoke with her now at the offices of the legislature informed her politely that Sheikh Sheriff was not in town; neither was he expected back for several weeks. As the man at the airport had informed her, this almond-eyed official also warned, "I doubt, miss, that even should you find the oasis in the hills, Ali Sheriff will see you."

Alex glanced at Raj, but now he was standing in the background. Alex persisted politely. "I must find him, and I believe that he will see me. Can you tell me how I might go about looking for him?"

The young official glanced at her skeptically for a moment, saw the blaze of determination in her eyes and sighed. He pulled a map out of his desk drawer and spread it across his desk. "Sheriff's oasis is in a little valley in a cluster of hills just before the mountain range. You will note that you must travel inland,

46

and I'm afraid there are no roads as of now into that sector of the country. You must go by what we call desert taxi—camel."

Alex hated camels. Ever since her first trip to Egypt, when she had been about six years old and been bitten by one of the obstinate beasts, she had despised them. But there were still places in Egypt that could only be reached by such crude transportation, and she was a staunch believer in accepting the inevitable.

She swallowed and blinked rapidly, eyeing the young man levelly. "How long will it take?"

"Oh, almost a full day's ride."

A day on a camel. Oh, Dad, she wondered, how could you have done this to me?

"How can we go about renting a camel?"

The young Arabian stared at her again, obviously uncomfortable. "Miss, I don't think you understand the situation. There are miles of desert between here and the oasis. Very rough terrain, and . . . a certain rough element. We are a religious and honorable people, but you must bear in mind that we are just making our way into the twentieth century." He grimaced and continued softly. "Our laws are very different from yours; I would not feel safe about your going, being a woman."

Alex stared at him in return, then said with quiet force, "I must reach Sheriff—a man's life is at stake."

"And I must warn you that you are a rarity in our country. Your eyes are so very blue . . . your face so fair. You must be blond. The color of your hair would make you a valuable prize— a unique addition to a sheikh's harem."

Alex nervously stuffed a stray strand of her hair back beneath the hood of her robe. "Oh, come on!" she said with a laugh. "I can't believe that kidnapping could actually be legal!"

"Not exactly legal, but perhaps unstoppable." He shrugged unhappily, as if she had forced him to carry a great weight upon his shoulders. "You must realize that we are ruled by the emirs of our seven provinces. And beneath those emirs, within the provinces, there are many sheikhs. Ali Sur Sheriff happens to be very powerful, and he is also a cultured man. But many of our tribes live by the old laws; they are independent and proud. They can disappear into the desert at will. And," he added gravely, "you must remember that even Sheriff is a Bedouin sheikh—total law within his own realm."

"But there are many Americans here!" Alex protested. "American industries have interests in the oil drilling—"

"Which centers in certain places. In town, miss, you have nothing to fear. Perhaps you have nothing to fear anywhere. I just don't know . . ."

"But *you* will know that I'm out there!" Alex knew she was pleading, and she was aware that a certain amount of pretty pleading just might work in her favor. It didn't particularly bother her to use feminine wiles when the occasion warranted. She had fought it out in a man's world long enough to believe it only prudent to take the advantage when she saw it.

"Oh, please! I will not be alone! I will be in the company of my male companion, young Raj here!" she murmured huskily, giving him her most liquid gaze from beneath the shade of her lashes. "You really must help me. It is a life-or-death situation!"

The young Arab sighed a last time and gave in. "I cannot stop you."

"Then you will help me?"

"Yes. But your coloring worries me."

"I'll make sure my hair stays covered!" Alex promised.

"And keep those robes about you—not only for protection from overzealous Bedouins, but from the sun."

Alex smiled. "I have spent a great deal of time in Egypt. I am very familiar with the heat of the Arabian sun. Now, please, tell me what we must do."

"I can arrange for camels. Be back here in an hour and I will have you set with your 'taxis.' "

Alex gave a covertly triumphant smile to Raj. Just a little while, and they would be on their way.

They walked the streets until they found a little café in a small hotel and Raj ordered heavy, aromatic Arabian coffee. When they were seated upon brick benches in the slim shade of a spidery tree, Raj watched her with open, honest curiosity.

"Why is it that you must reach Ali Sur Sheriff, Dr. Randall?"

Alex chuckled softly at his careful use of her title. "Raj, if you just call me Alex, you won't have your tongue tripping each time you want to talk to me."

Raj flushed and lowered his almond eyes. "As you wish, Alex. Why must you reach the sheikh?"

"It's as I told the sergeant," Alex replied, staring into the darkness of her coffee. "A man's life is at stake."

Raj's voice was tinged with a strange anger when he replied. "Then why isn't there a man helping you? Have you no husband?"

Alex's fingers wound tightly around her small white cup. "I am divorced," she said aloud, more coolly than she meant to. But she had suddenly discovered that she hadn't given Wayne a single thought in the last twenty-four hours. She had been frantic when she first realized Jim had disappeared, but she had still thought of Wayne, wishing she could find him just so he might help her. She had tried to reach him through the Luxor hotel that had been the return address on his letter, but she had been informed that he had checked out. And then she had tried, and tried and tried and tried, to reach D'Alesio.

D'Alesio! The thought of the man's *name* could send her blood boiling. But it had been since that absurd encounter in his bathroom that she had found it difficult even to conjure Wayne's face to her mind's eye.

"I'm sorry," Raj said stiffly.

Alex realized she had been cold and rude and that the cordial Arab youth deserved none of her animosity.

Only D'Alesio did, who had forced her into a one-day camel ride in a country where just being a female made her a secondary person—and fair game for emirs and sheikhs!

Alex impulsively took one of the young man's hands between her own. "Raj, I am sorry, I didn't mean to snap at you." She hesitated for a moment. "Raj," she said worriedly, "if something should go wrong—if any of these fanatical Bedouins should come around—would you be in danger?"

"No!" he said quickly. Was it too quickly? He lowered his eyes and stared into his coffee. "No. I am an Arab, and a Muslim. I am safe in this country."

49

"I wouldn't like to place you in danger," Alex said softly.

For the first time in their acquaintance, Raj questioned the wisdom of his friend Dan D'Alesio. What was it he believed this woman was hiding? He kept his long lashes lowered as he took a sip of his coffee, not aware that he was shrugging physically as he was mentally. D'Alesio was an honorable man; he would not hurt the woman. And despite his growing education and association with the many Western foreigners who stayed at the Victoria, Raj was an Arab and a Muslim.

This sweet and gentle creature with the hidden core of steel was a woman—one who should be cared for by a man. D'Alesio was certainly a man. If he felt the woman must be taught that she could not take the risks her headstrong nature dictated, then she must be taught that lesson.

He finished his coffee and smiled. "The innkeeper's number-one wife is preparing a meal for us to take. I believe we need to see if it is ready, and be on our way. Our hour is about up."

"Yes, it is," Alex said eagerly, slipping her linen veil back over the lower portion of her face. Raj started off to find the innkeeper's number-one wife, and she followed more slowly, muttering. "If I have to get on a damn camel for a day, I might as well get on the damn thing!"

She started as she saw Raj stare back at her with amazement and disapproval. "Well, I hate camels!" she murmured defensively.

I must be going nuts, she thought bitterly. I'm paying the man a fortune, then I'm apologizing because I'm cursing—because I'm a woman!

She ground her teeth, thinking fervently how very, very grateful she was that she hadn't been born a Muslim in an Arab country. Someone—some man—probably would have shot her by now!

The sun, the sand and the monotonous and miserable gait of her monotonous and miserable camel seemed endless. She and Raj had given up trying to converse hours ago; the effort was too draining. Alex's rear section was in a state of pain she had never imagined possible, and she had the feeling her bottom was bruised blue. She felt as if sand were permanently ingrained in every pore of her body. It had permeated her clothing, her eyes, her nose, her mouth, her scalp. The sun was so torturous that she could hardly bear it. There had been moments when she was sure she would start screaming from the never-ending, tedious ride. But she was afraid that if she opened her mouth to scream, her throat would fill with sand. Heat stroke, she thought mournfully as she envisioned a scene in which she ripped off the ridiculous robes she was wearing and plunged into a suddenly available Lake Michigan—one clogged with winter ice.

Only two things kept her from really going crazy. One was the belief that her father was alive, but that he was in danger. He had told her to get to the sheikh, and so she had to do so. And then there was D'Alesio. She would have walked across the whole desert to shove his words about her back down his throat.

Alex closed her eyes against the sun. Her camel was following Raj's camel; it needed no guidance from her.

Oh, Dad! she thought. Just a little over two weeks ago everything was a fantasy! We were going to make the find of the decade—of the century! And I was going to see Wayne today, and he might have changed, Jim, he really might have! He knows now that although I love him, I will not be with him unless I believe in him.

Her thoughts then shifted to Jim's enigmatic statement about the puzzle pieces. And she prayed again that Jim was alive. Dad, I'd ride camels all day every day for the rest of my life just to see your face, she quietly vowed as she closed her eyes tightly.

Alex reopened her eyes and reached for her sheepskin canteen. Impatiently ripping the linen veil from her face, she took a long sip of water. She caught Raj's eyes upon her as he twisted around on the camels single hump. "Go easy, Dr. Alex, not too much at a time," he warned.

Alex nodded dispiritedly and recapped the canteen. She thought of how she'd love to be sitting in the air-conditioned Cairo Hilton, sipping at a gigantic Scotch and water. She could imagine the size of the glass; there would be a single shot of Scotch and a full sixteen ounces of water. And ice. Lots and lots of ice. . . .

She blinked, laughing inwardly at herself. It was easy to see how people fell prey to mirages in the desert. She had actually managed to implant the picture of a tall, frosted glass into the sand dune ahead.

"Lucky we haven't hit any storms!" Raj called.

"Yes, lucky!" Alex called back. She allowed her eyes to close again. God, how she hated camels! She could smell this one even in the open air. When she had mounted, she had been sure his huge eyes had stared at her malevolently, and he had let out an earsplitting bray. He had, she believed, tried to nip, but his owner, anxious for the rental money, had given him a sharp crack with the whip. He's really not a mean camel, she tried to tell herself. He's just a camel.

She opened her eyes again. For a minute the endless sand and dunes and blue heat-waved sky seemed to merge.

Then she saw him, and he was another mirage. She laughed out loud, because of course he was a mirage, and she had conjured him because of her ridiculous conversation with Kelly.

His robes were black, and he rode a black horse—an Arabian stallion, a beautiful animal, its mane and tail flying high in the air. He appeared alone at first, scimitar slashing and gleaming in the blinding sun, black robes flying to make him one with the extraordinary horse. He rode toward them from a distant dune, the sand kicking up behind him.

He was a figure right out of the Arabian nights, sweeping across the desert with a blood-curdling chant upon his lips, a chant that rose as he was joined by other horsemen as they appeared over the dune.

He was, of course, a mirage. Alex thought so at first even as Raj turned to her again, his eyes wide with—was it alarm or curiosity? Yes, even as her camel collided with Raj's halted beast, she thought it was a mirage. It wasn't until her camel— stupid, stupid beast—balked and honked out a ridiculous noise and hopped and swayed so suddenly that she went teetering off her high perch into the sand far below with a mind-shattering impact that she realized it *wasn't* a figment of her imagination.

Dazed and covered with sand, she stared in disbelief as he kept coming, the stallion seeming to fly across the dunes, the man part

52

of a distant, mysterious past. She didn't think to be alarmed at first, or even to worry if the nine-foot fall from the camel's back had left her in one piece. She simply stared.

She stumbled to her feet, spitting sand, as the man and the mount, with the seven or so retainers behind him, circled her, their frightening Arabic hoots and cries and chants piercing the silence of the desert. The beauty of the approach had been so startling it had seemed to take place in slow motion; suddenly everything seemed to happen at once.

Her camel balked again and ran away with feet flying awkwardly, and she was standing alone. Some riders approached Raj, and he called out something panicky in Arabic as he was led away between them.

And then *he*, still upon his magnificent stallion, was staring at her. His eyes were coal flames. They sizzled beneath the sun; they seemed to set fire to her soul. His skin was the bronze of a Bedouin; his thick mustache and beard covered a chin of insolent, angular strength. His brows were heavy and bushy, his nose prominent with a hawkish hook. And when he smiled, slowly, insolently, arrogantly, his teeth were perfect and white against the full mouth and dark beard.

"What do you want!" Alex demanded, hoping her voice held the defiance her trembling body lacked. He just stared at her, still smiling. Who was he? she wondered, again bemoaning the fact that she had chosen hieroglyphics over Arabic continually in school. Atop the stallion, the man with the dark Arabic eyes and haunting facial contours was a more formidable opponent than she had ever expected to face. No, he wasn't just formidable. This man was terrifying.

"You made my camel run away!" she snapped, drawing desperately on whatever bravado she could summon. "You do realize that it is terribly rude to burst upon people this way—"

She didn't get any further. The sinewed muscles in the stallion's haunches convulsed, and the horse was moving—toward her.

"Now wait a minute . . ." Alex automatically began to back up. It did her no good. The horse broke into a prance and moved directly beside her, and even as she turned like a cornered deer, floundering in the sand and scrambling to flee, the man's arms caught her squarely around the middle and she felt herself being hoisted through the air and precariously balanced belly-down over the shoulders of the stallion. The man snapped out a single word in Arabic, and the animal's muscles bunched beneath her. She grabbed desperately at the saddle trimmings for balance as they broke into a canter.

It was difficult to talk; it was difficult to do anything other than pray that she would not fly off the racing horse, and try to draw air rather than sand into her lungs.

And yet, despite the rise of basic survival instincts, Alex found strength somewhere to scream out her rage. "You can't do this to me! I'm an American. Stop this horse! Let me go at once. I'll have the embassy on you for this! I'll call out the entire United Nations!"

Laughter, full, deep, rich and husky, was his only response. Eventually she tired after she had called him every name she could thing of—her vocabulary of profanities was quite extensive after all the years she had spent with her father and predominantly male workers. She threatened him with everything from being boiled alive to being drawn and quartered. Then she even remembered a few phrases in Arabic, two of which her father had taught her when she had begun to comb the bazaars of Cairo with him in search of authentic antiquities. *"Ibiid yaedaek! Kif wae illae sae' asrokh."* Keep your hands to yourself! Stop or I'll scream!

Great words. They might have an effect upon a wayward youth in a crowded bazaar, but it was blatantly obvious this maniacal Arab couldn't care less whether she screamed or not. There were certainly no *bolis*, police, around to help her.

She grew more and more angry—and frightened. No, Alex, she warned herself, don't be frightened! Stay mad! Don't let this man know you are anything but indignant and furious.

He merely grew more amused.

And she fell silent, focusing her inward curses upon some vague form of punishment for Kelly, who, it seemed, had wished this entire bizarre occurrence upon her. And when she finished cursing Kelly, she cursed Jim for having sent her to Sheriff, and

54

when she finished cursing Jim, she started again with her greatest, most vicious vengeance upon the true root of her present humiliation—D'Alesio!

She knew there was no way that she could be imagining this. Not when every inch of her flesh was being jounced and bruised; not when the sand flew around her, blinding her, pelting her skin; not when she could feel the heat and lather of the stallion and the broad steely hand of the insolent Arab, splayed across her back, holding her firmly.

It had to end. She was bruised from head to toe. She wasn't terribly sure she would ever walk again. It seemed that she had swallowed half the desert.

The racing horse had slowed to a more agonizing trot. A second later the animal halted, and she would have fallen were it not for the power of the hand upon her back. She tried to look up and blink the blinding sand from her eyes.

They were . . . somewhere. A vast number of tents stretched before her, a relief from the monotony of the desert. Grass grew in tufts at the stallion's hooves; she could hazily make out a cluster of date-nut trees. From somewhere nearby came the blessed sound of splashing water and children's laughter.

An oasis. They had reached an oasis. And the tents were large and numerous.

They had stopped in front of a particular tent, she realized quickly. A young woman greeted the Arab who was holding her with soft, quiet curiosity. She was adorned in beautiful silks, from the gauze veil that enhanced the beauty of her face rather than hid it, to her tight jewel-encrusted bodice and sheer ballooning trousers.

Alex suddenly felt herself plucked upward again by a grip about her abdomen, as easily as if she were a kitten gripped by a mother cat. And then she was set—plopped, actually—on her feet. To her vast relief, she was able to control the spinning of her mind and body and stand without falling.

She turned furiously to the man. "I demand—"

He broke in unceremoniously, not addressing her but the young Arabian woman. In the rapid brushfire of words that

55

passed between the two, Alex could make out only one word: *haemmaem*. Bath . . . *bath!*

"You bastard!" Alex shrieked, fighting tears of rage and disbelief. The arrogant Bedouin had insolently abducted her and raked her across the sands, and now he had the nerve to command that she have a bath. She wanted to scream with incredulity, humiliation, fury and fear.

She did start screaming, her fists clutched tightly to her sides. The Arab gave her a suave, cool smile, flicked his stallion's haunches lightly with his whip and trotted smoothly away.

CHAPTER FOUR

Alex's reaction was spontaneous. Blind rage brought power to her bruised limbs; she stooped to fill her hands with sand and tore after the horseman, coming within five feet of the prancing stallion. To her great satisfaction, the Arab was taken by surprise as she tore in front of him and showered him with the sand—and a few strident curses for good measure.

Her temporary victory was washed away in the tidal fury of his dark eyes. He blinked only once, dismounted from his horse and started after her with swift, calculated steps. Instinctively Alex turned to run, but she didn't know in which direction to head. She took off, but too late. The steel vise of his arms came around, catching her, hefting her up and over his shoulder with effortless agility. Very close to tears, she shrieked and pounded on his back, all to no avail. His strong, assured gait brought her back to the tent and inside the goatskin flap.

She landed unceremoniously on an already bruised section of her derriere with her now unpinned hair creating a tangled and blinding web before her eyes. Struggling for breath, she tossed back her hair in time to see her abductor stalking from the tent, her final view of him being of his black-draped back.

She lunged to her feet to accost him again, but even as she rose, two large and swarthy Bedouins passed before her, bowing and moving toward the flap. They were smiling, but the message in their eyes was firm; she needed no translation to realize that they were guards and would obstruct her forcefully were she to attempt an exit.

Biting down on her lip to quell the tears that rose within her,

Alex tried desperately to regain some composure and assess her situation logically.

Logically! Dear God, it wasn't a classroom, it wasn't even an ancient tomb with hieroglyphics to be analyzed and transcribed. She had been taken prisoner in the middle of an alien desert, by a dark and apparently all-powerful Bedouin, who had ordered that she have a bath.

Oh, dear God! This was impossible; outrageous. No, it wasn't impossible, because it was happening.

Don't panic, Alex. Don't panic. She realized suddenly that she was studiously chewing the nail of her left forefinger. She quickly wrenched her fingertip from her mouth and spun around to survey the tent.

Again, all she could think of was Arabian nights. The floor was sand, but over the sand beautifully woven Persian rugs were scattered. There was a massive canopied bed with silk coverings and a multitude of throw pillows; larger pillows decked the floor around an especially large rug. Turkish coffee brewed in a canister above a small fire at the far end of the rug; a tray with dates and nuts and fruits sat near it. Several divans, also decked in colorful silks, rounded out the room; spaced between them were teakwood tables and trunks.

It was an exotically beautiful place, she thought fleetingly. Even the inner skin of the tent had been dressed in billowing silk. The colors were those of the rainbow, bright and yet soft.

And in the far rear of the tent, silently watching Alex, was the stunningly pretty Arab girl. Her eyes were large and sympathetic as she stood quietly beside the tent's one other accessory—a large, ornately embossed metal bathtub with four huge feet that resembled those of a jackal.

Steam rose in fragrant mists from the tub. The girl inclined her head slightly toward Alex and swept her arm invitingly across the rise of the mist.

Alex crossed her arms firmly over her chest, tapping her fingers upon her arms. She smiled grimly. "Not on your life," she said with sweet, unfaltering determination.

The girl appeared to be sincerely upset. She spoke quickly in husky tones to Alex, but all Alex could make out was the Arabic

58

for "please," *min fadlak.* The girl again motioned to the tub, her expression pleading.

Alex shook her head. "I'm sorry. No."

The huge, doelike eyes of the girl became both sad and resigned. With delicate little steps she started toward the tent flap.

Alex heard her soft Arabic as she began speaking to the Bedouin bruisers. A second later both men ducked beneath the flap and stood behind the girl as she again addressed Alex in sorrowful tones.

For several seconds Alex stared at her blankly, wondering what on earth the girl was saying and once more lamenting her sketchy Arabic. Then the girl lifted her hands in a universal gesture of exasperation. The two men started toward Alex, and everything the young woman had been trying to say became crystal clear. She could step into the tub of her own accord—or she could receive some assistance from the bruisers.

Alex immediately leaped backward, lifting her hand toward the men. "*Kiff! Kiff!*" she exclaimed, thankful she remembered the word for "stop." The men paused, and she wished heatedly that she could smash both their faces as they smiled their superior amusement.

Everyone in the tent knew she was going to step into the bath under her own power. Bowing like amiable housemen pleased to have served her, they backed out of the tent, only to take up their positions on either side of it once more.

Alex grated her teeth and stared with animosity at the Arab girl, who continued to survey her sorrowfully. She attempted to smile, and Alex sighed. Begrudging every step she took, she gingerly approached the tub.

Even in high school and college Alex had never been the type to run around the girls' locker room nude. It bothered her to disrobe with the young Arab girl near, but she knew it would bother her a great deal more to be forcibly disrobed by the pair of guard dogs. With little finesse she ditched her Arabian robes and scrambled from the khaki trousers and shirt she wore beneath them, then crawled hastily and with even less grace into the elaborate tub. At first the impact of the heated water on her flesh almost made her cry out, but after the initial shock, the permeating, soothing heat felt delicious. Alex closed her eyes for a moment, savoring the relaxation of her bruised and abused muscles.

Her eyes flew open again as she felt a touch upon her arm. The young Arab woman stood beside her.

Touch me again, Alex thought, and you'll be in for a fit you won't believe.

But the woman merely handed her a vial and touched her own hair. Shampoo, Alex thought, nodding as she accepted the vial. The woman moved away discreetly and took a kneeling position upon the center rug to check the brewing coffee.

The water in the tub was oiled. It smelled faintly and pleasantly of almond and jasmine, and the feel against her skin was luxurious after the scorching sun and blistering sand.

It was absurd to appreciate being forced to take a bath, but for a brief moment of gratitude, Alex was thankful. A large Greek sponge floated upon the surface of the water, and she realized quickly that soap was within the sponge.

She had no choice but to take the bath, she might as well enjoy it. No choice . . . Alex scrubbed her skin with a fury as she again fought desperately to be calm and analytical. Where was she? In an oasis—an oasis in the direction she had been traveling. It was logical to assume that this oasis was the domain of Ali Sur Sheriff. Had it been the powerful sheikh himself who had abducted her? But she knew that Sheriff spoke English; he had, if memory served her, spent time in the United States. And even the official in Abu Dhabi had assured her Sheriff was civilized.

Alex ducked her head beneath the water to wet her hair. When she recalled the man who had so crudely abducted her, she felt strange little shivers of déjà vu, as if she had seen him before. There had been something about his eyes, the piercing, coal-black stare . . .

It was as if the answer to a riddle was evading her.

No, she thought, working the shampoo from the vial through her hair. She knew no Bedouins in this tiny country. Until recently the United Arab Emirates had been nothing but interesting reading to her when its strange conflicts of past poverty and modern wealth were mentioned in the financial pages.

There was something familiar about the man because he was an Arab and she had been in Egypt for the past two and a half weeks. The Arabs tended to have beautiful, mesmerizing eyes.

Oh Lord, Alex thought, I'm sitting here worrying about a man's eyes when I'm in more trouble than I've ever been in during my entire life.

Was the man Sheriff? If so, why wouldn't he talk to her? What did he want from her? He probably just wants to find out who I am and why I am trespassing on his lands, she reasoned. I'll explain the entire situation, and if he *is* Sheriff, I will have reached him; and if he isn't Sheriff, then surely he can tell me *how* to reach him.

Logical, Alex, beautifully logical. What if he's just a backward tribesman, determined to grant you a permanent place in his harem? Eight years of education just to become an ornament. . . .

The idea made her feel as cold as ice despite the heat of the water, which still steamed. Alex felt suddenly as if she were drowning, and she clenched her teeth, swallowed and took several deep, long breaths to fight away the panic.

A softly spoken word alerted her to the Arab woman's presence nearby. Alex opened her eyes to see that a large linen towel was being offered her. She accepted the towel, and as the girl turned away again, she rose and wrapped herself within its massive folds. She squeezed the water from her hair as best she could and fluffed it vigorously with the towel.

Her thoughts returned uncomfortably to the expert Bedouin horseman who had, in Kelly's ridiculously prophetic words, swept her away. Why would a man have a woman bathed in fragrance if he didn't want . . . She shivered and forced her mind from panic. No, no, no . . . there had to be a way out. She had to find Jim. Someone would help her.

Rajman! Where was Rajman? What had happened to him when he had been escorted away?

For a moment she was tempted to bolt out of the tent clad only in the towel and race straight back into the desert. Only the sharp mental reminder that the bowing brutes outside the tent

61

flap would merely catch her and physically restrain her kept her from behaving so foolishly.

Night would come. If she was quiet, if she watched, she would find a way to escape. Her sense of direction wasn't that hot in Chicago; in the desert it would definitely be worse. But they had come from the northeast. The Persian Gulf was to the northeast, and even here the sun rose in the east and set in the west. If she could just get hold of a horse—a horse, please, God, not one of those stupid, traitorous camels.

The Arab woman was speaking softly again. Alex glanced her way to see that she was sweeping her arm in the direction of the bed, with its billowing silk canopy. Upon the spread was a peculiar assortment of clothing. The girl nodded with a warm smile beneath her gauze veil, as if she was pleased she had made Alex understand. She swept her arm again in the direction of the Persian rug and the brewing coffee, mimed that Alex should eat and started bowing out of the tent.

A second later Alex was left alone—within the tent. Outside, she knew, the guard dogs remained.

Not wanting to be caught in the towel should she receive another visitor, Alex hurried to the bed. The outfit assembled for her was not that of a belly dancer—but it was not much better. At any other time in her life she would have marveled at the beauty of the color and texture of the cloth. In her present situation a touch of the soft, sheer silk, patterned in trousers and midriff blouse, made shivers start attacking her spine with debilitating frequency.

A swatch of her still-damp hair suddenly fell in front of her eyes, and she was tempted to pull it out. She had been warned about her hair. But she had dutifully kept it covered! No one seeing her monotonous trek across the desert could have observed anything out of the ordinary. The insolent Bedouin horseman had, in fact, come after her from the front, as if he had known someone would be coming. Impossible. She had arrived only this morning. She had taken the most direct route possible.

Oh, God! What did any of it matter? She was a prisoner, bathed and perfumed as carefully as a farmer fed a steer for the marketplace. Marketplace. Oh, Lord. The Koran recognized slavery. She knew that much about the Islam religion. It was something one might chuckle about in the civilized safety of a Chicago apartment. A man could have four wives, and he could own slaves. They were to be fairly treated, and they were allowed to buy their freedom!

Was she going to be put up for some kind of auction?

She was shaking profusely. Stay calm, Alex, stay calm, she warned herself. But it was almost impossible to stay calm under the circumstances. She was a mature, self-respecting, confident Ph.D. She had spent years of her life studying, and learning to hold her own inoffensively and excel graciously in a man's world. And she was being reduced to this!

No, no! Someone would find her. She couln't simply disappear into the desert. There had to be some kind of local law. The official in Abu Dhabi knew she was out in the desert. Yet he had been the one to warn her.

Alex picked up the silks from the bed in a sudden fury and sent them flying across the sand floor and throw rugs. Such garments might be appropriate for certain Arabian women, but she was an American! She would wear her own khaki cotton outfit. If she didn't continue to take herself seriously and maintain an outraged dignity, she would be playing right into his hands.

She stalked back toward the bathtub, where she had disrobed so hastily, only to discover her own clothing gone. A wave of frustrated fury swept over her and she kicked the huge metal tub—only to stub her toes. Swearing out loud, she hobbled back to the bed and started picking up the silks that were strewn at its base.

She was so engrossed that she didn't notice the tent flap open; neither did she hear the quiet entrance of the black-robed Bedouin with the fire-dark eyes. Nor did she notice the smile of pure, patronizing amusement that filtered across his handsome features.

She allowed the towel to fall in a rumpled heap to the floor and, still muttering curses beneath her breath with a vengeance, started to adjust the silks.

He hadn't been able to help smiling when he heard her curses. She was in the exact predicament in which she deserved to be, or at least she thought she was. But his smile also held a twinge of begrudging admiration. Despite everything, she was still fighting, still determined. He felt a small shade of remorse for what he had done as he watched her chin rise slightly as her lips trembled, but he quickly squashed his remorse. She was actually damned lucky that she had received only one hell of a scare and was not going to receive worse.

His smile faded suddenly as his eyes traveled over her body as she stood.

She had a gorgeous back, absolutely gorgeous. Her skin was a beautiful shade between ivory and rose, flushed as it was from the bath. Her shoulders were slender but very straight; the blades, rippling beneath her flesh, enticed a man's hands to touch. Her spine was indented in intriguing shadow, her waist tucked in neatly and trimly at the end of a long, graceful and shapely torso. She had little dimples—further shadow allure—just above the spot where her buttocks swelled to full, firm crests, neither too little nor too much, padded just perfectly to give shape without bulk. Her legs were long and lithe and sleek—again, perfect. Not heavy but not thin, shapely and nicely, lightly sinewed.

She dipped and bent, swearing softly still, to step into the trousers, and he was afforded a partial glance at her breasts. They were like the rest of her—full, high and firm and tipped by peaks a deep and provocative shade of rose. He saw that the shadows and angles of her collarbones were as elegant as the shape of her back; they were fine and delicate and delineated. His smile slipped back into existence as he watched her dust off the soles of her feet before stepping into the pants. Her nose wrinkled slightly as she did so. In the middle of the desert, cursing her little heart away at the fates, she was meticulously finicky.

She straightened, and his view of her superbly shaped back— which narrowed to a hand span at the waist and flared prettily again at the hips—was obscured as the silk bodice slipped over her shoulders. It didn't matter. The silk didn't conceal as much as it enhanced. And besides, the vision he had just witnessed was indelibly ingrained upon his mind as surely as if he had been branded for life.

His smile suddenly became dry and rueful. For a moment he had wished he were a wild Bedouin sheikh, answerable to no laws but his own and those of Allah. Something of the ages had coiled within him, a savage, primitive, male and undeniable desire simply to ravish and possess, and in possessing, gaining and taking and holding all that was simply beautiful and desirable.

No head games, no pretense, no lies, no illusion or disillusion. Simple possession, simple giving, simple taking.

His smile again faded. He wasn't a desert sheikh. He was bound by the morals of his world. And she wasn't simply a woman. She was the witch who had a soaring temper and determination of her own; she was the sophisticated upstart who had invaded his privacy, who had viciously threatened him, who had insolently declared she would do exactly what she wanted to do.

And she also belonged to Jim Crosby. He could only assume she was his mistress, and he had to afford Crosby a certain envy. Crosby was a striking man himself; it was logical that he should attract a bright and beautiful woman. Well, for such beauty one man naturally envied another. As for her temper, Crosby was welcome to it. He would warrant that had she been abducted by a true roving sheikh, that gentleman of the desert would see to it that she spent her time in the harem with her mouth taped shut!

Alex glanced indignantly at her silk costuming. She was covered from head to toe, but somehow she would have felt more dressed in a string bikini. This was a far cry from the robes and galabias she had seen worn by the fellahin or peasant women along the banks of the Nile. But, she thought with a hint of woeful comfort, at least she was not going to be attacked in the bathtub. Her attire might be almost decadent, but decadent was better than none at all.

It was a prickling along her spine and a subtle new scent upon the heavy air that alerted her to the fact that she was no longer alone. And she knew instantly, without conscious thought, that the intruder was not the Arab girl. The scent on the air was that of sandalwood and musk, and it was uniquely, ruggedly, hypnotically—male.

Alex spun quickly to find her coal-eyed captor standing perfectly still just inside the flap of the tent. He watched her with cool assessment—and no apology whatsoever.

She was definitely discomfited (wishing one could hide in a large paper bag was definitely "discomfited") and unnerved. Caught totally off guard, she wondered how long he had been standing there. Feeling terribly self-conscious, she was tempted to drop to her knees to wrap her arms around herself.

She stood as still as he, willing herself not to jerk or tremble or react. Mentally and then physically she squared her shoulders and lifted her chin, hoping the haughty, determined actions would allow her to speak with a haughty and determined voice.

"Who are you? I demand to know who you are!"

Her dignity disappeared when she stamped her foot after her last command, and she could feel the hysteria building inside her. It was almost impossible for her to curb the feelings. She was in a tent in an oasis God-knew-where, perfumed and bathed and dressed in an absurd costume, and facing the crazy Bedouin with the smoldering laser eyes who had brought her to her present condition.

"Who are you?" she shrieked. Why didn't he answer her? Even if he didn't understand English, he had to understand that she was furiously upset. And why was it that as soon as she needed it, she went blank on the sketchy knowledge of Arabic that she did have? Only one phrase would come to her mind—*Aenae imbasett giddaen,* which meant, "I've enjoyed myself tremendously." And she surely didn't want to say something like that.

While she stood in furious frustration, fists clenched at her sides, she tried desperately to recall a few more words in Arabic. Feeling tense and wounded didn't help a bit; it created an entire mental block. And then, while she still struggled, he casually started walking forward and spoke. "I might ask you the same question."

Dan wondered dryly if he had managed something vaguely similar to an Arabic accent. He doubted it. But then Ali Sheriff didn't speak English with an Arabic accent. If Ali's speech was accented at all, it was with a slight British twist, since he had spent a year in prep school in London before entering Yale.

"You speak English."

It was an exhalation of breath; it was an accusation. Dan lowered his lashes and kneeled before the still boiling coffee so she wouldn't see the grin that refused to be suppressed. His Arabic accent might not be the best, but apparently she didn't know it.

"Yes," he said dryly, "I speak English."

She should have stayed calm, but she didn't. The hysteria rising within her bubbled over with a new vengeance. She was scared half out of her wits, and being so terrified made her defensive, which made her bluster. "Then if you understand me, you'd better understand just what can happen to you for what you've done to me! I am an American, and what you're guilty of is kidnapping. Kidnapping is a federal offense. They can execute people for doing things like this—"

She broke off just as his eyes rose to meet hers.

Am I crazy? she wondered with horror. I'm threatening him while he still holds all the cards. And it was very evident that he knew he did. His stare was sharp and piercing and cold, and hinted of an anger barely tempered by disdainful amusement.

"This is not the United States," he said quietly.

Chills swept over her as she was trapped again by that strange feeling of déjà vu. She knew no one in the United Arab Emirates, and yet she could have sworn she had seen his eyes before, felt that contact, heard that deep, husky voice.

Calling upon every reserve of willpower within herself, Alex inhaled and exhaled and attempted to start over, diplomatically.

"Yes, you're right. This is not the United States. But please, if you will just tell me who you are . . ."

He rose and came toward her once more, a dry, grim smile tightening the fullness of his mouth. "That will depend upon who is asking."

He stopped right in front of her, and she suddenly found that her throat was terribly dry and her lips were desert parched. That faint aroma of sandalwood and musk and masculinity seemed as overwhelming as his black-clad physique before her. She could feel his breath against her cheek, and she could faintly detect the added scents of mint and Turkish tobacco. She noted vaguely that his large hands were neatly groomed, that the shoulders beneath the black robe were very broad.

And yet all these were secondary to the feeling of being electrically charged simply by being near him. She had to swallow to attempt to speak, and all the while her eyes were locked with his, and she was keenly, painfully aware that all that lay between them was a matter of inches and that all that protected her was that misty gauze of silk.

"Alex," she managed to choke out. "My name is—*Ismi* —Alex Randall." Great, now that she knew he could speak English, she was remembering some basic Arabic. "Dr. Alex Randall."

He smiled with a slightly derisive crook of his lip as he cocked a brow mockingly. "Dr. Alex Randall," he repeated softly. "You are very nervous, Dr. Alex Randall. Come and sit down and drink something. You must be very, very thirsty."

Alex nodded jerkily. She was thirsty, agonizingly thirsty. But despite herself, she jumped as his hand came down upon her upper arm. He smiled again, fully aware of her reaction and mocking her for it. She ground down hard on her teeth for control and forced her feet to move as he led her to the crimson divan nearest the central Persian rug.

"Sit, Dr. Alex Randall."

Alex sat uneasily upon the edge of the divan, folding her hands nervously in her lap. Be diplomatic—but forceful, she told herself. "I have told you who I am. Now, please, answer my questions."

"Ahh . . . but you haven't told me who you are," he corrected pleasantly. He poured her a little ceramic cup of the rich, thrice-boiled coffee, and she had the feeling that even as he hunched with coordinated agility to perform the little task, he was watching her. "You have given me a name that tells me nothing."

Her temper flared again when it shouldn't have. Alex drank her coffee in a gulp, burning her mouth and adding fuel to the flames of indignation seething within her. "A name is a hell of a lot more than you've given me!"

He still smiled—which, combined with that smoldering jet sizzle in his eyes, was a sure sign of danger. He rose and sat beside her, lifting her damp and tangled hair from her neck. "Dr. Alex Randall," he murmured. "No. Here you are not Dr. Alex Randall. Here you are nothing more than a woman with a very pretty shade of hair and light eyes—a valuable combination."

Alex wished dearly that she could slap his hand. She felt his touch with her entire body. That electricity was within him; it was within his fingertips. It shot through her nerves from head to toe, searing a heated path to her very center.

She clenched her folded palms, digging her own nails into her flesh. Don't! she warned herself. Don't strike out, don't react at all.

"I am a scholar of some repute," she said softly, trying to block out that feel of lightly callused fingertips upon her nape. "There are people . . ." She caught her breath for a moment as his fingertips stroked her shoulders, trailed slowly—excruciatingly slowly—down her spine, vertebra by vertebra. "There are people who know where I was—ah—" She gasped as those roving fingers splayed caressingly over the small of her back, almost absently and innocently massaging her hips and buttocks. His eyes had remained upon hers as she spoke and as he moved. The light in them was still one of amusement. His countenance was a rigid deadpan, but his eyes—they did register his amusement and challenge. He was taunting her, she knew, discovering how far he could push, how she was going to handle the situation.

"What was that?" he asked politely.

"What?" Alex demanded in confusion.

"There are people who know where I was, uh . . ." he mimicked.

"Oh, ah." Alex swallowed. She closed her eyes briefly and cleared her throat, then smiled sweetly at him while she reached behind her to capture his hand and set it upon his own lap gently but firmly.

"There are people who know exactly where I was heading

69

today. You see, you must release me immediately—" She broke off again as she watched his long fingers begin a new trek from her kneecap upward along her thigh. The touch was so like a lap of fire that she longed to shriek again and bolt in pure panic. But she did nothing for a moment, mesmerized as she watched those trailing fingers.

"You were saying?"

Polite inquiry again; as if nothing at all were happening.

Alex caught his fingers again as they began an intimate climb upward along her inner thigh. It was either that or scream.

Flattery, she thought desperately. He was not fighting her attempts to fend him off; he was taking her actions with surprisingly good grace. She held his hand, which seemed to burn with a coal fire as great as that within his eyes, and smiled sweetly. "You are Islam, sir—a man who submits to God. Surely your Allah cannot condone your taking prisoner—"

"An unbeliever in the true faith," he finished for her solemnly. "No, my God will not mind. The Koran even allows us to make war in the cause of the one true faith."

She was getting nowhere, and panic was rising within her again. His gaze and his touch were like the hypnotic power of a cobra. She was desperate to get away, and yet she was not repulsed. She felt as if she were being drowned in quicksand, and if she didn't get out while her head was still above the surface, she would be forever enmeshed.

And he was a kidnapping, cocky, insolent, superior bastard!

The outrage of the situation once again rose to outweigh careful diplomacy. Still fighting for control, Alex dropped the hand she held and sprang to her feet, moving across the tent.

"Who are you and just what do you intend to do with me?" she demanded with a show of bravado. Unfortunately, her last words quivered.

He was behind her quickly—too quickly—his hands once more caressing her shoulders, his fingers slipping beneath the silk to touch her bare flesh.

"You still have not told me who you really are, or why you are here in the desert," he reminded her smoothly.

Behind her, he was able to smile freely. He could feel her

shivering beneath his touch—he had definitely taught her a lesson. Let her spout all the controlled dignity she could manage, he knew he had her scared—very scared. It was unlikely that she would do anything so reckless again as cross an alien desert alone.

Yes, he was definitely getting to her. But he had to be an idiot masochist himself!

It was difficult to tell where the silk left off and where her flesh began. She was warm and incredibly vibrant and softly, femininely alive. The perfumes supplied for her bath were about to drive him crazy, and he realized ruefully now that he kept touching not to taunt, but because he was compelled to touch. Who is torturing whom here, he wondered vaguely.

His hands suddenly dropped to his sides. He felt a yearning within him—a natural but painful yearning that was an instinctive, physical thing, a heated arousal, which this woman, in this state of dress, would evoke in any halfway healthy male. But it went deeper than that. He felt strangely as if sparks had flared and met, negative and positive, forming a perfect whole. He sensed within her a subtle but deep sensuality, and it was tempting, terribly tempting, to play out his role to the hilt. He wanted her so badly that simply the scent of her, the touch of her, sent a haze saturating his mind against all else.

He turned abruptly away from her, grinding his own teeth, balling his fingers tightly into his palms. He was being a fool, letting desire for a beautiful woman cloud the objective mind he had nurtured so carefully. He had learned his lesson once; women came to him now, and he took care to appreciate them for what they were without losing his heart. He did not become an idiot over a nice pair of legs . . . or a rear . . . or an enticing chest . . . or rare amber-lime eyes or stardust hair.

Crosby's woman! he reminded himself, and the reminder straightened him out. He needed to make her realize that she had behaved foolishly, then pack her back home to some elegant little house in the suburbs. Except he wanted to know first just what she knew, just what her relationship with Crosby was.

A man did not, he chastised himself firmly, fall into lust with

71

a respected friend's woman—even if he was ready to throttle her half the time.

"I am looking for Ali Sur Sheriff," she finally said softly, her back still to him. Then she spun around, and the silks and her hair floated beautifully about her. "Are you Ali Sur Sheriff?"

He walked back toward her, remembering his resolutions. He saw the defiant demand in her eyes—eyes fringed by those unbelievably dark and thick lashes—and he suddenly found himself smiling again. He had tortured her and himself enough, he reasoned. Then, perversely, he changed his mind. Not quite enough.

He slipped his hands around the swan column of ivory that was her neck. With his thumbs he caressed her cheekbones as she stared at him with tense expectancy. His fingers combed through her hair, tilting her face to his, pulling her close, so close that they both became acutely aware of exactly what they were: a man and a woman, alone, touching.

Alex felt as if she had been drugged. She was furious; she had never felt so powerless. She was so accustomed to being heard when she spoke, to having social codes rule the actions of the stronger male, that she still refused to accept what was happening. And yet even as she drew her hands between them to press against his chest, she knew that she didn't protest out of loathing.

She tried to tell herself that she was trying to reach him with diplomacy—and to an extent that was true. She wasn't going to be able to stop this man if he chose to do anything. A struggle would leave her the loser—and her loss would be all the greater coupled with the indignity of a skirmish.

But there was more to it than that. Analytically. Oh, yes, analytically. She felt again that electricity that coursed from him, and she felt the heat that emanated from his tightly muscled body. That scent, so pleasant and yet so masculine, was part of the drug, as were the cobra eyes that mesmerized.

He was from a world she didn't understand, a world totally against the equality of the sexes. She certainly couldn't say she liked the man—surely she hated him! And yet he drew a certain respect, a certain admiration. There was simply something basic, raw and primitive about him; a rugged strength and sexuality that inexplicably existed.

72

And as he held her, capturing her eyes, she felt that sexuality as if no cloth existed between them as barriers. More basically than words could ever communicate, that sizzling contact spoke.

She didn't want it. It was more humiliating than anything that had been done to her because it was a feeling from within herself. It frightened her to the core. No, it terrified her, it was quicksand. And she would never accept his insolence, could never accept being used.

Her hands pressed furiously against his chest as he continued to hold her close, his eyes a curious enigma as they studied hers.

Let her go, D'Alesio, he warned himself. Remember Crosby.

"What are you doing?" Alex gasped weakly, trying to break his hold and tear her eyes away from the hypnotism of his.

He smiled, his teeth flashing white against the bronze of his skin and the darkness of his beard and mustache. "Just trying to decide whether I shall keep you myself or have you sold at the next auction."

He released her with that cool smile still in place and turned away. He shrugged. "I think you would be worth more on the auction block," he said idly.

"What?" Alex breathed. If she had a dagger, she truly might have killed him at that moment. She was literally being played with like a toy, and now this despicable man was casually finding her lacking.

Dan found it difficult not to laugh. She might be a Ph.D., she might be the most sophisticated woman in the world—but she had been insulted to the core because a "Bedouin" had held her and decided she might not be worth keeping!

He kept walking across the tent, his head lowered, his hand to his mouth to hide his secret smile. "But we shall see. . . ." he murmured quickly and nonchalantly, turning back to her in time to note that she had first become a snowy shade of white and then flushed to a becoming shade of red. "Tell me exactly what you are doing out here, and why you traveled across a desert to reach Sheriff."

"Are you Sheriff?"

"I am the one asking the questions here."

Still tense and more explosive with anger than she thought a person could be and still live, Alex replied tersely and condescendingly. "I doubt if you would understand."

"Try me."

She exhaled through clenched teeth. "I am looking for Sheriff because a man named James Crosby has disappeared."

"Go on."

"In his last letter to me Jim Crosby said that I should get in touch with Ali Sur Sheriff should anything happen."

Alex was startled to see the Bedouin's brows rise with both surprise and concern. His dark lashes lowered quickly over his eyes.

"And who is this Crosby to you? Why do you take stupid risks on his behalf?"

"Because he is my father," Alex said simply.

"Your *what?*"

The question was so vehement that for a moment she didn't notice that the Arabic accent had left the husky voice.

"Jim Crosby is my father, he is missing, and I am trying to contact Sheriff in hopes of finding him."

To Alex's shock and consternation, the Bedouin suddenly started to laugh. She watched with amazement as the man wandered to the nearest divan and sat, still laughing. And then, as she stared at him, certain now that it was he and not she who was crazy, he lifted a hand to his mustache.

The hair peeled away with a little tug, as did the beard with his next motion, and then a portion of the thick brows. She saw that the man's flesh was really light bronze and not a deeper, darker color.

"D'Alesio!" It was a hiss of surprise, and the most savage fury Alex had ever experienced in her life. Spontaneously her muscles bunched and contracted. She leaped like a shot at him, with only one thought in mind—that of shredding him to ribbons.

74

CHAPTER FIVE

The hurtling impetus of her charge caught him off guard and off balance. Together they seemed to soar through the air and crash to the ground in a tangled heap.

He had never experienced anything quite like her fury; she was like a small tornado. Psychiatrists often said that the insane could be inhumanly strong; at that moment he was convinced she had to be at least half insane. He didn't want to hurt her—but neither did he feel like having his eyes gouged out.

"Now, listen," he muttered impatiently, seeking to secure a grasp on her flailing wrists, "I know you must be angry, but how the hell do you think I felt, having a woman standing in my bathroom?"

Apparently insanity had closed her eardrums.

"I know you're mad"—he ducked to avoid a nicely placed blow from her fist—"but you can't carry on like this—"

"You scurvy bastard!" she shrieked. "I have never seen more contemptible behavior in my life. You uncivilized, uncouth son of a—"

"Stop right there!" he exploded, giving up all effort to parry her hostility without fighting back. He shifted his weight quickly, sprawling atop her and catching her wrists in a grip of vengeance. "Stop it, 'Doctor'—or you *will* find yourself on an auction block! This is an Arab, Muslim country where women are wives, concubines or slaves! They do not yell and shriek at men, and I will not have my position here made untenable by your temper!"

He had her wrists, and once they were secured, she couldn't possibly move them. But neither did she intend to shut up. "This

75

may not be the United States, but you, Mr. D'Alesio, are an American, and I promise you I will find a way to have you brought up on charges—"

Dan dragged her wrists together to secure them with one hand so that he could press the other across her mouth.

"Press charges at a later date, will you? I'm serious. I know you're angry. But I didn't do what I did merely to hurt or embarrass you. You had a lesson to learn. You went trekking right over land that belonged to Hamdi. If he had gotten to you, Dr. Randall, you could have spent the rest of your life singing 'Yankee Doodle Dandy' and he wouldn't have given a damn. Don't you realize the foolish risks you were—ouch! You little bitch!"

Apparently she didn't understand. She had bitten him.

"I could kill you!" she hissed. "I could honest to God kill—"

She couldn't finish the sentence because he clamped his hand over her mouth again. "Fine!" he whispered back harshly. "You could kill me. But I have no intention of letting you do so, and you bite me again like a child and I'll treat you like one and let you have exactly what you deserve—a good paddling."

At the moment Alex didn't care what he threatened. She was so infuriated she had no thought for possible repercussions. But she was also powerless to do or say anything. His left hand was a solid clamp on her wrists, and his right hand was equally effective over her mouth. He had arched and tightened his fingers so that she couldn't bite again. She couldn't even kick him, not with his solidly muscled weight on top of her. So she lay there, seething. Eventually he would have to release her.

Except that eventually could be a long, long time, and he seemed perfectly content to stare at her and wait. She hadn't the patience for the game. Her temper soared again, and she tried to tell him just how despicable he was. All that came out was muffled gibberish, and she succeeded only in affording him further amusement.

"Listen to me, *Dr.* Randall!" he finally broke in. "Perhaps you have a right to be mad. But think about your own actions! What right did you have to break in on me. I at least gave you time to get out of the bathtub! And you were so damned sure you knew all about the desert! Well, you don't know all about the desert—not here, anyway, Doctor! There is a hell of a lot worse that could have happened to you."

She started raving again, as best she could with a clamped mouth.

Dan sighed patiently, deciding to try another tack. "Why didn't you just tell me you were Jim's daughter in your first letter? Don't you realize it was because of your father that I didn't want to be bothered? I was too worried about Jim to consider anything else."

Alex finally quieted. He sounded sincere. He was worried about her father. And wasn't that what all this was about? She still wanted to kill him—he had thoroughly enjoyed every minute of taunting her. But he was right; she simply wasn't going to be able to do anything to him at the moment. He would be wise, however, to watch his back when she was in the vicinity.

"Besides which," he added quietly, "if you want to meet Ali, you had better calm down. He isn't especially fond of American women. He married one right after college, and she took him for enough to feed a whole tribe for a decade."

Alex remained still, staring into the dark eyes that held hers in their searing gaze. Slowly, very slowly, he removed his hand from her mouth. When she remained quiet, merely gasping slightly to gulp more air, he rolled his weight off her, sitting cross-legged beside her as he continued to watch her warily. Feeling as if she had just been through an electric blender, Alex pulled herself to a sitting position, watching him every bit as warily as he watched her.

It was he who spoke first. "Alex . . . Alexis?"

She shook her head. "Think, D'Alesio," she said disdainfully. "My father is an Egyptologist. Alexandria."

"Then why don't you sign your damn letters 'Alexandria'? And why do you go by the name Randall?"

Alex broke the hold of his eyes and sighed as she gingerly rubbed her wrists. "Randall is my married name. It never occurred to me that you could possibly be so rude as to ignore an urgent letter!"

"I didn't ignore it!" Dan snapped.

Alex shrugged.

"Where the hell is *Mr.* Randall?"

"I—I'm divorced," Alex muttered. "And there isn't a Mr. Randall anywhere—there's another Dr. Randall. I—I've never used my father's name because we're in the same field."

"You are an Egyptologist?"

"Of course!" Alex said with irritation.

"Just checking. You don't look like one."

"Oh, really?" she murmured coolly. "I never realized Egyptologists 'looked' like anything."

He stood, ignoring her caustic remark. With a small grimace he tore the "hook"—expertly applied putty—from his nose. He rubbed his face ruefully, and Alex saw how easily the dark makeup rubbed off.

How could I have fallen for it? she asked herself incredulously. She had the immediate, bitter answer to her own question. Because D'Alesio was good—as good at disguise as he was at journalism. She hated to grant him either fact, but it was always best to acknowledge the strengths of one's enemy.

As she silently watched him, he picked up a clean towel and dipped it into a porcelain washbasin near the bed and studiously scrubbed his face. Still idly holding the towel, he wandered back to her and sat on the carpet, pouring himself another cup of the aromatic coffee. He stared at her again as he sipped his coffee, his face once more familiar. He shook his head slightly as if in disbelief. "Jim's daughter." His brows knit in bafflement. "How old are you?"

"Twenty-six," Alex said, anticipating his raised-brow reaction. "I know—my father is only forty-four." She shrugged. "I was the result of a high school romance. My parents married before my father even began in Egyptology." She hesitated a moment, then shrugged again. "My mother walked out on my father and me when I was just a few months old. Jim managed to keep me and take care of me while studying and working at the same time. Needless to say, Mr. D'Alesio, I adore my father. I would battle you—or every sheikh and emir in a thousand deserts—if it would lead me to him."

D'Alesio lowered his lashes and sipped his coffee. He should have known she was his daughter. Crosby had hair that same soft gold color. But his features were angular, and hers were so delicate.

"Your father told you to get hold of Ali?"

"Yes."

"How? When?"

Alex bit her lip for a second, considering telling him to go to hell—*she* would talk to Sheriff. But he seemed honestly concerned, and no matter what her feelings toward him were, if he could offer any help, she would accept it.

"I got a letter from him on the fifth. He said, exactly, 'if anything goes wrong, get hold of Sheriff. A few things are making me a little nervous.' "

Dan was silent for several seconds, his fingers idly tapping the rug as he mused over her words. "Sounds like he knew something was up somewhere."

Alex waved a hand impatiently in the air. "Obviously. But this must be Sheriff's oasis. If I could just talk to him—"

"You're going to talk to Sheriff," Dan said dryly. "But he isn't going to be able to help you much. I planned on coming out here as soon as I got back to Cairo after your father didn't show in the Valley of the Kings. I've already talked to Ali, and he doesn't know anything."

Alarm rose in Alex's voice. "But Jim was here—I know he was here. He called me from Abu Dhabi—"

"When!" The sharp edge in his voice irritated Alex, but she merely shot him a hostile glance and then responded. "On the fifth—the night I got his letter."

"What did he say?"

Alex frowned, forgetting for a moment that she despised D'Alesio. "He—he said that I had the puzzle pieces. I wasn't sure what he was talking about, so I asked him to repeat himself."

"And?"

"And . . . nothing. The line went dead."

Dan set his coffee cup down on the rug and stood. Alex watched as he began to pace the confines of the tent, thinking that in his black robes he reminded her of an extremely tall

79

panther. He was constant energy; terribly alive, terribly vital. From the coal of his eyes to the smooth agility of his muscled limbs, he was vibrant and electric. Still wishing she could kill him—or at least see him hanged by his toes from a tree for the next ten years—she couldn't fight his compelling attraction. As he moved, her eyes followed him.

He stopped pacing, and Alex felt as if her soul were being impaled when he abruptly turned to stare back into her eyes.

"You know for a fact that he was in Abu Dhabi when he called?"

"Yes. I tried to get him back through the international operator."

"Do you have any idea what he might have meant by 'puzzle pieces'?"

Alex hesitated only a second. "Yes. I think he was talking about the dig—the expedition. The letter he had written was all about the way he had discovered historical 'clues' that fit. He wasn't worried about months or years of digging; he was certain he knew exactly where the tomb would be."

"You don't know?"

Alex shook her head with a grimace.

"But 'you have all the puzzle pieces.' "

"I—I suppose. But you have to realize these pieces are all in a haystack. I believe I might be able to find them—"

"Who else knows you have these pieces?"

Alex stared at him with marked annoyance. He asked questions like a drill sergeant.

"Would you answer me, please?" He read her expression, and then sighed. "Alex, I'm as determined as you are to find your father." She was still sitting on the sand, and he walked to her to offer his hand. She stared at it without touching it for a long time, then accepted his assistance in getting up. "I know you're angry. I was angry myself when I started this thing. I do not like being surprised in my bathtub. Neither do I like being threatened."

Alex lifted her chin and smiled sweetly. "I wasn't threatening you, D'Alesio, I was making promises. You can count on the fact that you'll never film my father's work now."

The hand that held hers tightened until she felt her bones would crack, but the man towering a little bit too close to her smiled.

"Blackmail, Dr. Randall?"

"Fact, D'Alesio."

"I wouldn't count on that. But let's not worry about filming right now, shall we? We have to find your father."

Alex arched a brow and wished that he weren't quite so tall and that she weren't clad in flimsy silks. "If you're not worrying about your precious film, D'Alesio, what are you worrying about?"

"A man," he replied coolly. "A friend—a brilliant scientist. But mostly, Dr. Randall, a man. A human being."

Alex lowered her head and pulled her hand from his grasp. She turned and walked away from him, wondering how it was possible to so despise a person and still admire him. And still feel that he was exceptionally attractive. More than attractive—magnetic. She had never met a man before whom she had wanted so much to touch, simply because of an element of sexuality so strong that it appealed to something that was physical, beyond emotion. She had known desire, but that had been understandable. She had been in love. She certainly wasn't in love with D'Alesio. And of all the men in the world for her to discover she found irresistible on a primitive level . . .

In her present state of confusion, it was more than she could handle. She had even felt it when she had thought him a wild desert kidnapper; now, seeing him as he really was, it only grew stronger.

"All right." His voice snapped out once again like that of a drill master. "What then?"

"What then?"

"What happened then? What did you do? Did you look for Jim? Or did you just sit around in your hotel room waiting to pounce upon me in the bathtub?"

"You son of—"

"Un-unh, Doctor! Not productive. I want to know everything that happened after the phone call until we met."

"You already know!" Alex flared with renewed fury. "All

81

right, D'Alesio, you want to know everything? I flew to Paris the next morning. Transferred flights and arrived in Cairo. I waited for Jim for almost four hours. Then I went to the Hilton. I gave everyone I could the third degree. No one knew for sure when they had seen him last. I called the police; they said he wasn't missing long enough to be a 'missing person.' I called you—a true effort in futility. I went to the museum. I called every professor my dad might know, thinking he might have gotten in touch with someone. I combed the tourist attractions and shops. I heard you'd gone down the Nile; I followed. You came back up the Nile. I followed. And then—as you know—I was tossed bodily out of your hotel room. I flew here—and was bodily attacked." Her voice kept rising as she spoke. Repeating all that had happened made her temper flame like a brushfire.

"Alex," D'Alesio said quietly, impressed despite himself with the loyalty and dogged determination of this particular powder puff. "If we're going to solve anything, we're going to have to call a truce."

She turned back to him. "A truce? You're crazy."

He laughed, and she felt as if she were even touched by the husky sound of his voice. "Truce, Doctor. We can hardly get anywhere when you're being hostile and uncooperative."

"Mr. D'Alesio, I can hardly help feeling hostile."

He stared at her, hands on hips, then suddenly laughed again. "Would it make you feel any better if I let you clobber me?"

She should, of course, say no. She had always hated violence, considering skirmishes beneath her. But she found she couldn't simply decline dignity. It would make her—childishly perhaps, but truthfully—happier to just give him one good crack.

"Yes, D'Alesio," she said quietly. "It would make me feel much better."

"All right."

"All right what?"

"Come over and clobber me."

Was he joking? Was it another trick? There was only one way to find out. Alex walked over to him and hesitantly lifted her eyes to his.

82

He lifted his hands and dropped them. "At your convenience."

She hesitated a second longer, then surprised even herself with the strength with which she hooked her right fist against his jaw. He gazed at her with eyes both startled and wry as he rubbed his chin. "I hope that did make you happy, Doctor, because you're not going to get another offer." He bypassed her, still massaging his jaw as he headed for the tent flap. She should have appreciated the way he glanced back at her warily over a shoulder, but she was busy rubbing her sore knuckles.

"You do pack a wallop for a powder puff," he muttered.

Alex suddenly realized he was heading out of the tent. "Where are you going?" she demanded. "I thought this was all to make me more cooperative."

"I'm going to go explain to Ali who you are, maybe keep you from having to explain a few things twice. Then I'm going to take a bath. I'll come back to bring you something to eat later, while Ali is at evening prayer. Then I'll take you to him."

"Wait!" Alex rushed after him to catch his arm and stop him. He looked from her hand on his arm to her eyes, and she flushed unaccountably and released him. "Raj—what happened to my young guide? If you've pulled something over on me, D'Alesio, it's one thing, but if you've done anything to that young boy . . ."

Her voice trailed away as she saw one of his slow, devastating smiles slip across his face, and she looked at him queryingly. "Raj is fine, *Dr.* Randall," he assured her. She had never heard anyone make such a taunt of her title before. "Rajman works for me."

Her eyes started to narrow; Dan watched the way her well-shaped lips pursed and thinned.

It was her "dangerous" expression, he thought dryly. The amber in her eyes began to spark against the green, and the color seemed to become gold before his eyes. In another second she would start flailing around with right-hook punches, and he had already learned she could deliver one with venom.

"See ya later, Doc!" he said with a laugh, and before she could vent any more steam upon him, he slipped out through the tent flap.

"Wait!" Alex called sharply again, springing after him. "Later? D'Alesio, get back here! What am I supposed to be doing while you have a leisurely afternoon?"

He didn't hear her—or if did, he was choosing to ignore her. Alex tried to exit the tent and follow him to demand a showdown, but she was met by her Arabian guard dogs as soon as she touched the flap. Still smiling politely, they nevertheless solidly blocked her way.

Alex stood quite still and stared from one man to the other. She smiled sweetly at them and tried a *Min fadlak*, which could mean either "please" or "excuse me."

They didn't budge. They merely shook their dark heads sorrowfully.

Alex spun and reentered the tent with seething frustration, wishing it were possible to slam a tent flap.

She crossed her arms over her chest and tapped her foot against the sand in several moments of simple frustration. Then she sighed, and her eyes lit upon the coffeepot and the tray of fruits and dates and nuts. What she would have liked was her giant Scotch and soda, with several lemon twists floating above the ice and bubbling water. But it was highly unlikely she would be enjoying such a luxury soon. Even she knew the Muslims were total abstainers; they didn't even drink wine.

She sat on the Persian rug and noticed with delight that several perfect mangoes were nestled prettily within the platter. She reached for one of the fruits and bit into it, enjoying the sweet, grainy texture. Just as she was reaching for the small coffeepot to pour herself another demitasse cup of the rich and aromatic brew, the tent flap suddenly whipped open.

Dan D'Alesio, his rakish smile in place, stepped in as she stared up at him. He threw something across the space between them and it landed a foot from her. Her eyes automatically followed the object. It was a brush.

"You wanted something to do," he said with a dry shrug. "Well, please, do something with your hair. You look like the madwoman of Chaillot."

The brush went hurtling back across the tent—but the flap had closed a second time and the missile crashed harmlessly against silk and goatskin. Alex could hear the soft echo of his throaty laughter as he moved away, and she spent the next ten minutes thinking of calamities, natural and premeditated, that might befall Daniel D'Alesio.

But eventually, with little choice of anything else to do, she finished her mango and coffee. And her eyes wandered back to the brush lying on the ground. She was dying to brush out her hair where it had dried in tangles. And it seemed absurd to spite herself just because D'Alesio was the rudest individual she had ever met. Besides, she was going to have to learn to ignore D'Alesio. It was an abhorrent thought, but it appeared she was going to need him. Her father's life was at stake. If D'Alesio were a two-humped camel and he could help find Jim, she would learn to tolerate a two-humped camel.

She rose and retrieved the brush, then studiously gave her hair far more than the customary hundred strokes. Then, with time still weighing on her hands, she eyed the canopied bed with its inviting silken coverings.

It should have been in a harem. The bed itself seemed to offer exotic sensual delights. But it also looked invitingly comfortable, beckoningly comfortable. It seemed to reach out and promise comfort to her tired and sore muscles. Shrugging and glancing uneasily at the still tent flap, Alex crawled on top of the sheer, cool silks and pulled several of the little pillows against herself. She didn't think she would sleep—her mind was still in a seething muddle over the events of the day. And she was becoming more and more worried about Jim. If Sheriff had no answers, where would she go? She had thought ahead no further than to seek out the sheikh. She had prayed that simply finding him would be the miraculous answer to all her problems.

But if he couldn't help her, she might be back at square one. No, D'Alesio was as determined as she to find Jim, and despite everything, that was a strange comfort.

The bed did prove to be very, very comfortable. Cocooned in the soft coolness of the sheets and embraced by the plush pillows, Alex finally slept.

* * *

She awoke while dreaming of lamb stew. A succulent aroma rose in her mind so strongly that she could smell it on the air. With a start she realized she wasn't dreaming. The tent was filled with a spicy, delicious scent. Jerking around, she discovered that D'Alesio was back. Cross-legged on the Persian rug, he was watching her with idle interest as he chewed food from a crockery bowl in his hands.

Irritated that he had come in while she had been sleeping, and not liking the feeling of vulnerability it gave her, Alex snapped, "You might learn to knock!"

He cocked a brow high and queried, "How does one knock at a tent?"

Alex swung her feet around to the floor and was again annoyed to realize she still felt only half dressed. "Now that the joke is over, Mr. D'Alesio, do you think you could return my own clothing?"

"Sorry; it's being laundered."

Alex rose, gritting her teeth. "You're really enjoying this, aren't you?"

He shrugged. "Perhaps. I have never liked being threatened, and, Doctor, you do have a talent with threats."

"Promises," Alex corrected coolly. "And sorry—I have never liked being treated like a child or a toy."

"Then you'll be happy to hear that I'm packing you up and sending you home as soon as I think I've heard anything helpful you might have to say."

"What?" Alex demanded, approaching him furiously. With him seated, she felt momentarily at an advantage. But he stood as she reached him and planted his hands as firmly upon his hips as hers were planted upon her own. And instead of looking down at him, she was looking up again.

"You heard me," he said firmly. "You're going home. This is simply no place for you to be. Now sit down and have something to eat."

He sat again and picked up his bowl as if the matter were settled. Alex remained standing a moment longer in helpless

86

rage, then sat across from him. She tried to remind herself that a man like D'Alesio had to be treated with kid gloves.

There was a large covered pot between them. Alex calmly lifted the cover and glanced about for utensils. D'Alesio handed her a second dish and she ladled some of the stew into it. She recovered the pot and said with quiet determination, "Mr. D'Alesio, I am not leaving the Middle East until I find my father."

He issued a small explosion of exasperation. "Lady, where are your brains? You want to have me boiled alive for what I did to you, and that was nothing but a warning! Alex! I will do everything in my power to find your father."

"I will not leave," she said stubbornly. She didn't look at his face. She barely knew the man, and yet she knew his power. She was discovering that he did have a few human streaks, but he still considered his words unquestionably to be law. And he had a way of making one falter into believing him, into accepting him. That power, his power, she tried to tell herself, came from his eyes, as if they had a separate, occult force all their own like a mystical jet stone. If she didn't look into his eyes, she could carry off her own aplomb more easily.

"You will leave," he returned shortly. He reached across her suddenly and she flinched, then relaxed as she realized he was merely reaching behind her for a large satchel. From it he withdrew a bottle of mineral water and stoneware cups. Her eyes involuntarily met his as he handed her a cup and she shivered slightly, aware that he had noticed and registered her flinch.

"Don't you realize that you shouldn't be here?" he asked irritably.

"D'Alesio, the only danger I've come across is you!"

To her surprise, he smiled with a small shrug. "Whatever the danger is, Doctor, you should leave before it gets too hot." He sipped his water and nudged the bowl of food she held. "Come on, Doctor, the stew is excellent. And if you eat it all up like a good little girl, I'll take you to Sheriff."

Apparently they had both dropped the argument for the moment. Alex obediently bit into the stew, which was excellent, with no protest. If she was about to meet Sheriff, she wasn't going to attempt to spite D'Alesio, no matter how condescending his attitude.

Before they left the tent, she put on the Moroccan slippers that had been left with the silk garments. Dan supplied her with a heavier robe to cover the thin silks. He also took it upon himself to secure a swath of material over her hair and a veil over her lower face. "When in Rome. . . ." he murmured as she chaffed beneath his ministrations.

"Are you quite through?" Alex asked impatiently.

"Quite." He laughed in return. He lifted the tent flap for her, and she preceded him out. The two bruisers she was coming to think of as Abbott and Costello didn't make a move except to incline their heads in a barely perceptible fashion toward Dan D'Alesio. They maintained their crossed-armed stances, a bitter reminder to Alex that she would be returned to the tent and once more guarded when her interview was finished.

The sun was fast fading in the western sky, and the color of the desert and the oasis was beautiful. The sizzling heat of the day was gone; night was coming to the desert, with its kiss of blissful coolness. Alex paused just outside the tent to feel the strange beauty of the night. She could no longer hear the laughter of children, but she could somehow feel the serenity of the camp. Past the closest array of tents, Alex could see glimpses of the water, aqua against the magenta sky, shaded and protected by numerous palms. The beautiful aqua water, the lifeline of the people.

Only a few of the Bedouins were about: men in neutral galabrias tethering horses and camels for the night, a few women in their modest robes wandering back from the waters of the oasis with pots for evening ablutions. It was a quiet time for the Bedouins; even the animals seemed to know it. Alex felt as if she had been taken back centuries, as if she had stumbled upon an era of tranquillity and beauty. The desert was as it had been through the millennia—not even the power of man could change it.

She suddenly felt D'Alesio's hand on her elbow. "It is beautiful," he said quietly, as if she had spoken aloud. And for a moment she felt as if they had hit upon a strange chord of complete harmony. In this vista where the tents seemed to stretch in grandeur for miles and miles against a magenta sky, where the air was silent except for the occasional bleat of a goat or bray of a camel, they had found something to share—an appreciation for a way of life that defied time itself.

Alex nodded, surprised to find that her throat was dry and she was unable to answer. He slipped his hand into hers and began walking. Then, as if the moment had brought them too close, he teased, "You should be three paces behind me, but I'll grant you a concession this once."

"Kind of you, D'Alesio," Alex murmured caustically.

"I thought so."

She bit back a reply because she saw they had passed before a tent about a hundred yards east of hers. Dan lifted the flap and ushered her inside.

CHAPTER SIX

Ali Sur Sheriff was waiting.

He was real, and he was handsome, and he was civil—and restrained; a far cry from a crazy Bedouin racing across the desert to abduct hapless blondes.

He was smiling, and Alex thought she had never seen such a beautiful smile. The Arab was dressed like Dan, in black desert robes, but he was a small man—or perhaps only when compared with D'Alesio. His skin was a dark bronze; his eyes were chocolate. He had a small mustache and an elegantly clipped goatee. With his smile, sparkling eyes and quiet, unassuming manner, he was a striking man. His voice, when he spoke, was also quiet and cultured.

"Dr. Randall. I am pleased to welcome you to my home."

His clipped English was perfect—so perfect, he should have been speaking in a British parliament. Alex shot Dan D'Alesio a hostile glance as she wondered whether she should bow, stand still or what. The problem was solved for her as Ali Sur Sheriff approached her with both hands extended, catching hers, and leading her on into the center of his tent, where a large rug again lay prominently across the sand floor. Boiling coffee and an array of pastries were set nearby.

The elegance of her tent was nothing in comparison to his. It seemed to Alex that the sheikh's tent was as large as a football field. It also had rugs and throw pillows and divans, but practical concessions had been added for the busy sheikh. There were large wood wardrobes in the far left section, a conference table and secretary to the right. Oil lamps sat upon various chests, and a graceful chandelier sat upon the conference table, a dozen candles burning brightly from its elegant holders.

Alex took all this in as Sheriff seated her. Then her eyes were only for the sheikh. It struck her as odd that he seemed to be such a gentle man, that his eyes could be touched by such kindness when he was a man of such unlimited power. But in those same kind eyes she found her answer—Ali Sur Sheriff was a man at peace within himself.

D'Alesio took a seat beside her, facing Ali Sheriff. Alex was both irritated and perversely pleased. She was coming to know the man, and at the moment he was a bit like a lifeline. He didn't touch her, but she could feel the pulse, the current of his presence; she could inhale the pleasant scent of sandalwood and musk that was so male, so solid, so subtle and yet stirring.

The sheikh poured the coffee, and when he handed out fine porcelain cups to Dan and Alex, he lit a water pipe. Alex had seen the pipes many times in Cairo; they were as social as coffee. He offered her the pipe and she hesitated, wondering if she should risk a hacking cough for the next hour to avoid insulting the sheikh, or simply to explain that she didn't smoke.

Dan settled the problem for her—smoothly, she had to admit. He reached past her for the pipe. "Alex doesn't smoke, Ali. All American women don't have bad habits!"

Sheriff smiled. "Alex . . . I understand from my friend that you are Jim's daughter."

"Yes," Alex murmured, feeling comfortable in the sheikh's presence, and yet a little lost. "I—my father wrote me a letter that I received just before I left the States. In that letter he told me that I must find you if something went wrong. Since then, as you know, my father has disappeared. I have come here, praying that you would be able to help me."

Sheriff inhaled on his water pipe and exhaled slowly. "I know this now, of course. But I did not know Jim had disappeared until Dan arrived here last night. I am very worried. Now, please, tell me everything that has happened, everything that you have done."

Alex did so, repeating all that she had told Dan, forcing herself to speak slowly and patiently. It was easier to talk to

Ali—she didn't continually feel the urge to kill him—and so she was able to be thorough and systematic.

But when she finished speaking, Ali was shaking his head unhappily. "I am very worried," he repeated softly.

Alex caught and held her breath. This was it. She had come to Sheriff praying for her miracle, and he knew nothing. What had she been expecting—a magician who could pull her father out of a hat?

She exhaled, trying not to cry. But before she could begin to speak, Sheriff did. "I do not know why your father told you to come to me, Alex. But we will work on that puzzle. I know that he felt there would be competition if his plans were known too soon. And I think he suspected someone—or some group—in particular. Your father's work can be dangerous, Alex. There are people who—well, people willing to kill for the riches produced by such an expedition. People, too, who are interested not so much in money but in glory."

"Alex," Dan interjected. "I believe Jim sent you to Ali, through me, because he believed we would have the power to find him. You cannot do so. If something has happened to your father . . ."

Dan's voice trailed away, and Ali picked up softly. "You must accept the fact that your father may be dead."

"No!" She hadn't meant to shriek at the man with the gentle eyes. She had simply done so because she couldn't accept the fact that her father might be dead. Sheriff, however, took no offense.

"Please, Alex, do not upset yourself. I say this only because you must be prepared for all possibilities—and because I agree with Dan. You must go home. If your father was abducted or—hurt, you could also be in danger. And this is no place for a woman such as yourself."

"Sheikh Sheriff," Alex said as calmly and firmly as she could, "I must find my father. I have spent a great deal of time in Egypt—in Cairo, Thebes and Luxor. Granted, I know little of your country, but then we might discover that my father's trail leads back to Egypt, and I am very familiar with Egypt!"

Alex noted with annoyance that Sheriff and D'Alesio exchanged quick glances. A silent communication passed between

92

them that left her baffled, but she didn't have much time to wonder because Sheriff spoke again, asking her to tell him anything she could think of that might be relevant. As Dan and he listened, Alex repeated the pertinent paragraph of the letter, then told both men about the strange phone call that had been so abruptly cut off. When she finished speaking, Sheriff stroked his goatee for several seconds, musing over her words.

"Your father was with me for several days, you know," he said, inhaling upon his pipe and slowly exhaling a flume of pleasantly scented smoke. "You are sure he called from Abu Dhabi?"

"I'm positive," Alex said, "because I tried to trace the call when we were cut off. I didn't worry about it at the time because I know the telephone systems here are—" She paused, not wanting to insult the sheikh, but Ali laughed.

"Our phone systems are terrible! Ah, well, progress takes time!"

"All right," Dan interrupted softly. "We know that Jim was in Abu Dhabi on the fifth. What we don't know is what happened from there. We have to find out if—if he left the country."

Sheriff nodded and clapped his hands. A man immediately appeared in the tent. Sheriff spoke quickly; the man nodded and disappeared as quickly as he had come.

"A rider will go out tonight," Sheriff explained. He glanced at Dan. "Jim was to see Haman before he left. Tomorrow you and I will ride out to see my old rival and find out what happened there."

"Haman?" Alex spoke up quickly. "My father mentioned Haman in his letter. He said that Haman had become very interested in him because you were financing his expedition. But if you were financing the expedition, why would my father go to Haman?"

Sheriff tapped his chin for a moment before answering. "Your father is interested in more than ancient treasures, Alex. He is interested in people. Egypt holds the vast riches of history, but her people suffer in poverty more vast. Here in the United Arab Emirates many of us have become almost obscenely wealthy. Now, to understand what I will say next, you must understand those of us who are of Islam. We are beholden to care for those who are less fortunate than ourselves. Allah entrusts us with the care of our brethren. I had promised your father more than the financing for the expedition; I promised him a large endowment for several new schools in Luxor and West Thebes. As a Muslim and as an Arab, I must take it unto my heart to provide for those Arabs less fortunate than I. Do you understand this, Dr. Randall?"

Alex nodded, touched again by the marvelous gentility of this powerful man.

"Your father told Haman about this, and Haman said that he would like to speak with him further. So your father planned to see Haman. He thought—rightfully—that a generous contribution by Haman, given perhaps merely to spite me, would still benefit the children of Egypt."

"Oh," Alex said softly. "But I don't believe my father trusted him!"

"Haman," Dan D'Alesio offered dryly, "is a slippery old fox. No halfway intelligent man would trust him!"

Sheriff grimaced. "That is true. But we will check with him tomorrow." He sighed. "Haman can be like a child. He very much wants to be in on your father's discovery. Perhaps he believed if he dogged Jim long enough, Jim would give in to him and allow him to be there for the dig—so that he might be announced to the world as a great man. I do not know how far Haman would go to achieve these ends, and although I do not think him capable of murder, I don't think kidnapping would be beneath him. I also think that my friend Haman is a very persistent man—"

"You think he may be holding my father?"

"No." Ali shook his head. "But I do not exclude the possibility. I think Haman might have something to say to help us; that is all that I feel for certain."

D'Alesio turned to stare directly at Alex. "I want you to think about those 'puzzle pieces' a bit. Are you sure you don't know anything more than you've told us?"

Alex shook her head. "I don't think so."

"Alex," Dan said quietly. "I think your father was trying to

94

protect you. Neither Ali nor I knew that Jim had a daughter until today. He kept silent and vague about his 'assistant.' We all know that there exists a tremendous black market for Egyptian antiquities. There are private collectors throughout the world who will pay ungodly sums for authentic pieces. Alex, at that level, Jim's life—your life—could be in danger. I think Jim was trying to protect you to the last minute—but I think he was also telling you that you can find the tomb."

"I—I suppose that could be so," Alex murmured. "Except that I don't think I can!"

"Probably not," D'Alesio said, unaware that his offhand comment made her instantly bristle. "But the point that frightens me is that someone else may think you can. All the more reason we have to get you out of here as quickly as possible."

"I'm not going anywhere—"

"Doctor—Alex—" Sheriff had the most fascinating way of saying her name, with the accent softly on the "x." Alex dragged her tumultuous eyes from Dan's to meet the sheikh's.

"I want you out of here as quickly as possible. You are in danger right here—and it has nothing to do with what might happen in Egypt at all! Among us you are an extraordinary woman. You must understand that here women may be bartered and sold. I fear that you may enrapture one of my own men! You are unattached, and therefore you are—how shall I say it?—free for the taking! Now, I can, of course, control my own tribe. But it is possible that rumors of your arrival are already spreading. You will be a temptation others may not be able to resist. I do not wish to go to war with my fellow countrymen when such a thing may be avoided."

"But—but—" Alex protested, feeling guilty and yet determined. "I cannot believe that someone would actually—I mean, I understand that your women are also valued and highly protected! And I've always understood that abducting a man's woman was a crime for which one man might kill another. Surely no man would chance that with you—"

"Dr. Randall, all know that Ali Sur Sheriff already has four wives and that he doesn't keep slaves or a harem." His dark eyes sparkled mischievously with a light that was still kind but also that of a healthy and lusty male. "If I could make you a fifth wife, Alex, I would gladly do so, but the Koran allows us only four. Therefore, you are not safe. Not here, and—if Haman does have anything to do with this—you will not be safe in Egypt. Even as your protector, I cannot always be with you."

Alex silently digested his words. She bit her lip and made a last effort. "Sheikh Ali Sur Sheriff, I must be here! Don't you see? I cannot go home without my father! I must know—" She cut herself off. She had been about to say, "whether he is alive or dead," but she couldn't voice the words. Instead she started over. "There might still be something in my mind that I haven't realized—another clue! Please, please, at least think this over!"

Again, one of those communicative glances passed between Sheriff and D'Alesio. "I will think on it," the sheikh said.

Alex was sinkingly sure that the words had been said to humor her. She felt as if she would explode with the unfairness of the situation. She could understand Ali—this was his world; he had been raised to see women as chattel, and in his experience with American women, it was apparent he had found little pleasure.

D'Alesio was another story. He was simply in a situation in which he could flaunt his chauvinism, and he was enjoying doing so. She would really love to see him . . .

She bit her lip softly as the two began to exchange a few words in Arabic. It was true, she had to admit grudgingly, that they both seemed concerned for her. Yes, she even had to give that credit to D'Alesio.

"I am sorry," the sheikh apologized quickly. "There are some things that only make sense in one language, you understand."

"Certainly," Alex murmured, sweeping her lashes over her eyes. Certainly, my foot! she thought. She had seen a soft smile creep onto Ali's lips, and she knew that he was aware of exactly how she had come into his camp, and that he found the entire incident amusing.

She never remembered hating any male with such venom before in her life as she did D'Alesio, even when she had fought to keep her head above water in her profession.

The sheikh rose. Alex's interview was at an end and there wasn't a thing in the world she could do about it. She offered her hand to the sheikh, and he accepted it. "We will speak again in the morning," he promised her.

"Thank you," Alex said dispiritedly.

D'Alesio's hand was upon her arm again, and she accepted it with weary resignation. Maybe in the morning. . . .

The tent was a blur to her as she left it, fighting tears. She had come though all this to finally meet Sheriff—only to be packed up and sent off as if she were a statue herself. Not that either Sheriff or D'Alesio could force her to go home. They could, perhaps, force her out of the United Arab Emirates, but she would go on to Egypt, and they couldn't stop her. If the answer to her father's disappearance lay with Haman, she couldn't—absolutely couldn't—leave. It was all so unfair! Just because she was an unattached woman. . . .

Bile rose in her stomach, and for a moment her hate extended to her ex-husband. If he had only been there when she had needed him, she wouldn't be alone and unattached now.

"Here we are, Doctor," Daniel D'Alesio said, and Alex realized she had walked blindly with him back to her own tent. She had barely even noted that Abbott and Costello were still standing sentinel outside the flap. But they were still there and she had known they would be.

"Why are those two goons still standing there?" she demanded sharply.

"For your own safety," Dan replied firmly, adding casually, "Have a nice sleep. I'll see you in the morning."

"Sleep?" she murmured vaguely, wondering herself at first why she was staring at him so peculiarly. "I slept all afternoon. It's early."

D'Alesio shrugged. "Well, you can sleep or twiddle your thumbs. I'd try to entertain you, but I promised Ali a poker game—he picked up a real penchant for poker at Yale."

"I thought Muslims were not allowed to gamble."

"We don't gamble; we play for matchsticks."

She was still staring at him, slowly realizing that an embryo of an idea was growing within her. He frowned suddenly, and she was treated to the sharpening of his jet eyes and the wary knitting of his brows.

"D'Alesio . . ." she murmured slowly, despising herself for what she was about to request. It was still too easy to remember how he had grappled with her, abducted her, and taunted her. And held her. Mesmerized her with that electric power. His touch was quicksand; he was terrifying. He was the enemy, but he was also the only friend she had.

"What?" he demanded impatiently.

Alex swallowed, not allowing herself to clear her throat. Her palms felt clammy and her mouth dry. She tried to sound entirely casual. "You're not married, are you?"

"What's that got to do with—oh, no!" His teeth flashed white across his mocking features as he laughed dryly. "Oh, no, Doctor! I have no intention of marrying you merely to keep a time bomb around!"

"It wouldn't be for real!" Alex protested. "Lord knows, I despise you! And it's my own neck—"

"Leave it to a woman who would break into a man's bathroom to demand that he marry her while informing him she despises him!"

"I'm sorry . . ."

"Forget it."

"I can't!"

Something of her determination sounded through the two simple words. Dan crossed his arms over his chest and leaned back slightly, watching her with an amused and mocking curiosity.

"Sorry," he said again softly. "I never make a deal that doesn't hold some benefit for me. This one spells only one thing: trouble."

He turned and started walking out of the tent.

"Wait!" Alex pleaded.

He stopped and turned to her with arched brows.

"At least tell me you'll think about it."

His answer was not long in coming.

"No," he said firmly. "I will *not* think about it." He chuckled suddenly, leaving Alex with no idea of whether he next was speaking seriously or merely tauntingly, as if daring her, calling her bluff.

"Change the proposal to a proposition, Doctor, and we might be in business. I'm not the marrying kind, but even for a proposition, you'd have to be very, very persuasive." He cocked a brow with a dry humor that left her staring at him blankly at first, incredulous, and then ready to hurtle herself at him again in blind fury.

"Get out of here, you—"

He laughed easily. "I'm going, Doctor. Good night."

He exited the tent to head back for his poker game.

Alex spent the next several minutes trying to cool her temper, and then she spent the next several hours staring at the silk billowing from the canopy over her bed.

Somewhere stars were shining over an Arabian night.

To Alex, darkness had never been more bleak.

CHAPTER SEVEN

It *was* possible to knock at a tent flap.

Alex woke with little disorientation to hear a soft rapping against the tent. She shot up from the silken cocoon of the bed, gazing about for a quick covering to slip over the very sheer nightgown she had discovered the night before, then reached for the light silk morning robe someone had thoughtfully left at the foot of her bed. She automatically smoothed back her hair while walking toward the flap.

Her early-morning visitor was none other than the sheikh. He entered with a wide smile and a cheerful good morning, and clapped his hands lightly so that his entrance was immediately followed by that of the young Arab woman she had seen the previous day. The girl carried a silver tray with various covered dishes.

"I have brought you some breakfast," Ali Sur Sheriff announced politely. His smile became deeper, and Alex was impressed with the nonchalance of his natural charm. "It is not the custom within our tribe to dine with our women, but since you have so obligingly accustomed yourself to our world, I shall accustom myself to yours. Besides, that is one pleasure I miss when I am not in the West—that of breakfasting with a beautiful face before me."

Alex grinned at his compliment without demurring. Though the sheikh might be faithful to his four wives, he was a man with a natural way with women. For a man of his religion and race, he had a strangely respectful and gentle attitude. "Thank you," she murmured as the tray was set down and the inevitable Arabian coffee was set to heat by the young woman. Alex was next offered a steaming and fragrant cloth to cleanse her face and hands. She murmured a *Min fadlak,* and the lovely Arabian smiled brightly beneath her veil.

Sheriff caught the girl's hand when she would have quietly departed. "Dr. Randall, you must formally meet Shahalla. She is my number-one wife."

The girl flushed and shyly lowered her head. "How do you do, Shahalla," Alex murmured, aware that the girl spoke no English but assuming she would recognize the tone of greeting. She wondered with an edge of rebellion if Shahalla shouldn't be offended. The sheikh was breakfasting with her, when he wouldn't do so with his own wife.

But Alex couldn't afford to be offended herself, or to say anything about women's rights. It was not the time or place, and she needed to wedge her own way into Ali Sur Sheriff's good graces. Somehow she had to convince him that she should stay!

The girl said something back in Arabic, smiled at Sheriff, and continued on out of the tent.

"She is a very beautiful girl," Alex told Sheriff, "with a lovely name."

"Yes," Sheriff said, taking his place on the Persian rug. "Shahalla is a blessing from Allah." He glanced up at Alex. "You will join me, please."

Alex quickly sat in front of him. The sheikh began to prepare her a plate. "Here . . . we have traditional 'fool.' You know what this is?"

"Black beans, I believe," Alex murmured.

"Yes!" Sheriff seemed pleased with her knowledge. "And, of course, a serving of our white cheeses . . . some halava—a sugary type of confection—and some of the very best falafel you will ever taste! Shahalla is an excellent cook."

Alex accepted the plate. She had seen the Arabic dishes listed on many menus before, but she had always opted for the security of the bacon and eggs offered by the various Egyptian hotels she had stayed in—hotels that catered to tourists. Smiling at Sheriff, she decided to test her stomach on the falafel first.

It was excellent—crispy, delicious. Surprise must have registered on her face because Sheriff laughed and said proudly, "Dr.

Randall, I told you Shahalla was one of the finest cooks in the world!"

Alex flushed, then laughed along with him. "I must admit, Sheikh Sheriff, that for all my time in Egypt, I have neglected to allow my taste buds to explore. This is wonderful. What is it?"

"Falafel is merely fool, ground and fried. It is the spices and care in preparation that make it so palatable."

"Then you are blessed, Ali Sur Sheriff," Alex said lightly, "for your wife is beautiful and surely talented."

He was staring at her with a peculiar twinkle in his eyes. "You are not offended?"

Alex frowned. "I don't know what you mean."

Sheriff extended an all-encompassing arm about the tent. "By our life-style."

"No, of course not. Why would I be?"

"You are an American—and a doctor in a rare field. Surely we seem archaic to you!"

Alex hesitated, forming her reply carefully. "This is, yes, a very different way of life. I could not accept your standards because I was not raised in them. I am my father's only child. He raised me to believe in myself, and to work for what I wanted out of life. It is hard for an American woman to accept others of her sex being thought of only as second-class citizens. But it is not my right to judge your life—or the lives of your wives. Shahalla appears to be very happy."

Sheriff thoughtfully chewed upon his falafel and bit down on a soft piece of white cheese before speaking again. "I was married to an American woman once. Perhaps if she had been more like you, my life would now be different. Ah, well, that is all in the past. And now, if you don't mind, I would like to learn more about Alexandria Crosby Randall. Why are you divorced?"

Alex flushed slightly at the inquisitive and forthright question. Had another man asked her something so personal, she would have been offended. But it was difficult to resent the query from the sheikh with the dark and gentle eyes.

"It is hard to say," she told him with a grimace and a shrug. "My husband—my ex-husband—is also an Egyptologist. We were married while I was still working toward my doctorate. It's

102

strange," Alex mused, casting a wry glance at Sheriff, "but one would have thought we would have been perfect for each other—two people with a passion for a dead and ancient past! But once I graduated and took a position with a museum, things started . . . they just started going wrong. We quarreled over everything. And—" Alex broke off suddenly, staring at Sheriff. How did one explain to a man with four wives how she had been unable to handle Wayne's admissions that he had been casually sleeping around.

"Please," Ali murmured, "go on."

Alex smiled softly. "You have been around the world, I understand, Ali, so I am sure that you understand we believe in monogamous marriages. My husband told me he had been sleeping with women he had met in various nightclubs—and that he would continue to do so unless I gave up my job and promised that I would—that I would be at home for his convenience at all times."

Sheriff was laughing. Alex felt a heated anger growing within her, but the sheikh apologized quickly. "I am not laughing at your problem but at your reticence in explaining it to me—and your choice of words!" He moved to pour the coffee, which was well heated by now. "So, your husband was not worth your staying home for?"

Alex sipped her coffee while debating how to answer the question. "Ali, I loved him very much. I still love him. It's very difficult to explain. I worked very hard for my doctorate, and I care very much about my work. I don't think that I am a fanatical liberationist—I love keeping a home, and I love to cook. But I am also a trained Egyptologist. To give up my work would be to give up part of myself. Wayne always knew that part of me existed. It's possible to be so insanely in love that you'll promise to change anything, but I don't believe that can really help a relationship. If you try to change too strenuously, you will eventually grow to resent the person who caused you to lose so much. I never worked ridiculous hours, and our home was always a home. Can you understand that I did love Wayne but also knew that a lopsided partnership couldn't last?"

Sheriff contemplatively stirred more sugar into his coffee.

"Yes," he murmured. "I can understand that." He sipped his coffee again, and his expression told Alex that the sugar content was perfect. "I was curious, you see, because our friend Dan mentioned to me over our poker game last night that you asked him to marry you."

Alex had been sipping her own coffee. To her dismay, she choked and gasped and sprayed the Persian rug with her coffee. She grasped hastily for a napkin to sop up the mess.

Sheriff caught her hand. "Please do not worry—it can be cleaned. I did not mean to startle you so."

"I—I—" Alex stuttered. "I didn't believe that Mr. D'Alesio would bring up such a subject."

"You are not very fond of my friend, are you, Alex?"

"Well—I—I—" What could she say? She needed the sheikh, as she needed Dan. She certainly didn't want to offend the sheikh by telling him she found D'Alesio to be a royal bastard.

"You are still angry over his charade of yesterday." Sheriff shrugged. "If we had known you were Jim's daughter . . . but we didn't, and what is done, is done."

Alex pretended a deep interest in her coffee. Sheriff hadn't been around when D'Alesio had thrown her out of his hotel room, and he hadn't heard D'Alesio laugh over her marriage proposal; neither had he been the one who was terrified and humiliated during the little "charade."

"Have you finished?" Sheriff inquired politely.

Alex glanced at her plate in surprise. She had finished, barely tasting what she was eating after that first bite. She had been so carefully weighing all her answers because she wanted to become Sheriff's friend. She had to get him to change his mind about insisting she leave the UAE.

"Yes, I have finished, thank you," Alex said politely.

"Then come; you will walk with me. It is early yet. In another hour or so I must start off for Haman's with Dan, but until then . . ." He shrugged with his beautiful smile in place, teeth brilliantly white against his skin and dashing mustache. "Your own clothing has been laundered and returned. You will find it in the trunk beside your bed. If you wish to dress, I will wait outside for you."

Alex quickly stood, murmuring a thank you.

Ali bowed and ducked beneath the flap. Alex quickly found her clothes where he had said they would be, dressed gratefully in lightning time and rejoined him.

"We will walk to the water," he told her.

Alex noticed as they left her tent that Abbott and Costello were gone, but that they had been replaced by a new set of guards. Laurel and Hardy, she mentally dubbed the second pair. Laurel and Hardy followed behind them at a discreet distance.

Whereas nighttime had been peaceful and quiet, the morning was full of bustling activity. Boys and young girls tended flocks of sheep and goats, herding them through the trails between the tents toward the meager grasslands. Women were busy in front of their tents, gathering laundry, dousing cooking fires. An old man repaired a rent in his goatskin abode.

"Many of my tribesmen belong to the armed forces of the United Arab Emirates," Ali explained as he led Alex along the trail to the water, the life center of the oasis. All whom they passed—male, female, child and adult—bowed graciously to the sheikh and stared quickly and curiously at her, but not long enough to be rude.

Water never appeared more beautiful than it did at an outpost in the desert. It shimmered aqua and the blue beneath the sun; it was one of the most beautiful sights Alex had ever seen. Young children were playing in it; women were washing clothes along the sandy banks.

Ali stooped to cup a handful of the liquid life, allowing it to drip through his fingers. "This must seem most strange to you, Dr. Randall," he murmured. He glanced at her and grimaced. "But as you say, we are what we were raised to be. I have seen the majority of the world, Alex, and yet this—this place with no plumbing, no electricity—is where I choose to be. Oil has made us rich. But progress cannot be bought in a day or even in a year. It comes with time. And even then one must wonder how much progress he wishes to purchase! And oil! Across the Persian Gulf, the Iranians and the Iraqis murder one another for oil, for these riches . . ."

He stood, and his handsome face twisted into a grimace. "I

love it here, Alex Randall. We are one of the last bastions of a truly romantic past. We offer perhaps the last of the Arabian nights. In time roads will sweep across the desert. We will build a railroad, and we will erect fine colleges. Our medicine will improve, and we will breed teachers and poets and scientists. We will join the contemporary world." His grimace became a soft smile. "I begrudge that time coming, Alex, because all this will be gone—the simple beauty of water, the splendor of the horses racing across the sand, the honor that belongs only to men with simple needs."

Alex hadn't realized that she had reached out to touch him until her hand came into contact with his cheek. He glanced at her quickly and caught her hand, and as he read the empathy in her eyes, he lightly kissed the back of her hand, as if he were a French diplomat rather than a desert chieftain.

"I tell you all this," Ali said, "because I still think it would be best if you were to go home. Our world is very different; I do not wish it to prove dangerous for you. However, I have given this situation serious contemplation. Marriage," he teased her, eyes twinkling, "is a bit drastic. And I am the sheikh—the Arab. My name must stand to protect you. But it is not enough. Responsibility comes with power, and I already have grave responsibilities. Dan must therefore tell me that he will agree to be personally responsible for you—that he will be your protector. If he will do that"—Ali lifted his hands slightly—"then I too will agree that you may stay. Hopefully, between the two of us, you should be safe."

Alex stooped to trail her fingers through the water. "Ali, I wish you would realize that I am responsible for myself. It is my choice to take risks, and it is my responsibility to accept the consequences. You . . ." Her voice became involuntarily husky and her breath seemed to catch in her heart for a moment. "You must try to understand. My father is my family. He is everything to me. I cannot leave without knowing—"

"I do understand," Sheriff interrupted quietly. "But your being in danger will not help your father. The desert has strange laws, Alex. In our religion we believe in an eye for an eye. We believe in our customs, a way of life incredibly old. And also, in

106

our blood, we believe in our wants and our desires and our tribes. We still hold fast to a wild beauty, Alex, but with it, we can also be dangerous to outsiders."

Alex shook her head and touched the surface of the water again. "I don't understand you, Ali."

He laughed. "You are an exceptionally beautiful and unique woman, Alex—and willful! You need a lot of protection. Go work on D'Alesio again. You are a strong woman, yes, but still, as I said, a beautiful one! Surely you can charm a man! Dan is very self-sufficient and accustomed to his independence. It will not be easy for him to feel he must slow down for a woman, but still . . . he is a man, Alex. And if you wish to stay, I am afraid that I must insist we also have his agreement."

"But he'll never—" Alex broke off abruptly. She had been about to plead again that she was responsible for herself, but she realized her plea would fall upon deaf ears. Ali had decided. She was wasting her time trying to do anything other than confront D'Alesio again and beg and threaten until she forced him to agree.

"I won't have much time to 'work' on him, I'm afraid," Alex muttered. "Not if you two are leaving in an hour."

"Then if I may," Ali said lightly, "I will suggest that you start now!"

Alex glanced at up at the sheikh, then sprang to her feet with determination. "Where is he?"

Ali Sur Sheriff tossed back his head and laughed. "In the tent beyond yours, almost behind it. Go and wake him up. He is wasting the morning away."

Alex hesitated a second, then spun to walk back upon the trail that had brought them to the water's edge.

"Alex Randall!" the sheikh called after her.

She paused on her toes and spun back to face him.

"Good luck. I find you to be fascinating. I would enjoy having you as a guest much longer."

Ali Sur Sheriff watched as the beautiful girl smiled, saluted him with a wave and turned to race off again.

She had something, he mused, something very special. And then he laughed again, because although he found himself growing fond of the American woman and did enjoy her company, he still logically felt she would be better off away from the Middle East, away from Cairo. For all they knew, Crosby might have been murdered.

But although he liked and admired her, and felt a great empathy for her, his actions were for the friend he loved like a brother. There were times when he might have been in grave trouble in the States. Dan, with his eloquent way with words and keen sense of danger, had pulled him out of many scrapes. And when he had broken up with his American wife, Dan had flown across two continents to help him and be beside him. But now, he felt, it was Dan who needed help—whether Dan thought so or not!

Dan had always managed women so easily. He was striking, he was a celebrity and he had a certain innate and primitively rugged sexuality that appealed instantly to the opposite sex.

He was a man basically unaware of his natural assets; he was always so intensely involved with the world that he would never have stopped to worry about his effect on people. Affairs came easily and naturally and usually ended when he moved on.

But what was it, Ali wondered, that seemed to come to all men? Was it age? Or the world itself. To most men came a time when they began to long for something solid, to need more than excitement, to crave a family and a home. With him that fulfillment had come with the acquisitions of his wives, one by one. With Dan, of course, fulfillment would be different. He was essentially a one-woman man, Ali was sure, simply looking for the right woman.

That one woman could be Alexandria Randall. Oh, they appeared to clash like oil and water, but there was something else there, something that touched the air like electricity when they were together. Yes, Alex might very well be just what Dan needed, the perfect mate for him, body and soul. She was strong like the desert sun, yet gentle like the night breezes that cooled and soothed its heat. And, Ali thought a bit angrily, she deserved more of a man than what she had had. D'Alesio would never feel threatened by the strengths or intelligence of another person. He would admire such qualities, encourage them to their full potential.

108

I am trying to play Allah, Ali chastised himself. I am using my power to manipulate. He shrugged with a grin. What good was power if one didn't occasionally use it? He had his responsibilities; he also deserved his enjoyments. And he was going to enjoy the electric storms to come, he thought with a laugh. Ah, yes, sparks were destined to fly.

He laughed aloud suddenly, wondering if Dan wouldn't be tempted to come striding down to the water to give him a good right hook across the jaw if he knew his life was being manipulated. But Ali could be pretty damn good at guileless innocence when he chose.

And Crosby was missing. Ali owed the man's daughter his protection. And he was going to need help. Who really could protect the girl better than Dan D'Alesio? And what better could he do for his friend than to hand him a sun-gold beauty.

Ali still chuckled lightly to himself as he started back for his own tent. One hundred years ago his forefathers would have made a similar gift to a respected friend. Poor Dr. Randall! She would be so terribly offended if she knew.

Little tiny prickles suddenly seemed to accost his skin, a sure warning that he was not alone. He jerked around, drawn instantly from a comfortable sleep. "Oh, Jesus!" he muttered, raking his fingers through his hair. "You again."

She was sitting demurely at his kneecaps.

"Who else was I expecting?" he muttered in dry exasperation to the silken canopy above his head.

"Ali told me to wake you," Alex said defensively.

"Of course," Dan muttered caustically. "My bathroom . . . my bed. Maybe I ought to marry you. At least I wouldn't be so startled to find you in all these places."

Her lashes lowered and she stared silently at her hands. "Actually," she began, "that—"

"Forget it," Dan interrupted roughly. "I was being sarcastic. And can't you ever take those damn things off?"

"I don't want to marry you, D'Alesio," she said a bit smugly. "All I need is—" She broke off as her eyes rose with startled surprise to meet his. "What things?"

"Those lashes."

"No, I can't take them off. They're attached to my eyelids."

Dan sat up and leaned closer to her, studiously inspecting her eyes. "They *are* for real!"

"Of course they're real! What kind of idiot would run around the desert with false eyelashes!"

Dan suddenly laughed. "You don't want me to answer that. But listen, since you're sitting on my bed—and I sleep in the buff—why don't you be sweet and bring me a cup of coffee."

She was about to snap that he could get his own damn coffee when she remembered she was trying to charm him. She gave him a disarming smile and hopped off the bed.

His tent was set up exactly like hers—rugs, silks, divans and a center section with a Persian rug where meals were taken. Apparently someone catered to the needs of Ali Sur Sheriff's American friend. Coffee brewed in a tiny pot, and an elegant silver tray of covered dishes awaited his pleasure.

Alex poured one of the delicate ceramic cups full of coffee and brought it back to Dan, taking a seat once more on the edge of the bed.

"Listen to me, will you please, D'Al—Dan?" Not waiting for an affirmative reply, Alex rushed into her list of arguments. "Ali has finally agreed that I might stay—"

"Great. Then you're his problem."

"I'm not anyone's problem!" Alex snapped, biting her lip as she remembered how cool and cajoling she had meant to be. How she wished she could tell him that he didn't matter a damn! But he did. Ali wouldn't let her stay without Dan's say-so, and she could hardly do battle with the sheikh on his own lands.

"There's a small catch," she murmured uncomfortably.

"Oh?"

"Ali says I can stay if you agree to—uh—personally protect me."

"Then you're leaving, because I don't agree."

"You bastard!" she hissed, forgetting again that Ali had suggested charm. "D'Alesio, you need me! I swear you'll never film a thing my father does if you don't help me!"

There was a dangerous narrowing and a heated sizzle in the

depths of his eyes, but Alex was too incensed to heed the warning.

"Blackmail again, Doctor?"

"Blackmail, threat, whatever you choose to call it."

She was startled when his fingers suddenly wound into her hair and tugged so that she found her face an inch away from his. "Wrong move, Doctor. I work only by my own credentials. James Crosby knows my brand of professionalism. And I'm sure he'll understand that it's a hell of a lot easier traipsing around a desert without a rope of a powder puff—"

"Damnit!" Alex jerked her hair from his grasp, fighting the tears that were rising to her eyes. He hadn't hurt her; she was merely getting so desperate. "You don't have to do anything except tell Ali that you don't care if I stay. Surely you can be that accommodating—"

"That's what you call accommodating, Doctor?" Dan interrupted cryptically.

"Of course," Alex murmured impatiently, wondering why, when she once again wanted to strangle him, she was focusing on the dark hair that tufted across his broad chest rather than on his eyes. It was an attractive chest. She found that she was staring at its rise and fall, watching that slight ripple of muscle that went along with his breathing.

"I've been accommodating enough already. I don't want a leech around my neck. Always with me, always a pain."

Alex tore her eyes from his chest to laugh disdainfully. Cool your temper, she warned herself. Stop threatening; try to be reasonable. "Mr. D'Alesio, I assure you I will not be a leech. I have no interest in you. Until this all happened with—with Jim—I was planning on meeting my ex-husband in Luxor. That meeting has been delayed, but I'm still counting on its taking place. Look, all I want to do is be allowed to stay in the desert—"

She broke off as Dan suddenly stuck his cup beneath her nose. He smiled. "I'd like more coffee."

Alex frowned. "It's still half full."

"One never finishes Arabian coffee. The bottom is all grounds."

Cajole him, Alex reminded herself. She silently took the cup

111

and got up to refill it. He accepted it from her when she returned, watching her with his dark eyes fathomlessly brilliant and a hint of a grin tugging at his lips. He drank the coffee quickly and solemnly handed her back the cup. Alex gritted her teeth and returned it to the tray. When she turned back to the bed, Dan was rolling over, taking half the sheet with him. Alex was treated to a view of a firmly molded back and the upper part of very firm, very nicely shaped buttocks.

"You really haven't a shred of decency," she snapped, forgetting about cajolery again for the unnerving moment.

"Hey, it's my bed. You're the one with the indecent habit of intruding upon a man's privacy. Rub my back, will you? If you do, I'll think about your request."

The last was sweetly phrased; it was also a challenge and a warning. With his face turned from hers, Alex allowed herself to chew on her thumbnail nervously. What was she doing, anyway? Allowing him to play her along? Or was he seriously considering helping her? She remembered his mocking words about propositions the night before and semifroze, trembling in a way she didn't quite understand and certainly didn't like.

"Uh-hum." Dan cleared his throat loudly. Alex bared her teeth behind his back and then clenched them tightly before gingerly taking a closer position and beginning to massage between his shoulder blades.

Why was she doing this? she wondered again through clenched teeth. Jim . . . Jim was why she was doing this. Because she loved him so very much. He had been more than her father. He had loved and cared for her alone, struggling through everything with a baby in diapers, staying up nights, being both mother and father because he would not give up his baby daughter. And all the years as she grew up, he was there with her, bringing her to Egypt, sharing with her the wonders of the ancient world, exulting in her quick mind and the appreciation she too could give all the things he loved.

She would sell her soul to the devil for him. And there probably wasn't much difference between D'Alesio and the devil, she thought wryly as she allowed her frustration to make her massage an excellent one. Not that it was that difficult. His back held

112

a fascination for her fingers. She could feel the tension and power within his muscular frame, the electric heat of his skin. He was a man in superb shape, and it was—scientifically—intriguing to feel the fine, exceptional tone of his strongly sculpted body.

"So . . . your ex-husband is running around Egypt," Dan murmured, twisting slightly so that he could see her face from the corner of his eye. "Why isn't he with you if you're trying to reconcile?"

"I couldn't find him."

"No wonder," Dan muttered. "He's probably in deep hiding. Un-unh-unh!" he warned as Alex's nails automatically curved over his flesh. "You want something from me, remember?"

Alex carefully untensed her fingers.

"Right shoulder. And go ahead, scratch—just do it gently!"

Alex scratched his shoulder blade.

"Down a little . . . ahh . . . toward my spine . . . good, good, you do have a few talents! Now down a little more. . . ."

She was already down to the small of his back. Another inch and she would be massaging a nicely shaped rear end.

"You really ought to rot in hell!" Alex exploded suddenly, jerking away and pulling the sheet higher up on his body. He rolled over again to smile at her. She didn't return the smile.

"Will you tell Ali I can stay or not?" she demanded, the fire in her eyes sparking them to a sizzling gold.

His smile faded only slightly. His eyes were unreadable jet. "No."

"Why, you—you never intended even to think about it!" Alex accused furiously. "You made me go through all that—"

"All what?" he exploded in return, dark eyes narrowing. "You try to threaten me and blackmail me. You want to become a thorn in my side and yet it's a total imposition for you to scratch my back?"

"Go to hell!" Alex repeated. She spun about, momentarily defeated, tears threatening behind her eyes as she blindly stumbled for his tent flap. Without Dan, without Ali, she would be searching blindly, only able to pray that they would cover every possible clue.

"Alex, stop!"

113

The command in his voice was simply another insult added to injury. She kept walking.

"Alex!"

When the second thundering of his voice didn't stop her, Dan shot out of the bed, a sudden surge of conflicting emotions exploding in turmoil in his mind.

He didn't want to be involved with a woman, and God in heaven, he didn't want this stunning blonde—Crosby's daughter —running around the desert. He wanted her out of the UAE and he didn't want her in Cairo; he wanted her home, out of reach of all possible danger. Antiquities were a big black market business in Cairo and throughout the world; such huge sums were involved that murder easily became part of business. If something had happened to Crosby, Alex could be in far more danger than that offered by a fat, licentious, neighboring sheikh. But this woman had a head like a brick wall. She was determined to stay, determined to find her father. In a way, he could understand how she could trust no one else with the task. She loved Jim Crosby as no one else could.

And Dan was suddenly aware that she had come to mean something to him—what, he wasn't sure. Yes, he was. He wanted her, desired her with a craving unlike anything he had ever experienced before. He couldn't trust himself. . . . Trust himself? Hell, what for? She was of age. And he was certain—absurdly certain, since he was also sure she would like to tie him to a tree and wield a bullwhip against him—that she felt it, too. She should be whipped like an obstinate child. She was as stubborn as a mule, headstrong.

Being near her unleashed a tumult in him. He was shaking with anger, driven from within to a whipped fury. If she would only go home. . . . Her courage and determination were admirable, but there were also certain realities to be faced.

He was a man who could be impatient and brusque, sometimes taunting and mocking but seldom, if ever, maliciously cruel. Yet now he caught her arm with a vengeance, jerking her around so hard that she literally spun into his arms. Her head snapped back as she brought her hands to his arms, struggling against his biceps. Her eyes, glittering with their mixture of lime and amber

114

that could sizzle to pure gold, met his. They were hostile, furiously angry—and beginning to brim with tears.

"Damnit, D'Alesio!" she choked out. "Let me go!" The man was stark naked and he felt as hot and vibrant as an active volcano as she was forcibly crushed against him. He was making it almost impossible for her to fight the tears of frustration and anger and despair that welled beneath her lids.

He was making it difficult for her to think, to do anything other than feel his harsh steel strength and overwhelming heat. She felt as if she were gasping for air just to breathe, struggling against a massive wave of dizziness, combating the roaring that seemed to rush in her ears.

"D'Alesio!" she managed to hiss. "Haven't you a shred of modesty?"

He hadn't thought about his state of undress when he leaped from the bed, but now it seemed to him a further lever to shock her into dropping her insane ideas. Because if he couldn't get her to leave, he would have to join in her insanity. Damn Ali! What was in his fool head that he thought she could be safe.

With her pressed so close against him that he could feel the furious pounding of her heart, the fullness of her breasts, even the hard-tipped peaks of her nipples despite her clothing, he realized vaguely that he was lost. He wanted to throttle her; he would never forgive himself if something happened to her. Somehow, though she was trouble, she was unique. A tumultuous dilemma, and God help him, he couldn't control the desire that shot through him and manifested itself physically when he held her so, feeling that thundercloud, furious pace of her heart.

He laughed dryly, with no humor. "Doctor, you are a card. The joker, to be specific. You invade my privacy and then stand there spewing out how distasteful you find my nudity. Well, Doctor, I gave you your answers last night. You want something from me? Let's lay it all on the line. You are a pain. Accommodating you is going to be a pain. I'll put it this way, sweetheart —I did tell you how I don't make deals that don't offer me certain benefits. You want to stay—you get to stay. On my terms. And that means that you see a hell of a lot of nudity. . . ." He insinuatingly trailed a hand with wide splayed fingers down her spine, stopping at the small of her back to press her even closer to him, grinding her hips against his. "You're an appealing female," he said with casual bluntness. "I'll handle your being here. I'll be your token male protector. But I'll expect the benefits of being that male."

She didn't blink; she didn't look away. She didn't redden; neither did a muscle within her aristocratic features twitch.

If it weren't for the fact that the furious pounding of her heart skipped a beat, he would have been certain she hadn't heard him. Now she could really tell him to go to hell, but she would also be forced to leave.

She was no longer pressing against him, but standing dead still. Her nails had curved inward slightly; he could feel them against his arms.

"Then you'll do it?" she inquired blandly. "You'll give Ali the okay?"

"Yes," he told her, feeling a husky contraction in his throat. "But did you understand the price? Sell your soul to the devil—and you do pay up. You'll be mine, Doctor, for the duration—till the bitter end."

"Yes, D'Alesio, I understand you. I have no problems with comprehension. You want me to sleep with you."

"Continually, while we're together," he warned her flatly.

"So I assumed."

"You're willing to accept that?" His hold on her slackened as he rigidly controlled his surprise from registering in his face.

"Whatever it takes, D'Alesio," she said smoothly. "Whatever it takes. I *would* sell my soul to the devil at this point."

D'Alesio laughed. "You only have to sleep with him."

She slipped easily out of his loosened hold and turned once again for the tent flap, stopping as she reached it, her head slightly lowered. "I'm going to tell Ali that you've agreed."

She was staying, he thought incredulously. He had attempted to call her bluff—but he now knew that there had been no bluff. He also knew that he had not been bluffing himself. They had sealed a pact. If he was going to be with her, he was going to have to have her.

She hesitated just a second, and her eyes flashed defiantly at

116

his. "If it won't trouble you too much, I would appreciate it if you don't demand immediate payment. I do have to talk to Ali, and he is eager to get started for Haman's."

Turning once more with a haughty squaring of her shoulders, she slipped outside the tent.

Dan stared after her for several seconds, wondering whether to laugh or curse God, Allah and every deity that had ever ruled over the pharaohs of Egypt. He chose to laugh. What else was there, really, to do. If nothing else, his life would prove interesting, certainly more entertaining then he had allowed it to be for some time.

Was she assuming that he would give in, become a nice moral gentleman now that the point was made? He couldn't if he wanted to. They had made a deal, and he intended to see that she lived up fully to her part of it. She had made her devil's pact with her eyes wide open, and if he was the devil, he damned well was going to collect. He would have to, or drive himself crazy. And, he sobered at the thought, he would be going crazy enough trying to make sure that he did protect her when he didn't even know from what direction danger could come.

Damn her! Damn her tenacious, temperamental soul and sweet, too-seductive form straight to hell!

117

INTERLUDE

UPI—July 24

EGYPTOLOGIST DISAPPEARS UPON BRINK OF DISCOVERY

Dr. James Crosby disappeared just days before he was due to start excavations in a remote sector of the Valley of the Kings.

Crosby's daughter, Dr. Alexandria Randall, reported him missing to Egyptian authorities when he failed to meet her as scheduled at the Cairo airport on July 6. Dr. Crosby was also reported missing to authorities in Luxor when he failed to appear as scheduled in the Valley of the Kings.

The authorities have no leads in the case and admit that they are baffled by Dr. Crosby's disappearance. They have been unable to determine if Crosby disappeared in the United Arab Emirates or in Egypt.

Therefore the dig has been canceled. Crosby guarded whatever information he had concerning the existence of Anelokep's tomb. It is known, however, that he believed it existed within the realm of the known cliff and rock tombs where not only the pharaohs of the New Kingdom but many of the nobles of the time were buried as well.

Because of the phenomenal black market in Egyptian antiquities, it is feared that Dr. Crosby has met with foul play.

Neither Crosby's daughter nor Dan D'Alesio, the journalist scheduled to record the find, can be reached for comment. Reputable sources state that both have entered the United Arab Emirates in hopes of gaining information from

Sheikh Ali Sur Sheriff, the multimillionaire responsible for the expedition—and the last man known to have seen Crosby.

Dr. Wayne Randall, another Egyptologist of repute and the divorced husband of Alexandria Randall, was, however, available for comment. He had been doing independent research outside Luxor when he heard of James Crosby's disappearance.

"I fully intend to do everything in my power to find Dr. Crosby. As soon as I am able to locate Dr. Alexandria Randall, we will solve this thing together. We were to have met here [Luxor] today for personal reasons; I know now that she is following any clue she can grasp in hopes of unraveling the mystery."

In view of Crosby's disappearance, scholars across the academic world are debating the possibility of Dr. Crosby's daughter sharing his information.

When approached with this question, Dr. Wayne Randall replied, "I believe it is possible. I will know when I see my wife. If she does know her father's secrets, I can promise you that we will, together, find that tomb against any odds, in honor of Dr. Crosby."

Wayne Randall's determination is not shared by all in the academic world; some noted Egyptologists and archaeologists are of the opinion that Alexandria Randall would be in grave danger were she to attempt to walk in her father's footsteps.

Newspapers, tabloids and various other media are reviving the question so prominent in the 1920s when the tomb of Tutankhamen was opened: Is there truly a 'Curse of the Pharaohs'? Tragedy did follow in the lives of many of the principal players in that expedition. The debate between the supernatural and the law of coincidence is being once again raised.

The handsome blond man read the paper by the light of his powerful battery-operated torch. Jim Crosby illuminated the

119

text over and over again, line by line, swearing fervently under his breath as he read the words of Wayne Randall's statements.

A sound overhead pierced through his soft but vehement mutterings. He automatically switched his light off and froze, listening. The blackness that surrounded him became so complete it was impossible to see his own hand even an inch from his eyes.

For several minutes he waited, but he heard nothing more. The sound, he decided, had merely been the shifting of sand. Still, he waited awhile longer before relighting his torch, musing idly as he did so that it made little difference. The light from his torch could never be seen unless someone was so close that it wouldn't matter anyway.

He started staring at the paper again. This time he focused on the names of Alexandria Randall and Dan D'Alesio. Were they together? He hoped so. Oh, Alex, he thought, I never meant to place you in danger.

If she was with Dan and the sheikh, she would be amply protected, he was sure. But what if something had gone wrong? What if Alex didn't realize quite what she held? Worse, much worse, what if she didn't realize where the danger lay? It was so unlikely that she would see.

Groaning softly, he leaned his head back against the limestone wall. He had to have faith. In D'Alesio. And in an Arab sheikh.

CHAPTER EIGHT

There were ten riders in the caravan that would cross the desert to the small oasis of Omar Khi Haman. The journey would take no more than two and half hours, so the men were able to ride upon the swift and beautiful Arabian horses that were the pride of Ali Sur Sheriff; but since many gifts would be brought, numerous camels in the elegant trappings of Sheikh Sheriff would accompany the horsemen. At the head of the caravan would be Ali Sur Sheriff—and Dan D'Alesio. And Alex was there to watch the preparations.

Ali hadn't appeared surprised when Alex told him Dan had agreed to her staying. He had merely nodded—and told her that she must be with Dan or him any time she veered away from the oasis. "I cannot be with you all the time, so when I am not, Dan must be," he had told her quietly.

Alex wondered what Ali must think had transpired between her and Dan. Dan alternated between a barely concealed hostility and a taunting mockery each time they spoke. And she—she was holding desperately to a cool and aloof dignity.

Standing in silence as she watched the camel packs being secured to the beasts of burden, Alex started violently as she felt the light touch of his fingers run along the side of her neck. She turned, and a shade of her panic must have shown in her eyes, for he smiled slightly with dry amusement.

"Interesting," he said.

"What?" she murmured defensively.

He touched the little gold sphinx earring that dangled from her left lobe, and Alex wondered bitterly if he was commenting on her jewelry or enjoying the fact that he could so easily make her a nervous wreck as soon as her guard was down. "Very pretty," he murmured, meeting her eyes with his, which seemed to gleam with a dazzling jet that might truly belong to the devil. "Sexy."

She was still for a moment, fighting the mercury that ripped along her spine at his mere words. Then she gave him a cool smile that was entirely apathetic. "Glad you like it, D'Alesio. I wouldn't want you to be shortchanged."

He laughed, and his laughter was genuine, and the mercury seemed to race along her spine again.

But his laughter ebbed as he reached for her hand and slipped a heavy ring upon her finger, speaking before she could protest. "Ali thought it would be a good idea if his people considered you spoken for. Wear this; it's kind of like a brand, if you know what I mean."

She almost hit him—almost. She controlled her impulse when she saw the muscles of his shoulders tighten.

"Thank you," she managed calmly.

He inclined his head briefly, then left her, as if he had grown tired of taunting her and was once again bitter.

Only moments later the men were ready to leave.

Alex had spent most of her time earlier pleading to accompany them, but both Ali and Dan had been firm. Dan had mentioned then that she was lucky she was being allowed to stay in the UAE at all.

She stood within the confusion, near Dan, watching as he mounted the black stallion he had ridden the day before. He was dressed again in black desert robes, as was Ali. And as antagonistic as she was feeling toward him, she had to admit he made a handsome, romantic figure. He was minus the beard, nose putty and dark makeup today, and next to Ali, it was obvious that he was not an Arab. But it was equally obvious that he was a man at ease and familiar with his surroundings, a confident power wherever he might be. Both he and Ali were striking and charismatic men, ruggedly assured, ruggedly masculine and arresting with that essence of being so basically male.

Strange, she thought vaguely, that she should come across two such vital and volatile men together. Both had a quality that even

Wayne lacked; it was something about their eyes, a determination to take the world by the horns and damn the consequences. They shared a love of life, a determination to make every minute count.

Alex worked the ring nervously around her finger, then glanced down at it. Yale, 1973. What am I doing? she thought, panic rising again. She was getting in so deep. He was quicksand, just as her father had said. All she could think of was D'Alesio as a man, and she didn't want to think of him in that way. Neither did she want to think about his words in the tent or her response to them. It would be one thing if she could think of herself as being noble. But though she really would have done almost anything, it wasn't nobility that robbed her of breath when he held her. It wasn't nobility that made her ache inwardly because his touch created mercury within her body, and it wasn't nobility that made her mind go blank and allow her instincts to take over with a yearning that seemed to lap as a tiny fire might, catching hold of something within her that threatened to burn to wild, consuming proportions.

It is not him, it is me, she thought. She had been alone for over a year, and in that year, though she had met pleasant and attractive men, she had never met one like D'Alesio.

Still, the conflicting feelings she had for him were very upsetting to her. She had been so sure she was still in love with Wayne, and if she was, how was it possible for her to be so attracted to D'Alesio, of all men? In her entire life no one had ever managed to cause her such humiliation, to treat her so crudely, or to raise her temper over the boiling point so quickly. And while she was half hypnotized by him physically, she was still, in a remote corner of her mind, thinking how lovely it would be to see the man in stocks, with herself given free rein to hurl rotten tomatoes at his strong, angular features.

She started as she realized he was seated upon the stallion and staring down at her. The horse was prancing slightly, ready to be off, and the dust was covering her slippered feet. She hadn't even noticed.

She felt a little catch in her throat as she guiltily thought she should be thinking about her father and not at whatever plight

123

she had gotten herself into. Impulsively she reached up for the broad hands that easily held the reins.

"Don't trust Haman," she said quickly. "I know he must know something! Please don't let him—"

"Alex, whatever Haman does or doesn't know, Ali and I will find out," Dan said firmly.

"I'd really feel better if I was along—"

"Forget it—and let's not go through it again." When his mind was set, his features made him appear to be as implacable as granite.

Alex bit her lip unhappily and looked at the ground. "It's just . . . it's just that it's going to be so hard to be here all day, wondering. I don't know what to do with myself."

He leaned down from the saddle and lifted her chin so that their faces were almost touching. His lips cut a humorless grin across his jaw, one that didn't touch the hard granite of his features or the endless jet of his eyes. His tone was bitter, but as Alex felt tremors erupt all along her spine, she wondered if the bitterness was directed at her or at himself.

"I'll tell you what to do all day. Take a long, long bath. Shampoo your hair again. Do whatever you do to your nails. Because tonight you pay up, my love, and this particular devil likes his souls to be clean and fresh and sweetly perfumed and feeling like silk."

He released her chin, and a barely perceptible nudge of his knee against the stallion's flanks sent the horse prancing forward.

Alex felt as if a thundering tidal surge had washed over her. Blood seemed to rush to the extremities of her body in heated waves. She wanted to kill him; she wanted to stop the stirring sensation that he created within her with mere words.

"Some of the children will be taking the sheep to the grass plains on the other side of the oasis. Perhaps you would enjoy going with them. The view of the mountains is beautiful from there, and Rajman may escort you so that you are not alone."

As Alex glanced up a second time to see that Ali had paused before her, she wondered how much of the recent exchange he

124

had heard. She tried to smile. "Perhaps I shall go with them. Thank you."

"And you will find your things in your tent." Ali winked. "That camel that ran away from you just happened to run right into camp."

She kept smiling through clenched teeth. It would be absurd to try to explain to Ali that he'd had no right aiding and abetting D'Alesio in the little charade he had perpetrated against her.

The caravan started off. Alex watched the departure of men, horses and camels until they disappeared over a dune. Then she shrugged and turned to return to her tent.

She almost stepped over Rajman.

"You!" she muttered with hostility, her eyes narrowed menacingly. "You traitorous jackal!"

"Please, please!" Rajman protested, falling into step with her as she marched past him toward her tent. "Please, you must understand. Mr. Dan knew you were coming out to the desert, and that it could be dangerous. In Cairo just last week they had an article in the newspaper about an English girl, a daughter of one oil worker, who disappeared in the desert. It wasn't here, I grant you; I believe it was in Saudi Arabia. But Westerners just don't understand the nature of the sheikhdoms! You must believe that Mr. D'Alesio didn't want you hurt—"

"Hmmph!" Alex sniffed. She entered her tent and snapped the flap closed behind her, but Rajman remained on the outside, pleading with her.

"Dr. Alex, please do not be angry with me. You needed the help of Sheikh Sheriff, and you needed Mr. D'Alesio. Now you have both, and you are no longer a woman alone. Please, you must forgive poor Rajman! I would have had a part in nothing that would have hurt you!"

Alex had been pacing the tent. At his last beseeching, she jerked the tent flap back open. "I assure you, young man, that that journey across the sand slung over the saddle was very painful indeed."

"Yes, ma'am," Rajman said, hanging his head.

"And falling off that damned camel was not a ton of fun."

"Yes, ma'am," Rajman repeated humbly.

Out of the corner of her eye Alex noticed that her day guards, Laurel and Hardy, were attempting to approach the tent unobtrusively. Apparently they were to follow her wherever she went. Her annoyance with Rajman suddenly shifted to the guards. She jerked the young Egyptian into the tent with her.

"I forgive you," she stated with little generosity. She didn't feel much like forgiving anyone associated with D'Alesio, but she could hardly blame the youth for his loyalty to a man he apparently knew well. Besides, Ali had said Rajman might "escort" her out to the grass plains with the children, and she hoped that meant she could shake her guards for a while. They were beginning to make her feel claustrophobic. And the last thing she intended to do was spend the day taking another long bath. She had the childish urge to roll in the sand for an hour before D'Alesio was due back.

"I need to find a few things," Alex said abruptly. "Then you and I will accompany the children and the sheep."

Rajman bowed with delight. "That's wonderful, Dr. Alex! You will give me this chance to atone for myself!"

"Raj, please quit bowing. You're making me nervous. Just wait one minute. . . ."

She discovered that all her things had indeed been returned to the tent. Strange, but she had never worried about her passport, only the mimeographed documents she carried. Within those documents lay at least half of the puzzle pieces, and if she was to spend the day without going mad worrying about what was happening with Haman, she would need something in which to engross her mind. A search into the New Kingdom hieroglyphics would certainly call for her total concentration.

An hour later she and Raj were sitting beneath the spotty shade of a date nut palm. The grass plains were hardly what she had expected from the descriptive name given the spot.

She would have called it the sand plains. The grass, what there was of it, grew in scattered tufts over a large area about a mile from the oasis. There was dense greenery only on the land immediately bordering the oasis. Ali's Bedouins were actually no longer wanderers; the sheikh had been introducing methods of

126

irrigation that allowed them to maintain their homestead within the oasis.

The sheep, however, seemed quite content with the straggly little tufts of grass that grew here. And as Ali had said, there was a beautiful view of the mountains rising in the distance to the south.

"What lies over the mountains?" Alex asked Raj before pulling out her notebook to set to work.

"Oman," Raj replied with a smile. "A country smaller even than the United Arab Emirates, but almost as rich!" He shook his head at fate. "Egypt has the riches of history; this peninsula has the riches of oil." He gave Alex a wide, white-toothed smile. "Pity we Egyptians didn't have more of the oil to go with the history!"

Alex grimaced in reply. She had to agree with Rajman. Here, or at least with Ali's tribe, the method of life was a century backward, but it was grace of custom that had been preserved, not poverty.

She had seen tremendous poverty in Egypt—poverty that clung to the children, to the scalpers at the tourist attractions, to the men who eked out a living along the Nile, to the women who grew old years before their time.

Jim had cared about the people of Egypt as he had cared about its treasures. He sought the tomb of Anelokep not for personal gain, but for the Egyptian government. The treasures from the past belonged to Egypt, but they could be viewed and appreciated by the world. And each time such an exhibit went on loan, the income derived from its showing came back to the people.

"It is a pity," Alex murmured aloud. She glanced at the sheep, ambling about their grazing grounds, apparently oblivious to the heat. In contrast to the voluminous robes and galabrias worn by the adults, the four boys who tended the flock, youths ranging from seven to ten years old, Alex assumed, were half naked. Their slender young bodies were as lithe and agile as those of the sheep as they hopped about occasionally to urge a stray back to the fold.

"All is the will of Allah," Rajman said, shrugging with fatalistic acceptance. He idly chewed a blade of grass and lay back against the dune, resting his head upon his folded arms. He closed his eyes against the sun and then twisted toward Alex, opening one. "If it is the will of Allah," he said softly, "we will find your father."

Alex smiled and nodded. It is *my* will to find him, she thought, and God help me, I will do so. Alex believed that fate—and God—were partial to those willing to help themselves along.

Rajman yawned. "Do you care if I take a catnap?"

"No, take a nap," Alex said, subduing the smile that sprang to her lips. She needed to study the hieroglyphics, and it would be much easier to study if Raj wasn't chattering away.

Except that when Raj stopped chattering, her mind began to drive her crazy again. Sitting upon the cliff, she suddenly became so angry she wanted to throw something—at D'Alesio. He had refused so adamantly to marry her—but he was more than willing to go to bed with her. Not that she had really wanted to marry him, but it was the principle of the thing. The most galling part about it all was that she was not horrified, she was not noble—she wanted him. And it didn't gel at all with her emotions.

"Oh, God," she groaned aloud. "This is not productive." Neither was it comfortable. It seemed that beneath the desert sun she was besieged with chills, then riddled with heat. And she was so very, very nervous. Read! Work! she commanded herself. Think of Jim.

That thought finally did it. She could not make time pass. She could not make the evening come any faster by dwelling upon both dread and feverish anticipation.

She pulled out her notebook and studied the translations she had already made. The first was from a wall relief taken from one of the temples in Luxor. It was a prayer offered to Osiris, and the wall painting above the words had been that of Anelokep in his guise as that god.

Hieroglyphics were tricky because certain symbols could be translated several ways. There could be vast differences in interpretation and therefore confusion among such words as "under," "behind" and "after."

Anelokep had ruled after the boy king Tutankhamen, but long

128

before the great king Seti I. He was eighteenth dynasty, as was Tut, and among the Theban kings who had rejoined Upper and Lower Egypt. Dozens and dozens of kings and great nobles had been interred within the cliffs of the Valley of the Kings, but as well as those esteemed graves, there were catacombs full of the mummies of the poor people. In fact, Alex assumed that within that sprawling area of carved rock and cliffs and caves there were literally millions of mummy remains, centuries of an ancient civilization, a gluttony of death.

Tutankhamen's tomb had become a tourist attraction, but before Howard Carter, the English archaeologist, discovered the tomb, there had been nothing but sand where the crowds now walked daily. Time had done what most often the priests could not: given the tomb a natural barrier. Carter had dug for years to find the sixteen steps that led to Tut's comparatively small and modest tomb.

Alex glanced down at the notes she had made. "Forever shall you sleep eternal, Anelokep, King of Upper and Lower Egypt, Pharaoh, divine ruler who has made us and kept us one. In sight of (or in view of, or viewed by, or beneath the view of) the great (grand, powerful) lady shall you lie as your soul rules into eternity, joining the gods."

Alex sat back and stared up at the sun, then shielded her eyes against it, letting her mind review the history of ancient Egypt. At the dawning of the New Kingdom, the pharaohs, as mengods, had begun to come closer to the people. With the establishment of the Valley of the Kings, there had arisen the problem of allowing the people into the temples of the kings to perform various deeds of sacrifice in honor of that particular ruler's afterlife, while still hiding the actual burial site and the treasures needed for that afterlife. Numerous tombs were robbed in antiquity; Anelokep didn't intend to be plundered while he lay by as a hapless mummy. Therefore it wasn't time that hid his tomb but the cleverness of his priests and builders. They had created a puzzle, and she held the puzzle pieces.

Alex had become so involved with her work that she had been listening to the strange noise a long time before it registered in her mind. Then, as the whirring overhead became more persistent, she stared disbelievingly into the sky. There was a helicopter overhead. In the quiet of the desert it appeared as absurd as a spaceship with little green men hovering over the Sears Tower.

The glare of the sun upon the metal was blinding as Alex tried to study it, but shielding her eyes as it came nearer and lower, she became sure that it was a modern and expensive craft— small, sleek, and efficient—except that it appeared the pilot was either drunk or flying high on something else.

The boys who had been tending the sheep were staring upward, as stupefied as she, while the startled sheep began to *baa* and disappear in various directions.

Alex tapped Rajman's arm. "Raj!"

The craft hovered closer and closer to the ground, creating miniature sandstorms as it approached. Alex frowned deeply in consternation. Then a little thud hammered in her heart. Perhaps the helicopter had come from town; perhaps they were coming out to find her with news of her father.

She absently tapped Rajman again. He didn't respond, and she nudged him again. This time she received a reply: a loud, rattling snore.

The helicopter landed, and a spray of sand filled the air. The right-hand door opened. More absurd than the ultramodern chopper landing in the time-preserved desert were the three men who wobbled and hopped out of the open, swinging door. They were in full Arab dress, their galabrias all a dun color similar to that of the sand.

"Raj!"

The men were coming straight at her, and she realized belatedly that they had honed in on her position from the sky while she was blissfully unaware, her only concern being ancient symbols.

"Raj!" This time she half slugged him. How had he slept through the obnoxious roaring of the helicopter blades, Alex wondered bitterly.

Her punch finally woke him. He blinked and frowned in confusion, then smiled at her as if she were a bit crazy for waking him so crudely.

Some nap, Alex thought fleetingly.

"What—" Raj began, but then he did hear the whip of the

blades and he stared toward the helicopter and the Arabs making their fast approach.

"Allah be merciful!" he breathed, spellbound as she had been for an instant.

"Raj, who are they? Are they government men? Raj!"

His eyes turned to her, and they held no speculation, only panic. "Government—no. I think—get up, Alex, and run. Run toward the oasis and start screaming as loud as you can."

"But Raj—"

"Do it, Alex!"

"What about you?"

"They don't want me, and I don't believe they'll hurt me. I'll try to stall them. Head back for the oasis and scream for help as loud as you can. Please, Alex, I beg of you—*run!*"

Alex stared beseechingly at Raj, then at the three Arabs who were approaching too quickly, then miserably back to Raj.

He stood and dragged her to her feet. Her precious notebook fell unheeded to the sand. Raj gave her a little push. "Run, Alex!"

Suddenly her feet took flight. In wild panic she started racing across the dunes. She twisted her head to see over her shoulder and realized that she had started running too late; the Arabs knew how to run on the sand, she didn't. Their shoes were made for the sand; she still wore the delicate Moroccan slippers.

Raj, who did attempt to stall the men, was simply knocked down.

Alex turned her eyes back toward the oasis and discovered a new burst of strength. Her heart was hammering like a drumbeat, and sharp needles of pain shot through her legs. But she was young and in good tone, and she began to believe she could outrun the men until she tripped over the hem of the long robe she wore. Sprawling and rolling in the sand, she heard the thudding of footsteps against the earth and knew she had been caught. As she scrambled to stand, a large woven blanket was thrown over her and she was rolled in it. With her arms secured to her body, her legs useless, and her head slightly exposed, she was easily hauled like a sack of potatoes and carried over one of the men's shoulders. She could vaguely hear his labored breathing.

She hadn't had time yet to be really frightened; now she was too stunned to fully assimilate fear. Her first feeling was, strangely, exasperation. Not again, not again, this is getting ridiculous.

She could only see patches of the world as she was jostled along. A spit of sand, a tuft of grass, the trunk of a date nut. And then even those swatches were gone as she heard the whirling of the chopper blades. She was stuffed through the door and onto the small floor of the helicopter.

She heard screams then; furious Arabic chants, bloodcurdling war cries. Struggling fiercely with her wrapping, she managed to sit up and see out the window.

The men of Ali Sur Sheriff were coming. They rode, they ran, scimitars gleaming in the sun, an occasional rifle letting off a thunderous shot.

They were coming for her. Apparently one of the shepherd boys had heard her cries and had run back to the camp. For a moment she appreciated the beauty and passion of the people. Their sheikh had taken her in, and therefore she was one of them. They would fight for her; they would, if need be, die for her. But there was to be no battle, and for that Alex was glad. The helicopter gained altitude recklessly, and the tribal fighters of Ali Sur Sheriff were left behind in the sandstorm created by the chopper's departure.

A hand roughly pushed her back to the floor, and there was little Alex could do. She still couldn't comprehend what was going on, but she wasn't terribly frightened about whatever it was. She was too busy being terrified by the crazy lurch and swing of the helicopter. Muslims were abstainers, but she could have sworn the pilot was drunk. His comrades were shouting fiercely in Arabic; the pilot was shouting fiercely back. And still the helicopter lurched and swayed, losing altitude, gaining altitude.

There was only one prayer upon Alex's lips, and that was that she would survive the insane flight.

Ali Sur Sheriff was a devout man. At high noon, when the sun blazed ferociously straight overhead, the caravan halted. It was time for prayer. The men rolled out their rugs and faced Mecca upon their knees. In deference to his friend, Dan too kneeled in the sand, lowering his head in silence. Perhaps something of the holy quality of the moment got to him, or perhaps he finally gave himself time to think. But while he had been thinking about Alex with bitterness all morning—despite their "terms," she had cornered him and he wasn't fond of being cornered—he was suddenly possessed with the ardent desire to laugh. He had been worried about her and James Crosby. The many threats she had made had pricked him like barbs, and he had been goaded into making a deal he didn't want.

But he was realizing, as his smile deepened, that he liked Dr. Alex Randall. True, half the time he was tempted either to throttle her or hog-tie and gag her; but there was more to her than that angelic blond beauty. She was as stubborn as a mule and as tenacious as a desert cactus, but she was also vibrantly beautiful and possessed of that natural, subtle but oh so appealing sensuality. Her determination, honesty and loyalty—and that fervent devotion she bore her father—were extraordinary qualities, Dan thought, in a woman of her beauty.

He lowered his head farther as he felt his grin spreading. The arrangement was becoming very appealing to him. He was eager to reach Haman's, and determined to learn what he could. And very, very eager to return for the night.

A sound suddenly permeated his thoughts, and he looked quizzically toward the sun. A small helicopter was flying overhead, hopping dangerously across the pure blue of the cloudless sky. His frown returned to his features as he studied the disappearing vehicle as it careened westward. A helicopter? Out here?

"It is the Christian," Ali said with a laugh, "who stays longest on his knees. Are you that badly in need of spiritual guidance?"

Dan grinned and rose, startled to realize that he had been staring after the helicopter for a long time. "Ali, what's a chopper doing out here?"

"Another toy," Ali said, shrugging. He stared up into the sky and then pointed northward across the horizon. "Like that toy."

Straining his eyes, Dan could make out a large pink heap half covered by desert sand. Squinting more, he realized he was staring at a large pink Cadillac. With surprise he turned back to Ali.

"Haman!" Ali laughed. "The chopper must be another amusement, like that Cadillac. He has so much money that he doesn't know what to do with it. Every once in a while he buys a big American car, drives it around until it runs out of gas, overheats or stalls, and then just leaves it. He can buy another if he wishes."

Dan laughed. "That's one way to save on repair bills." He shook his head, thinking Haman could use a financial consultant. Ali, he believed, was worth billions rather than millions, and yet he had a sense of constructive expense and waste. But then Ali had been educated in Britain and the United States and he had traveled enough to realize that even his resources could not cure some of the world's poverty. He had set goals for his riches, with the belief that charity began at home, then extended as far as was feasible.

"You think the chopper was Haman's?" Dan asked.

Ali shrugged and smiled. "Who else would have such crazy pilots?"

Dan laughed along with Ali. The Arab clapped his hand against Dan's back and they joked about "Haman's Desert Flight Training School" as they returned to their horses to continue their ride.

Alex was deposited rudely on the floor in a tent not unlike the one she had come to consider hers at Ali's oasis.

As she fumbled furiously to dislodge herself from the cumbersome blanket, she heard loud commands snapped out in Arabic. The words were spoken so swiftly that she could make out nothing.

As she finally managed to swing the blanket off her shoulders, she saw two of the three Arabs who had shared the wild ride with her backing out of the tent, bowing strenuously as they did so.

Hope and Crosby, she thought fleetingly, *The Road to Morocco.* But her moment of dry humor didn't last long, because her eyes naturally riveted on the man who had been shouting commands. He was seated on a pillow, or rather his inestimable weight was spread over several pillows on a massive divan. He was dark, with beady little eyes in a fleshy face. His chin would be described as triple rather than double. He wore a merry, very self-satisfied smile, as well he might, for he was attended by four lithe and lovely young women. One merely sat near a tray of coffee and sweets, ready to move at his slightest command. Another kept the heat from his face with a large fan of exotic bird feathers. One kneeled before his bare feet, gently caring for toes that were fat as sausages, and the last stood by to mop his brow and jowls with a swath of cloth when they dampened despite the constant fanning.

Alex was so amazed at the scene that she just stared with her mouth gaping for several seconds. She thought such things had gone out with the last great sultans of Persia.

Haman, Haman, Haman. The name began to ripple through her mind as she remembered her father's letter. This fat sheikh had to be Haman, and he did indeed exist just as Jim had described him. It was ironic, she thought. She had wanted to come here today, and here she was.

But this wasn't what she had had in mind. Haman's licentious smile informed her exactly what *he* had in mind—and she wanted no part of it.

Dan had been right; there were much worse things that could happen than the warning he had given her, and one of them was happening right now.

Alex stood, warily watching Haman. He was too fat to run or exert himself, she thought quickly. And his girls didn't look the type to engage in a fight.

She smiled at the sheikh sweetly—then bolted for the tent flap. She was immediately returned. Two of her original captors caught her and lifted her by either elbow to deposit her once more in a heap before Haman.

The fat man waved away his bevy of beauties and lifted his bulk with surprising agility. Alex sprang to her feet as he approached her, backing away. She backed into the skin of the tent, and found herself trapped.

He lifted a hand, his eyes awed, and reached for her hair. Alex slapped the hand away in panic. "Keep your fat paws off me!" she shouted in panic. "Ali—Ali Sur Sheriff will come for me!"

This did not impress Haman. He had started smiling when she had knocked his hand away; now he laughed, holding his massive belly as he did so. Alex ducked around him, muscles bunched, fists clenched as she returned his scrutiny.

He watched her, then doubled over in laughter again. When he sobered, he was still smiling. He muttered something in Arabic, out of which Alex could fathom only a few words, but enough to give her an idea of their meaning along with his gesticulations.

Haman was fascinated by blondes, and he enjoyed a woman with spirit.

Oh, God, Alex thought, this was one road show she had to get out of! But though she was tempted to give Haman an hysterical tongue-lashing, she controlled herself. There was hope. Ali and Dan were somewhere near at this very moment. If she could just play for time and then find some way to make a big-enough racket. . . .

Haman clapped his hands. The men returned to take her by either elbow once more and drag her along. Instinct made her fight. Despite her resolutions, she was pulled away biting and kicking and furiously attempting to twist and turn to viciously spew her saltiest venom upon Omar Khi Haman.

She didn't see much of the trail she traversed because she was busily trying to evade the hands of her captors, who returned her curses in Arabic each time she managed a painful bite, kick or scratch. She did, however, vaguely notice and register the fact that there was a fenced corral behind Haman's tent and to the left. Several Arabian horses roamed freely within it, but there were also three with saddles and reins tethered to the fence.

She was suddenly pitched into another tent, her two "escorts" obviously pleased to be letting her go. The impetus of their toss brought her to her knees.

This tent was filled with women of all ages, shapes and sizes. But if Alex had expected help or reprieve from members of her own sex, she was sadly mistaken. Two of the ladies—big, husky women who appeared in their late forties—reached for her. They

136

had grips more powerful than those of the Arab men. They pulled her to her feet, and one of them reached for the hem of her robe.

"No!" Alex snapped furiously. There were titters of laughter throughout the tent. The middle-aged woman didn't stop in her efforts for a second. So much for her own sex, Alex thought dryly. She lashed out with a foot, and the heavy-set Arabian woman fell to the floor on her derriere. "No, damnit, and I mean it!" Alex raged.

When the woman fell, Alex looked behind her. History seemed to be repeating itself in outrageous fashion. Another bathtub awaited her, this one absurdly modern. It had all the proper connections attached to it, except that there was no plumbing.

Alex had obviously angered the woman she had knocked over. She stood, and for an absurd moment Alex thought she looked like a dragon. If she had started breathing fire, Alex wouldn't have been one bit surprised. The woman's hand suddenly flew through the air and hit her cheek, sending her sprawling once more.

Alex had never engaged in even a playground fight as a child. It seemed incredulous that she was trapped in a tent with this monster female, but she wasn't about to let the hefty Arabian get away with physical abuse. She was younger and much more agile. She leaped back to her feet with her head spinning, fully intending that her tormentor would receive a good right hook to the jaw.

Except all hell broke loose, and so quickly, that afterward she wasn't sure how she had finally been dumped in the tub. All she knew was that the entire tent of hefties and beauties had wound up in the act. Silk-covered pillows had flown and feathers had riddled the air. And she had finally been divested of her clothing. Apparently if Haman ordered one bathed, one was bathed.

Alex was tempted to cry as she was submerged in the bath, but she couldn't allow herself to do so. Trying to regain her lost dignity, she went rigid as her hair was shampooed and gawked over by every one of the ten or so women and girls in the tent. She ground her teeth and withdrew into her mind, strenuously

137

reminding herself that she was a fool to expend energy with no hope of escape when it was much wiser to remain calm until she saw opportunity. And Dan and Ali would be coming; they could not be far away. . . .

Somehow she survived the bath, and the strenuous scrubbing given her by the dragon lady. She was cocooned in a massive towel, and her hair was studiously dried with another. And then she was given a set of ridiculous silk clothing similar to what Dan had given her.

Dragon Lady was in no mood for a further squabble. She veiled her face modestly (Alex wondered why her ferocious mug would need to be hidden, unless it was for the benefit of the observer!) and tucked her head outside the tent, calling for someone. While they waited, Alex was offered a heavier robe to wear over the silks.

The two men returned. Dragon Lady accompanied Alex and her escort to a new tent. Alex was crudely pushed into the tent. It was small, and although it also had a center rug with a tray of fruits, its largest and most dominant accessory was a large silk- and fur-covered bed.

Dragon Lady stayed only long enough to snatch back the heavy robe. Then Alex was left alone, but as she had been at Ali's, she was guarded by a pair of goons. Except that now she would have loved to see Ali's goons, the ones who were to protect her rather than guard her.

"I have to get out of this asylum!" she tried to tell herself without shaking or collapsing in useless tears.

She glanced nervously at the bed and thought of the fat and repulsive sheikh Haman and felt her breakfast sour dangerously in her stomach. If D'Alesio could only rescue her from such a fate, Alex thought woefully, she would cheerfully spend the rest of her life enjoying his glorious nudity.

She tiptoed carefully to the tent flap, to discover that she had been right. She was guarded by the two men. An attempt to leave by such an avenue would be foolhardy.

Glancing desperately about the room, Alex paid sharp attention to the structure of the tent. One large pole held up the skins in the center; the circumference was ringed by smaller poles at strategic locations. As in the tents at Ali's oasis, this too was sided in silks. But as far as she could tell, there was nothing to hold the actual skins to the ground except in those places where they were attached to the sustaining poles.

Alex took a hesitant glance over her shoulder. Things were quiet outside the closed flap. Catching her breath for a moment, she walked to the rear of the tent and fell to her knees, inspecting the juncture of the skins with the ground. The skins were stretched tight, and were restraining in that aspect. But she could get her fingers beneath them, and then her hand, and then her wrist.

She glanced over her shoulder again, feeling that her breathing had become harsh and shallow with fear and anticipation. The entrance was still quiet, but how long would it remain so?

If she waited, Dan and Ali would be here. But what if they didn't come in time? Or worse still, what if there was absolutely no way to let them know she was here?

A mental image of the many jowls of Sheikh Haman was the deciding factor. Alex strained furiously against the skins, drawing them ever farther, inch by inch, from the ground. She finally created enough space to be able to worm her body beneath them.

Alex slipped her head under the skins and quickly surveyed the area. More tents stretched before her, and she could hear muted conversation from afar. But she couldn't see anyone. Desperately she flattened her body against the ground and shimmied beneath the skins.

CHAPTER NINE

Alex hovered close to the ground as she tried to assimilate her surroundings. She could hear occasional spurts of conversation, and every once in a while the Arab voices would rise. She began to creep around the tent, pausing with a catch in her breath when she saw two men passing. They didn't give her a glance; they were the ones involved in the heated conversation she had been hearing. They passed on, heading deeper into the camp.

She tried to orient herself in relation to the horse corral she had seen. It was, she assured herself with confidence, to her left. But she couldn't merely walk down to it; the guards would be upon her like a swarm of flies.

Perplexed, she rocked upon the balls of her feet and glanced nervously to her rear and the haphazard rows of tents. Several had lines stretched between them with clothes hung out to dry in the hot afternoon sun. The heat, she surmised, was the lucky factor that was presently keeping the camp so quiet.

But she couldn't stay where she was long; someone was bound to come along and see her. Glancing speculatively at the closest clothesline about a hundred feet away, she decided she was going to have to make a run for it. Creeping quietly around the tent again, she bolted across the open space, praying no one's first, second, third or fourth wife was going to make an untimely appearance to bring in her laundry.

Gasping for breath, she reached the line and sheltered herself within the drying folds of a tattered galabria in a dull-color tan. She could hear soft voices from the nearest tent, and she realized she had to act. She slipped the garment from the line and over her head and grabbed at the next nearest piece of material. It was

140

another galabria, but she wrapped it quickly around her head and then sprinted toward the next tent to the left before the owners of the first should discover their clothesline ravaged.

Now stop jumping around! she warned herself. When she walked, she had to do so casually. She had to pretend she had every right to be sauntering through the camp. If she kept her head lowered she should be okay; it seemed apparent that it was the lunch hour and therefore there were few people about.

It was difficult to convince herself not to hide, but she was sure that a furtive appearance would draw far more attention than a confident one. And from where she was now, she could hear the occasional whinny of a horse. She had been correct—the corral was still just a little to her left.

Squaring her shoulders, she lowered her head and pulled the material close over her forehead. Walking swiftly, she entered the main trail. Her blood seemed to freeze when she saw a man walking toward her, but she forced herself to keep walking steadily. The man passed her. Alex allowed a pent-up breath to escape and hurried on, willing herself not to break into a telltale run.

She reached the corral and saw only two horses tethered to the fence, while the others roamed freely. Slipping fingers damp with perspiration over the crude latch, she released it and slipped inside. The horses ignored her. It occurred to her that she should leave the gate open in the hope that the rest of the horses would bolt to freedom along with the bridled mount she chose.

Following that logic, Alex first released a beautiful bay gelding from his tie before grasping the reins of the second tethered horse, a chestnut with a dark, flowing mane. She eyed the creature's back nervously, praying that she would be able to leap up onto it. Luck had been with her so far; if she could just mount the horse . . .

Just as she was congratulating herself, her luck suddenly soured. She heard a loud shout and turned to see a man racing for her. The horse's owner, no doubt. Alex couldn't dwell upon that worry. She grasped the reins and a handful of mane and swung her leg with all the vigor she could summon.

Her landing upon the creature's back was less than graceful, but she made it. The horse started moving as she lay against his neck, struggling for balance. But she achieved that balance and dug her heels fervently into the animal's flanks, making a mad dash for the open gate. As she had hoped, the other horses in the corral followed. They were pressed one against another in their flurry to bolt.

The Arab tried to push the gate shut, but the impetus of the horses was too strong. He fell back, scrambling in the sand and gasping for breath. But by then his shouts had been heard and the once-quiet camp was suddenly alive with humanity. Alex tried to race down the trail in front of the corral, but so many people were milling about that her horse reared and refused to go forward. She managed to turn the animal by straining at the reins, and attempted to forge a trail through the tents.

She had not chosen a particularly agreeable mount. Neither was she anywhere near an expert horsewoman. Between her fumbling attempts at control and the horse's confusion, they managed only to drag down one of the smaller tents.

Now it seemed that the camp swarmed with shouting people, all coming from different directions. Alex jerked desperately at the reins, trying to keep the horse from tripping and throwing her as he pawed at the tent fabric that billowed around his hoofs. His knees buckled, but Alex managed to drag him back up. She spun around again, knocked down a furious mullah, and nudged the horse forward once more. They bolted together, then raced a hundred yards before coming into contact with a herd of goats. The goats protested with panicky bleats and began running amuck through the camp.

Alex noted vaguely that more of the smaller tents were falling and that women were shrieking as they crawled out of their collapsing homes. Absolute pandemonium had broken loose.

There was no sense attempting to ride through the incensed goats. Alex clung to the neck of the horse as he reared high in protest and plunged his forelegs back to the ground. Without her command, the animal spun about. Her knees lost their precarious hold on his bare flanks and she careened dangerously close to the ground. Then the horse bolted forward, and she lost her grip entirely, falling amid the melee of goats. She instinctively raised her arms above her face. Miraculously, the stampeding animals veered around her.

When the thundering past her ears quieted, she slowly moved her arms and opened her eyes.

She was surrounded by furious Arabs, among them the fat sheikh himself. He took a step closer to her and launched into a screaming verbal assault, shaking his fist at her. Alex just lay there and listened desolately. She had had her chance, and she had blown it.

It was no surprise to her when two of the men stepped forward past the sheikh and wrenched her to her feet. The sheikh was still ranting threats, his clenched fist pounding the air.

Fat Omar Khi Haman was definitely no longer smiling. His dark face had gone red with his flush of blood, and his jowls were shaking like molds of Jell-O.

He really is mad, Alex thought, adding to herself, of course he's really mad. I—a woman—have just destroyed half his camp. She was too dazed and dispirited to care.

Suddenly she was saved from his rancor by another shout from the distant entrance to his personal tent. Alex regained interest and vitality as she saw everyone look toward the desert horizon. She narrowed her lids and strained her eyes, but she could see nothing but sand. Still, she knew these desert dwellers could read far more from the sand than she.

The sheikh stared off to the horizon, then glanced back at Alex, issuing orders. She heard something about the helicopter, and two men rushed off. Then a sausage-fat finger pointed to her, and she felt the two pairs of hands upon her arms tighten, and then she was being hauled back toward the tent from which she had so recently obtained her freedom.

A bolt of energy suddenly surged through her with renewed hope. The horizon! They had all been pointing off to the desert. Dan! It had to be D'Alesio and Ali arriving!

She gave a furious twist to her arm and momentarily eluded one of her captors. She lashed out wildly at him, managing to throw a few good punches before her arm was captured again. She didn't give up. All the way back to the tent she balked,

143

kicked and struggled, even managing to sink her teeth into the wrist of the man on her left.

She was half wild with exhilaration. They would throw her into her tent, and then she would wait, and when she was sure the riders had reached the oasis camp of Haman, she would scream bloody murder.

Except that they didn't just throw her into the tent. They dragged her in and still didn't release her. Her eyes widened with horrified alarm, and she immediately began screaming in panic when she was hauled to the bed.

A hand clamped over her mouth, and one of the Arabs used his weight to hold her down as his companion secured one of her flailing fists and tied her wrist to the bedpost. Despite the fact that she fought like a wild woman, and despite the considerable damage she caused her tormentors, she shortly found herself bound hand and foot to the bed. For a terrified second she thought she was about to be sexually assaulted right then. But as one of her captors stuffed a rag into her mouth and secured it around her head, she realized she was merely being carefully restrained—and thoroughly quieted.

The men barely glanced at her when their task was complete. They turned quickly and left her behind.

Alex worked against her bonds furiously but succeeded in doing nothing but chafing her wrists. The dirty rag was nauseating her, and she had to take deep breaths and swallow carefully not to be sick. Eventually she exhausted herself and lay still, staring dismally at the silk that billowed from the canopy over the bed.

They were there. Ali and Dan were there, within shouting distance from her. But they didn't even know she was here. They would carry out their business, and they would turn around to ride home. And she would be left in the fat sausage-fingered hands of an insanely angry Omar Khi Haman.

Tears pricked furiously at her eyelids, and she closed her eyes. She didn't want to cry. But she was about to start shaking in the futility of silent sobs.

Ali Sheriff was frowning.

"What is it?" Dan demanded.

Ali lifted a hand and pointed to the oasis camp, which looked miniature in the distance. "Something is going on."

Dan stared in the direction indicated, and his brows were furrowed in confusion. Even at this distance he could see that the camp was in chaos. Horses and goats were running loose. Several of the miniature-looking tents were flattened. It was the lunch hour, usually a quiet time in the Bedouin camps.

"I wonder what happened," Dan murmured.

"So do I," Ali agreed. "Haman is usually so—ordered."

Dan felt a strange trickle of unease tingling along his spine. He glanced toward the sky, as if seeing the helicopter again, but of course he didn't. Something disturbed him about the turn of events, but he wasn't quite sure what. He flicked his reins over his horse's neck, and the spirited Arabian bunched his well-muscled haunches. "Let's move a little faster, shall we?" Dan suggested.

The animals had been caught and resequestered by the time they reached the camp. The sand trails of the oasis were once again quiet.

Too quiet, Dan thought.

And Haman greeted them himself, a little too effervescently. He hugged Ali as if he were a long-lost friend instead of a cold-war enemy, and gave Dan, whom he'd only met once or twice before, a magnanimous American handshake. He dragged them into his tent almost before they had a chance to dismount from their horses.

Seated on the rug in Haman's quarters, Dan and Ali were immediately offered juice and coffee. Dan gritted his teeth and bore with the custom, knowing that no business could be spoken of until the hospitalities had been afforded.

Haman himself brought up the question of their visit. "My friends," he asked with a too-wide, too-magnanimous grin, "what brings you here across the desert in this heat?"

Ali was sipping a sweet orangeade, and Dan replied. "We are looking for the American, James Crosby. He told Ali he would

145

come to see you before heading into the city. He has disappeared since leaving Ali. Can you tell us if he made it here?"

To Dan's surprise, Haman seemed relieved by his vein of questioning. "Yes," Haman said quite frankly. "James Crosby did come here. We enjoyed several nights of conversation together." The fat sheikh's smile became very self-pleased. "I pledged Crosby a large sum in Egyptian pounds for his project with the schoolchildren."

"When did he leave?" Dan demanded tensely.

Haman waved his fat fingers in the air. "Two—two and a half—three weeks ago. I do not keep track of the time. It has no meaning for me."

"But he definitely left?"

Haman's beady little eyes became mere slits in his bulbous face. "Of course he left. What do you imply?"

Ali broke in on the conversation. "We imply nothing, Haman. We are merely very worried and need any information you can give us. But that will wait a moment." Ali shot Dan a warning glance. "I have brought you gifts, Sheikh Haman. Some very special French cheeses, some linen from Belgium and some of those American Devil Dogs you are so very fond of."

Haman beamed and clapped his hands. A servant immediately appeared, and Haman ordered that they unpack the caravan.

"I saw your new helicopter," Ali said idly as the parcels were brought into the tent. "It is a nice toy."

"I do not have a helicopter," Haman said. He had been pawing about in a parcel, but it seemed to Dan that he spoke tensely and that his greedy fingers and back became stiff.

He is lying. Why would he lie? Dan wondered. "You seem to have had some trouble here today," Dan said pleasantly.

Haman shrugged, but Dan sensed the same stiffness.

"One of my stallions went a little crazy," Haman said swiftly. He procured a Devil Dog from the pack and eagerly bit into it. He glanced at Dan then and abruptly started offering information. "I can tell you that Crosby is no longer in the country. I had him followed to Abu Dhabi. He hired a private plane."

Dan and Ali exchanged glances. Haman had originally had no

146

intention of offering them this information. Why was he suddenly being so generous?"

"Why did you have him followed?" Ali asked.

Haman shrugged. "To offer my services if need be."

Dan stared down at his coffee. To offer services? Dan doubted it. More likely Haman wanted to be in on the find, if there was one.

"Where did Crosby go?" Ali asked. "If you were having him followed, it seems remarkable to me that you do not know."

Again Haman shrugged. "My men lost him," he growled. "James Crosby was talking on the phone at the airport at Abu Dhabi." Haman paused with a bit of wonder, and Dan understood. Getting a line out of Abu Dhabi was a miracle itself.

"And then?" Dan urged.

Haman took another bite of his Devil Dog. Dan was tempted to slap the chocolate pastry out of the man's meaty hands. He felt his entire body tense as he fought for control.

Haman began to speak again, and Dan was fraught with frustration. Haman's Arabic was strangely accented, and when he spoke through a mouthful of food, Dan had to strain for comprehension.

"Zaid, who followed Crosby—and was severely upbraided for losing the man—said that Crosby must have believed he was being followed. But not by Zaid. Zaid swears Crosby never saw him. He said Crosby was talking, then, suddenly looking at something, he slammed the phone down. He disappeared into the airport crowd so quickly that Zaid lost him."

"Perhaps," Ali said slowly, "we could speak with Zaid."

Surprisingly, Haman was quite agreeable. He clapped his hands, and his servant once more appeared. While Haman ordered that Zaid be brought to the tent, Dan idly sipped his coffee and glanced around the tent, wondering what it was that was wrong that he simply couldn't put his finger on.

It was then that he noticed the earring.

At first it was only a speck of gold against the sand. It lay not two feet from him, five inches from the edge of the rug. Dan glanced sharply at Haman. He was still rattling on to his servant. Inching his hand over, Dan closed his fingers over the gold.

147

Shielding his find with his body, he opened his hand at his side and casually glanced down. His blood seemed to boil within him, creating a wash of heat that spread like wildfire from his legs to his head. There was no mistaking the earring. It was a tiny sphinx suspended from a delicate gold loop. There could be no second set of earrings like this, not out here, anyway, and he could remember all too clearly how he had touched the little bob that morning as it hung suspended from Alex's ear.

Haman and Ali were talking again. He did not hear them as he fought for control. It suddenly made sense. The helicopter that Haman claimed he did not own, the information about Crosby that he had offered so willingly—Haman! Dan could not stop himself from shuddering with rage as he envisioned the obese trickster thinking he could have Alex. Wave after wave of fury struck him. His anger was such that he thought he could easily kill. His first temptation, barely restrained, was to jump to his feet and strangle the jowled bastard with his bare hands. But he couldn't do that. He had to find Alex first.

If Haman had touched her, Dan thought he would go berserk and at a minimum break the ridiculous hook nose that sat in the fat face. And then he would break each finger one by one.

He shook himself slightly, trying to rid his eyes of the blood-red fury that seemed to half blind him. He realized he had never felt quite so possessive before in his life. The assault had been done to him; Alex was his. And this morning, when he had agreed to protect her, he had decreed somewhere in his heart that only he would have her, love her, discover the seductive mysteries of those strange gold eyes, the silk feel of her golden hair; only he would know the embrace of her femininity, the sleek curve of her back, the enticing dimples, the feel of her full breasts in his hands, the tangle of her long, shapely limbs with his.
. . .

The desert is getting to me, he told himself. Alex Randall was just a woman, albeit an extraordinary one. But she was his responsibility, as of that morning, and he owed her more now than he ever had when she had just been James Crosby's daughter.

It wasn't a matter of debt; he had agreed to protect her and

148

more than any true Arab sheikh before him, Dan felt a killing rage. But he had to control it. He had no doubt that he was furious enough to leap at Haman and kill him outright. But then he might lose Alex altogether and put Ali and his riders in grave danger. The Bedouins would arise to avenge Haman; he was their sheikh even if he was nothing but a fat caricature of a man, and both desert and Muslim justice called for an eye for an eye. He would create a slaughter if he acted out his primal and instinctive vengeance.

A few seconds later Dan had himself under control. He looked up at Haman and waited for a break in the ostensibly casual conversation that he was carrying on with Ali on the benefits of a certain strain of sheep. When there was a lull Dan said very casually, "Did you hear that there was an American woman with hair the color of the sun and the moon combined who stays with Ali?"

Haman stiffened; he definitely became even more tense. A bead of perspiration broke out upon his fleshy upper lip.

Ali was staring at Dan as if he had gone crazy, his expression implying he was an idiot to mention Alex to this man with the insatiable appetite for women.

"No . . ." Haman began, but then shrugged and tried to smile innocently. "Wait—yes, perhaps I did. One of my cousins works in Abu Dhabi on the road systems they wish to improve. I believe he did mention that an American woman had arrived and was seeking Sheriff." He glanced guilelessly at Ali. "Then she did arrive?"

"Yes," Ali, lost, murmured.

"Ah," said Haman with a wide, beaming smile as his tent flap opened. "Here is Zaid. Now he will answer all your questions."

Dan noticed that the unusually tall Arab had fresh scratch marks across his face. He felt his muscles heat and tense again.

He rose. "Ali, I will leave the discussion with Zaid to you." He inclined his head politely to the Arab. "I believe that my horse was going lame. I need to check on him."

"There is no need of that," Haman said graciously. "You are welcome to any of my mounts, and my stables are as fair as those of my friend Ali Sur Sheriff."

149

"I am sure that is true," Dan said politely through clenched teeth. "But this horse is very special to me. He is an especially noble and valiant steed, and I would check on him myself before leaving."

Ali was staring at him as if he had indeed gone entirely berserk and was ready for a padded cell. They had ridden all this way to find out about Crosby and they were learning more than they had ever hoped. And Dan was walking out on the information.

Before Ali could protest, Dan bowed his way out of the tent. So as not to create suspicion, he sauntered straight down the trail that led to the corral where the horses and camels had been taken to be cooled and watered. Ali's riders were seated idly about the fence. Dan joined them and made a show of checking his horse.

Ali's nephew, Ahman, was among the riders. For the benefit of any of Haman's men who might have followed him, Dan spoke loudly to Ahman, beseeching him to come to the horse. When Ahman was bent beside him, studying the Arabian stallion's hoof, Dan began to whisper. "I have reason to believe that Haman has stolen Alex. I'm going to try and find her. There are, I'm sure, only two of Haman's keepers here at the corral. You must engage them in conversation so that I can slip away."

Ahman's dark eyes first registered surprise, then understanding and dark fury. Though women were second-class citizens, they were also very prized possessions. Ahman took the abduction personally, since Alex had been accepted by his sheikh and was thus a possession of his tribe.

He wasted no words with Dan but nodded, his expressive eyes grave. He began speaking once more about the horse, then turned and found the two horse tenders with his eyes. He somehow relayed the message silently to his comrades, and as Dan watched covertly, Haman's two men were drawn into deep conversations with Ali's riders. Dan whipped across the sand and grass-tufted trail to disappear into the maze of tents.

At first he had the overwhelming feeling that he was looking for a needle in a haystack. The tents seemed to stretch forever. But with his dark robes it was easy enough for him to lower his head and begin a brisk walk among them. His naturally tan complexion had been darkened by the sun, and his eyes were as dark as those of any Arab's. Unless he was accosted straight on, he could probably move about unnoticed. But he had to move fast. One way or another, he would have to return to Haman's tent soon.

He was near the area where the two tents were down. Glancing surreptitiously around, he decided no one was near and stooped to stare at the fallen skins. Hoofprints marred them. Perhaps Haman hadn't been lying; it appeared a horse might have gone berserk. That didn't particularly matter. He was holding the earring that could only be Alex's.

From his stooped position he heard the sound of feminine laughter coming from his right. Moving stealthily, he followed the sound. Cautiously he tested the tent flap.

There were several women in the tent, but none of them was Alex. He smiled dryly as he realized he had come across Haman's harem, reportedly one of the finest in all the Arabian countries. For a second he was tempted to explore his find, but he reminded himself that no woman was worth his neck.

Except the one that he had somehow become saddled with, the one who had become an obsession for him. The one he had discovered he simply had to have because he had become so physically bewitched that his need to possess her was like the need for water to a body burning with fever.

He ducked away from the harem tent. Deeper into the scattered rows of tents, he could see that the majority of them were strung with laundry. Haman, he was sure, would not tolerate laundry strung from the tent where he would keep his blond prize—and come to claim her.

And then Dan knew exactly where he would find her. There was only one tent in the quiet camp with a man stationed in front of it.

Dan skirted quickly from tent to tent until he was behind the one he sought. Then he followed the circumference silently until he was directly behind the Arab guard. Slipping the knife he always carried while in the desert from its sheath at his calf, he sprang at the guard, one arm holding the man in a viselike grip while he brought the knife to the Arab's throat. "One word," he whispered in Arabic, "and your blood will run."

151

The Arab, his dark eyes rolling with fright, barely nodded for fear of slicing his neck on the blade.

"Is she in there?" Dan demanded.

Again the Arab gave a barely perceptible nod.

"Has she been touched?" Dan unintentionally brought the blade closer to the man's flesh as his muscles knotted with tension.

"Min fadlak," the man whispered. *"Min fadlak . . ."*

Dan pulled the blade away, and the terrified Arab let out a spew of information like a fountain. "No, no, she has not been touched. She is like the cobra, that one, she has caused nothing but disaster! The entire harem was in shambles, and then she made chaos out of the animals and the tent and the tribe! Even Haman is wondering what he has gotten himself into—Zaid bears the scars of her fury upon his face."

All of a sudden Dan felt a lightness sweep over him, and he was tempted to laugh. He didn't dare. He had to put the fear of Allah into the man before him. "I am going to let you live—for the moment," he told the Arab tersely. "But"—he pressed his fingernail firmly into the Arab's neck and prayed his absurd story would be believed—"I have just injected you with a new American weapon. It is a poison that will kill you slowly and agonizingly if it is not properly removed within thirty minutes. Now you will stand here and not move, not speak to anyone except in casual greeting, until I say so. Do you understand?"

The Arab was shaking like a leaf blown in winter. He nodded, his eyes dark with a terror that reached his soul. Satisfied, Dan left him and slipped inside the tent.

He paused as soon as he entered, covering his mouth as a wide grin split across his features despite the situation.

She was tied to the bed and gagged, but not even her circumstances kept the gold blaze from her eyes as she studiously wriggled her wrists and impatiently tapped a foot at the same time against the canopy column.

She should have been in tears; she wasn't.

Certain now that he could make things work out, Dan approached her slowly. She was still so undaunted and defiant that

152

he couldn't resist the temptation to tease.

She saw him, and her eyes widened and her frame began wriggling in a new fury for release. Dan crossed his arms over his chest and allowed her to see his smile.

"You know," he told her, sitting idly on the bed at her hip, "I think Haman might be the one man to have the right idea. This is the quietest I've ever seen you—and the first time you haven't been causing trouble!"

Her muffled murmurings beneath the gag became heated. Dan assessed her slowly from head to toe. She certainly had the body for light and sheer silks. Even with the gag around her mouth she looked stunning and exotically desirable. Rage shot through him again as he thought of Haman, but he studiously tempered that rage. He couldn't provoke a slaughter.

She was murmuring herself hoarse, and he knew she was demanding that he free her. He cooled his rage with a dry laugh. "I can't untie you. I have to go demand that you be returned to me. But don't worry—we will bring you back." He ran his hand along her ribs, left bare by the harem outfit, to the little gold chain she wore around her waist. "Do you think," he murmured huskily, "that any self-respecting man would allow his number-one woman to be touched by the likes of Haman?" At that moment he was struck with a deep pain himself that wound heatedly inside him. A flash of fire seemed to sweep through him. He wanted her as he had never wanted a woman before. It was a gnawing that ate at his insides, and it was compounded by the suggestive beauty of the way she was garbed. The Arabs, he thought wryly, did have marvelously erotic customs.

He stood quickly, reminding himself that he had to get her out of there. The murderous rage in her eyes made him chuckle softly again. "Just think of how good I'm going to look to you tonight in comparison!"

If eyes could really shoot daggers, Dan thought dryly, he would have been cut to ribbons.

He ducked swiftly out of the tent and confronted the guard again. The man kept touching his neck, his eyes still wide with terror.

"That woman is mine," Dan said sternly. "And I intend to get her back without bloodshed. You will not mention that I have been here. Do you understand? When she is returned to me, I will see that you do not die."

The Arab shook his head fervently up and down. "I will never, never breathe a word. Haman has no right to steal a woman; he has more than Allah allows to begin with. But he is my sheikh; I must obey."

"I understand," Dan said grimly. "But this time you will keep quiet."

The Arab was still nodding his head as Dan walked away. He was, Dan thought dryly, probably furiously counting the minutes.

Dan didn't bother to return to the corral. He stalked straight for Haman's tents and belligerently cut through the quiet conversation going on between Ali, Zaid and Haman.

He was glad of his height at that moment, as he was able to stare furiously and menacingly down upon the fat sheikh with his arms firmly crossed over his chest. He knew he appeared threatening.

"Omar Khi Haman! I believe that you are holding the American woman. She is my fiancée—intended to be my number-one wife—and I demand that she be returned to me immediately."

Haman's dark skin paled to an ashen color. Ali spun about in righteous fury.

"Haman! Is this true?"

Haman stuttered. Actually, he held the cards; Ali had ten men counting himself and Dan, while Haman had his entire tribe. But looking at Dan D'Alesio, Haman feared for his own life. What was the vengeance of his tribe if he lay in a pool of his own blood?

"I did not know that she was to be your wife, Dan D'Alesio," Haman said quickly. "I would never have taken her. And of course, now that I know she is intended to be your wife—"

"Number-one wife!" Dan roared in interruption, knowing he must still remember where he was.

"Yes, yes," Haman simpered. "Number-one wife. I will, of course, make restitution." Resentment touched his eyes for a

154

moment. "I return her to you gladly, D'Alesio, for that one, she is nothing but trouble! Since she has been here she has disrupted my entire harem and caused great destruction. You are welcome to her."

Dan was ready to laugh again. Haman was right; he was no match for Dr. Alexandria Randall! But he retained his stern expression and demanded, despite his knowledge, "Has she been touched?" It was a point of honor, and retribution had to be handled so.

"By Allah, I swear it, no," Haman assured him a little wistfully. "Please, I will return her with a flock of my finest sheep, and ten proven camels of the most pliant of dispositions."

"Twenty camels," Dan bartered.

"Fifteen," Haman bargained in return. "She is a beautiful and unusual woman, but she is also old."

Anything over eighteen would be old to Haman. Dan didn't correct him. "All right," he agreed, feigning a certain disgruntlement. "I will accept fifteen camels. But you will bring my woman to me now."

"Yes, yes, of course." Haman then glanced nervously at Ali, who was awaiting his next offer. "I invaded your oasis, Ali Sur Sheriff," the fat sheikh said humbly. It was a grave crime to invade the lands of another sheikh—and get caught red-handed. Especially when that sheikh was as powerful as Ali. "And for that I ask Allah's forgiveness, and yours. Please accept from me another twenty camels—"

"Twenty-five," Ali said firmly.

"Twenty-five," Haman agreed, "and ten of my finest stallions."

"Ten stallions," Ali mused. Then he bowed gravely. "When the woman is returned, untouched, I will accept your gifts."

Haman himself left the tent, followed by Zaid, who nervously held his hand to his injured cheek.

Ali stared at Dan incredulously. "Alex is here? How? How did you know?"

"I'll explain later," Dan said quickly. "Did you find out everything you could about Jim?"

155

"Yes. I have some information that may help us."

"Good," Dan said. "Let's get Alex back then and get the hell out of here."

Ali nodded gravely. "I am glad you were able to act with restraint, my friend. You bargained well with Haman. Killing him would have been a calamity."

Dan nodded in return. It was a strange world. Except for the possible consequences—many lives ridiculously lost—Ali wouldn't have cared in the least if he had killed Haman. Murder and honor took on different dimensions here.

Haman returned, followed by Zaid and the Arab guard who had stood outside the the tent where Dan found Alex. Between them Zaid and the guard, who still mirrored his terror though his dark eyes, carried a struggling burden wrapped in a blanket.

"She is dangerous," Haman apologized to Dan.

The writhing burden was placed upon the floor. Seconds later a furious Alex emerged. She sprang from the floor as if catapulted and launched herself at Dan, tears forming in her eyes.

"How could you have left me like that! Left me, to be taken again in that stinking blanket by these—"

Her words became incoherent as she flailed against him. Dan caught her wrists, not angry but both amused and a little proud that she had come out of it all still fighting.

But he couldn't afford so much as a smile. He would lose his credibility and respect as a man if he allowed her to rail against him and physically attack him in front of these men. And if they lost an iota of respect right now while they were still in Haman's domain, they could be in serious trouble.

He glanced at Haman and grimaced and winked. "Throw the blanket back on her, will you? You are right, Sheikh Omar Khi Haman. She is nothing but trouble. But—she is mine. It is the will of Allah."

She was shrieking like a wild thing as she was trundled back into the blanket. Dan left the tent with her packed over his shoulder.

Someone had alerted the caravan to be ready to move. Dan was about to mount his horse with Alex still over his shoulder

156

when the Arab guard came racing out of Haman's tent, tears streaming down his face. He fell to his knees at Dan's feet.

"Please, *please!* Oh, by the mercy of Allah! Am I dying? Am I dying already? Have I hope? Please, remove this new American weapon from my neck! I am a man with three wives and ten children, I am a good Muslim, I am a good man!"

Dan had forgotten all about him. The poor man was as white as death itself. Dan shifted his weight to hold his writhing package firmly against his shoulder with one hand so that he could use the other to pretend to pluck his "weapon" from the man's neck. "You're fine now," he told the Arab.

He turned away as the man, still clutching his neck with uncertainty, praying fervently, thanked him profusely. "I will live?" he called after Dan. "Please, the poison—how much . . . ?"

"The poison didn't get through," Dan called back over his shoulder. "You will definitely live." He was trying very hard not to chuckle, and also to reassure the half-crazed Arab. Dan glanced back once. He lowered his gaze quickly. The man was finally regaining a healthy color.

It was difficult to mount his horse with Alex still over his shoulder, but he didn't want to chance freeing her until they were out of the desert domain of Omar Khi Haman. Dan saw Ali's eyes twinkling merrily as he watched Dan strain to mount. Ali didn't interfere or help, either because he didn't want to make Dan look less a man or, more likely, simply because he was finding the spectacle too amusing.

Dan groaned silently as he made it to his horse. He had done so smoothly, but he was also sure he had strained every muscle in his shoulders and back.

"Let's go," he growled to Ali, and with a smart kick against his horse's flank, he was off.

Ali raced alongside him, the rest of his men falling behind. "Tell me something!" he shouted against the stir of the wind they created.

"What?"

"What was that 'American secret weapon'?"

Dan laughed despite the ride ahead of them and his aching muscles. "Ingenuity!" he shouted back. "American ingenuity!"

Then he sobered. His blanketed "fiancée" was squirming like a snake, and he could hear her muffled pleas. Very soon he was going to have to release her, and he wasn't sure he wouldn't rather face a score of cobras.

CHAPTER TEN

A cool breeze wafting in from the Persian Gulf with the coming of twilight touched her cheeks like a soft caress as she stood at the open window. Below her she could see a blanket of brilliant green spotted by rainbow colors: Sheikh Ali Sur Sheriff's town palace gardens. The place was beautiful, and in direct contrast with the desert. Beyond the palace walls were the streets of Abu Dhabi. Camels, donkey carts and horses traversed the roads, but so did automobiles. The majority of the people who rushed home from their businesses were in Arab dress, but there were a number of smart European business suits to be seen also.

There was even an occasional female who walked past in the distance in Western dress. Some of these women, Alex knew, were the wives of diplomats, or employees of the various Western concerns within the city. But some of them were actually Arabian women; women who were being educated, women who might one day bring about change in an ancient way of life.

Ali did not resent the change he deemed to be inevitable. For one thing, he didn't believe it would come in his lifetime. He spoke of the Bedouin way of life with a little sigh and great wistfulness, as if he would miss it dearly were it to be taken from him, but he would also tell her with pride that modern highways were being planned across the land, that the newspapers and fledgling television stations were flourishing, and that one day modern plumbing and electricity would stretch as far as his desert hideaway, the oasis he called his own.

She had come to know a great deal about both Ali and Dan in the last twenty-four hours—mainly that both were very human. She had been a bit surprised to find herself fed and then

159

shipped off to bed upon their return to Ali's camp, both men having decided for her that she had to be exhausted. She had nervously asked Dan if she was not expected to pay up, but she had seen a warmth in the jet fire of his eyes when he answered that she had never noticed there before. He had given his deep, husky chuckle, and she seemed a bit taken aback when he had announced, "Really, Alex, I'm not a sadist!"

She had slept like one dead, to awake in the morning to discover that he had slept with her. The indentations in the sheets and the pillow beside her were still warm. In a bit of confusion she wondered if something had gone on after all, but she quickly dismissed such a notion. If a man such as Dan D'Alesio had held her with anything more than simple comfort, she would have known.

Alex had learned almost immediately upon awakening that they were leaving, heading back toward the city. And she was thankful that their route back was to be far different from the way she had first come to Ali's oasis. The camel ride to the Gulf was less than two hours, and from there they had traveled the coast on Ali's French superluxury yacht. She had tried to ask questions aboard the yacht, but both Ali and Dan had insisted that she enjoy the beauty of the voyage.

And she had enjoyed it. She didn't think she had ever seen anything more beautiful than the shimmering turquoise of the Persian Gulf. And the yacht had been so lovely, so modern, it had taken her mind so distantly from the camp of Omar Khi Haman that she could remember her experiences only vaguely, as if they had happened to someone else.

Dan had spent the majority of the short sea voyage engrossed in plans which he said he would shortly explain to her. And so she had spent the hours chatting with Ali and learning more about him and his way of life. Although he was the most devout of Muslims and totally abstained from alcoholic beverages himself, he kept a well-stocked bar aboard and she was given the gigantic Scotch and mineral water she had dreamed about when the desert had so parched her throat. It was even topped with a number of lemon twists.

Alex became so relaxed in his company that she asked him if

he would mind a very personal question, and when he smilingly assured her he would not mind at all, she had demanded to know how he could possibly love all his wives, and how they could accept sharing him. Ali had enjoyed the question. He had explained that much like the American Mormons, Muhammad had founded his religion with a shortage of healthy young men. Wars and blood feuds had been costing the Near and Far East their manpower for centuries. Muhammad, being chaste and caring, had probably decided it was better for women to share their husbands than to have their lives reduced to the status of whores.

"Many Muslim men take only one wife," Ali said, his eyes twinkling. "To many men, Christian and Muslim alike, one wife is more than enough! But for me the old system works. For one, I can afford four wives! And my ladies are all very different. Shahalla loves the nomadic life and she prefers to await me at the oasis. Hima loves London, and so she keeps our home there. Delia is in the United States and becoming very modern, I might add, but still charmingly loyal; and Zana you will meet in town. All my wives have children who fill their time, except for Shahalla, my youngest, who, we ecstatically believe now, will present me with a ninth child in the spring. Everyone, however, returns to the desert when we celebrate Ramadan, the Muslim month of fasting. And so our heritage is retained while we also move forward."

Alex had shaken her head a bit, thinking of how unbearable it had been to learn that she shared Wayne with other women. Ali, as if reading her mind, had touched her hand with a soft smile. "You were raised very differently, Alex, and you should never expect less than total fidelity from your mate." He smiled at her strangely, and Alex wondered again just how much of what had passed between her and Dan the Arab knew. Ali continually behaved as if she and Dan had become lovers for a lifetime.

Ali was a man of principle, yet it often seemed that he would humor Daniel D'Alesio no matter what. Ali had been involved with Dan's charade when she had first come to the desert. She didn't, however, feel like arguing with him when the day was so beautiful and the gulf so tranquil. She might have told Ali then that until just a few days ago, she had been fervently hoping to see the man who had once been her husband. But Wayne too seemed incredibly distant. Only Ali, the yacht, his cordial servants and Dan D'Alesio—oh, definitely Dan D'Alesio—seemed to her to be real.

Hero worship, she chided herself. She would have fallen a little bit in love with any man who rescued her from Omar Khi Haman. But Ali too had rescued her, and Ali was a fascinating and charismatic man. She liked him; she felt as if he had become, almost instantly, an old and dear friend.

But she didn't feel that static electricity with Ali, or the almost overwhelming desire to reach out and touch him. She was, she had to admit, afraid of Dan. She was nervous around him; her spine was assaulted by continual heated ripples. She was waiting for his touch, for his demand, half determined that she would somehow avoid him, half longing for him to demand that the devil receive his due.

And when she allowed her mind to dwell on him, she became worried sick all over again about her father. But both Ali and Dan professed their belief—to her, at least—that James Crosby was alive. And she believed them, because she had to.

She had felt a bit solemn when they docked in the port at Abu Dhabi Town. Ali had pointed across the gulf and reminded her that Iran and Iraq were at war, and that differences in religious belief were as hot as the demand for oil. He had also explained to her how the Persian Gulf and the Gulf of Oman were considered to be a jugular vein. A war that racked the entire world could break out if the gulfs were ever blockaded, because the proportion of the world's oil shipped through these bodies of water was astronomical.

Alex felt a little shiver when she thought of such things, more than she ever had before. Because of Dan. Because he climbed the hills in Afghanistan, because he filmed from the Iraqi border. Because he was always where there could be danger.

But now, as she stood at the window she wasn't thinking about the Iran–Iraq conflict; she wasn't even thinking about her father as the soft breeze touched her face. She kept thinking about Dan, and it was making her a wreck!

She had been given an entire suite of rooms within the palace, which had been built with the best of both the ancient and the modern worlds. There was a deep whirlpool in the bathroom, which was decorated in beautiful blue mosaics, and the rugs that dotted the tiled floor were plush fur. The bed was a modern king-size—but it was covered in rich silks and offered another billowing canopy.

She couldn't keep her eyes off the bed, but each time she glanced at it, she hurriedly looked away.

Physically she wanted Dan. She was fascinated by him in a way she had never been fascinated before. More fascinated, she admitted guiltily, than she had ever been by Wayne.

How could she have forgotten Wayne? How could she feel this overwhelming need for a man she barely knew? But she did know him; he had become her life.

A tap sounded at the ivory-embedded door to the outer chamber. Alex jumped, then stilled her beating heart and swept through the salon with its water pipe, divans—and well-stocked refrigerator—to the door.

She was greeted with a low bow from one of Ali's turbaned servants. "The sheikh and Mr. D'Alesio wish for you to join them now," the man said with a gracious smile. "If it is convenient, I will lead you to them."

"Yes," Alex murmured, annoyed that she was flustered. "Yes, of course it is convenient."

Her heart began to thud, because she was about to hear all that they had discovered about her father—and because she was about to see Dan.

Ali's servant bowed again, and Alex automatically bowed back and began to follow him. She was glad she had a guide. Ali's palace swept on and on, seemingly forever. Each room was luxurious, each hall a masterpiece of romantic building techniques. Minarets adorned the palace as they might a mosque, affording tiny tower rooms with stained-glass views into the garden. The corridors all surrounded a courtyard with a beautifully flowing fountain, but despite the logical layout, Alex doubted if she would be able to find her way to Ali's office alone.

The servant left her at the finely carved door to the office. Alex thanked him, then paused a second with her hand on the brass knob.

She was in her own clothing this evening, but something had led her to follow custom to a degree. She wore a floor-length dress with long, flowing sleeves and a high Chinese collar. Her hair was free, and feminine vanity had compelled her to shampoo it thoroughly with a scented lotion left her in the bathroom. She had enjoyed the whirlpool with its warm scented oil too, and at the moment she knew she looked her best. Her hair was very light over the blue silk of the gown, and she had dispensed with any makeup, feeling certain that the desert sun had colored her cheeks naturally.

Why, she wondered fleetingly, had she taken such great pains? Because of D'Alesio, and because, she admitted, of her own ego. In a matter of days they had become intensely involved. But as intense as the days had been—and as intense as they might become—there had to be a future, and a day of reckoning. Dan had often been the subject of a number of columns in the pages of various newspapers and magazines, always linked with a different and beautiful woman. And he was, she was certain, as electrically attractive to other women as he was to her. He was too vibrant, too vital, too ruggedly *male* not to be!

And she did still love Wayne, didn't she? When this strange Arabian world was in the past, she would come back to earth and know that her life must go on. She would, she was sure, find Wayne in Egypt. And she would explain merely that it had been absolutely necessary to rely upon Dan D'Alesio. If there was anything to explain . . . well, she simply wouldn't explain. She was a little ashamed of herself for wanting the intimacy she had bargained for, but she was also—when she was not busy chastising herself—a little defiant. Wayne had been sleeping God knew where; she owed herself an outside affair. Kelly had been right about one thing—Wayne had been the only man she had ever known. Wasn't it only just that she too should discover something else of the sexual world?

164

Just? If she loved Wayne, why was she worried about justice? It was a childish emotion. But it was there. Because she wanted D'Alesio. Because his dark eyes gave her shivers, because his laugh could make her feel as if she had been warmed by a fire. Because he could irritate beyond reason, but ride across the desert on a black stallion when the going got rough.

"Alex? Are you all right?"

She had stood outside the door for so long that it had suddenly swung open. Ali was staring at her with soulful Arabian eyes full of concern.

"I'm, ah, fine," she murmured, smiling weakly and sailing on into the room as if she hadn't been standing as still and blank-eyed as a statue at the door.

Dan, staring out at the garden from a long, slatted window as she had been, turned to her as she entered the room. He smiled as he saw her, his hands clasped idly behind his back. She was such an enigma, such a fascinating woman of contradictions. He remembered unwrapping her from her blanket cocoon and being certain that she was going to give him holy hell. But she had been dignified and subdued, apologizing sweetly for having put them all in danger. She had simply been so terrified, bound in a tent that belonged to Haman. Her shudder had been very eloquent. He had longed to take her into his arms and assure her that he would protect her forever.

But it hadn't been the right time or the right place, and she might easily have thought him a bit crazy. But it had been nice to ride back together; she had sat before him on the magnificent black Arabian stallion, and her back had pressed comfortably against his chest for the entire journey. He had never felt such vast tenderness for a woman—any woman.

Upon their return he had taken a single glance at her delicate features and seen the purple smudges beneath her eyes. "Do you know what you're going to do?" he had demanded.

"Well, I'm not taking another bath!" she had declared emphatically.

"No." Dan had laughed. "You're going to bed. But maybe you should take a bath. You do have the slight aroma of sheep about you!"

She had been indignant to hear that she had been worth only fifteen camels because of her age, but she had laughed when Dan had assured her he could have demanded a score of stallions if she'd only been a young virgin.

"Sorry," she had informed him with a quirk of humor. "I'm afraid I was very normally married."

And then she sobered and asked him about their deal. He had wanted to tell her that he would never do anything to hurt her.

His smile deepened as he watched her now. When he had crawled in beside her last night, he had noticed that she had taken another bath and that she smelled deliciously of jasmine.

"Sit down, Alex," he told her softly as Ali led her into the room. She did so, curling her feet beneath her as she gracefully sank to one of the lush pillows on the floor.

His heartbeat quickened as he watched her. Last night he had lain awake in agony, held in check by his own whirling emotions. He didn't think he could bear another night without touching her, yet he knew he couldn't force her to keep their bargain. Still, he believed she felt the same sexual current that he did. Despite her independence and quick temper and wit, he was certain that she was as compelled as he. Watching her now, he couldn't help but believe that she had dressed to please him. Her hair appeared as gold silk against the gown, which was concealing and yet suggestive. Her head was lowered, but he could see the quick rise and fall of her breasts and he had to fight back a primitive urge to trounce Ali out of the room and attack her then and there, baring those full ripe breasts to his view and touch.

"We're going to tell you all that we know and what we think should be done now," he said aloud, walking across the room and sitting on another plush pillow that had been drawn near hers on the rug.

Ali joined them and sat on the third pillow. "Wait until our meal has been served," he cautioned.

Dan nodded. They were quiet until a turbaned man and a veiled woman had brought in a tray with rice, aromatic lamb shish kebabs and a light-looking salad of several kinds of lettuce.

Dan could barely smell the food. She was scented again with sensual bath oils that also carried subtly through the air that

166

natural feminine scent that was hers alone, unique, fascinating, compelling, hypnotic, stirring . . . Capable of driving him right up a wall.

They were alone. Ali fixed the plates, and Dan began talking. "We know that your father left the country. Zaid was able to tell us from where he had hired his plane, and we found the pilot. He entered Egypt at Luxor. From there we—we don't know. But we also learned from Zaid that your father knew someone was following him. Before he made his phone call—before he wrote his letter."

"And," Ali said quietly, swallowing a piece of his lamb before continuing, "I believe I know why your father was determined that you find me through Dan."

Alex had been having a difficult time fighting the spell of the man so close beside her. She had barely tasted her food, and only the fact that they spoke of her father kept her senses from total abandon.

"Why?" she asked, suddenly springing full swing into logic.

"Because of the puzzle pieces. I think your father intended you to go ahead with the expedition."

"But I—I don't know where the tomb is! Jim didn't tell me what he had discovered, only that he was convinced he knew where it had to be through his research. And it still might not have been that easy for him to find it. The desert has changed in three thousand years. There could be mountains of sand—"

"Alex," Dan interrupted quietly, "obviously your father did know something. Something that someone else considered price-less. Enough to perhaps send your father into hiding."

He had left out the obvious. Enough to kill for.

Alex was glad that he had. As long as she could believe Jim was only in hiding or perhaps being held prisoner somewhere, she was okay. She couldn't imagine any other possibility. A shudder rippled through her, and she turned to Dan.

"I still don't understand."

"Listen, Alex," Dan said tensely, "Jim made a point of calling you—at a time when it was next to impossible to make a call—to tell you that you had the puzzle pieces. He also forewarned you that in the event of trouble, you were to get to Ali—through me.

Neither of us had even known of your existence until you arrived. But he knew us; he knew Ali would support the endeavor, he knew that I would see it through with you. It doesn't make me particularly happy, but I think it's obvious Jim intended you to take over his expedition."

Alex frowned. "Why does it make you unhappy?"

Dan hesitated a moment, scowling darkly. "Because a woman is trouble."

"I am not trouble—"

"Two sheikhdoms almost went to war over you," he reminded her bluntly.

"But it's not my fault Haman is a sick old lecherous man—"

"Hey! Hey!" Ali interrupted. With a wry smile he added, "No squabbling, children. Take advice from a man who has managed to find peace with four wives. The past is best left alone. Alex, blond beauty can make you a very dangerous lady. Dan, we have made our decisions, and the past is the past. We must go forward from here."

"Yeah," Dan said dryly. But he spoke to Alex matter-of-factly again. "Okay, you don't know where the tomb is. But you do have the puzzle pieces. Think you can find what Jim was after?"

"I suppose it's possible," she said slowly, and then excitement rose in her voice. "If anyone can think like Jim, it has to be me."

"Precisely!" Ali agreed.

"And," Dan added dryly, "as soon as we reach Cairo, we announce that we are replanning the expedition."

"Which in a way," Ali said unhappily, "makes you bait, Alex."

"Bait?"

"If someone was after Jim—"

"It isn't an *if*," Dan charged irritably. "Alex, you are going to be in danger. Whoever got hold of your father—or whoever your father ran from—doesn't want anyone finding that tomb. Or perhaps he—or they—do want it found, but they want to claim the discovery for themselves." Dan sighed, placing his plate on the tray and gulping down a cup of coffee in one mouthful, dregs and all. "You will be bait, Alex. Announcing that you have all your father's documentation and heading on into the

Valley of the Kings should draw all the riffraff from the rafters. They'll be after you. But Ali and I have been over it and over it, and I don't think we have any other choice of action—except to leave your father's disappearance to the police and hope that within that struggling bureau of red tape they find him. Of course, the U.S. might step in with its own agents—"

"But the CIA are seldom trained in Egyptology!" Ali said.

"Neither would they care as deeply as you do," Dan said softly. "Or as much as Ali and I."

"The choice," Ali said, "is still yours."

"That's right," Dan announced rather coldly. "I don't like this one bit. But as I've said, we can't come up with anything better. Still, if you have the slightest hesitation . . ."

Alex placed her plate too upon the silver serving tray. She stood and smiled at them both. "Gentlemen, when do we leave for Cairo?"

Ali and Dan exchanged glances and shrugged. "Tomorrow morning," Ali told her. "I've already wired the curator of the museum to be ready to assist you with whatever you may need."

"I have one problem," Alex said. "I was studying photocopies in my notebook of some of the relevant hieroglyphics when Haman's goons—"

"We have the notebook," Dan said, and his voice sounded strangely distant and very cold. "Rajman saved it all for you."

"Oh," Alex said simply. "Then I guess I'm all set. How long do I have to really solve this puzzle?"

She asked the question of Dan, but he was busy pouring himself more coffee and ignored her.

"I think about a week," Ali said. "We can't stall too long. The men your father hired as workers are still waiting in Luxor. We'll lose all credibility if we don't move quickly. And I believe that something will happen before we actually have to prove we know what we're doing."

"Carter dug for years," Dan said absently. "We can easily dig for a long time without looking suspicious."

What was wrong with him? Alex wondered. He had smiled very nicely when she entered, then turned into a growling bear, and now he sounded as if nothing made much difference to him one way or another. She was suddenly anxious to be away from him.

"Well, then," she said lightly, "if everything is settled, I think I'll leave you two. I'm still very tired." Why, she asked herself with irritation, had she said the last so nervously.

Ali and Dan both stood. "Yes," Ali said, "you have been through much in the last few days." He stopped to pick up a tiny bell from the tray and ring it lightly. "My wife will take you back to your rooms."

Ali walked her back to the door. His Abu Dhabi Town wife was just outside the door. Like Shahalla, Zana was a lovely woman, perhaps ten years older than her desert counterpart. Silently she inclined her head toward Ali and then Alex.

Her heart began to beat a little erratically as she bowed back. Had Dan lost interest in her? Had all his threats and promises and deals been nothing but bluff to unnerve her? She suddenly hoped so, because she realized how very afraid of him she was.

"I'll be right up, Alex," the man of her thoughts suddenly called out casually. Her heart seemed to skip several beats. He could be so nonchalant. So cool. As if he were saying, "I'll be up to discuss the weather in just a few minutes. . . ."

But perhaps things were just that casual for Dan D'Alesio. He had to be accustomed to the fast lane, and Kelly had repeatedly assured Alex that she was archaic.

She was following Ali's wife through the vast and beautiful corridors to the finely carved door of her suite. And then she was saying good night and smiling and bowing again. And then closing her door, and wondering why there wasn't a good bolt for it.

Alex walked through the suite to the bedroom and the window with its tiny balcony. The drapes were sheer white and they drifted around her as she lifted her face to welcome the breeze.

The worst part of torture, as long philosophized, was the expectation of things to come. D'Alesio was apparently aware of that philosophy. He had her on pins and needles, knowing what she wanted, not knowing what she wanted, anxious, afraid, confused. . . . "Damnit!" she exploded to the crescent moon that spread its silvery shadow throughout the room. "If we could only have done with it. . . ." Then what? Would her worst fears be realized? Would she find it all too easy to need him, to long for his touch?

"Now that's hardly what I call a romantic attitude!"

Alex spun around so quickly at the throaty chuckle that she almost lost her balance on the tiny balcony. She grasped desperately at the molded railings, but she wouldn't have fallen, couldn't have fallen, because he reached her with the same silent speed that had brought him into the room.

Breathlessly Alex stared into dark eyes, into the jet depths of mystery as seductively eternal as time. His arms were around her, his hands laced at her spine to hold her. Her own hands rested upon his shoulders, an instinctive gesture to hold fast to security. But was he security? Or loss and pain more devastating than any she had yet to know.

The moonlight cast a strange glow upon his rugged features and eyes. The jet eyes seemed to sparkle, and as he flashed her a smile with perfect white teeth, she wondered for a fanciful moment if she hadn't indeed signed a pact with the devil. He pressed her more closely to him and a spasm of chills created a riot along her spine. She tried to breathe normally, but the harder she tried, the more evident it became that she was gasping for each short breath.

"Doctor," he murmured, "has anyone ever told you that in the moonlight your eyes are like pure gold against velvet green? They are a picture of something far more intriguing than the greatest treasures of Egypt, brighter than the sun, deeper than the moon. . . ."

She had become so hypnotized by the husky silk of his voice and the pearl-white flash of his teeth against his bronze complexion that she was taken entirely off guard when his lips touched hers. They brushed so lightly against her that she couldn't think to protest, only marvel that a mouth that could appear so firm could touch her with such tenderness. His lips were like gossamer, so enticing and persuasive that instinctively she responded and pressed closer to him. She could feel acutely the heat of his body as if every nerve in her own had found new sensitivity, as if something within her had become alive as it had never been before.

The soft provocation of his mouth had been a snare more deadly than that of a delicately woven spider's web. She had stepped into the trap. Fascination had been too great to resist, and when she pressed her lips to his in return, silken enticement became ardent demand. His kiss became an inferno that ignited as it consumed. It swept her breath away; it left her trembling with weakness, burning with a strength only applicable to the need to feel more and more of him. The current, the tension, the heat were his. Only by this fusion could she find the strength to stand.

His tongue parted the barrier of her teeth, teased along the ridge of her mouth, played coaxingly with hers, dove deeply to explore and plunder and savor the farthest recesses of her mouth. And then withdrew. Only to circle her lips. To allow his mouth to shower kisses over her cheeks and find her mouth again. To nibble kisses against it, to breach the barrier of her lips and teeth once more with ravenous hunger. To drink and drink of this nectar, as if he would never have his fill.

Alex's fingers dug into the fabric of his shirt, into the muscle beneath as she clung to him, fast losing all reason as she was swept into a storm of whirling fire. He held her steady with one hand still upon the small of her back, as if he knew she would fall without his support. But he brought his other hand trailing up her spine, sensitizing it anew, to thread his fingers into her hair. Perhaps he didn't know that he didn't need to hold her so, that she had been snared by the magic in his eyes. Perhaps it was merely her unleashed hunger.

But he held her, and held her, and held her in the moonlight, and that soft glow caressed them as did the soft breeze from the Persian Gulf. Time seemed either to stand still or to stretch into the dark eternity of the desert as he kissed her, alternately ravaging her mouth to its ultimate depths, then kissing her face with the softest of enticements, finding her eyes, her temples, her chin, her throat, so alabaster in the silver veil of the moon.

He could feel her trembling. He could feel the ardent pounding of her heart. Or was it his own, drumming double time? It didn't matter. All he knew was that she was responding to him, clinging to him, allowing—no, not allowing but accepting, savoring—his advances. And while he wondered how he had ever allowed any woman to touch a chord of need so deep within him, he was also wondering if there had been a woman alive before who could drive a man so insane. Had any woman before touched the very air around her with such a sweetly seductive fragrance, had skin that could actually rival silk, had the power to curve so perfectly against a man's body that she became both an inescapable lure and a sensual enigma.

The moon slipped behind a cloud, and they were bathed in a darkness in which it was hard to tell that two people stood upon the balcony. But maybe they weren't two; maybe they had become one.

The moon reappeared. It bathed them in new silvery light.

He finally broke away from her, yet held her still, his fingers firmly wound into the sun-and-moon hair at her nape as he compelled her eyes the same way he had compelled her lips.

"I've never even kissed you before . . ." he mused softly, watching as she struggled to lengthen her gasping breaths. Her lips glistened with the moisture of his kiss, and they were full and swollen and inviting all over again.

She swallowed, and her golden eyes closed to shut him out. Another shudder rent her body and he felt her stiffen. He was losing her, and he couldn't understand why. He knew she wanted him, knew that the fires spread through her as they did through him—special fires, the type so rarely experienced that they deserved to be cherished, recognized, honored and carefully tended.

Anger suddenly gripped him as he became sure that she was thinking of her ex-husband. Ali had shown him the Cairo paper that had carried the UPI article.

Randall. The man who had cheated on her; the man who didn't have the confidence to allow her brilliant mind free reign. The man who, if Zaid and Haman were right about certain speculations, had been very much upon Jim Crosby's mind in those last few days before his disappearance.

173

Convulsively his fist clenched, tightening his grip upon her hair.

"Shall we move inside, Doctor?" he inquired with a biting cynicism he had never intended.

Her tongue, such a tiny, delicate thing to create such infinite pleasure, darted nervously over her lips. Her eyes became flashing beacons of indignant defiance.

"Shall we, D'Alesio?" she demanded coolly. "I can't believe that a man such as yourself can really find the need to demand a—relationship with a woman simply because she made a deal in desperation."

His breath seemed to catch hard in his chest with a slamming of his heart. He stood still as he stared at her, his jet eyes never wavering. But for a moment he wondered, and he knew he could never force her, and he knew that she was right.

He was equally sure that it would never be force. As he paused he could feel the soft rasp of her breath, the pattering of her heart which raced unchecked, touching his as did the full, firm mounds of her breasts. Mounds that were peaked with hard, pouting little nubs he could feel against his flesh despite the silk of her gown and the cotton of his shirt.

He suddenly started laughing, chuckling deeply. "Start believing, Randall," he told her with a full, wicked smile. And he released her—only to slip his arms back around her at the strategic points from which to sweep her into his arms.

She gasped, but her hands laced around his neck. He saw the gold flash of her eyes in the moonlight, and the defiance was gone. Her gaze was a little uncertain, a little wistful, a little lost. "We're really going through with this?" she murmured as he strode surely with her to the silk-covered bed with its exotic canopies.

"Damn right, Ms. Randall," he told her softly. His firm, silent stride brought them closer to the bed.

CHAPTER ELEVEN

"It's not Ms. Randall," she reminded him quietly. "It's *Dr.* Randall!"

"It's both, I believe," he replied, smiling as he laid her upon the silk covers and stretched his length beside hers. There was a small bronze loop attached to the oriental gown's zipper high against the hollow of her throat. He pulled the loop slowly, pausing to press his lips first against that enticing indentation between her collarbones. Then he followed the line of flesh bared to him with the slow creep of the zipper, pressing his lips against the valley of her breasts, while not yet touching the mounds. Her fingers caught in his hair, clenching tightly but convulsively as tremor after tremor shot through her, not in any attempt to stop the slow caress of his mouth.

He traced her lower ribs lightly with his tongue and patterned another dizzying line along the concave line beneath her ribs to her waist. Below that he found her navel and gave it great attention, probing it with his tongue until she was certain he had actually reached inside her. Her fingers caught and uncaught in his hair, pulling, releasing, pulling again as she expelled a soft moan she had never meant to utter.

The zipper halted just inches below her navel. He traced the tip of his tongue to that point, teasing along the side of the material. He felt her like quicksilver beneath him; she trembled, flesh and limbs coming alive at his ardent touch.

Pulling himself upward, he stared into the liquid gold of her eyes. They were wide, slightly dilated. Her lips were parted, invitingly moist. He touched them again with his own and felt the sweet dart of her tongue against them. Her fingers now wound around his neck, deserted that pose and clutched his shoulders, roamed over his back.

He broke the kiss and traced the contours of her cheeks with his finger, marveling at the soft texture, at the exquisite line of bone structure. His finger trailed along her throat. Then he slipped his hands beneath the material that clung to her shoulders, drawing her up so that he could slip the sleeves from her arms. For a moment he paused, drinking in the sight of her in the moonlight, savoring the silver play upon shadow and and angle, soft mound and hidden delight. Her breathing was almost silent, and yet he could hear it, the softest of rasping, quick, heightened, sensual, enticing. It caused her breasts to rise high and fall rapidly in that silver glow, and he thought he had never seen anything more like finest alabaster than the quality of her skin. Or felt anything softer.

He crushed her against him, impatient with his own shirt because it lay between them, but more determined to draw the robe from beneath her that still held the curve of her hips and the shapely length of her legs from his view, from his touch. Sweeping her hard to him, he slipped his hand along her back, loath to release that touch, needing to in order to splay his fingers low over her hips, lift her and tear away the silk garment completely. It flew unheeded to the floor.

He was consumed with both impatience and a fervent desire to draw the moments out into eternity. He was loath to release her, and yet to shed his own garments he had to. And she was still clad in the Moroccan slippers he had given her at Ali's, and a pair of peach-froth bikini panties. The panties alone were enough to drive a man half mad.

He laid her gently back against the pillows and ripped off half the buttons in his haste to remove his shirt, jerking the tails from the confinement of his belt. But as his shirt flew to the floor, he noticed that she had edged off her own slippers with the toes of each foot. Her eyes were half slits in the moonlight; the lashes that he could have sworn were too long, too dark, to be real were creating crescents of the most ancient mystique against the ivory of her cheeks. She wouldn't stare directly at him, neither would she quite smile, but the steady inhalation and exhalation of breath that brought her firm, rouge-crested breasts high and then low again signaled him clearly that she still wasn't protesting. And her lips were still parted, moist, puffed and pouted in their sweet, clear shape.

As if spellbound anew, he lowered his mouth to her lips again but didn't quite touch them. He circled them with just the tip of his tongue, then delved lightly, coaxingly into her mouth. The delicate pink tip of her tongue moved tentatively to touch his, taste it, savor it and draw back to her mouth, creating a staggering fusion. But as he kissed her this time, he wrenched his shoes from his feet and draped a leg over hers. And when the kiss broke he could no longer fight the allure of her breasts and he took them into his palms, holding them, allowing that slightly rough flesh to graze the nipples to hard, darkening peaks. He lowered his mouth over one while still grazing the other, and the moan she emitted was ardent and aching rather than soft. As if giving over to sensation, she arched high against him, and he felt a slow undulation begin within her hips, a seduction all the more erotic because it was simply the decree of nature. And as he caressed her breasts with hands and lips and tongue and teeth, that sweet writhing that swept away his mind became more ardent, more beckoning, more inviting.

He continued to massage her breasts with his mouth, teasing them lightly with unhurried flicks of his tongue, drawing upon the nipples more urgently, more demandingly, while following the curve of her body with his palm, appreciating, cherishing the slender line of her waist, the fanning flare of her hips, the indentation of her lower belly. He slipped his fingers beneath the elastic band of her peach panties and followed that line over and over. He barely noticed that her hands were kneading his shoulders, her fingers stroking, clawing, massaging, finding the heat of naked flesh as compelling as he was.

He followed the path of his fingers and hand with his lips then, reverently enjoying the angle of her hip, her belly. He no longer teased beneath the line of the peach elastic but tugged gently upon it, drawing it from her slowly, excruciatingly slowly, from hips to thighs, over her kneecaps, finally over her feet. And then he began the trek back, kissing her toes, sliding his tongue between them, along the arch of her foot, her calf, the tender shadowland of her upper thigh to the ultimate heart of sensual sensation within her. Moonlight secrets, the enigma of femininity. He had lost all control of his mind, but in that loss he loved her as he had never known love before, believing that he had never known a woman so uniquely feminine, so uniquely beautiful, from golden head to toe. He wanted her as he had never wanted a woman before, but with that wanting he became obsessed with being wanted every bit as voraciously in return. And in the whispers that came to him, the cries that were soft silken beseechings upon the silver of enchanted air, he was rewarded. She called his name, she begged him, she arched herself to him and tried only upon occasion to wrest herself from the ecstasy that was just a little bit of agony and would result in ultimate rapture.

"Please!" she gasped again, and she was curling to him, dragging at his hair, his shoulders, pulling him back into her arms. And though she wouldn't look at him, her fingers played along his back like butterfly wings and her lips were hungrily against his shoulders. She nipped lightly, she kissed him, following his shoulder to his neck, his neck to his broad, hair-roughened chest, his chest to his chin, to his lips. He held his lips melded to hers and reached for his belt buckle, delighted when he found her fingers already there. Fire raged through him at her touch, like wave after wave of hot volcanic lava. Together they divested him of jeans and briefs and clung together, deliriously locking together in that first complete touch of flesh against flesh. And then her fingers, delicate fingers, feminine fingers, soft and yet demanding, were running feverishly over him, exploring his back, his chest, his hips. Responding to his soft-spoken commands, finding the blazing desire that was wonderful, uniquely hers and hers alone, beautiful and fulfilling in itself because she had elicited its ardent growth.

The scent of jasmine was on the air, soft and subtle, and it mingled with the breeze and the provocative, sweetly unique scent that was her special essence.

He suddenly groaned deeply and grasped the golden tendrils of her hair, holding her face between his palms as he brought them back full-length upon the bed. "Oh, Alexandria . . ." he whispered, and she had never heard her name spoken with such command or with such tenderness. Never had she been held so masterfully, coaxed into such vibrant, needing response. Never had she been so swept away that all that mattered was the man, the sensation, the beauty and the awe.

But he was fighting for logic, fighting to worry. "I have to protect you," he whispered, but not even words could dim the silver desire that swept through her.

Life was strange, she thought with a fleeting poignancy. Not long ago she had protected herself, because of Wayne. She was not with Wayne, and yet she had found this rare wonder—Dan. And then she was thinking no more, because she couldn't bear the interruption against the beauty of sensation.

"No," she murmured huskily, "I take pills."

Not even for that murmur could she stop tasting him. She spoke in gasps as her lips hovered, touched and hovered again over his. She wrapped her arms around his shoulders and arched high against him, yearning for him to fill the hungry void within her, to ease the delicious and desperate need.

But still he wouldn't take her. The jet of his eyes was surely that of the devil's in the moonlight.

"You are not being forced into a bargain," he told her hoarsely.

Alex pressed her face into the curve of his neck, unable to look at him. She moaned and murmured brokenly, "Surely that is— obvious. Why are you doing this to me? You must know . . .?"

He couldn't bear the soft reproach of her voice, yet he had to see her eyes. He caught her face between his hands and smiled tenderly as he gently drove his knee between her legs and situated his weight between them, entrapping her.

"Yes," he said softly, "I know. I had to make sure that we both knew."

And he embraced her with all the tenderness in the world as his masculinity breached all her barriers, a thrust as hard and full and certain as his arms were tender. She cried out at the shuddering impact, unwittingly digging the crescents of her nails into his shoulders. He shuddered himself and held still, frightened that he had hurt her.

"Alex . . ."

"Oh, Daniel . . ."

Her silk and ivory legs twined around him and he felt the sweetest of embraces. And he was free. The dam of restraint broke with the tidal wave of desire, a storm that was both fury and peace. Flesh burned and melded to flesh while their souls flew to the cadence of the ages.

And with each thrust of velvet, Alex lost a little more of her mind, of her heart. Within her, he touched her heart. He was as real and as strong as the earth, and yet he lifted her beyond it, taking her further than she had ever been before. And while she relished him—the length of him, the fingers that threaded hers, holding them on either side of her, the electric current of life and vital masculinity that created spontaneous fire within her—she also soared, aware that their fires had risen to meet and diminish the light of the moon, of the stars.

It was a little bit like dying, yet while taking part in that dying, finding a sunburst of life more vibrant than any known.

The fire reached a glorious peak, sizzled in rapture. Molten heat washing through her, through him, mingled and filled her even as she began the sweet descent back to silken sheets. And even those moments, following the precious few of incredibly brilliant ecstasy, were beautiful as she had never known them before. Because she had never heard her name shouted so hoarsely yet triumphantly, demandingly, tenderly. Neither had she ever been held with such reverence, filled still as the molten rivers of their abandon warmed her, nor held so tenderly, so consumingly.

And still nothing mattered. Only the beauty of the night, the air of silver essence, the breeze that cooled them.

The man who held her was tender as only a man of strength could be tender, still giving, telling her even now, with the heat of passion passing, that she was beautiful, stunning . . . perfect.

There was a lot to be said; neither attempted to talk. They simply lay entwined, glistening flesh against flesh, savoring the sweetness of the aftermath. And in time fulfillment, satisfaction and complete, exhausted contentment took their toll, and they slept.

Alex awoke with a slight start, wondering only momentarily why she was naked and yet so wonderfully warm.

He was curled against her back, his arm draped around her and his hand casually nestled against her waist.

The moonlight still filled the room with its magical touch of silver.

Alex moved very carefully, certain that he would wake with very little provocation. She froze when she felt him begin to shift, then shifted quickly and pressed her warmth against his again. She didn't want him waking—not yet.

She wanted to think, but more than that, she wanted to study him, every line, every nuance—the man, the awesome, perfectly toned animal that lay within that man. Somehow she wanted to attempt to explore his heart and mind through his face, and also to gorge herself upon the length of contours and angles and flesh and muscles of the man who had given her such intense ecstasy while demanding and taking with such a contrast of strength and tenderness that she had never felt so wondrously feminine.

He might have been a bronze statue in the moonlight, she thought. That shimmering glow captured the bulge of his muscles that seemed so trim and fluid when he was awake, moving with his constant vitality. He was lean, but built like solid rock. She smiled slightly as she thought that he was beautiful—and that he would probably be quite indignant to hear himself so described.

But he was. Long and trim and yet sinewed, the mounds and indentations of his shoulders, arms and back were clearly delineated by light and shadow. His buttocks were firm, shaped very nicely, and his thighs, too, were hard but nicely shaped. Sleep gave his appearance a certain peace, a youthfulness, but it couldn't hide the energy that created the fluid grace of his body.

She glanced with fascination at his hands. The nails were clipped short and were meticulously clean. Little tufts of dark hair curled over the fingers, before and after the knuckles. The fingertips were lightly callused, which was to be expected; he didn't sit at a desk. He lived what he reported. They were, she thought with a little ripple of remembered pleasure, wonderful hands. The veins were blue against the sun-dark color of his skin, covered again by a light smattering of jet-black hair. They were long hands, she decided assessingly, actually broad too, but appearing slender because of their length.

He shifted slightly and draped a leg over hers again, and she held her breath and quickly closed her eyes. But she heard his deep breathing and opened her eyes again, studying his chest. Beneath his collarbones the curling dark chest hair was lush and rich. It tapered along with his waist to a single slender line and flared again below his waist. With his leg cast over hers, she couldn't follow the vision any farther. It didn't matter. It was ingrained within her memory.

He was beautiful, physically superb. And with a touch of feminine ego, she thrilled with the knowledge that he had been hers, and that whatever came, whatever the future brought, she would have the precious memory of their time together.

Tonight had surpassed deals; it had gone beyond her own consciousness. It rent her mind with confusion, because she couldn't believe she could have fallen out of love with Wayne, and yet she was, admittedly, more than a little bit in love with Dan D'Alesio. Fantasy? Perhaps. He was an enigma, he was strength; he was the man who had ridden across the desert upon a black stallion to sweep her into his arms. He was a force larger than life, and it was impossible not to be swept away.

Yet at the same time she had to hold on to a piece of reality. She had to go to Egypt; she had to find her father.

And he would be with her. All the way. In that she trusted him implicitly. And no matter what they found, he would be there with her, whether they would share triumph and joy or the pain of discovery if something had happened to Jim. She couldn't accept that possibility; she had to have faith. And right now she had to step back to earth. She had left the desert behind; she would also eventually leave Egypt behind. She would be back, of course; Egypt was part of her life. But that other part of her life would take over again, the part that was simple, uneventful. She would rise in the morning, fight the traffic on Michigan

Avenue, spend the day secluded with co-workers and fragments of a civilization long dead.

And perhaps she and Wayne could put the pieces of their lives back together. It was strange, but it didn't seem to matter so much anymore. In fact, at the moment she really couldn't remember his face. It was probably much more aquiline than the countenance she stared upon now. Wayne's nose was perfectly straight. It did, admittedly, lack the character of the slightly crooked one before her.

Even in sleep Dan D'Alesio emitted character. And even in sleep his jaw was firm and strong, his lips nicely sensual, his dark brows and lashes full of intrigue and fascination.

Yes, she was in a little bit of love, maybe more than she cared to admit. But hadn't that been what she was afraid of all along? Neither had been able to deny the sexual tension that had rippled between them, but even when she had envisioned the most barbaric tortures for him, she had had the insight to be afraid. Because it would be too easy to care too much.

She didn't want to deny tonight. Neither did she want to deny anything else that could come between them. But she was going to die a little bit again when it was over, because he would eternally hold a piece of her heart, and a piece of her soul. She would never be able to see moonlight again without remembering him, without recalling again and again this night of soft breezes from the Persian Gulf and exotic, magical enchantment within the mosaic palace of an Arabian sheikh. Even silk. The feel of silk would remind her; a scent of sandalwood and musk upon the air. . . . And yet. Brown so deep it became midnight, flashing with fire, with sunlight. . . . With sparkling amusement —as it was now.

How long had he had been watching her watching him, she wondered with a surge of panic.

"I do hope I pass muster!" he said with a laugh, securing her chin when she would have dipped it low to avoid the probing gaze of his eyes. "Well, I have to be better than Haman, don't I?"

Alex raised her lashes and met his eyes. "Certainly," she said a bit primly, but adding an impish taunt she couldn't resist, "But that doesn't say much. A baboon would be preferable to Haman."

Dan laughed and ruffled her hair and pulled her tightly against him. "Thanks a lot. I'm better than Haman—but on a level with a baboon. Ah, well, such is life!"

Her face rested against his chest, and she liked the rich, warm scent of him and the way his hair tickled her cheek. She liked everything about him, about the moment, and she wished desperately that she could capture time and store it in a bottle to relive over and over again. She would have imagined that she would feel awkward; she didn't. She loved being with him, feeling his arms around her, casual and yet secure, so intimate, so . . . natural. He was a rogue in his way—he had tossed her rather crudely out of his Cairo hotel room—but even if he were the devil, surely even the devil deserved his due.

Devil, rogue, prince of the desert—he was also her Rock of Gibraltar, and though she would never let him know, she would hoard greedily all that fate allotted them.

He stroked her cheek softly, and his voice was husky when he spoke. "I think I'll be a little more gallant. You do by far outshine any beauty ever to reign in the finest of harems. And I thank you, with all of my heart, for tonight."

Alex frowned at the sound of his words, trying to twist to read his eyes. She would never have expected such a poetic statement from him, and she couldn't quite believe that he meant his pretty compliment. But then she also didn't want to believe that he was quite so tender, or quite so demanding, with every woman.

Before she could seek his eyes, he sat up, bringing her with him. "I wouldn't be at all surprised to find a bottle of champagne in the ice box. Want some?"

"I—yes, thank you, I suppose so."

Alex was a little surprised to see him jump easily from the bed and walk silently out of the bedroom to the salon. A bit selfconsciously, she ripped the covers from beneath her and dragged them up to her chin as she waited for his return.

He did return with champagne, and two chilled glasses. He seemed completely at ease with his nudity as he sat on the bed, smiled at her and twisted the cork. Alex jumped slightly as the cork popped and Dan lithely moved backward to keep a short gush of the frothing champagne from spilling over the sheets.

"Love champagne," he murmured, licking his thumb absently, "but not on the bed." He handed Alex the glass, and as she instinctively reached for it, she lost the barrier of silk she had drawn between them.

Dan laughed, and the sound was deep and pleasantly throaty. Alex glanced at him, biting her lip unwittingly as she flushed a pale pink.

"Doctor," he teased, pouring the champagne, "upon our first meeting you barged into my bathroom, where I was rather innocently naked. You barged into my bed, where, once again, I was innocently naked, to demand that I marry you. And now that we have finally been most thoroughly intimate, you would deny me the pleasure of your nudity? Really, Dr. Randall, that doesn't seem at all fair. Besides," he added dryly, "it's a bit late and ridiculous, don't you think?"

Alex lowered her lashes and ignored his question as she sipped her champagne, but she didn't make any mad grabs for the sheets. Instead she headed for seemingly safer ground. "Dan, what do you think will happen in Cairo?"

He shrugged. "It depends on what you mean." He smiled softly in the dim-glowing light. "But I believe sincerely—and don't ask me why—that your father is alive." He chuckled suddenly. "What I do find difficult to believe is that Crosby is your father. I should probably be ashamed of myself. He's not a hell of a lot older than I am."

Alex forgot the situation and laughed. "Don't feel too much like a child molester!" she charged him. "Jim isn't a lot older than I am, either."

They laughed together, and then Dan suddenly sobered. "What happened to your first marriage?"

Alex felt her laughter fade away, her smile go stiff and then disappear. Then she shrugged and drained her champagne glass, to have it instantly refilled. "Are you trying to make me inebriated?" she demanded, attempting to regain the lightness they had shared. "I guarantee you, the story isn't worth the effort and you've already . . ."

185

"Had my way with you?" he queried. "The story is worth it to me. Tell me what happened."

"Sometimes I don't know," Alex murmured, studying the rim of her glass and running her forefinger around it. "Our marriage looked terrific on paper. Two Egyptologists—and Egyptologists, I guarantee you, are often lucky to have interested friends, much less spouses! But . . ." Alex gnawed on her lip and shrugged again. "Wayne never believed I actually wanted to work, which was strange. Sometimes I think he married me because of my father, strange as it may sound. I think he wanted to be James Crosby's son-in-law without any interference from James Crosby's daughter. And then at other times, I question myself. We didn't actually split up over the work bit. We, ah . . ."

"Go on."

Alex continued to stare at her glass rim. But she had downed her first glass of champagne quickly, and it felt as if the bubbles had gone straight to her brain. For some reason it didn't seem so terribly awkward to try to put into words the secrets, doubts and pain of her heart.

"Rumor reached me—or perhaps I should say several rumors reached me—about Wayne's extramarital activities. I didn't want to believe the rumors at first; I suppose I couldn't accept the fact that Wayne didn't love me as I loved him. Anyway, it was eventually what I didn't hear that finally made me ask him. My colleagues at the museum," she explained, "suddenly started becoming silent when I walked into a room. Wayne was going a bit hot and evidently heavy with a tour director. When I did hear about that, I challenged him, ready to believe him if he denied it. Except he didn't deny it. I suppose he thought I had him red-handed, which I didn't. To make a long story short, Wayne told me it was my fault. If I stayed home and used my education to support his work, none of it would have ever happened. A wife should be 'convenient'—not gone for fifty hours a week, and certainly not planning expeditions, unless it was to stand behind her husband."

Alex broke off suddenly and tossed down her second glass of champagne. She was going to have one hell of a headache in the morning, she warned herself woefully. But at the moment it didn't matter. The room was too beautiful, the night was too beautiful, and it was strangely wonderful to tell it all to Dan D'Alesio. And at the moment she felt good. She smiled a little wistfully and lethargically handed him her glass as she stretched out beside him, cradling her pillow. "What do you think?" she demanded. "Was it all my fault?"

Dan set the glasses down and stretched beside her, gently cradling her in his arms and hiding a wry smile. A few glasses of champagne and all the rough edges of her spiky temperament smoothed away. Her eyes, heavy lidded, were sweetly sensual, and the sleek, fluid curve of her body was even more so.

He made a mental note to himself to remember to pack a couple of cases of good vintage champagne for the expedition into the Valley of the Kings. Oh, those desert nights . . .

"No, I don't think it was all your fault. Unless you tried to leave Wayne at home with an apron tied around him and a sponge mop in his hand; did you?"

"No," Alex said with a giggle. "I'm not a brilliant cook, but a decent one, and I'm fanatically neat—"

"I believe that," Dan said solemnly. "And I repeat, I doubt that it was all your fault. Things are very seldom all one person's fault to begin with. In your case, though, it sounds as if Wayne deserved a ninety-percent share of the blame. You don't marry a 'Doctor' without expecting her to 'doctor' something. Granted, the vast change in sex roles in the past years has been hard on many relationships, but most men learn to cope. I don't think anyone—male or female—wants to change basic sexuality. Besides, it sounds to me as if you were doing all the work on the home front—hardly robbing anyone of masculinity. When two people work, two people should be putting in. But you were cooking, you were keeping the home, and I can personally guarantee that there are no doubts whatsoever as to your complete femininity, and your absolutely marvelous effect upon masculinity."

He kissed her nose lightly with the last words and began stroking his fingertips over her body from her shoulders to her lower abdomen, slowly, soothingly, and yet arousingly. Alex caught her breath, trying to ignore the subtle taunting of his fingers. She had given honest answers; she wanted a few herself.

"What about you?"

His dark eyes were following the trail of his hands, but he lifted and dropped a brow and she knew he had heard the question. "What about me?"

"You—ah—never married."

"No."

It was getting difficult to talk, but his reply maddened her. Why? She had no ties on him.

"Why?"

"Hmmm?" He seemed fascinated and totally distracted by the angle of her hip.

"Why haven't you ever married?"

"Oh . . . lots of reasons. I travel continually, and I haven't met too many females I think I would trust—or women who would want to share my life-style. I'm a loner; I like being unhampered. And mainly, I suppose, because I never met a woman with whom I was sure I wanted to share my life. Until death do us part, you know."

"I see," Alex murmured a bit resentfully, attempting to roll away from him. But he rolled with her, keeping her a prisoner beneath his carefully balanced weight.

"I can see your point of view," she said analytically, trying to maintain a uninterested cool despite the fact that they both knew she had been irritated by his reply. "The field is large, isn't it, Mr. D'Alesio? And you play it quite well. Magazines continually picture you with exotic beauties. But don't you ever miss any of them?"

His eyes caught hers, and he smiled devilishly. "Certainly not at the moment."

"I'm serious, Dan."

"So am I."

He dipped his head to kiss her, then kissed her again, slowly, as if he were taking all the time in the world now to explore and analyze.

He drew his lips from hers a second time and answered her. "Quite seriously, my love," he murmured, seeming to bathe her with a warm glow with the simple husky use of the endearment, "I can't ever imagine missing anyone when I'm with you."

Alex caught her breath. Was it real? Or was it a line he might be very adept at using?

He started moving his kisses over her throat, then lower, to leisurely taste and savor her breasts.

Alex tried to catch his hair and to continue speaking rationally.

"Dan . . . do you believe that people change? I mean, change their beliefs, their ideas on commitment?"

He raised his head, and his weight settled over hers as he cupped her face between his hands. "No," he said blandly.

"But—"

"But what? There are no 'buts.' Not now. . . ."

Get a grip on yourself, Dan warned himself. He could feel his temper rising because he knew she was questioning him because of her ex-husband. He hated the man without knowing him. And what was going to happen when they got back to Egypt? Randall would be waiting with his promises of changing. Dan didn't believe in any of those changes. Alex had been open, willing to take blame. And it didn't appear as if Randall had ever had anything to complain about. And worse than that, according to Haman and Zaid, James Crosby was concerned about his son-in-law's too-convenient habit of stumbling upon him. Randall just might have something to do with Jim's disappearance.

At best Randall was a parasite, and it was possible that he was far worse. And somehow, Dan thought grimly, he was going to make sure Alex didn't manage to reconcile her past marriage.

He knew that what the two of them had together was special. He had sensed it before he ever touched her; and now he had proof that the electricity between them was a certain magic that comes seldom in a lifetime. And he knew he could sweep her into that magic, take her to silver clouds where the fusion of their bodies swept away all else. He could give her more than she had lost. He just had to keep reminding her. . . .

She was frowning slightly, but he had no idea that she had taken his anger and vehemence in an entirely different way.

He cares about me—but not enough. He wants me, but not

involvement, Alex thought, and it was surprising just how painful the thought was. He was coming to mean far too much to her. She was a fool, because he had blatantly declared he would never change. She closed her eyes against the pain she had not expected to experience—and the desire to have more with him than she had ever admitted to herself. And then she closed her mind against the future. They were together now, and she had no intention of even attempting to pretend that she didn't want him, that he couldn't touch her and create a wildfire. At the moment he was hers, just as she was his. And for the first time in her life, she couldn't really give a damn about morals or issues. She was willing to live only for the moment—and whatever moments there might be.

"I really don't want to discuss your past or mine, Wayne or any other women. I admit I have met my share of lovely females, but not one who could in any way compare with you. You go beyond beautiful, Alex," he said huskily, shaking her head slightly between his palms to make his point.

She smiled. "Mr. D'Alesio, you do have a talent with eloquence. Are you so complimentary to all women?"

"Nope," he said gravely. "Only the ones I capture on the desert and seduce into passionate affairs."

"Really?" Alex murmured.

"Really. . . ."

He shifted his body above hers, and she gasped and shuddered deliciously as he entered her a second time. It was a surprise, but a beautiful surprise, one that swept her mind away as her body trembled in delight and instinctively responded to his. Wave upon wave of deliciousness washed over her as his body moved in a melding rhythm with hers. "I want to make love all night," he whispered to her.

His mouth, lips, teeth and tongue captured hers. She gasped for each breath, which he whispered he loved, because each breath arched her more tightly against him. And in the end it was silver magic again, and they lay together again, entwined and content.

Eventually he shifted. Alex smiled lazily and closed her eyes and adjusted herself luxuriously against the silk sheets. She felt his whisper against her ear. "What are you doing?"

"Falling asleep!" she said with a laugh.

"The night," he said indignantly, "is nowhere near over."

Alex laughed softly. "We're supposed to head for Cairo first thing in the morning. Ali—"

"Ali?" Dan queried with a dry laugh. "I promise you, Ali will not insist upon leaving first thing in the morning. He's been in the desert with Shahalla, and his 'town' wife has been alone a long while. His are equal-opportunity marriages, I'll have you know."

Alex's smile spread across her cheeks, and she warily opened her eyes. Dan was standing with the champagne tucked under his arm and the glasses in his left hand. He reached for her hand with his right. "Come on," he told her huskily.

"Where?"

"The hot tub, of course! This is the perfect Arabian night. The moon is silver, the air is soft and fragrant. We're surrounded by the exotic beauty of a sheikh's palace. Tiles, mosaics, silks—and an incredibly sensual, golden beauty. You can't expect me to waste all this, can you?"

Alex couldn't help laughing again. "Dan, I'm not even sure I can walk."

"No problem," he assured her, dipping low to the bed and balancing the bottle and glasses as he swept her into his free arm. "I'll carry you. Now, circle your arms around my neck. . . ."

Still giggling delightedly, Alex did so, loving the ease with which he held her, unable to resist the jet eyes that held hers in dark enchantment. Unable to deny that she, too, wanted the spell to last forever, and equally unable to deny that she loved even the simple body contact between them, the heated strength of his shoulders and arms, the crisp tease of his hair-roughened chest against the vulnerable softness of hers.

They were in the land of exotic enchantments. And it was a mystically beautiful Arabian night.

191

INTERLUDE

UPI—July 28

DR. ALEXANDRIA RANDALL TO PROCEED WITH
EXPEDITION

Late yesterday afternoon Dr. Alexandria Randall reentered Egypt, accompanied by Sheikh Ali Sur Sheriff of the United Arab Emirates and Daniel D'Alesio, to announce her plans to resume the expedition planned by Dr. James Crosby before his disappearance on July 6.

After finishing research preparations in Cairo for the next week, the trio will set up headquarters in Luxor while preparing for the dig in the Valley of the Kings.

When asked if she was certain she knew where her father had been intending to go, Dr. Randall replied, "Of course. My father and I have always worked very closely together. It may take time, but hopefully our information is such that we will be able to zero in immediately on the correct area."

Asked if she believes her father has met with foul play, Dr. Randall answered, "No. I believe my father is alive and well, but for reasons of his own, keeping himself unavailable."

"We will not accept the possibility of foul play unless such evidence becomes irrefutable," said Daniel D'Alesio. "And unless such evidence does come to us, we will continue to search for him in all good faith. However, due to Dr. Crosby's disappearance, Dr. Randall will be given twenty-four-hour protection."

"There are those," reports Sheikh Ali Sur Sheriff, "whose

192

only interest in the study of the past is their current desire to fill their own pockets or place their names in the annals of history. Since Dr. Crosby has disappeared, we find it prudent to guard not only Dr. Randall but that information she alone has deciphered."

Two men read the article with intense interest.
Both were in the Necropolis of Luxor, in very different places.

Wayne Randall read the paper furiously. When he finished the article, he ripped the paper to shreds, then berated himself for the action. D'Alesio! How involved was she with the man?

D'Alesio, announcing that Alex would be protected by him.

Somehow he had to get through. Alex still loved him, he was certain. Somehow he would manage to see her.

Wayne Randall sat down to calculate how to handle the unexpected turn of events. It should all have gone so smoothly. Alex should have come to him.

Dr. James Crosby read the paper by the light of his torch. And then he tossed it into the air as he laughed.

"I knew," he mumbled joyously to himself, "that one of them in that threesome had to have some sense!"

The waiting would be almost over.

He sat in the dirt again, trembling for a moment in relief. Then a smile lit his features and he picked up the dusty paper again.

You did well, my friend D'Alesio, he mused. I just hope you know that you are holding one of the most ancient forms of treasure a man can find.

He bit his lip broodingly. Take care of her, D'Alesio, he implored silently, I have to trust you to do so. And it's only just beginning. . . .

CHAPTER TWELVE

From the height of the balcony of their group of suites in the Hilton (Ali had insisted that they needed separate suites), Alex stared out across the distance to the Great Pyramids of Giza. She was glad to be back in Egypt—even if she left the suite only long enough to spirit herself into the Cairo Museum for the day and then back into virtual hiding. Dan and Ali had chosen the Hilton because Ali's Cairo home would be too obvious a place for curiosity seekers to find them, and the Victoria was also a bad choice because Dan was known to frequent that quaint establishment. The Hilton might be the third most obvious establishment, but they had to stay somewhere, and in this case obvious was also inconspicuous because the Hilton was so crowded with tourists. They could come and go with the crowds.

Cairo was always magical to Alex. It was often dirty, riddled with the poor, the bullet scars of recent wars and a mixture of peoples that was simply fascinating. The old stood along with the new. Where other ancient cultures were measured in centuries, that of Egypt was measured in millennia.

It was a wonderful place, with the cries of the muezzins calling the people of Islam to prayer, the hawkers on the streets shouting loudly, the fellahin grabbing on to the buses as they jerked their noisy way down the streets. Below her people were rushing about, concerned with business. And in the distance, rising like magic, were the pyramids.

Alex smiled as she felt a warm touch on her shoulders drawing her back against Dan. Night was falling; the air was golden and it seemed that the ancient stone structures were shining as if in sunlight.

"They are amazing, aren't they?" Alex murmured with a touch of awe.

"Umm," Dan agreed. He slipped his arms around her waist and pointed to the largest. "Whose is that?"

"Khufu—or Cheops," Alex returned with a soft smile. She had spent the last week trying to describe the intricate dynasties of the ancient Egyptians to Dan, and in many ways he was surprisingly astute. But he could never remember the name of the pharaoh who had built the largest of the three pyramids of Giza.

"Don't smirk at me," Dan protested, even though he couldn't see her face. "I've got it now. Khufu—fourth dynasty. Hated by the priests because he cut back on sacrifices. Actually he wasn't such a bad guy. He knew that the living needed the sacrifices more than the dead, and that the priests were getting rich on the sacrifices. Also, it's possible that his hundred thousand workers travailed during the months when agriculture was at a standstill, and therefore that he fed the peasant workers when they might otherwise have starved."

"Very good!" Alex laughed. "Except that it's all still speculation. Herodotus didn't write quite so nicely of Khufu."

"Ah, but he was a tourist to the land."

"I'll tell you, D'Alesio," Alex teased, "you certainly are trainable."

"Thanks."

"You're welcome. Oh, Dan, it is a beautiful view, isn't it?"

"Very," he agreed, resting his chin on the top of her head. "And you know what? Just because it's so beautiful, I'm going to take you out to dinner."

"Really?" Alex spun about in delight. They had met a few determined reporters at the airport, but since then they had kept such low profiles that they were almost flat.

In a way, she had loved the time. She would never have believed, after their first meeting, that she and Dan could be not only ardent lovers but the most congenial of friends. Often serious and brooding, Dan had a marvelous sensitivity and a wonderful sense of humor. He would sit with her as she delved through tedious work at the museum, and returned with her

195

when the day was done, determined that she not be out of his sight. He would know when she was excited and encourage that excitement, and he would know when she was depressed and cajole her from that depression, often angering her first but then causing her to laugh until she would wind up in his arms.

Their nights beneath the Egyptian moon lost none of their magic or splendor.

But in a week Alex had seen no one but the curator and professor assistant at the museum, Dan, Ali and Rajman, who had returned to his native land just hours after they did.

Rajman performed a very specific duty, which his hotel training had left him well equipped to handle. He was the buffer zone. He filtered all calls and kept stragglers off their floor. Alex had become vaguely aware that Ali had other men around them. She and Dan were always followed to the museum and were always followed home. And when they would all meet for dinner and progress talks in the evening, she knew men stood outside the saloon door.

When she mentioned the eerie feeling being so guarded gave her, Dan had replied firmly. "We don't know yet what happened to Jim. Until we do know, I'm grateful that Ali has the wealth and power to keep his goon squad around you at all times."

Now Dan glanced into her eagerly shining eyes and smiled. "Really. We've probably been around long enough for the excitement to die down. And we'll go to a small, out-of-the-way restaurant that one of Raj's cousins owns. We should be okay."

"Wonderful!" Alex spun away from him and headed for the bedroom, which was supposedly hers but in actuality shared with Dan. "If we're actually going out, I'm going to dress!"

Dan kept smiling as he watched her scamper through the salon with the lithe yet regal tread he had come to love. Then his smile slowly faded. There were so many things he was keeping from her.

He had never mentioned the newspaper article Ali had shown him, in which Wayne Randall had claimed he intended to work with his "wife" on finding James Crosby. And he never even attempted to tell himself that the reason was the possibility of Randall being a suspect. He had nothing to go on in that direction except Haman's insistence that Jim Crosby had been very wary of his ex-son-in-law. But Haman was still the most suspicious figure around. He was in Egypt now himself; Ali had informed Dan that Haman's men had been following his own men who had been trailing every movement Dan and Alex made.

It was a confusing puzzle, still nowhere near being solved. But as for Wayne Randall. . . . He had been trying to get through to Alex all week. And Dan hadn't felt a qualm about having Raj keep the man at bay.

Unconsciously Dan clenched his fists as he stared out at distant Giza from the balcony. He wondered bitterly what Alex's reaction would be when she did discover that her ex-husband had been trying to contact her. She would probably be furious that he had kept her from Randall, and then determined to find a way to throw herself back into his arms.

A slight breeze ruffled the dark hair over his forehead as he stood there, as stiff as the faraway Sphinx. He didn't have an overall plan, and he couldn't define what he wanted for the future. At the moment, he was simply determined that Alex should not return to Randall. They had made a deal, he told himself harshly. She was his until they saw the whole thing through. And he'd be damned if he'd allow another man—any man—so much as to touch her while she was—under his protection.

That was the logic he would admit to.

Inside, where the fires raged, where primal human emotion and desire reigned supreme, he was simply a man who had claimed a woman, beautiful, tempestuous, bright—and sweetly, wonderfully sensual. From the first time he had taken her, covering her soft ivory nakedness with his own hard bronze body, he had claimed her for himself alone with a fierce and elemental possessiveness more ancient than the civilizations of Egypt.

She could be the most prim, the most elegant, the most sophisticated of women. . . . But he could touch her, whisper in her ear, and she would spin into his arms, her eyes brilliant with lime and amber, sensually shaded by those incredible lashes, and become the most beguiling wanton, trembling, then sweetly giving, opening to him like a golden burst of the sun.

No! Damnit! He was going to make sure she didn't get back with Randall, a man capable of emotionally abusing this rarest of prizes who had loved him.

Dan was surprised to discover as pain riddled the side of his fist that he had crashed it against the railing. Ruefully he rubbed it, gave himself a little shake and wandered into the salon. He poured himself a shot of Scotch and leaned casually against the portable bar. Getting a little carried away here, aren't you, D'Alesio? He sipped his drink and smiled as he remembered how he had once rudely tossed her out of his rooms. He had thought of her as a powder puff, not realizing that Alexandria Randall was a lady as beautiful on the inside as she was on the outside. Ali had forced him to see.

He laughed out loud and lifted his glass to the air. "To you, Ali, you old scoundrel. Conniving, manipulative—and so charming about it!"

He hadn't realized until this moment just how much Alex had come to mean to him, how he changed daily because of her. For the first time he wanted something more than what he had. He wanted something permanent. He never tired of her—of touching her, of just being near her, hearing her voice. . . .

There was a tap at the door, and Dan automatically issued a "Come in." It was Ali, as he had expected. What he hadn't expected was the secretive way Ali moved into the room, looking about the place.

"What is it?" Dan asked with a frown.

"Where's Alex?" Ali countered.

"Dressing." Dan automatically lowered his voice. "Why, what's up?"

Ali sighed. "I had really begun to suspect Haman was the culprit in this situation," he said, delving into the bar and pouring himself a soda. "Brother," he mumbled, "if I weren't such a stinking good Muslim, I could really go for a drink."

"Ali! What's happened?"

"You and Alex were trailed today—and not only by my men and Haman's men."

"Are you sure?"

"Positive. You know I don't allow my people to slip up."

198

"By whom?"

"Well, we can say that the gang is all here."

"Wayne Randall?"

"That's right."

Dan shrugged. "Randall has been around all week. You know he keeps trying to call Alex. It isn't really a great shock that he was following her."

"Not shocking," Ali agreed. "But very interesting."

"Interesting, yes." Dan grimaced. "But it takes us back to the same puzzle. Jim has disappeared. But Haman is still sniffing around, and Randall—who Haman says made Crosby very nervous—is also on our tail. If the two men we suspect are following us, then what did happen to Jim?"

Ali was quiet for a minute.

"There's the obvious solution," he finally said softly. "Jim could be dead. Perhaps he died by mistake—someone perhaps tried to force information out of him and he refused to cooperate. With him gone, that same someone would need Alex."

Dan glanced at the bedroom door, assuring himself that it was still closed and Alex was out of range to hear their conversation.

"I don't believe that, Ali," he said softly. "I have a gut feeling that Crosby is alive, and hoping we will find him. I believe he knew that someone was after him, and that he couldn't get help. Someone wants in on that dig badly. The question is—who? Haman kidnapped Alex; I sincerely doubt that his principles extend too far. But from all I can gather on Randall, his morals are nonexistent. What do you think?"

Ali chuckled softly. "I think, my friend, that you would be very happy to put Wayne Randall behind bars."

Dan scowled and then shrugged. "That's probably true. But I'm trying to be objective. What do you think Haman is doing? Does he want to be involved so badly that he would resort to murder? If not, what is he doing here, following us?"

Again Ali hesitated before answering.

"I do not think that Haman would resort to murder—but then we don't know that anyone has been murdered. I think Haman feels he can perhaps deal with Crosby if he is found, offer Crosby a large sum of money if he will just allow him to participate—be in the background, perhaps—when the expedition goes into full swing."

"Or perhaps he wants Alex back," Dan said uneasily.

Ali exhaled a long breath. "I do not trust Haman where Alex is concerned. We are not in the desert now. It is easy to abduct a woman in Cairo and disappear into a dark, winding alley. But whether Haman would take Alex again—or merely try to use her to get close to the expedition—I do not know. While he does nothing wrong or illegal, we can do nothing except watch. Strange. . . ."

"What?"

"Perhaps I am prejudiced against Randall myself. For no sound reason I feel that Haman is just an annoyance, strenuously seeking a little glory. I worry more about Randall."

"So do I," Dan murmured.

Ali smiled secretively.

"Would you quit grinning like a damned cat!" Dan exclaimed.

"You are very protective," Ali commented. "Admirable. But you are also possessive."

"Thanks to your conniving."

"I didn't connive—"

"The hell you didn't!" Dan laughed at Ali's professed innocence.

"Alexandria needed total protection. More than I could give her. She needed the protection of a possessive man. Of a lover."

"Sure," Dan said with a grin. Then he sobered suddenly. "With all these people running around, do you still think it's safe to go out to dinner?"

Ali shrugged. "Nothing's going to happen in downtown Cairo. Besides, nothing is going to happen until someone finds something out. All these people following Alex are just going to keep following her until she leads somewhere."

"Yeah, you're right," Dan mused. "And it's time we stop playing quite so safe. We won't learn anything if we don't dangle a little bait."

"Precisely," Ali agreed. "Tonight we get to see who will crawl out of the woodwork. By the way, do we have any idea where we will be leading with our bait when we reach the Valley of the Kings?"

"No," Dan said with a grimace. "Even Alex doesn't know yet."

"Know what?" Alex suddenly demanded, appearing at the bedroom door. Dan felt his heart take a little leap when he saw her. She was dressed in black for the evening, a soft knit with a high collar and billowing sleeves. It was secured at her waist with a wide belt, above which the material hugged her form attractively and below flared with a swaying grace. High-heeled black sandals drew special attention to the length of her shapely nyloned legs, and her hair, against the black of the dress, appeared as soft and tempting as a gold-streaked cloud.

Dan noted with a raised brow that Ali as well as himself had become momentarily tongue-tied.

"Know what?" Alex persisted, apparently unaware of the stir she had caused them both.

Ali cleared his throat and gazed at Dan with an apologetic grimace. "That somewhere in the back of your mind you might know where the tomb is," he said a bit gruffly.

"Oh," Alex murmured, sweeping her lashes low over her cheeks as she shook her head unhappily. "No, Ali, I don't think I do," she said apologetically.

Dan set down his glass and approached her, offering his arm. "Let's forget the tomb for the evening, shall we, Dr. Randall? You look ravishing—so ravishing that if we don't get out of here quickly, my better nature will fail me and I'll discover that I have one appetite surpassing the desire for dinner. . . ."

Alex flushed at his compliment and glanced over his shoulder at Ali. "Don't tease, Dan," she murmured lightly.

"Who was teasing?" he said with a groan. "And don't mind Ali. He's a big boy with four wives—although I'm sure at the moment he is wishing he were totally unattached." Dan glanced with a wry smile at Ali as he began to lead Alex to the door. She was surprised when his head lowered to hers as they walked and his whisper seemed to sear her ear.

"But then you're not unattached either, Alex. Remember that."

Alex quickly jerked her eyes to him in surprise, but Dan was staring straight ahead, his countenance as fathomless as the granite she sometimes thought he must be partially composed of.

What had he meant? she wondered, her blood suddenly seeming to take a tingling race through her veins.

She quickly squelched whatever dreams were blossoming in her heart. He meant that they had made a deal. He had said that she was his for the duration—until it was all over—that was what he had meant.

She unobtrusively bit into her lower lip and cast the man beside her a surreptitious glance. He was striking tonight; exceptionally so. He was in black, which had made her choose the color herself. She smiled slightly as she remembered him in the black desert robes—so different from the suit he wore with the matching vest and tailored cream shirt, yet also worn with such a natural flair. He could be in any costume, any guise, and he would still be naturally striking, but the European suit fit his tall frame to a devastating T. It amplified his innate electricity; he appeared both elegant and rugged. And when his eyes lit upon her, the devil-jet within them was given further fire from the midnight darkness of his attire.

Alex glanced hastily ahead of her, strictly reminding herself that the man she was admiring was Daniel D'Alesio. He was hers to borrow, not to keep. She had walked into everything with her eyes wide open, determined to be mature, to accept and enjoy the magic of the affair and accept—if not enjoy—the fact that she was involved in an affair created by expediency, nothing more.

I am in love with Wayne, she tried to tell herself as they walked. And as soon as I am able to find him, I'll explain everything . . . not everything! . . . almost everything, and he will be reality and maybe, just maybe, we will have both learned and we can create a real world between us again. What I feel for Dan is hero worship. I am not really in love with him and I will be mature enough to smile and bow out.

Ass! She chided herself. You are in love with him. And you will never, never forget what he can do to you with a glance, with a touch. Wayne could never in a thousand years make you feel what you feel with him.

Alex clenched her fingers around her evening bag. Dan was an experienced lover; he could whisper things to drive her wild, and encourage her to totally uninhibited abandon with his husky murmurs of all that she did and was that he loved. But he didn't love *her*. He was an extraordinary man, capable of great giving, and she was a fool—no, an idiot—if she expected his appreciation of her to be any greater.

Wayne! She screamed the name aloud in her mind. Strange, but there had been a time she hadn't dare think about him because of the pain. And now she had to force herself to think about him to avoid pain.

Despite the growing darkness, the streets were busy. Egyptians tended to dine late, and the restaurants were flourishing. Alex was accustomed to the stares they drew as she, Dan and Ali walked the short distance to the restaurant. Tourism was big in Cairo, but Westerners were still a bit of an anomaly to the populace. On her first trip as a child, she had been frightened when people were fascinated by her hair and wanted to touch it. She was no longer frightened, nor was she a child. Nor was anyone likely to attempt to touch her when she walked with Dan and Ali. They were both men who seemed to radiate danger.

Ali had drawn to her other side as they walked, and he and Dan had been talking, although Alex had no idea what they had been talking about. She hadn't realized how absorbed she had been in her own thoughts until Dan pulled on her arm. "Whoa, Doctor! This is it. We're here."

A dark and rather foreboding alley led to the restaurant. But once they were inside the building, everything was lovely. The tables were covered in snowy white linen, with gleaming silver placed upon them. The lighting was subdued but not dim, and soft Arabic chatter could be heard along with the sound of dinner utensils clinking against china. They were seated by Rajman's cousin, a slender young man with dark eyes as soulful as Raj's. He gave them a table in a corner bordered on both sides by high wooden dividers adorned with hanging plants.

Dan said that Raj had suggested they have seafood, since his cousin's place was known for having the freshest in Cairo. Alex and Ali both agreed to the idea of a mixed shellfish platter, and they placed their orders for drinks and entrées at the same time. Their drinks appeared promptly; the entrées would take longer. Alex sipped at her Scotch and tried simply to relax and forget about her confused relationships. She could feel Dan's eyes on her, but she pretended not to notice.

His left arm was behind her, on the upholstery of their booth. He brought it around and gently ruffled her hair against her temple. "Why are you brooding?" he asked quietly.

"I—I'm not," she lied, smiling across the table at Ali. "I've just been thinking—about the eighteenth dynasty."

"Why don't you think aloud?" Ali suggested.

Alex shrugged. "It was a strange time," she murmured, sucking the Scotch off her swizzle stick and idly twiddling it with her fingers. "Right before the eighteenth dynasty, there was the Second Intermediate Period. Egypt had been in chaos—the last pharaoh had been very weak, Upper and Lower Egypt had split, and a people called the Hyksos had invaded and seized power. The eighteenth-dynasty pharaohs were princes of Thebes who seized power back. Two pharaohs died expelling the Hyksos; then Ahmos drove them out of the country. Amenhotep I followed Ahmos, and his tomb was robbed in antiquity. Anyway, you eventually have Pharaoh Ikhnaton, who decided to worship Aton rather than Amon Ra. The first was the actual, physical disc of the sun, while Ra refered to something more abstract, more spiritual. Ikhnaton made a little bit of a mess of his reign, devoting himself to his new religion. He moved his capital and then refused to leave it. Consequently there was a downfall of power in the northern provinces. He was followed by one boy king and then another. Here is where Tut comes in—Tut-ankh-Amen, who reinstated the old religion. Tut was followed by Ay, and then Horemheb. Horemheb, dated his reign back from Amenhotep III, ignoring Tut, Ikhnaton, Ay, Smenkh-ka-Ré—and our own Anelokep. But because Anelokep fits right in there, he should be near Tut. But I don't believe he is. Something is off, and for some reason I think it has to do with Hatshepshut."

Dan stared at her blankly, as did Ali. "Marvelous," Dan said dryly. "Who the hell was he?"

"Not he," Alex corrected with a small smile. "She."

204

"She?"

"Ummm. You might be surprised, Mr. D'Alesio, to learn that the royal line passed through the females. A man could only become pharaoh by marrying the heiress. Which is why the family trees were so crazy. A pharaoh had to marry his own daughter—and whatever other *females* came after her—if he wanted to continue to be pharaoh after the death of his 'Great Wife.'"

"Really?" Dan exclaimed, and Alex laughed.

"Really!" she assured him. "And if a son wanted to be pharaoh after his father, he had to marry his mother quickly, and then his sisters."

"And you think my marriages are strange!" Ali said with a laugh.

Alex shrugged. "Hatshepshut more or less co-reigned with her father, whom she must have married upon her mother's death. He was Thutmose I. And then she was married to Thutmose II, and Thutmose III—"

"And then Anelokep?" Ali interrupted.

"No." Alex shook her head. "She lived a long time before Anelokep!"

Dan laughed at Alex and Ali's confusion. "I think what Ali is getting at is this—what does Hatshepshut have to do with anything?"

"I'm not sure yet. But there are references to her in all the available hieroglyphics and records pertaining to Anelokep's burial."

Dan was gazing at her steadily, and Alex saw a peculiar light suddenly blaze in his eyes. "You do know what it is, Alex."

"I don't—"

"You don't think that you do, but it is there. Just keep thinking about her and talking about her."

Their food arrived as Dan finished the sentence, and Alex stared mournfully down at her plate. She glanced back at Dan. "I'd rather think about shrimp."

"I didn't mean that you should force it," he said quietly. "But talk out loud about what you're thinking." He chuckled softly. "You may consider me a bimbo as far as Egyptology goes, but

Ali and I make marvelous listeners, and the questions we ask may actually help."

"Don't forget, Alex," Ali said, clasping her hand across the table, "we leave tomorrow to set up in Luxor."

Alex nodded. She hadn't forgotten, and she had copied everything she thought might possibly help from the museum. The cordial staff had photographed all the broken pieces of the ancient walls and the granite slabs that might possibly contain anything in reference to her needs. "There's nothing much else I can do in Cairo anyway," she murmured. She bit into one of the shrimp swimming in an aromatic concoction of butter, garlic and various herbs. It was delicious. She tasted a scallop, grateful that both Dan and Ali spoke and read Arabic and had made the purely Egyptian restaurant available to her.

She glanced up suddenly to see that both men were watching her. She frowned, returning their scrutiny. "What is it?" she demanded with exasperation. "Have I got parsley on my nose or something?"

The two exchanged glances, laughed, then sighed and relaxed. "I guess we were both waiting for you to suddenly hit upon the main clue," Dan said apologetically.

Alex grinned and shook her head. "Sorry," she murmured. "You should both eat; the platter is delicious."

Dan lifted a brow wryly in Ali's direction and began to eat. As soon as Ali automatically joined in, Alex smiled, swallowed another scallop and began talking.

"Hatshepshut was very remarkable. Although future pharaohs ignored her in their records, she claimed to rule as king, and she probably did! Thutmose II reigned only thirteen years, and while Thutmose III was still just a lad, she was virtually pharaoh. Her temple at Deir el Bahri is not only magnificent but renowned for its fascinating sculpture and inscriptions. Egypt was at peace at this time; building and trade flourished." Alex smiled. Ali and Dan had both stopped eating again. "The royal lady did maintain a little of the power she claimed into eternity: she was not buried in the Valley of the Queens but in the Valley of the Kings."

Still smiling sweetly, Alex returned to her own meal. She

watched covertly as Dan and Ali shrugged at one another and started eating again.

Then she was no longer smiling as she ate because she was overwhelmed by frustration. Why can't I see what Jim meant for me to see? she wondered. She had all the puzzle pieces. She had been staring at them day after day, and she still didn't understand. And she had to solve the puzzle. If she did, she could find Jim. She knew it.

She had to find the tomb, and she had to find him. And when they were together they would share the dream of cataloging and clearing the ancient treasures of the Egyptians. And her deal with Dan would be over, but she would still have to see him day after day because he would be filming. . . .

Alex set down her fork as her appetite suddenly left her. How would she be able to stand seeing him day after day after they had lived together so intimately? She chanced a glance in his direction, to see that he was staring across the room, strange emotions filtering across his face. She followed his line of vision.

They had been so engrossed and so secluded at their intimate table that Alex had noticed nothing past Ali's handsome face. Now she realized that the woman who had taken the table cater-corner from theirs was watching them. No, not them—Dan. And Dan was staring back.

For no explicable reason Alex felt a shivering panic touch the base of her spine. She tried to assess the feeling, but it actually needed no assessment.

The small, chic brunette was probably the most beautiful woman Alex had ever seen. Her eyes were huge and blue, her cheekbones high, her face a perfect oval. She smiled slowly, and Alex thought miserably that she had never seen anyone do such a simple thing with such appealing sensuality.

"Excuse me," Dan said suddenly.

Alex moved her eyes from the woman to Dan as he rose and approached the table. He bent low to speak to her, and her smile broadened, displaying deep, matching dimples in both cheeks.

There was suddenly a sharp grip on Alex's frozen hand, and she turned then to Ali with surprise. She had forgotten he was sitting right across the table from her.

207

"She's just an old friend," Ali said softly. "Dan is being polite."

"Old friend—or old flame?" Alex queried sweetly, forcing a casual smile to her lips."

Ali shrugged. "All men have pasts."

"D'Alesio certainly seems to." Alex sipped her wine, amazed at the depth of jealousy that raged within her. Jealousy . . . and pain. But she had always known she was a fool to become involved with Dan. No strings. But Ali knew that she had become involved, and she couldn't bear the look he was giving her now—one of empathy strangely combined with amusement and—pleasure! Ali was glad to see that she was upset because Dan was speaking intimately with another woman.

"Ali," she said quietly, sipping her wine again and then running a finger idly around the rim of her glass. "Dan is most welcome to his past—and to his future. You of all people are aware of the circumstances regarding our . . ."

"Affair." She had almost said "affair." And of course that was all it was. But somehow she couldn't say that word. And for some reason she was very ridiculously blushing crazily, because of course Ali was very aware that she and Dan had been sleeping together since that night in his palace.

"Our being together," she finished a bit lamely. "Really, Ali, you have no need to look at me like that. I'm an adult. Quite old enough to know what I'm doing. And where I'm going when this—including Dan—is all over."

"Do you, Alexandria?" Ali queried softly.

"Of course, Ali," Alex said, and sighed, managing to sound quite exasperated. Then she gave Ali a brilliant smile and began idly chattering, carefully keeping her eyes from Dan and the brunette. She heard herself muttering something to him about how pathetic the dreams of the ancient pharaohs became when their sad-looking decayed remains were unshrouded and unwound and put on public display. "Ramses II, with colossi all over Egypt, lies in a room in a case with rows and rows of other mummies around him! Think how horrified he would be to see himself in such company!"

Ali laughed and responded, but they both knew the conversation was brittle. Alex kept trying not to glance toward the other table; she couldn't help glancing in that direction now and then. And for all her mature logic, she felt as if she had been slammed against a brick wall as she watched Dan. His right hand was placed upon the back of the woman's chair; his left hand was on the table, and his stance appeared very intimate. His brow was slightly furrowed as he spoke in reply to something, but Alex couldn't begin to read the emotion in his jet eyes or tense features. The woman reached up with blood-red nails to touch his shoulder, and her fingers ran over the lapels of his dinner jacket.

Alex wanted to scream.

She tried to remember that she was talking to Ali. "The . . . uh . . . pharaoh, when alive, was referred to as the living king. When dead, he became the . . . uh . . . god king because it was believed he actually became Osiris—"

"Alex!" Ali interrupted, grinning. "Dan is being polite to an old friend, nothing more."

"Ali!" Alex responded in kind. "I told you, it makes no difference to me."

Ali had no chance to reply, as Dan chose that moment to return to their table. Alex wondered desperately how to appear polite and mildly interested in his friendship, not as if jealousy was eating away at her and she would dearly love to smash his face into his dinner."

"Old friend?" she inquired sweetly as he slipped in beside her.

"Acquaintance," he replied briefly.

She must have managed to sound nonchalant—perhaps too nonchalant. Because Dan didn't say another word about the woman who still sat at the table near them. He launched into a discussion with Ali on the supplies they would need to procure when they reached Luxor.

Alex barely heard the words they exchanged. She felt her anger rising like lava in a volcano. She had no ties on him, but damnit, he was with her. And he had still excused himself—oh, politely, of course—to wander over to another woman. He hadn't really done anything, her more logical sense told her. He had merely said hello to a woman—albeit a very beautiful, very sensual woman—and then returned to the table. He hadn't left her stranded in the middle of the street.

She still wanted to kill him, and it was frightening, terrifying to think of how terribly involved she was to feel such pain. And she wasn't normally jealous. She had trusted Wayne against all odds, because she had believed he loved her.

Dan did care for her. That was what hurt. They shared so much that was so special to her that was just a way of life to him. . . .

". . . be right back."

Alex started guiltily as she realized Ali was talking to her and smiling. She watched him blankly as he left the table and then jerked as if she had been burned as Dan's arm came around her shoulder.

"What in the world is the matter with you?" Dan demanded tensely.

"I . . . uh . . . I don't feel like being mauled at the moment," Alex replied, wincing inwardly as the words left her mouth.

"Mauled?" He lifted a querying brow.

"I'm sorry; I really want to be left alone."

She was already wishing fervently that she could kick herself when he chuckled huskily, inclining his head to whisper in her ear. "Doctor, the lady is merely an old acquaintance. I don't, I'm afraid, remember her name, and therefore an introduction would have been impossible."

"You don't even remember her name!"

"Alex, I said 'acquaintance,' not—"

"Are we ready?" Ali queried, appearing at the table again. "I think we'd best get back if we want to make an early start in the morning."

"I'm definitely ready," Alex murmured, moving swiftly to her feet. To her annoyance, Dan was right beside her, taking her arm with one of his unbreakable holds. Alex waited until they were out of the restaurant to whisper at him vehemently.

"I'd appreciate it if you would drop the vise grip now," Alex hissed as they stepped into the Egyptian night.

Ali, behind them, suddenly exclaimed. "Allah be merciful! A full Egyptian moon. And tonight was made for trouble."

210

"What?" Alex asked, trying to see what Ali was talking about, but Dan pulled her around and more tightly into his arms. "It is a full moon, sweetheart." His voice was low and husky, yet she had the strange feeling it would carry on the night air. "It's good luck to kiss beneath the Egyptian moon . . . did I ever tell you that?"

He claimed her lips in an outrageous kiss, one impossible to repel. Definitely a full moon, she thought irritably, and D'Alesio is turning into the werewolf of Cairo.

Still sizzling with righteous anger and certain he had lost his mind to so accost her when she was ready to kill him, Alex brought her hands against his chest. But his embrace was one of steel; he had no intention of letting her go. Neither did it seem possible to twist her lips from his, although it wasn't quite a kiss. He was merely holding her—tensely. "Dan!" she said, her words muffled against his mouth.

"Alex!" A shocked plea suddenly sounded in the night. The strangled voice she heard was a familiar one. Very shocked, hurt, angry. Wayne's voice.

She broke away from Dan. His eyes were holding hers with a demanding challenge. She met them with fury, attempting to twist out of his arms to see the man she hadn't seen in a year, the ex-husband she had been so sure she had loved . . . would love again when the sudden tempest of her life left and reality returned.

Wayne.

And very vaguely Alex could hear Ali's dry voice behind them. "What a surprise. . . ."

Dan released her abruptly, and she was able to turn.

Wayne, with a somewhat ghastly expression on his face, was standing before them. Alex searched desperately for something to say.

Dan took the initiative. "You must be Wayne Randall. Sorry we haven't been able to return your calls. It's been crazy, getting ready for the dig and gathering last-minute data."

Wayne, his handsome face pale and sullen but knit into a tight mask of determination, ignored Dan. "Alex, I have to talk to you. D'Alesio, I need to speak with my wife alone—"

211

"Dan," Alex began, trying to extricate herself from his grasp. "I really do need to talk to Wayne, to exp—"

"Sorry," Dan said coolly, a grim smile whitening his lips, the jet of his eyes seeming to be a blowtorch that sizzled all it came in contact with. "Randall, she's not your wife. Not anymore. And she's with me. And I don't intend to leave her in your keeping for two seconds. Now if you'll excuse us—"

"No way, D'Alesio!" Wayne thundered furiously. His beautiful blue eyes were like ice chips as he suddenly took a wild punch at Dan.

Wayne was no fighter. He was a scholar, Alex thought sadly. Handsome, head in the clouds, tall, thin, his light hair constantly ruffled. He was no match for D'Alesio.

The punch almost hit Alex, and she suddenly found herself tossed into Ali's arms.

"I'd stop there, Randall," Dan, to his credit, warned.

Wayne was too berserk to stop. He aimed another punch, which Dan neatly sidestepped.

"Stop it!" Alex heard herself screech out.

"Ali, take her home," Dan said absently, warily eyeing Wayne for his next move.

"Ali, you let go of me!" Alex demanded with reproach.

He wouldn't have released her; not after Dan's command. But it didn't matter. Wayne made another lunge at Dan, and Dan finally struck back. Wayne landed on the sidewalk, rubbing his cheek without rising, but shouting out, "I'll kill you, D'Alesio!"

"Sure," Dan agreed absently, stepping past him and jerking Alex's arm back from Ali.

Alex was furious. Dan had just proved that she meant no more to him than any other woman, just a possession. He was capable of being charming to any female of the species. She knew without a doubt that she needed to cling to her past. When the devastation of losing Dan befell her, she would need some dream to cling to. Her dream was Wayne. And he had tried to fight for her. Dan was just such a damn lug.

"You idiot!" she raged at Dan. "You might have hurt him! Let me go. I want to talk to him. Let me explain—"

"Not on your life, Doctor. You're with me because you wanted to be. And I warned you it would be to the finish."

"But I have to explain—" Alex was flailing at him, trying to break his grasp.

"Sorry, Doctor."

He was pale beneath the bronze of his flesh; his eyes were a deep and furiously burning jet. His voice was calm, cool. But with his last words he shrugged and dipped, butting her midriff and tossing her over his shoulder, heedless of the passersby in the streets and the small audience they were drawing.

"We're going back to our room, Doctor," he murmured flatly.

He was halfway down the street as he uttered the words, despite her fervent, pounding protests.

To top it all off, she could still hear Wayne's cursed threats in the background and, from closer behind them, Ali's soft, delighted laughter.

CHAPTER THIRTEEN

Cairo, Alex decided bitterly, was as much a man's town as Abu Dhabi.

It was difficult to remember that just two hours ago she had traversed the same streets, strolling along pleasantly between Dan and Ali, watching with idle enchantment the people who crowded the streets: Arabians, Nubians, southern Europeans, the occasional Western tourist. And it was just as difficult to remember how cordially she was usually treated by Egyptian men—the hotel concierges, restaurateurs, merchants, curators, guides, taxi drivers—because not one of them thought a thing of Dan lugging her—protesting—through the streets. They all seemed to think it some form of vast amusement, even the one policeman they passed. He laughed the hardest.

Alex protested until they reached the doors of the Hilton. She wasn't about to be carted through the lobby, and her whisper was both furious and vehement. "Put me down now, D'Alesio. I'll walk right next to your side. Just don't you dare bring me through that lobby like this."

He hadn't said a word during the entire walk; now he hesitated.

"I'm not going to run anywhere," Alex hissed. "I know damn well Ali and his—his—friends are right behind us. And believe me, D'Alesio, I have a few choice words to say to you myself that I don't particularly want heard by others!"

He set her down less than gently and gripped her elbow roughly. "As you wish. Let's proceed through the lobby."

Regaining her dignity as best she could. Alex lifted her chin and preceded him into the lobby, tightening her lips at the feel of the viselike grip of his fingers on her elbow.

They walked stone-faced and swiftly to the elevators. Ali was close behind them, but when the cage door opened, he stepped backward, offering Alex a dry smile. "I wouldn't get in on this one for all the oil in the Persian Gulf!" he swore with a grimace.

"But—" Alex's protest was cut off as the door eased closed. She was alone in the elevator with Dan. Why not? It was Dan she wanted to kill. But she had wanted Ali there. Because she did want to kill Dan, to rip him to pieces, and Ali might have been a stabilizing influence between them. And he would have stopped Dan from retaliating if she did go absolutely berserk and attempt to strangle him.

By mutual agreement they remained silent and not touching in the elevator. Not until the door to their suite was opened and then closed behind them did Alex let loose.

"D'Alesio," she raged venomously, stalking across the room and tossing her purse onto a sofa as she spun around it, making the piece of furniture both a barrier and a scapegoat as she dug her nails into the fabric of the high-rising back. "This is it! The last straw! The deals are over and done with. I could kill you. I could honest to God kill you. How could you do such a thing to me? It's all right for you to trot off and talk to an old acquaintance—whose name you don't even remember—but you not only keep me from talking to Wayne, you create an entire performance for him. You stabbed me in the back, Dan. I'm not a damned rug, and I'm not property! You knew I wanted a reconciliation! You made me look like an idiot first, and then you wouldn't even let me talk to Wayne. Not only that, you turn around like a prizefighter and knock him down—"

"Don't get on that!" Dan interrupted sharply, his tone deceptively quiet, his features tightly drawn as he stood just inside the door, his stance casual as he idly lit a cigarette. "The guy came at me twice before I hit him—in self-defense."

"Because you had me! What did you expect him to do? Say, 'Oh, excuse me, Mr. D'Alesio'?"

"Yeah," Dan said dryly, his eyes narrowing at her. "I guess I did."

215

"What? That's preposterous."

"How so, Doctor?"

Alex hadn't realized how angry Dan himself was until that moment, when he jerked out of his jacket and tossed it in a furious motion across a chair. "Doctor, you *are* with me. For the duration. Now I did nothing but say hello to that woman and trot right back to the table. I'll admit it was pleasant to realize that you might be jealous over me. But you are not going near Wayne Randall. We're talking a very different story here, my love, and we both know it. I repeat: you are with me now."

"Because we made a deal, Dan."

"And we both know we agreed upon certain stipulations." Alex was surprised he didn't strangle himself with the vehemence with which he ripped off his tie.

"Well, I want out of the deal."

"So that you can run after a man who cheated on you? Who didn't have the self-confidence to accept that his wife might be brighter in his field than he?"

"He may have changed—"

"A man who says he cheats because his wife works isn't going to change."

The possible truth of his statement did little to cool her wrath. "It's none of your business!" she snapped.

"You're my responsibility," he said in return, "and that makes it my business. You're not going to make a fool out of yourself on my time!"

Alex stood dead still for a moment, feeling her fury run through her bloodstream in static jerks. "Like I said, D'Alesio," she murmured through tightly clenched teeth, "the deal is off. I'm walking. And then it will be my time."

"And what about your father?"

Her head was spinning. Further pain clouded it, and suddenly, as angry as she was, she was ready to cry. "I can raise an expedition on my own," she said coolly, leaving her stance at the sofa to swerve around it and retrieve her purse. "I'll send for my things."

Only an idiot, she admonished herself seconds later, would have believed she could walk out the door just like that.

He allowed her to reach it, but then took only two steps to reach her and swing her back around to face him.

"You're not walking," he promised in a quiet but heated tone. "We went through all this at Ali's. The deal was that we see it through together. Just consider it a deal you really made with the devil, Doctor. No backing out once the papers are signed."

She stared at him, fighting back the absurd urge to cry that had seized her moments ago. She didn't really want to go, but she was wise enough to know that the delay would be even more painful. Until they saw it through; that was what he kept reminding her.

"Let me go!" she suddenly raged, banging her fists against his black-vested chest. You're the idiot, D'Alesio, she thought. Don't you realize that I'm falling in love with you and that's the worst fall that could ever happen? Into a black pit where there is never a landing, never any hope of anything except falling through eternity, broken into pieces against the jagged rocks of memory.

"I will not let you go!" he bellowed. "Never! Not back to that man. I can make you forget him, and if I damn well have to prove it, then so be it, that's what I'll damn well do!"

"What?" Alex shrieked, freezing her flailing fists. No, she thought desperately, don't touch me, not now, because I'm confused and vulnerable and I'll melt like hot lead.

"I can make you forget a man named Wayne Randall ever lived, Ms. Randall." His whisper was touched by both anger and determination as his lips hovered close to her ear. "I can promise you that I can make you call my name with a need more intense than any you ever felt for that man."

"No," Alex protested weakly. His words were a breath of heat and moisture, sending tiny shivers of arousal down her spine, all the more heightened because they knew one another well now, so well that her body automatically anticipated the delights of his expert hands and lips and hard-muscled body.

He released her, taking a step back to discard his vest as he held her with the jet demand in his eyes. For a moment she stood still, fighting the desire that his whisper alone could stir, the hypnotism of natural response. Her eyes were wide. She was already trembling.

"Oh, no!" she exclaimed, determined to sidestep him as he worked at the buttons of his immaculately tailored shirt.

She didn't make it around him; she hadn't expected that she would. But she'd had to try, for what remained of her heart.

He didn't just stop her, he lifted her into his arms. "You're fighting yourself, not me, Alex," he told her grimly as he stalked with her into the bedroom.

"Dan, please . . ."

He stood her up and pulled off the belt of her dress and slipped down the zipper despite her fumbling countermeasures to stop him. And before she could chatter out his name a second time, he had swept her onto the bed and his weight was partially over her as he surveyed her body in matching black bra and bikinis and nylons.

"Dan!" she shrieked out furiously as he lowered his head to nuzzle the ivory mound of her breast that stood firm above the low line of the French-cut bra. He ignored her, moving his lips lower to capture the nipple through the thin wisp of lace.

Alex swallowed convulsively. The intensity of fury that had raged through her rechanneled itself into desire. The moist persuasion of his mouth and the knowing, gentle graze of his teeth were so exotic over the lace that a flash of explosive heat instantly rendered her body into shudders. She caught her breath, knowing she had never wanted him with a more volatile need than at this moment.

"No . . ." she moaned quietly once more.

But he did know her, and he did know that he could make her cry out his name. He knew her every erogenous zone, and as if she were a delicate and custom-made musical instrument, he had learned how to play upon her to bring forth the most delightful and tempestuous of melodies.

He moved his kisses over her trembling torso, gentling her hips, teasing very soft and very feminine flesh again through the exotic touch of lace and silk. He felt her freeze and gasp as he delved within, felt her open sweetly to him.

And she called his name. Tenderly he removed her stockings,

218

then the lace and silk that had been erotic in the play but now created barriers against his need to have her completely. He rose to shed his black trousers and briefs, and she kneeled on the bed, burying her face against his chest as she murmured against it.

"This isn't fair to me, Dan . . ."

He dug his fingers through her hair and tilted her face to his. "It is fair, Alex," he murmured huskily. "The stipulations were all in the deal."

"Devil deal," she whispered in return. But her arms were circling around him, and he claimed her lips as he embraced her in return, bringing them both back to the bed. The tempest within her suddenly made her the aggressor, determined to touch him with delicate fingers and thirsting lips until he knew the wild extent of the hunger he had caused to curl within her.

He allowed her to take the lead, whispering how he loved it when she touched him, how good, how very, very good it all was. And all the while his hands found her, cradling her curves, exploring the ivory beauty of her flesh, breasts, hips, shoulders, thighs, until Alex straddled him, her hair a tangled fan that fell in wild, beguiling disorder over her breasts. He reached up to touch it, threading his fingers through it, drawing her face to his so that their mouths might meld as their bodies did. But when they broke the kiss, he swept her beneath him in a strong, fluid motion that didn't mar for a second the beauty of being one together or alter a stroke in the smoldering rhythm set by his velvet thrusts.

"Whisper my name, Alex," he murmured huskily to her.

"Dan. . . ." And she whispered it over and over, gasping as all that had been fury became the storm of unleashed passion. Smoldering fires grew to high-leaping flames, and the craving, the yearning, the beauty that was a sweet hunger that one prayed could go on and on while soaring toward its reward, exploded within them both like a heaven-reaching burst of fire sparks.

And she called his name again, a jagged but sweet refrain, embracing his heart as her slender limbs embraced his body. He smiled, shuddering slightly with the aftermath, as he rested his head against the dampness of her breasts, feeling himself drained, his life force filling her. And he knew then that he loved her, more deeply than he had loved before.

The knowledge was painful, especially since with the intimacy of their passion cooling, they were both silent, touching but inwardly withdrawing from each other. Lovemaking could be a respite, sometimes a beautiful respite that was a moment of heaven to cling to, but after the sweet fury of the storm, nothing had really changed.

He could make her forget Randall; yes, he could make her call out his name. But he couldn't erase the argument that had been the catalyst of the storm from either of their minds.

Dan sat up and drew his hands to his temples to rake his damp hair back against his head. He stood without glancing at Alex and walked to the closet to pull out his robe. With the terrycloth wrapped around him, he stepped onto the balcony, drawing in air as he stared out over Cairo, his fingers clenched over the wrought-iron railing.

What am I trying to do? he wondered. In the end, he wouldn't be able to stop Alex from returning to Randall.

Unless Randall was in on something. But he didn't want to mention to Alex just how possible that might be. He wanted her to see for herself. And maybe he was wrong; maybe it had been Haman trailing James Crosby all the time. Haman was devious and crooked enough to be up to anything.

None of that particularly mattered at the moment. What did matter was Alex. He was in love with her, totally, deeply. She was in love with another man. And he was using force to keep her away from him. What a fool. By stopping her, he would make her more and more determined to see Randall.

But he had to stop her just in case Randall was in on something rotten. He had to slit his own throat. Both Jim's and Alex's lives might be at stake. If he came out of it all looking like the heavy, he would have to take that chance, no matter what his personal feelings.

Dan glanced down at the streets of Cairo. There was little activity now. But out in the distance toward Giza, the Great Pyramids were still standing sentinel, wrapped in mystery by the darkness and the moon, guardians of Cairo's ancient past. They were a reminder of the wealth that lay in that past. And a reminder that modern man, as well as ancient man, would risk the death curses of the pharaohs, imprisonment or even life to possess the vast riches of gold and precious gems to be found within the sands.

Dan turned from the balcony and headed back into the bedroom. Alex had her back to his side of the bed and the covers pulled tightly over her shoulders. She wasn't sleeping.

He wondered if he should try to explain. He opened his mouth, then closed it. When he spoke to the back of her head, his voice was grating and harsh, which he hadn't intended at all. "I'm sorry, Alex. You did make a deal. But even if you hadn't, I couldn't allow you to talk to Randall now. Please don't try. I'll have to stop you."

She didn't reply. He slid out of his robe with a sigh and crawled beneath the sheets. She remained rigidly in her position, turned away from him, not touching.

Dan stayed on his own side, staring bleakly up at the ceiling. In time he slept, reminding himself that they would be in the Valley of the Kings tomorrow, searching, and making themselves the ultimate bait.

The phone was ringing. Still half asleep, her eyes refusing to open, Alex fumbled for the receiver. She touched a hand.

Her eyes finally opened. Dan had come around the bed to answer the phone. He glanced at her with little expression as he said, "Yes?" and then listened.

Alex gazed at the rugged angles of his face for moment, watching his eyes with their hard, unreadable jet, then lay back against her pillow, closing her eyes.

It would be useless to question him about the call. She felt safe to assume that she would never receive a phone call; she knew now that Dan had decreed that she not speak to anyone and therefore she wouldn't be able to. She didn't doubt that Wayne had been trying to get through to her for days, probably since they had reentered the country. But did it really make any difference? Dan was right; she was kidding herself if she thought

221

Wayne would ever change. But that didn't even make any difference.

"Yeah," Dan said, "put it through."

He placed his hand over the mouthpiece and shook Alex's shoulder. His eyes were steadfastly upon her.

"It's your ex-husband. Rajman says he insists upon speaking with you, and I think you may as well talk to him and straighten things out."

Alex reached jerkily for the phone, unable to believe that Dan was actually giving her the call. He had spent last night convincing her he would never allow her to talk to Wayne while he was around.

He stood after he handed the phone to her and walked naked like a great sleek cat to stare out the window.

She knew he would hear every word she said. Was he trusting her? she wondered.

"Hello," she said nervously.

"Alex! I can't believe I've gotten through to you! I'm going to talk fast, honey. I know D'Alesio must be holding you virtually a prisoner, and I know just as well that you can't be in love with him. It has something to do with your dad, Alex, I know. But listen to me—I can help you find Jim ten times better than him, honey. We'll find Jim and work on us, sweetheart, our marriage. I love you, honey. And I know you love me. Just give me the word, Alex, and I'll come pick you up—with the authorities, so we won't have any problems. Alex . . . are you there?"

Yes, she was there. She was holding the receiver so tightly it was amazing the plastic didn't crack in her hand. Such a short time ago his words would have meant everything in the world. But now they meant nothing. Because Dan was right. She would be a fool ever to trust Wayne again. And more than that, she was fooling herself cruelly if she believed she could use anyone to make her forget Dan.

"Alex? Alex, damnit, answer me. I need you, Alex."

She smiled slightly. There was already a peevish quality to Wayne's voice. He *needed* her, not the way a man should need a woman but because she was a convenience to him at this time.

She glanced at the window to see that Dan was staring at her,

222

arms crossed over his broad, dark-haired chest. His eyes were a challenge, but she wasn't cowering to that challenge. She simply told the truth.

"Wayne, I'm sorry. I have nothing to say to you. I'm working with Dan and Ali. I appreciate you caring about Jim, but we have everything in hand. I—I don't want to see you at all in Egypt."

"You can't mean that!" Wayne exploded. "Alex, I'm an Egyptologist too. If you're going after that tomb, you need me, not a wise-ass reporter. You have no right to do this, Alex. I deserve to be in on that tomb with you. And I'm warning you, Jim has already disappeared. Something could happen to you, Alex. I want to see you. I—" He paused for a moment, as if realizing the tone of his statements. "I love you, Alex."

"I'm sorry, Wayne," she said again with real regret, "but I don't love you anymore."

"I don't believe that!" Wayne said, his voice grating harshly. "That damn D'Alesio has done something—"

Dan suddenly strode back from the window and snatched the receiver from her hands. He spoke immediately into the mouthpiece. "You heard her, Randall. She doesn't love you anymore. Now leave her alone."

He placed the receiver down hard on the phone and glared at Alex. "Glad to see you can stick to a deal," he said dryly. He turned away from her and headed for the bathroom. "Call room service for breakfast. Then get your things together—only what you'll need in Luxor. Ali said he wanted to be out of here by ten. You can have the shower in five minutes."

Alex watched as his swift, agile stride took him away from her. She heard the slam of the bathroom door and bit down hard on her lip to keep from crying.

I might have been a fool to have loved Wayne, she thought miserably, but I'm an absolute idiot to be so in love with that arrogant SOB. But I am. And he thinks he threatened me into keeping up my part of the deal. Wrong, Mr. D'Alesio. But I'm probably much better off with you believing that. I don't think I could handle it if you knew the truth.

As he promised, he was out of the bathroom, freshly shaved and showered, in five minutes. She took a little longer.

They ate a private breakfast in tense silence. One hour later they were airborne in Ali's private jet, headed for Lower Egypt.

Alex gazed impatiently out of their suite window in Luxor. Across the Nile was the Valley of the Kings.

It was exciting to have come this far. Long ago, before the modern Egyptians had built on this land, the ancient Theban pharaohs had lived and ruled here. There were beautiful temples to be seen on this side of the bank, more carefully cared for by the Egyptian government every year. The temple at Luxor was indeed fantastic; just north lay Karnak, with its multitude of awesome sanctuaries, pylons and temples. All were wonderful; you could close your eyes and feel the splendor and mystery of the pharaohs and a civilization over three thousand years old.

But across the Nile was the Valley of the Kings, the cliffs rising to the sky, housing the vast area of hewn tomb after tomb, a place where the fertility of the Nile had no middle growth; there was life and greenery, and then there was desert. And the city of the dead. The Valley of Kings and the Valley of the Queens. There were so many tombs that the cliffs were almost like gigantic anthills, with underground passages leading to more underground passages.

Alex suddenly bit hard on her knuckles, wondering with marked irritation why she didn't seem to be able to unravel the puzzle facing her. And then she was swamped with depression. The Valley of the Kings had been so thoroughly searched. So many tombs had been found—those of Amenophis I, II and III, and the Thutmoses, Ramses III, Ay and Horemheb, Tutankhamen and even Hatshepshut, in the Valley of the Kings. Common graves had been found, tombs of noblemen had been found. It seemed impossible that Anelokep's tomb hadn't been discovered if it existed.

What was it that she was missing? she asked herself for the thousandth time. She didn't believe that mountains of sand could be covering the entrance to the tomb; her father had believed one could almost walk right into it without bothering to dig! It had to be more like the picture puzzles in which you stared at a landscape and were supposed to find the shapes of twelve fish hidden within the lines of the trees.

The door suddenly opened and slammed. It was Dan, returning from his trip with Ali to the authorities.

"We have permission to set up in the Valley," he told her stiffly.

"Wonderful," Alex replied, her tone as distant. "Are we going to make our camp this afternoon?"

"No." Dan shook his head. As she opened her mouth to ask why, he interrupted before she could speak. "You forget, Doctor, that we don't know where we're going yet. We need to stall for as much time as possible. And you can spend what's left of the afternoon and evening studying your notes to see what else you can come up with."

Alex turned back to stare out the window. "I don't think I can stand studying those notes anymore," she muttered.

"You have to," Dan said quietly. "It's the only chance we have."

She winced, remembering that it was Jim, not a royal tomb, that they were really looking for. She did have to look at the notes; she had to solve the puzzle. Because she had to find Jim.

"All right," she said glumly. "I'll start again."

Out of the corner of her eye she saw him turn toward the bedroom. As if he felt her looking at him, he answered her unspoken question. "I'm going to take a nap—for one, so that I don't disturb you. And also because I didn't get any sleep last night."

You think you didn't! Alex thought miserably. But she said nothing as he entered the bedroom and closed the door behind him.

For several moments she stayed where she was, staring out at the city, watching the still water of the Nile. Its surface was mirror smooth; there were no breezes to ripple the water.

How have we made such a mess of things? she wondered. She thought of how easy, how rapturous, how intimately comfortable it had been to live with Dan. What had gone wrong? How had everything become so stiff and distant? Was it merely because she had admitted to herself that she was in love with a man who was a loner, who wanted no shackles around his neck . . . no permanent involvement.

The fight had been over Wayne. But even after that fight, they had made love, and it had been both sweet and torrid. Which only went to prove, she thought sadly, that all problems certainly couldn't be solved in bed. Except that she would gladly sleep with him again, because it was all that she had to hang on to.

But last night he hadn't held her after they made love; they hadn't curled together into the long hours of the night. He had risen, he had left her, he had returned to issue his decree, and then he had lain stiffly on his own side of the bed. And the foot between them had become miles by this morning.

Tears started to well in her eyes, and she issued an impatient oath. If they could only find Jim; if she could at least have her father. . . .

"If I'm going to find Jim," she whispered aloud to herself, "I'm going to have to study until I find out what he knew."

Thus determined, she drew out her work and laid her notes before her on the old English desk. Soon her brow was knit in concentration.

For some reason she kept reading over the references to Hatshepshut, the queen who had claimed herself pharaoh and had herself buried in the Valley of the Kings. Alex puzzled over two other references to past queens—one of the Nefertitis (there had been several) and a second "great wife," Shenkah, of a little-known pharaoh.

Alex began to wonder if she was reading and interpreting the hieroglyphics correctly. The reference to Anelokep taken from one of the Karnak temple walls seemed very strange. It alluded to "the God Pharaoh"—the pharaoh when dead, reigning "between" Nefertiti and Shenkah. It didn't make any sense.

She realized she was chewing the paint off her pencil and distastefully placed her pencil on her notes and stretched. Glancing at her watch, she realized she had been studying for several hours. She stood and yawned and walked back to the window to stare longingly out at the Nile.

Eventually her eyes turned rebelliously to the bedroom door.

The man who had cost her a decent night's sleep was in there comfortably napping, while she racked her brain! Damn him! She glanced out the window, then back to the street. Maybe what she needed was some breathing space. Perhaps she couldn't think because her emotions were too involved. She was growing more and more worried about Jim, and she had discovered she was truly no longer in love with the ex-husband who had suddenly decided he wanted her back, while also discovering that she was desperately in love with the devil with whom she had made a blood pact.

Alex gnawed on her knuckle for a second, thinking he would be furious to wake and not find her in the room. She paled a little as she thought of the flaming temper he was capable of.

Then she smiled grimly. The hell with him. She was not his prisoner. She wanted to go downstairs and breathe the air of the Nile. She was certain Ali had plenty of men around. She would be safe. And if Dan didn't like it, so much the better. He would learn that she didn't simply follow his decrees.

With the decision made, she felt better. Grabbing her shoulder bag, she silently let herself out of the suite.

There was a row of shops near the hotel. After standing in front of the hotel and enjoying the air and the native hubbub of donkey-drawn carts and street hawkers, Alex turned her steps nonchalantly for the shops. Most of the antiquities displayed in the stores were fakes, but every once in a while it was possible to find something not only authentic but rare. A little browsing would be entertaining. But halfway down the street she froze in her tracks.

There was a man standing outside the first storefront, studying the display. He was differently dressed from the first time she had seen him—he was in a slightly rumpled European suit—but she would recognize his fat-jowled face and dark, beady eyes anywhere. Haman. Omar Khi Haman. And he wasn't alone, she saw with rising panic. Zaid was with him, and another of the goon squad, both men looking equally out of place and lethal in awkward business suits.

Alex hesitated only a second in her frozen state before spinning on her heels and starting back for the hotel at a brisk walk, looking studiously over her shoulder. She didn't believe Haman had seen her, but after her experiences with him, she couldn't control the fear that threatened to overwhelm her. Her walk turned to a run, and she glanced over her shoulder to see if he was in pursuit.

The street had suddenly become crowded. She couldn't see anyone chasing her, but neither could she see Haman or his men standing in front of the shop any longer. She scanned the crowd quickly, and her heart seemed to stop. Zaid had seen her. And Haman. They were pushing through the crowd. Haman was puffing and moving slowly. Zaid was fast gaining ground on her.

Half tripping in her nervous haste, Alex looked back again as she reached the door to the hotel lobby.

The door flew open without her pulling it. A hand suddenly descended on her arm, and she attempted to scream. Only a gasp came out. But as she stared stupidly at the hand on her arm, wondering how on earth Haman could have gotten in front of her, she realized it wasn't he or his goons after all. The flesh on the hand was pale.

She looked up slowly—into Wayne's face. Wayne's handsome face. Wayne's flashing green eyes. Wayne, only Wayne. . . .

Strange, but she really didn't feel a thing. It had been over a year since he had touched her, and she could honestly look at the face that should have been on a magazine cover without feeling a single thing. His touch meant nothing. Only one man in the world could make her blood sing with a look from devilish dark eyes, with a husky laugh, with the lightest of touches.

"Wayne," she said distantly. "What are you doing here?"

He smiled, and she vaguely thought that he knew he had an endearing all-American smile. "I've come for you, Alex. I know that D'Alesio was forcing you to say those things on the phone this morning."

For a second she felt her jaw drop. He was so sure of himself, smug, confident. He couldn't believe she had fallen out of love with him. It was probably unthinkable to Wayne that any woman would ever fall out of love with him.

"Wayne," she said patiently, "no one forced me to say what

I did. I'm with Dan because I want to be. I don't want to see you now, or ever again."

His smile faltered, then regained its brilliance. "Alex, I can't believe that. D'Alesio has some kind of hold over you, but we'll break that hold. You're coming with me, and then we'll find Jim."

"Wayne." His grip upon her was tightening painfully, and she impatiently tried to break it. "Wayne, I'm not hypnotized, I'm not under anyone's hold—"

"Come on."

Ignoring her protests, he started dragging her along. "Wayne!" Alex screamed out, digging at his unrelenting fingers with her free hand. "I'm serious."

She realized then that he was dragging her toward an automobile in the road, a black sedan with its engine running and a driver in the front seat. He had no intention of letting her go.

"Wayne, I mean it!" she cried, but she was coming irrevocably closer to the idling sedan.

"Alex, come on! Hurry. I'm trying to help you. Look."

She took the time to glance around in the direction Wayne indicated. Zaid had cleared the street crowd and was upon her.

Suddenly her other arm was grasped, and a torrent of angry Arabic was riddling the air.

She found herself becoming the rope in a terrifying game of tug-of-war. Something would have to give quickly. Haman would eventually puff his way to them, and it was doubtful Wayne was traveling entirely alone.

Ali and Dan certainly hadn't traveled alone. But where were the men of the desert chieftain when she needed them most: She was being used as a giant wishbone, and no one was coming to her defense.

Dan woke with a startled jerk. He glanced around the room, wondering what had awakened him. Nothing was amiss. His alarm clock was ticking quietly and steadily, but besides that, everything was silent. Too silent.

He bolted out of the bed and raced to the door and out into the salon of the suite.

Alex was gone.

Without going back into the bedroom to retrieve his shoes, Dan raced out of the suite, his heart hammering. Where had she gone? Damn, he should have warned her more fervently that she was in danger, that either her old enemy Haman or the ex-husband she loved had something to do with her father's disappearance.

A fine sweat broke out on his brow. When he got hold of her, he was going to kill her. But what if he couldn't find her? His mind went blank; chills riddled his perspiration-slicked body. If something happened to her he would go mad.

He forced himself to calm down, to remember that Ali's men had to be somewhere near her. They wouldn't allow anything to happen. And Raj should be near her, too, if she had left the hotel.

Dan met Rajman in the lobby. The Egyptian greeted him with a burst of confusion. "I was following her, and watching to see which fish would bite. But both fish went for the bait, Mr. D'Alesio. And she's out there now. We've been trying to make sense of it—"

Dan suddenly saw a hint of the commotion outside the lobby doors. "To hell with the sense of it!" he exclaimed, bolting past Rajman and out the lobby door.

Zaid and Wayne were in the midst of a heated argument; Dan wondered if either could understand the other, since Wayne was shouting in English and Zaid was shouting in Arabic. Alex was between them, staring from one to the other while furiously working at her wrists.

Dan could understand why Ali's men had taken so long to break it up. Alex was in no immediate danger while the men argued, and there might have been something to learn from the angry words.

As Dan watched, trying not to grin, Alex kicked Zaid in the shins and spun about to repeat the action upon her other heckler. The argument stopped as both men bellowed in pain—but neither released her.

The treasure she could lead them to, Dan thought wryly, was worth a little pain. The argument resumed again, but this time they began to pull on Alex's arms.

Dan narrowed his eyes. Across the street where the crowd had drawn to curiously watch the action, Omar Khi Haman, ridiculous in business attire, was also watching the proceedings.

It had gone far enough, Dan decided.

Out of the corner of his eye he could see Ali's cousin Ahman watching the proceedings, watching him for a cue to action. Dan nodded briefly. Ahman nodded in return and swept a compact revolver from beneath a fold of his galabria. A shot rang in the air, silencing the argument with its loud report.

Alex was as startled by the deafening sound of the gun as the two men holding her. Like them, she went dead still with the sudden shock.

It was then that Dan stepped forward. He was barefoot and bare-chested, and his dark hair was tousled over his forehead. But he had never appeared more menacing. Alex noted vaguely that she had never realized quite how tall he was until she saw him tower over both men, hostility crackling with electric tension from the dark depths of his eyes.

"Excuse me," he said smoothly, circling Alex's waist and drawing her from the hold of both men. "I'll remind you both that the lady is with me, and I don't appreciate her being accosted."

Zaid burst into a stream of angry Arabic. Dan listened. Alex squirmed to see his face, but she was drawn against him, the tip of her head beneath his chin. She was grateful that he held her; she was dizzy with the aftereffects of fear and confusion.

"Zaid says that you were trying to kidnap Alex, Randall. Is that true?" Dan suddenly demanded.

"Scurvy liar!" Wayne exploded. "For one, D'Alesio, I don't care what kind of lies you've fed Alex; she still belongs to me. And this Arab here was the one trying to abduct her—I was trying to save her from him!"

Dan said something to Zaid in Arabic. He flew into a stream of Arabic curses, finally lifting his arms in impotent exasperation, and turned to stalk down the street.

"Zaid said you are the liar, Randall," Dan said with polite inquiry.

"And you're going to listen to that Arab! The hell with you,

231

D'Alesio." Wayne's brows lifted slightly, and Alex twisted to see that she was surrounded. Ali and Rajman and two men she recognized from Ali's desert tribe were ranged behind Dan.

"You've asked for the trouble, D'Alesio," Wayne muttered suddenly. "Alex, this man is after nothing but a story. This is your last chance. Come with me or take the consequences. I promise you, someone is going to wind up hurt. Don't let it be you, because this tough has decided to use you."

She was surprised when Dan suddenly released her. She turned to see his eyes, flaming jet, staring into hers. "I'm not holding you, Alex. Randall, the choice is hers."

Alex stared from Dan to Wayne, her heart pounding painfully in her chest. Suddenly a knot seemed to form in her chest. She was being used by everyone. They were after the priceless treasure of the ancient tomb; all she wanted to do was find her father.

She took a step back from them both, overwhelmed by the ridiculous urge to burst into tears. "I think you should both rot in hell for an eternity," she said heatedly.

Then she spun around, blinded by the tears in her eyes, and pushed past Rajman and Ali and the tribesmen to reenter the hotel and race through the lobby to the elevator. She went straight to the suite and into the bedroom, slamming the door closed behind her. She was able to throw herself on the bed and bury her head in the pillow before the tears came.

They were cleansing. When the torrent ended, she did feel better. I will find my father, she promised herself. I'll expect nothing from any man; I'll use Dan and Ali as I've been used until Jim is found. Dead or alive.

Jim could be dead, but she didn't cry again with the admission. She just felt numb. It was a possibility she had to accept, even as she had to accept that she must work against it. One way or another she would find out what had happened to her father. And then she would put all this behind her—the curse of kings, the curse of men. The curse of being in love, and not knowing if she was being totally used in return.

Alex remained on the bed, lethargic and listless. Shadows began to fill the room. She had half expected Dan to come after her, furiously berating her for leaving the room, reminding her

232

that she was more trouble than a horde of cobras. But hours passed and he hadn't come near her. She didn't even know if he was in the suite, and she didn't know if she should care.

Her eyes closed and she fell into a restless sleep.

She was awakened while the moon still rode high in the ancient land of temples and the Nile. There was a single rap on the door.

It didn't open. She heard Dan's voice. Curiously, it wasn't riddled with the anger she had expected. It was soft and husky.

"Alex, if you ever walk out on me like that again, I'll—I'll wring your neck."

She closed her eyes. Was Dan, like everyone else, merely after the tomb? He didn't need money, and Alex believed he honestly cared for Jim. But he was a broadcast journalist; he lived on danger, on excitement, on the stories of the century. And he was very much a physical man, energy and vitality personified—a demanding lover, a giving lover, an all-consuming lover. . . . But his sexuality never stood in the way of his determination. He molded his needs to his current situation.

She was his at the moment. He could be the fury of a storm; he could be the tenderness of the lapping tide on a moonlit night.

He had done her a favor. He had taught her a few things about Wayne. He had taught her that she could be deeply, passionately involved with another man. He had taught her that she possessed a vast sensuality and a capacity for love far greater than she had ever known.

And he was sure to leave her devastated. He had threatened to wring her neck. His anger had been controlled, but it was still there: pride; male ego; his determination to find the tomb and James Crosby.

She was faintly surprised that he didn't bang down the door and wring her neck right then and there.

She heard his voice, soft, husky. "Please, Alex, don't do anything so dangerously foolish again."

She bit her lip, suddenly wishing that she hadn't bolted the door or that he would bang it down. He was capable of doing that, she knew. And she didn't have the courage to stand up and open it. She was feeling so very vulnerable. He would realize that she loved him, and he would probably be as blunt as he usually was. He wanted no ties.

She didn't open the door, and neither did he.

He left her alone for the entire night.

Alex lay awake, praying that he at least remained in the suite.

CHAPTER FOURTEEN

By nightfall in West Thebes, the vast cliffs and dips of the Valley of the Kings truly belonged to the world of the dead.

The tourists who came daily to traverse the known tombs of long-dead pharaohs had left. Only the villagers of Qurna remained; a people who eons ago had made their homes on the very cliffs that housed the tunneled chambers of the dead. The Egyptian government had been trying to move these villagers for years; doubtless they would keep trying for years to come, with the same lack of results.

Those who lived in Qurna were tenacious and obstinate—and wary of those they dealt with in the Valley of the Kings. The government officials Dan and Ali had contacted about their work had warned them to be leery of the villagers. But when night fell upon the encampment, the people of Qurna seemed as far away as the distant stars.

The tents that housed the expedition party were modern canvas affairs; battered tin coffeepots perked over open fires. They were once again upon the brink of the desert, but the circumstances were as different from those at Ali's camp in the oasis as night was from day. The simple, primitive beauty of the sheikhdom was lacking—the essence of elegance within the desert, the touch of silver, the feel of silk. No Arabian stallions raced these sands; donkeys and water bison were the beasts of burden. The modern world had so intervened that there could be nothing so simple as a sheikh ruling his people with love and patience.

Alex sighed as she stared out at the cliffs, mournful shadowlands in the dim light of the moon. This was it: the Valley of the Kings. It was a place of ancient magic and ritual, of culture—of intrigue and romance. The story of a civilization lay within the cliffs, a story that had begun to be unraveled in Paris in 1826 when Jean-François Champollion had founded the science of Egyptology by learning to decipher the ancient hieroglyphics, the knowledge of which had been sealed for some two thousand years.

Today they had explored the known tombs. She had gone through all the open tombs with Dan, Ali and Raj, and at Dan and Ali's gentle insistence, she had spoken the entire time. She had told them what she knew about the design of the chambers, the methods of mummification, the reigns of the pharaohs, the utensils taken into the tomb to remain with the dead pharaoh for his rebirth as a god. They studied doorways to see how granite blocks could seal the tombs; they studied every nook and cranny of the layouts. Alex explained that Tut's tomb had been so very hard to find because workers for Ramses II's tomb during the nineteenth dynasty had built their living quarters above the entrance to his tomb; years later sand and earth and rubble had hidden the sixteen steps that led to Tut's tomb.

During dinner she had pored over her books on Egyptology, showing the men page after page of the treasures discovered in Tutankhamen's tomb: the disassembled golden chariots, the death masks, the thrones, the caskets and coffers; finely carved figurines in ebony, alabaster and multicolored glass; cases for the sheep's-wool wigs worn in the day; bracelets, earrings, necklaces; an ivory papyrus smoother. The list was endless.

And Tut's tomb had been robbed in antiquity. Still, so little had been taken. The robbers must have been accosted in the act, and the tomb resealed.

Alex was sure that when they found Anelokep's tomb, they would discover that it too had been robbed sometime over the millennia. But if they were lucky, they would find it resealed, as Tut's had been.

She glanced up at the few stars that twinkled over the dismal night in vast necropolis. Here we are, Jim, and where are you? I have reached this point; we have announced that we will find the tomb. The world is waiting, and I still haven't the faintest idea of what I'm doing. I've studied all the plans, Jim. I walked the tombs today until my feet blistered. I've read until my eyes closed on me. And I still don't know what I'm doing. . . . The world is waiting, and I'm a fraud.

Alex stood and stretched and rubbed her derriere. The rock she had been sitting on was hard and jagged, but she had barely noticed when she had been swamped by her thoughts.

Suddenly everything bothered her. Her ankle itched and she couldn't scratch it because of her boots, but she didn't want to take off her boots because night might have brought out a number of scorpions or snakes. She glanced back toward the camp, wondering what had caused her to wander away in the first place.

Dan. Polite, solicitous. Cool.

The distant way he had looked at her all day made her wonder if they had ever been anything more than remote acquaintances.

She could see him clearly by the firelight before their tent. His dark head was bent over one of her books; occasionally he glanced up, his rugged features a study in concentration, to listen to something Ali or Raj was saying.

The five tribesmen of Ali's oasis who had accompanied them to Egypt were relaxing with the Theban workers. She could hear laughter from the group in front of one of the other sprawling tents. Altogether their party numbered fifteen. She was the only woman, but she had never felt more safe in her life. Ali had seen that she rested on a little pedestal where the men were concerned; Alex was warmed by his concern. If all else proved to be devastation from delving into the past, at least she would always be able to say that one good thing had happened—she had acquired Ali Sur Sheriff as a friend.

And Dan had been her friend. No, more than her friend. Her lover, a perfect mate for her tempestuous soul. There had been a time when they had laughed and challenged and gambled. Two adventurers, reckless, impetuous, willing to cast everything on a long shot.

It can't really be over, she thought. We're perfect for one another, if he would only realize it. . . . Perfect. The night in Ali's palace, the week in Cairo, high above the city, swept away to the heights of the clouds as the pyramids soared with them in the moonlit background.

Alex smiled faintly as she suddenly heard the refrain of modern music. Rajman was playing his tape recorder. The refrains of "Hang On, Sloopy" were ricocheting through the ancient Theban hills. It didn't matter. The music might be enough to wake the dead, but Alex had the strange feeling that no remaining mummified forms were going to stalk the cliffs.

She tensed as she suddenly heard the rustle of brush behind her. She wasn't more than a hundred yards from the camp; in the forlorn sanctity of this empty valley, even Ali and Dan had felt safe about allowing her to do a bit of wandering. It would be almost impossible for a man to sneak up on them.

But Alex had heard a noise. She spun around, her eyes attempting to pierce the darkness. "Who's there?" she demanded.

The noise came again, and with it a form out of the darkness. A small form, scampering toward Alex.

Alex poised to run, but before her legs could spring into action, she heard a softly phrased and accented "Please!"

Something made her stop curiously, her heart thudding. She stood perfectly still and waited as the small form approached her.

It was a woman—a petite, exceptionally beautiful Egyptian woman. Even in the moon and firelight, her eyes were green, her features smoothly chiseled, her face an alabaster mask.

"You are Alex?" the woman whispered, reaching into her dark linen robe.

"Yes," Alex murmured, watching the woman with a frown of confusion. Where had she come from? The village of Qurna?

"Here—please, you will take this."

Alex automatically reached for the offered package. It was wrapped in newspaper, but before she could open it, the woman turned to speed away.

"Wait!" Alex called. "Please, wait! What is this? Who are you?" She started to follow the Egyptian, but the petite beauty was as swift and sure on the jagged terrain as a gazelle. In seconds Alex had lost her in the darkness.

"Alex!"

She stopped as she heard Dan's thundering growl and the fall of his footsteps behind her. She had lost the woman, anyway.

"What are you doing, running off like this? I know you're the Egyptologist, but the snakes and scorpions and mosquitoes don't care a hell of a lot about knowledgeable degrees—"

"I'm not running off," Alex interrupted, exasperated with the sardonic quality of his voice. Ali came up behind Dan, and Alex smiled weakly at him. "I just received a mystery present."

"From whom?" Ali demanded.

"A woman . . . an Egyptian, I believe. I don't know. I was just standing there—there by that rock—and she walked up to me and handed me this." Alex stretched out her hand with the newspaper-wrapped bundle.

Dan's fingers gripped her upper arm firmly. "Let's take it over to the fire."

Seconds later the three of them were seated as she carefully undid the wrappings. When the paper was cleared from the small statuette, Alex emitted a stunned gasp.

It was about twelve inches high and solid gold—a pharaoh, standing with his staff and sepulchre. He wore a banded crown upon his head with tiny precious inlays of lapis lazuli to denote the vulture and the cobra—the insignia of Lower and Upper Egypt combined beneath one ruler. And at the base of the statuette were tiny hieratics. Alex strained against the darkness to read them.

"Is it real?" Ali demanded.

Dan nodded before Alex could answer. "It's real gold, all right."

"It's Anelokep!" Alex breathed with thundering excitement stealing her voice. "It's a piece that should have come from his tomb . . . See, there's his name, and his royal cartouche."

Although neither Dan nor Ali could read the symbols, they both politely stared as she pointed at the writing so painfully, so delicately, carved. Alex momentarily forgot the distance that had risen between her and Dan as she struggled for breath and coherency to speak again. "And there's mention of the queens here again—see—Hatshepshut! And here are the symbols for the two lesser queens I noticed the other day. This signifies god king—or dead king! This has to be from his tomb! Someone has found it!"

"Alex," Dan said quietly. "Tell us about the woman who gave it to you. Slowly. Say anything you can think of."

She took a deep breath, unable to take her eyes off the small statue. "I told you, I was just standing there, and then I heard a noise. I was about to start running, but she called my name—"

"How?" Dan interrupted.

"Alex. She called me Alex."

"Strange," Ali muttered. "What did she look like?"

"She was, uh—very pretty. About . . . I don't know, not terribly young. Not a child, at any rate. She was somewhere between my age and thirty-five, maybe. She was very petite, and her eyes were a beautiful green." Alex lifted her hands helplessly as she struggled for a better description. "She was . . . unique. Almost like a china doll."

Dan was looking at Ali. "She must have come from Qurna."

"Shall we take a ride?"

"Might as well. The villagers won't be friendly, but at least we speak their language."

"Wait a minute," Alex protested. "You're going to go into Qurna? Now?"

"If we're going to find her," Dan said dryly, "now seems to be the time."

"Then I'm going with you." Alex said stubbornly.

"No you're not," Dan said. "You're going to bed. Things are starting to get hot."

"You won't be able to find her without me," Alex protested. "And the statuette was given to me! If she sees me, she may talk; if she sees the two of you, she'll probably run away again."

Dan stood and planted his hands in his pockets. Alex recognized the determined sparkle of jet in his eyes. "You're not going, Alex. It's unlikely that we'll find this mystery woman of yours. She could find shelter in dozens of homes, and Qurna still harbors bands of murderers, rapists and thieves. Night isn't the best time for an American woman to be prowling around. You're going to bed."

He turned around and strode smoothly toward the single jeep

they had brought across the Nile. Alex compressed her lips furiously, ready to start after him. Ali caught her arm.

"He's right, Alex, Qurna could be dangerous for you. And Dan is worried about Haman and—" Alex glanced sharply at Ali, and he cut off whatever he had been about to say and started over. "Alex, don't forget that there has to be a reason for your father's disappearance. In camp you're protected."

"But Ali," Alex protested, trying to free her arm. "This is the first real clue we've had! We're so close. Ali, James Crosby is my father! Please."

Ali drew in a deep breath, and Alex was reminded that she faced not only one of the most wealthy and powerful men in the world but a Muslim sheikh—a man accustomed to being obeyed by women. He certainly wasn't going to help her defy Dan.

"Alex, Dan has told you where you will be safest. He is concerned for your welfare. You will obey him."

Ali released her, then turned to follow Dan. He yelled out a few orders in Arabic as he joined Dan in the jeep.

Alex noted that as the jeep drove away, Ahman and another of Ali's men wandered nearer the tent. Guard dogs again, she thought with a sigh. She was being left, and that was that. Law decreed by Daniel D'Alesio. She gritted her teeth and irritably entered her tent, ducking beneath the canvas A-frame. Damn Dan and damn Ali! She imagined a scene in which she had them both buried up to their necks in sand. And then she sat on her cot and started shaking. She shared the tent with Dan—naturally. But he would be sleeping feet away on his own narrow cot. And suddenly she needed intimacy with him more than she ever had before; they were so close to—to something. And she was terrified. What would they find? She needed Dan—his strength, his comfort. She wanted to shake him because she was so angry at having been left, but more than anything she wanted to crawl to him and beg that he be with her when the puzzle was unraveled.

Alex took her boots off and lay back on her cot. Ali had mentioned Haman. Did he think his old enemy was behind her father's disappearance? Who else? And why else would Haman have followed them to Egypt? He had sent Zaid after her the other night.

Chills began to race down her spine. She was guarded by a dozen men, but she was suddenly aware of the vastness of the graveyard in which they had camped. They hadn't seen Haman all day. In fact, he had done nothing but follow them, and Zaid had been no more guilty of accosting her than Wayne had been.

What a fiasco. Poor Wayne. He wanted in on some great discovery so badly.

But she couldn't dwell on Wayne; she had to worry about Haman. But he hadn't been around the Valley of the Kings today.

Thoughts kept revolving in Alex's mind. Haman. Wayne. Floor plans for royal tombs. Dan. She wanted him to come back so badly; she just wanted to know that he was in the tent. She would never sleep without him there, even if her only comfort was hearing him breathe.

But she did sleep. Her next coherent thought was that it was amazing how brightly the sun could shine through canvas.

Dan knicked his chin as he saw Alex emerge from the tent. He scowled, staring into the mirror he had braced on a travel pole. The tiny knick bled as if he had hit a main artery. His eyes suddenly met hers in the mirror and narrowed slightly.

He remembered the first time he had seen her in his bathroom, how he had thought her nothing but a powder puff in her sleek and elegant beige suit with matching hat.

On the expedition she dressed practically: khaki trousers, short-sleeved beige blouse, hair neatly caught at her nape in a simple elastic band. And yet she wore her practical clothing with as much flair as she did a business suit, a silken harem outfit, a chic black cocktail gown. So much a woman. Capable of roughing it with no frills when the occasion warranted; enjoying all that was feminine when she could.

He lowered his eyes for a moment as he rinsed his razor in the small plastic container attached to the pole beneath the mirror. She was approaching him, her hands casually stuffed in the

242

pockets of the khaki pants. He met her eyes again as he swiped more carefully at the shaving cream still on his left cheek.

"Well?" she demanded.

Dan noticed slight violet smudges beneath the unearthly sweep of her long, dark lashes. She looked a little pale too, he thought. The strain of worrying about her father was taking its toll, he felt, wishing desperately that he had a few sure answers to give her.

"Well what?" he queried.

"Did you find her?"

Dan dipped his face to rinse it in the water. He groped for the towel he had draped on a nearby fold-up chair. The towel was suddenly stuffed into his hands. He dried his face and studied her eyes as he draped the towel over his bare shoulders.

"Yes and no."

"Damnit, Dan, what does that mean?"

"Get a cup of coffee, will you?" he retorted, irritated with her tone. He knew what was coming: a spiel on how they might have found and held the woman if she had been along. "You can be a real shrew first thing in the morning."

He walked past her to the fire in front of the main tent. Rajman, proud of his expertise with frying eggs over the open fire, grinned up at him. "Breakfast in five minutes, Mr. Dan."

Alex had apparently stalked him, because she suddenly crashed into his back.

"Give Alex some coffee first, will you, Raj?"

"Certainly, certainly."

"Dan!" Alex demanded, pushing away from him and nodding her thanks to Raj as he handed her a cup of coffee.

"All right, Alex; we saw her. But we lost her."

"Oh, Dan!" Alex exclaimed with disgust. "I told you—"

"It wasn't Dan's fault." Ali made his quiet announcement, appearing suddenly beside Dan. "No matter what, we couldn't have brought you. Haman has taken up headquarters on the outskirts of Qurna and—"

"Ali," Alex protested. "I'm supposed to be bait! How are we going to draw anyone out if I'm not—"

"Alex," Ali said softly. "Bait is one thing. We don't want to hand you right over to whoever is behind all this. Especially since we've anounced that you know where the tomb is. Someone just might be willing to kill for that kind of information."

"That's right," Alex murmured defiantly. "And whoever this is may be holding my father, and that woman might have led us to him."

"Alex, I have a strange feeling the woman will try to find us—or you—again," Dan told her. "I told you, we did find her last night. She was right in the middle of the street."

"Watching Dan very studiously," Ali said.

"But when we started toward her, she disappeared into one of the alleys. And you know how the homes in that place wind through the hillside. I chased her, but she disappeared."

"But," Ali interrupted again, "I don't think she was running from Dan or me but from whoever might have been behind us. That's why I say she'll find us again." Ali suddenly laughed, dipping to accept a cup of coffee from Raj, who listened to the entire interchange with eyes flashing his excitement.

"She is," Ali mused to Alex, "an extraordinary woman—very beautiful, as you said. And I do think she was trying to convey some message to Dan when she first saw us."

"Perhaps she would like to be the first to create a harem for Dan!" Rajman piped up with a broad grin.

Dan and Ali both laughed. Alex glared at the lot of them with little humor and spun about to return to her tent. She heard Dan's dry comment in the background. "That's not a bad idea."

Alex muttered an oath beneath her breath and ducked into her tent. She wanted to study the statuette again. It was her only tangible link with the tomb—and her father.

They spent the day prowling the open tombs again. If nothing else, Alex decided, she would study the tunnels and chambers within the cliffs and hills and know for certain where Anelokep's tomb *wasn't*.

She was angry with Ali, but she was angrier with Dan, and so she chose to spend the hours linked with Ali. She didn't like remembering how much she had enjoyed seeing Dan that morning, shirtless, his broad back bronzed and gleaming beneath the sun, shaving foam covering his face. She had felt both little chills and a strange comfort to see him half naked. She could easily envision a life in which she awoke every morning to duck beneath his arm as he shaved to retrieve the toothpaste, at ease with one another.

It wasn't to be, she told herself solidly. It was never intended to be. Dan lived his own life, and it seemed as if even the calculated and demanding desire he had once felt for her was gone. She had been a conquest; the conquest had been conquered. Perhaps too easily. Perhaps she had become too jealous; perhaps they had fought too much.

They were in the tomb of Knut, a nobleman of the eighteenth dynasty, when she and Ali wandered back to the burial chamber alone. She was idly pointing out some exceptionally fine wall paintings depicting a scene of women making shat-cakes with huge containers of honey spread across the table. Kohl darkened the eyelids of the workers, and in the next picture, Tye, the wife of Knut, sat before a dressing table with the reeds of her eye paints spread before her. "It's easy simply from this one picture to date this tomb after the Intermediate period," Alex told Ali absently. "Those years were lean; eye paints were kept in hollow reeds. By the eighteenth dynasty the wealth of the land was flourishing again. See, here Tye is keeping her paints in containers of alabaster."

She pointed at the picture and turned to see that Ali was smiling at her. She frowned, and he laughed. "I'm sorry, Alex," he murmured, still smiling affectionately. "It's just that I was watching you, listening to you, and you're such a knowledgeable and independent lady! This must be very hard for you—Dan ordering you about, and me . . . well, me being an Arab and a Muslim and having four wives. . . ."

Alex lowered her eyelashes. "This is your world, Ali. And yes, sometimes I am eager to return to my own." And, she added silently, I'm not so terribly sure I'd mind Dan being so bluntly commanding if he did so out of love instead of plan and determination.

"Ah, Alex," Ali murmured. "They are different worlds. But think on this: we do cherish our women. We may seem chauvinistic to you, but in my land, the punishment for rape is usually quick decapitation. Women are also protected." He was silent for a moment, studying the paintings. "Alex, we are harsh because we care. I have grown very fond of you, and I believe Dan has fallen in love with you."

Alex felt her breath catch. For several seconds her heart pounded wildly; then she realized that she couldn't live on hope because of the words of a man's friend. "I think you're wrong, Ali," she said casually, walking to another wall. "Oh, I believe that Dan does care for me. Perhaps a lot. But not enough. Dan is too involved with the world to be involved with a woman. He likes to keep moving; he doesn't like the shackled feeling." Alex smiled at Ali with a little grimace. "I think Dan *would* be happy to have our mystery lady join his 'harem.' His international collection!"

Ali laughed. "Men and women can be such fools! It's a pity that it seems that I have forced the two of you together—but not into an honest confrontation. Ah, well, I can say nothing more to either of you, except perhaps this: Dan also believes that you are still in love with your ex-spouse. I do not believe that. But as I've said, you are both adults. You must come to your own conclusions. Adults—but also scared children. Americans!" he said, and laughed. "Always so worried about pride."

He turned away from the paintings and to the door that led from the burial chamber to a corridor and then to the antechamber. "Let's find the erstwhile Mr. D'Alesio, shall we, Dr. Randall?"

"Just one more moment," Alex murmured, pretending to stare at the wall again. "You go on ahead. I'll be right there."

She wasn't really seeing the ancient paintings. She was thinking about Ali's words. Dan has never said that he loves me, she thought sadly.

But I am in love with him, and perhaps the greatest injury I could do myself wouldn't be to lose my pride or to take a chance on a broken heart, but not to ever admit my feelings to him.

"Alll . . . lexxxx . . ."

Ice suddenly seemed to congeal her body from her head to her toes as she heard the eerie whisper within the burial chamber.

"Alllleeexxxxx!" The long, hissed whisper came again. She didn't dare turn to the corner of the chamber, the source of the sound, and yet she was compelled to turn. She wanted to scream; she couldn't. Terror brought the clamminess of the tomb to her flesh as she pivoted slowly and yet irrevocably to the darkness of the shadowed corner that was never touched by light.

Her sudden inhalation of breath was so sharp that it seemed to thunder throughout the chamber. She exhaled, feeling her mind spin with relief and then amazement. The whisper was coming from the Egyptian woman who had brought her the statuette.

Dizziness swept through Alex with her relief, and she was at first too grateful to discover that her name had been whispered by the woman to wonder how she could possibly have gotten into the chamber, when the corridor was behind Alex.

"Who are you?" Alex begged. "Please—"

She cut off her words as the woman suddenly rushed forward and gripped her hands. Alex stared downward as a tiny object was stuffed into her palm. "Thank you," she murmured stupidly, "but who are you? Where did you find the statuette of Anelokep? Please . . ."

The petite beauty with the glorious green eyes suddenly swept past her and into the corridor. Alex raced after her, but when she left the burial chamber and reached the corridor, it was empty. Alex kept running, out to the antechamber. It, too, was empty. Two other doors led to a shrine and a small treasury; both were empty of all life except that of ancient Egypt, depicted in the wall paintings.

Unable to believe that the woman had disappeared as if into thin air, Alex rechecked the chambers. Then she sighed and walked up the steps that would lead her out of the tomb, out of the realm of death and darkness.

Ali and Dan were awaiting her on the outer steps. Both jumped up with alarm at her expression.

"Did she pass here?" Alex gasped.

Ali and Dan exchanged glances that clearly denoted that she was a candidate for a nervous breakdown.

"Who, Alex?" Dan asked softly, catching her arms.

"The woman! She was there with me, in the tomb, and then she disappeared."

"We'd better head back to camp," Dan said. "It's been a long day."

Alex ripped her arms from his grasp. "Damnit, D'Alesio, I'm not crazy! She was there! And—" She suddenly remembered that her fingers were clenched around another gift from the woman. "Here!" She shoved the object triumphantly into Dan's hand.

His dark eyes stared down at the object, then sardonically back to hers. Alex frowned with confusion at his look. "What is it?" she demanded.

He opened his broad palm. Laying upon it was an ordinary chess piece—the white queen.

"She gave it to me!" Alex insisted. "She was there, the woman was there—"

"All right, Alex," Dan said softly. He had to believe the evidence of the chess piece, and yet he still sounded skeptical. "You saw this woman, but you say she isn't in the tomb, and she hasn't passed us." He reached out and took her arm. "Alex, she's either still in there or she disappeared into thin air."

"Then she is still there! Dan, I don't carry chess queens in my pocket!"

Dan smiled. He dropped her arm and headed for the tomb, then stared back at her. "Come on, Alex, let's look for the woman."

Biting her lip and lowering her eyes, Alex nervously started to follow him. Ali stood still, and Alex turned back to him. "Ali, are you coming?"

"No." He smiled devilishly. "I'll leave you two to solve the vanishing woman mystery. I'm going back to camp. I'll see you when you get there."

Dan's long strides made quick work of the tomb—antechamber, shrine, treasury and burial chamber. He met her back in the antechamber. "Alex, there is no one in here. And no one passed us."

"She was here," Alex persisted stubbornly. She stared down at the cheap plastic chess piece she held. The white queen. A

248

mysterious woman had suddenly appeared in a tomb to hand her the white queen, and then she had apparently disappeared.

"No!" Alex suddenly exclaimed aloud. "Dan, there must be a tunnel out of here!" He stared at her with jet eyes narrowing determinedly and arms crossing over his broad chest. In a moment she was going to find herself being removed bodily from the tomb.

"Dan, listen to me, please. People were buried among these cliffs for centuries—not just the pharaohs but nobles like Knut and even commoners. So many tombs were dug that they often hit upon another; there are just plain tunnels that run into other tunnels with mass graves of the poor. Everyone was mummified and buried with whatever ceremony his or her mourners could manage." He was walking toward her; in the damp space of the tomb she was suddenly reminded of how very alive he was, powerful, vibrant and vital. His heat and electricity seemed to radiate to her. He had decreed himself her keeper, and in another moment she would be swept into those strong arms and she would lose the will to fight because it would be so much easier to feel the security of his hold, the sweet beat of his heart as he commandeered her against his chest.

"Dan, please, let's check?" she whispered, praying he didn't touch her. She was close to forgetting they were in a tomb, forgetting that the search for the father she loved was at stake, and bursting into tears to tell him that she was in love with him and that if he would just hold her, nothing else would matter—even his apparent belief that the sun had finally made her crazy.

He halted, sighing in a very masculine fashion. "All right. How do we look for the one of these tunnels?"

"I—I'm not sure. The walls, I guess. Press along the walls."

He shrugged. "I'll start in the treasury. You take the shrine."

Alex nodded mutely.

After ten minutes she was hot and sticky and beginning to think she *was* crazy. The walls were solid rock. There was nothing in the shrine except paintings and rock walls. Biting her lip, she moved back into the antechamber.

The room was lit by a single bulb strung in the center with naked wiring. Alex noticed uneasily that the shadows in the chamber were growing more dense. Outside, night was falling. Soon the bulb in the tomb would cease to shine as the Valley of the Kings—as a tourist attraction—closed for the night. The feeling of chilling fear, of knowing they might all be in danger, that had swept through her with the whisper of her name descended over her again. She was ready and willing for Dan to drag her away.

"*Alex!*"

Her name was shouted with such tense excitement that she jumped, then raced to the far end of the corridor leading to the burial chamber.

Dan's long jeaned legs were stretched along the floor. She almost tripped over them. "It's here," he told her tersely. "You were right. Look—this block is cut. See, the rest of the wall is sheer—one piece with the hill. But this—it's limestone, not granite!"

He pushed upon the piece of rock to which he referred. It backed up several feet, made a grinding noise and then stopped, leaving a space large enough for a person to crawl through. "I'm going to follow it," Dan said, pushing through the opening feet first. "You stay here."

"I will not, and this time I mean it, and you haven't any of Ali's tribesmen around to act as guards!"

"Alex—"

"Dan, it's getting dark. I'm not staying here alone, and I'm not wandering back to camp alone! I'm coming with you."

Dan's eyes reflected meditative jet as he mulled over her words. "Okay," he said unhappily. He reached behind himself to retrieve the flashlight he had crammed halfway into his back pocket. "Let me get in all the way first, just in case."

Alex nervously waited as he crawled through the opening. Seconds seemed to pass as hours; then she heard his voice. "Come on," he said huskily.

Alex scrambled into position behind him, still clutching the tiny white queen chess piece in her hand. She slithered through the opening much more easily than Dan had, since she was so much smaller. A second later he was helping her to stand. The tunnel was small. Dan was stooping, since otherwise his head would hit the rock ceiling.

He trained his flashlight on the walls, then turned it off for a second. Alex almost protested, since she was sure they would be plunged into total blackness, but some light was seeping in from somewhere to make the tunnel gray and misty. Dan flicked the flashlight back on. "Let's go."

He trained the light ahead of them as they moved at a snail's pace. Alex's grip of his hand was a cold vise as they walked more deeply into the unknown. She gasped as she suddenly tripped over something.

"What is it?" Dan demanded, turning the light to her feet.

For the second time that day Alex would have screamed but she instantly realized that she had stumbled over a mummy. Its wooden coffin lay to the side; it had been dumped out as if some robber had searched quickly and then discarded it as worthless. The decaying wrappings were in tatters; the face was half uncovered, and an empty eye socket stared out at them with eerie reproach. Alex's foot still touched the leg; she moved it back, and the wound limb snapped and broke off from the brittle body.

"Oh, God! How awful for the body to be left like this."

"Come on," Dan said gently. "We'll notify the right authorities to pick him up when we get out of here."

Alex clamped her mouth shut and obeyed Dan, stepping over the pathetic remains of the violated mummy. She held onto to Dan's hand as they moved onward.

"Step carefully," Dan suddenly warned. "I think we've stumbled upon a common graveyard."

Alex nodded mutely, pressing her face between his shoulder blades. The tunnel had become wider, and both sides were lined with sarcophagi in various stages of upheaval. One open wood coffin held two bodies laid to rest head to toe. In other instances the mummified bodies had been dragged half out of their coffins and left in teetering positions. "And they thought they'd have eternal life. . . ." Dan murmured dryly.

"I know and it's awful that they've been desecrated this way," she said.

He turned for a moment to bring her head against his chest,

251

ruffling her hair with a tenderness she had dearly missed. "We must be getting near the end of this thing. More light is beginning to filter through."

"Yes, but it won't last much longer," Alex murmured. "It's getting dark outside."

Dan gripped her hand again. "Come on."

They kept walking. "How far have we gone?" Alex asked.

"I don't know," Dan murmured. "We've been winding in circles, going deeper, climbing again. Maybe a thousand yards all told. Alex, this is it. Look."

She glanced over his shoulder and breathed a long sigh of relief. The tunnel took another upward slant and then opened to the darkening sky; a small opening. She giggled suddenly, hoping Dan would manage to squeeze his broad shoulders through it.

"Laugh at me getting through that thing," Dan warned wryly, "and I'll let Ali teach me a few good measures in disciplining disrespectful women!"

"Sorry," Alex murmured with no remorse.

A moment later they reached the small opening. Dan pushed Alex up and through it. She found her footing on the rocky cliff, then stared around her as she waited for him to chin himself up and squeeze through. He was standing beside her as she tried to gauge their position in the starlit dusk.

They stood midway up a cliff in a tangle of dry grass. Straight across the narrow valley beneath them, she could see a new rise of cliffs. Alex gasped suddenly, realizing where they were. And then she started laughing.

Dan dragged her around to face him by the shoulders. "I swear I will think you are crazy shortly, Doctor. What are you laughing about?"

Alex gripped his shirt as he held her, smiling radiantly despite his comment. "I've got it, Dan! The last puzzle piece. We've hit the end of the Valley of the Kings. That's the beginning of the Valley of the *Queens*! Oh, don't you see, Dan? Remember. The queen, Hatshepshut, was buried in the Valley of the Kings! That was the reference—and Anelokep did just the reverse. Our mystery lady handed me the *queen*. Anelokep is buried in the Valley of the Queens! And I even know exactly where, just as Jim did.

252

The hieroglyphics did have the answer! He's buried between Nefertiti and Shenkah. I'm sure of it, Dan!"

He raised his brows skeptically, then couldn't help laughing in response to her enthusiasm. He kissed the tip of her nose. "Okay, Alex, I believe you. First thing in the morning—"

"No, Dan, now! Please! The walk won't take us thirty minutes and I've been there before and we're all alone and I can check out what I'm thinking. And oh, Dan! Please. We might find the answer to my father's disappearance and I can't possibly just go back to camp and sleep now when I might be this close to knowing something about Jim!"

Dan held her for a moment, feeling a tight squeeze within his heart. The agony within her voice when she spoke of her father was outweighing his better judgment. He couldn't bear the pain she had so valiantly contained so long.

"All right," he said lightly. He grimaced, dusting off his jeans as he took her hand. "There's going to be a full moon," he said dryly. "What's an Egyptian night with a full moon in the desert without a nice long walk among the old tombs?" He carefully began edging down the cliff, supporting her scramble after him. "I always did believe you were a romantic at heart. A walk through a mass graveyard. Wonderful."

"Oh, shut up, D'Alesio!" Alex groaned in reply. At the moment she didn't care how he teased her—as long as he was with her. Helping her, beside her. Ready to lend his support no matter what they found—her father . . . or the answer to James Crosby's disappearance. And please God, she prayed silently, let him be alive.

Her goal was within sight, and the tiny plastic chess queen was still gripped tightly in her fingers. It was the final piece in the jigsaw puzzle. In just moments she would be able to see the entire picture. And Dan would be with her. She tightened the grip of her fingers around his.

CHAPTER FIFTEEN

The moon cast a glow over the rock and rubble as they hurried across the valley.

"I don't know what you think you're going to find in the darkness, Alex," Dan warned as they approached the new set of the cliffs. "There can't be anything obvious; when Carter and Carnarvon were looking for Tut, they excavated everything in sight. And if we do find anything, we're still going to have to wait for tomorrow. The supervisor of antiquities is going to have to be notified, we're going to have to call in my film crew, and the Egyptian government is going to have to set up a guard system."

"I know," Alex murmured, huffing slightly to keep up with his pace. "It's just that I want to see what is where I think an entrance should be. . . ."

"We'll probably stumble into a pit of cobras," Dan muttered. But he was the one setting the pace, and he never released her hand. He suddenly stopped in the moonlight, staring at the strange line where the dark sky met the cliffs. "Where to, Doctor?"

Alex bit her lip for a second, orienting herself in the darkness. She closed her eyes to remember her last visit to the Valley of the Queens, envisioning the arrangements of the tombs in her mind. "Up . . ." she murmured slowly, then more excitedly. "Up—and to the left. We'll pass the entrance to Nefertiti's tomb first."

She was already scrambling up the rocks, dragging Dan along with her. They would come to a footpath, and then the steps, and then more steps to the entrance, sealed off for nighttime.

"It has to be just left of here, Dan. Let me have your flashlight."

Dan obligingly handed Alex his flashlight. Then he actually stood patiently for twenty minutes as she meticulously scanned the light over the landscape. And in all that time Alex could find nothing. Dan was right; if anything had been there, someone would have seen it years ago. But she stubbornly kept walking over the cliff, until she noticed suddenly that the outcropping of rock was wider at the tomb of the queen than it should have been. She had been inside the tomb, and if she remembered correctly, the antechamber was very narrow.

The roadway dipped into a deep and treacherous gully on the side of the tomb. "Dan! We've got to get down there!"

He sighed, but didn't argue. "All right, Alex, but we'll spend only another half hour here at most, agreed? The morning is a better time to explore."

"Agreed! Agreed!" Alex promised. She was already scrambling down the rocky incline. And at the bottom she found what she had been seeking.

A thicket of dry brambles was camouflaging the tiny opening —a hole even smaller than that of the tunnel opening they had stumbled out of. But Alex was suddenly sure she had found what she was looking for. It had gone unnoticed previously because it would be absurd to search for a tomb in a tomb.

She scratched her hands badly and ripped her trousers as she slid the last few feet.

"Would you please be careful?" she heard Dan chastise from behind her.

She spun on him. "Help me! We need to clear some of this rubble away!"

With a deep sigh he complied. The small opening widened enough for Alex to slip through. "Un-unh!" Dan stopped her when she would have started down. "I go first." He jiggled his brows in the moonlight. "Someone has to scare away the cobras and scorpions for the doctor."

His voice was tense, and Alex realized he was as excited as she was—just a little more practical. She bit her lip as she watched him descend into the hole, holding the flashlight firmly in his grip. She heard his feet thud as he hit the floor. A second later he called her.

"Lower yourself in. I'll catch you."

Alex lowered herself, clawing at the rock and sand around her. She felt Dan's hand span her waist and she was supported the next several feet until she could stand on the floor.

"Doctor," he said, and bowed dramatically as he released her, and then his jet eyes met hers with bright admiration. "I do believe you have found it!"

He swept the light around, and Alex caught her breath. Before them was a set of steps, but they were already in some type of outer chamber. The walls that surrounded them were the rock of the cliff. Only a break in the stone above had allowed them entrance. And at the end of the steps before them, two life-size statues of the pharaoh Anelokep guarded a door smothered in shadow—and marked with the royal seal of the pharaoh.

"Dear God!" Alex exclaimed at the sight of the statues. She began to tremble. They were in the right place; just the statues she stared upon were priceless. But apparently someone, at some time during the millennia, had tried to rob the tomb. That was why there was the entrance they were now in.

Dan's arms suddenly slipped around her, and he kissed her exuberantly on the lips. "Congragulations, Dr. Randall. And now, come on. We can't go any farther without proper excavation procedures and, more important, without help and security."

Alex nodded, biting her lip with disappointment. They had found the tomb—but no clue to Jim's whereabouts. What were you expecting, she charged herself, Jim waiting for you at the entrance?

"Alex?" Dan said gently. "We will find your father. Something will break when we start the excavation. We'll find the mystery woman, and we'll find Jim. I promise. You believe that, don't you?"

"Yes," she lied, clinging to him.

His lips brushed past her ear. "Are you okay?"

"Fine," she murmured. But she wasn't fine, and she was grateful that at least he was real, there, a living, breathing strength beside her. As always when she was near him, she could feel the pulse of his blood through his system, the pleasant scent of after shave combined with something very subtle but very male. She opened her mouth, ready at the entrance of the tomb to throw herself upon his strength and burst into tears and tell him how afraid she was, how she needed him, loved him, could only handle what was to come if he would hold her through it all.

Ridiculous. He did hold her, he did care for her and, being Dan, he would be with her as long as she needed him.

But she couldn't make an idiot of herself. There *were* certain strengths to be gained from retaining pride.

And the moment was passing. Dan bent to lift her so that she could reach the opening that was about ten feet above the chamber floor. "How are you going to get back up?" she asked as she grasped the sand and earth above her.

"Jump—I hope," he said and laughed. "I'll make it; just don't go running off without me."

She started to smile as she grasped and clawed her way back through the small opening, assisted by his push. "I guess we weren't the most brilliant of explorers," she murmured when she was halfway through the opening. "We should have brought a rope—"

Her words were suddenly cut off, and wide-eyed panic seized her along with the hand that suddenly and fiercely clamped over her mouth. She was dragged the rest of the way from the hole, her heart pounding fiercely, her fingers clawing at the hand that cut off her speech and left her struggling desperately for breath.

As she was dragged kicking and struggling from the entrance, she saw that three men were silently taking part in the capture: two black-clad Arabs and a third man, in black jeans and black shirt, were holding her.

She recognized the third man instantly with a wash of illness that threatened to steal her consciousness more than the loss of breath. Wayne.

"Alex?"

She heard Dan call her name, the thumping of his feet against the rock wall as he leaped for a hold on the rubbled circumference of the opening and balanced himself from below. She bit into the hand holding her mouth, screaming in her throat, attempting to warn him.

She managed to sink her teeth firmly into Wayne's hand, but he merely emitted a rough oath and threw her from him, sending her flying hard against the rocky ground. Scratches from the jagged pebbles tore her palms and cheek as she landed and scrambled to find her feet again. She turned to face Wayne; like his companions, he was carrying a gun, and it was aimed at her.

She didn't recognize the man standing before her. His handsome face was marred by a hardness that was cold, cruel and ruthless. His lips were drawn into a tight line; his face appeared pinched. "Get over here, Alex," he said softly. She ignored him, and he smiled, training the gun on the opening where Dan's strong bronzed hands and arms were visible, tensing to pull his weight up. Alex paled as she realized the man she had once thought she adored was dead serious—he would pull the trigger without a thought. Biting her lip, she stood, ignoring the Arabs as she walked toward her ex-husband. He pulled her back against his chest this time, and it took all her willpower not to cry out as he set the cold muzzle of the gun against her temple.

"Alex, damnit, answer me!"

She heard Dan's annoyance, then saw his eyes, his hard, frozen expression as his head lifted above the hole and he saw exactly why she wasn't answering. Time seemed suspended in the air. Then Dan crawled the rest of the way out of the opening and stood, apparently unsurprised and unruffled.

"Randall," he said with quiet disgust. "I was wondering when you would make your appearance."

Alex felt Wayne's shrug. "Wonder no more, D'Alesio. This is it."

Dan too shrugged in response, keeping a careful eye on Wayne's trigger finger. "I've got one question: Why? The money? The Egyptian government will get the majority of the treasure."

"Why?" Wayne laughed, and the sound was hard and cruel. "Not the money, D'Alesio, although there will be certain financial rewards that will come in handy. We don't all have the Midas touch, and we can't all be instant successes. No, D'Alesio,

I probably can't explain it to you, but Alex might understand. It's the fame. Something even you can't match. It's gaining immortality with the pharaohs, a permanent place in the history books."

Dan adjusted his stance, and despite the fact that the two Arabs stood behind Dan with their guns on him, Wayne flinched; Alex felt the cold steel boring against her head. "Move too fast again, D'Alesio, and you'll watch her die right here."

Dan lifted his hands, praying Randall didn't see the sweat breaking out on his brow, the cold fear that gripped him as he watched Alex's eyes, bright and wide and terror-filled, within her white features.

"I'm not moving, Randall, and she can't hurt you. You, uh, wanted her back, and now you've got her. You don't need that gun . . . there."

Wayne suddenly laughed. "You know, I did want her back. And if she had any sense, she would have come. And she would have led me to the tomb all on her own. I wouldn't have to kill her now. . . ."

Alex suddenly realized that she had been married to a madman. He was actually speaking with a certain regret. She swallowed, terrified that she was going to pass out.

"How did you find us now?" Alex was amazed that Dan could be speaking so calmly, so conversationally.

"I've been following you all along. I saw Sheriff leave you in the Valley of the Kings, and then I realized that you two weren't coming back out. I scoured the hills until I saw you again, and then I knew Alex had stumbled on something."

"One more question, Randall," Dan said tensely. "Where is Crosby?"

"That I don't know," Wayne said with a shrug. "I lost him out here one day. He must have fallen into one of these ancient tunnel holes and maybe met with a cobra. He knew I was following him, although I don't know whether he knew quite what I was up to. I kept telling him how I wanted to get back with Alex, but he still wouldn't let me in on it. His loss."

"How are you planning on getting away with Alex's and my disappearance?"

259

Wayne smiled again. "Easy—the curse of the pharaohs. The world expects terrible accidents to happen when people dip into ancient Egyptian tombs." The smile left Wayne's face. "Get back into the hole, D'Alesio. Now."

As Dan paused, Wayne tightened his grip upon Alex. "Pay attention, D'Alesio, and you can spend your last hours together. Give me any trouble and I'll shoot. You see, I'd just as soon not. I'd rather come back and 'discover' the tomb myself in about a week—and, of course, discover that the two of you died in the noble quest for knowledge. Force me and I'll pull the trigger. The little bitch chose you, D'Alesio, so now she can have you. For eternity, as they say."

Dan shook his head. "She didn't choose me, Randall. I forced her. Leave her out of this; you can come back together and discover the tomb—"

"Forget it, D'Alesio. I'm not an idiot. Even if she were still in love with me, I'm afraid Alex is a little too honorable for her own good. She'll blame me for her father—and for you. And she'd stab me in the back one night, if she hadn't gone to the authorities first. Now get in there. There's a trip gear right beneath that hole, a safety precaution. As soon as you two are back down there, I can release a granite block weighing a ton to seal you in. The Egyptians really were masterful architects. And they planned retributions just like you're about to receive for grave robbers. A rather fitting end, don't you think? Now jump, D'Alesio—unless you want to see Alex's head spattered on the rocks."

Dan shrugged and lowered himself back into the hole. A second later Alex heard the thump of his feet on the floor of the tomb. "Now you, sweetheart," Wayne whispered against her ear. He shoved her toward the hole. Her knees were wobbling so badly that she could barely walk and crawl to reach the hole. She tried to lower herself with fingers that were frozen and shaking. She couldn't hold on to the opening, and she fell into the darkness. She was sure she would break a dozen bones before being left to die, but Dan caught her in the blackness, buffering her fall with his strong arms and his weight.

"You should have stuck with wars and famine, D'Alesio!"

Wayne called down to them. "And Alex, sweetie, you should have stuck with me."

Alex thought numbly then that Wayne *hadn't* been a half-bad Egyptologist—he *had* found the ancient gear. She heard the whir of air as the massive granite began to slide downward within the chamber. She and Dan had to step backward to avoid being crushed beneath it as it slid smoothly into its slot, leaving them in total silence and darkness.

For a moment Alex merely stood still, but then she realized exactly what had happened and exactly what position they were in. Sealed in a tomb, locked in with the dead in a tiny, no-exit cubicle. In a matter of minutes? hours? their oxygen would run out.

She screamed, and the sound amplified and reverberated throughout the stone cubicle. It didn't matter; she screamed and screamed again, realizing that she was going to die.

"Alex!"

She was being fervently shaken, then wrapped in strong, warm arms. Dan's arms. She felt his heartbeat, the soft whisper of his breath against her cheek. She inhaled the musky masculine aroma of him: sandalwood. The scent she so loved.

"Oh, Dan!" She suddenly started babbling, knowing now, when it seemed all was lost, that petty things were so trivial. They were going to die, and she had never whispered how she loved him.

"Oh, Dan, I'm so sorry, so sorry I got you mixed up in all this. Dan, hold me, please, tight. I love you so much, I need you, I want to feel your touch until. . . ."

"What?" Dan murmured hoarsely. He had the advantage of not believing that they were destined to die; if they hadn't been carefully followed by Ali's must trusted men, Ali himself would be looking for them now. Dan's one concern had merely been to keep them both from getting shot.

He wanted to tell Alex that, but his words froze in his throat. They were sealed into the outer chamber of a cold and dank tomb many feet below the earth's surface, but suddenly it didn't matter a heck of a lot. He had just heard the sweetest music in the world.

"What did you say, Alex?" he demanded.

Her arms clung tightly around his shoulders. Her fingers were winding into his hair, touching his nape and shooting little jolts of need along his spine that were a sunburst in the darkness.

"I love you," she whispered feverishly again, pressing close to him. "Oh, Dan, I love you so much and now it's too late, and oh, Dan, hold me, love me, with whatever time we have left. . . ."

He should have told her that he didn't believe they were going to die. He should have. But it had been days since he had touched her . . . since their argument over Randall. And it was cold and dank and slimy within the rock, and they were both covered with dust and cobwebs and sand.

None of that mattered. She had whispered that she loved him. Her soft body was pressed against his, and he was more than willing to love her within the forbidding caress of the rock.

"Oh, Alex," he groaned, crushing her against him. He couldn't see her because of the darkness, but he could feel her. He showered the top of her head with kisses and slipped his hands beneath the hem of her shirt, splaying them over the silk of her back. He moved his fingers around to cup her breasts within the confines of her bra, grazing his thumbs lovingly over the nipples that stood erect and hard beneath the lace. And his lips came down to savor hers, hungrily, slowly, completely.

They were so involved with each other that neither heard the sound of rock scraping against rock. They were both stunned when they realized light was filtering through to them from the steps that led to the entrance of the second chamber.

Alex was facing the steps. Her eyes opened wide as Dan kissed her and she stiffened, terror once again permeating her bones. She broke the kiss and gasped out a scream.

The tomb itself was opening; the second sealed door was sliding open. She could think of nothing but the time and place; the ancient mystery and magic of Egypt; the curse of the pharaohs, the rebirth of the dead.

"Oh, my God . . . !"

Dan spun about at her cry, slipping his arms protectively around her as he shielded his eyes against the sudden light. And then he was clasping Alex in his arms as he stared down the steps, because she had passed out cold.

Then, to Dan's amazement, a voice boomed. "Good Lord, D'Alesio, I was hoping you would get together with my daughter, but you don't have to make love to her beneath my very nose!"

James Crosby, his blue eyes mischievously boyish, his blond hair tousled, was walking up the steps that led from the tomb, his huge battery-operated torch creating the light.

Alex screamed again when she came to; but her father's face was the first thing she saw, and after a moment of shrieking hysteria she realized that they were all alive and that it was indeed her father smiling down at her. Then she hugged him for at least ten minutes, yelling at him, scolding him for scaring her half to death, then asking a million questions that she gave him no chance to answer. Finally she calmed down and looked around her.

They were in the antechamber, and it was awe-inspiring. The room was stacked with coffers, guarded by statues; the walls were grooved with deep niches that held more finery; golden gods and goddesses, the pharaoh as Osiris, the pharaoh guarded by Mut, on and on ... her eyes couldn't even register the treasure of this, only the first room. But along with the treasure were several modern-day items—cotton sheets, a pillow, a portable electric grill.

"I don't get it, Crosby," Dan was saying, shaking his head. Alex realized that she had come to in the middle of a question-and-answer period between him and her father. "You've been living in the tomb all this time?"

"Umm." Jim Crosby sat with his arm around his daughter as he replied dryly. "When I went out to see Ali, I knew Haman was quite interested in my movements. But Haman didn't need money, and he isn't any archaeologist! I knew he was following me around, but that hadn't really bothered me." He hesitated a moment, glancing briefly and uncomfortably toward Alex. "Randall had been making me very nervous. He'd been too ingratiating, too determined to make me believe he wanted to get back with Alex and be a model husband. I didn't know how far he would go to be in on this find, but like I wrote you, honey"— he smiled as he tousled Alex's hair—"I was nervous. I tried to tell you where the tomb was without saying it over the phone or putting in on paper, just in case something did happen. And I told you to get to Dan and Ali because I knew you'd need protection."

"But why are you in the tomb, Dad? How have you been living?"

Jim Crosby smiled broadly. "Randall was following me the day I decided to check out my theory alone. He's had men crawling these cliffs since. I knew I was on to the tomb—and that Randall was on to me. And so when I tripped onto this—literally, I fell through the floor from the tomb above—I just stayed here." His eyes started twinkling in the reflection of the brilliant light from the torch. "I was seeing a certain young Egyptian woman, who happened to be with me. Her name is Lani Habu and she is a villager from Qurna. I decided that the only way to keep Wayne from either smuggling the goods out of the country or killing me to claim the find was to lay low, disappear—and pray that the three of you could get to me without anything else happening! If I emerged from the tomb, Randall would have found me. But he wouldn't know Lani from a dozen other Egyptian women. And so she brought me food and clothing and an occasional newspaper." He shook his head with a wry grin. "I was a little worried about the two of you getting together— knowing you both—but it appears you're getting along well."

Alex lowered her lashes, suddenly unable to answer as she remembered how she had thrown herself at Dan just moments ago, believing that the end had come. She wondered as blood rushed to her cheeks just how much of the scene her father had witnessed.

"It seems determined opposites attract," Dan said breezily. "Which reminds me, Crosby," Dan suddenly growled, "why didn't you ever tell Ali and me about your assistant being Alex— your own daughter?"

James Crosby looked mildly surprised. Of course, Alex thought, he didn't know that she had crossed a desert and been abducted first by Dan and then by Haman, to get to where she was now. He couldn't know that the very man who had helped her reach him had once bodily tossed her out of his hotel room.

"I didn't want Alex's name listed at first because of the danger involved. And then, as I said, knowing you both, I really didn't want either of you knowing too much about the other. You might have thought I was trying to play matchmaker, which I wasn't, really. Well, maybe just a bit. I thought you might be strong enough to keep Alex away from Wayne and, well . . . I know I shouldn't interfere, but I also knew enough about Wayne . . . oh, never mind! My motives were really for the best. And you're both here now."

Yes, Alex thought, we're both here now. And Dan did keep me from Wayne. At least he tried. And he was strong. Very strong. He made me love him.

Alex stood up suddenly. "Shouldn't we, ah, be doing something?"

Her father exhaled a long breath. "Yes. Now that we're all here, someone needs to get to the authorities. But it's going to be tricky. Randall is going to have people watching the cliffs."

Dan, sitting cross-legged in front of Crosby and continually staring about the room with awe, cleared his throat. "No one is getting out the way we came in. That granite block weighs at least a ton."

Jim Crosby shook his head, his boyish smile back in place. Dan found himself smiling in return as Crosby's look reminded him that he had once believed Crosby's daughter to be his mistress. It was easy now to see why. It was incomprehensible that this man could be the father of such a mature, sophisticated woman. Yet he was, and seeing them together more than proved it. They were both talking—reasonable and pragmatic already. And yet they seldom took their eyes off each other.

"There is another exit—out into the tomb above. But the problem is going to be getting out of the valley. I've no doubt Randall would shoot any of us on the spot," Jim replied.

"Well, Ali is out there somewhere, not far away," Dan said with a shrug. "I'm sure I can reach him."

265

"I don't know," Crosby protested. "Now that you're here, I can try getting out myself—"

"No way," Dan said firmly. "Crosby, I'm better suited for the job. I've crawled around a lot of war zones and I know when to drop and crawl on my belly. Show me the way out, and I'll go."

Alex bit her lip as she watched her father mulling over Dan's words. Suddenly she didn't want either of them leaving. She had just discovered her father alive; she couldn't lose him again. But thinking Dan might be a target for her ex-husband was also more than she could bear.

"Wait!" she exclaimed. "I was wrong—we shouldn't be doing anything. Dan, you said Ali was out there. Let's just wait until he gets to us."

Dan shook his head and stood. "No. If Ali is with the men he had trailing us, he may not know yet how deadly Randall is. I have to try to get to him. Jim, how do I get out of this mausoleum?"

"Left corridor over here—come on, I'll give you a boost."

Alex didn't get a chance to say any more. Dan didn't even say good-bye to her. Her father and Dan disappeared into the shadows, and then Dan was gone.

A moment later Jim walked into the antechamber and the glow of the torch. Alex tried to smile. He stretched out his arms to her, and she rushed into them. "Oh, honey," Jim murmured, "I was so worried about you. I can't tell you the hours I sat here wishing I had never gotten you involved."

"I—I'm fine, Jim, and I had to be involved," Alex murmured in return.

Jim grimaced as he released her, watching her nervous eyes follow the trail across the stone floor. The moments they waited, he knew, would seem like hours. He tried to talk to ease her mind.

He waved his arm to encompass the room. "Well, what do you think, Alex? Have you ever seen anything so staggering?" He laughed. "I can't tell you how itchy my hands have been. But I haven't touched a thing. We're going to have to work slowly and thoroughly, photographing, categorizing. It will probably take us months just to clear. . . ."

Jim was talking on, and Alex was grateful to her father, she knew what he was trying to do. But the situation was sinking through to her heart and mind more and more thoroughly. She had been in love with and married to a man who would have killed her without batting an eye. She had been ready to reconcile their marriage. And Dan was out there now trying to save all their lives from the madman she had been willing to love again.

She was caught in a turmoil of emotions she couldn't begin to sort out: gratitude—heartfelt gratitude to find Jim alive. Fear—the primal, instinctive fear of being beneath the ground in a shrine for a dead pharaoh. Fear for Dan. And pain, and shame, and humiliation. She had been more than an idiot, first with Wayne, and then with Dan. How could he ever care for a woman who had been so besotted by a man like Wayne? How had she ever been such a fool? There was suddenly only one thing she wanted to do—dig herself her own hole in the ground and crawl into it.

Jim was talking about unsealing the door to the actual burial chamber, musing over the various coffins that would house the mummy.

Alex suddenly burst into tears.

Jim stopped talking and wrapped her in his arms as if she were a little girl. He held her, rocking her, in the dank confines of the tomb, and she garbled out incoherent speech. "Oh, Dad, it's not that I'm not crazy with joy to see you . . . I am . . . but Wayne . . . and Dan . . . oh, Dad, I know how wonderful this find is, but I want to get away from Egypt. Just for a while. I want to be with you, I love you, but I want to get away so badly. I want Dan to be okay . . . I want to wake up and pretend it all never happened. . . ."

"Shhh," Jim consoled her. "Dan is going to be okay. That one is a cat who lands on all four feet. You're in love with him, honey, aren't you?"

"Yes. No. I don't know, Dad. I've got to get away—from the tombs, from . . . from everything."

"You will, sweetheart. You will." He just held her for a long, long time, then tried to speak again. "I've got a surprise for you, sweetheart. One I hope you'll like."

Alex tried to dry her eyes. She knew her face was a mess. Her tears had turned the dust on it to mud. She managed a weak smile as she pulled away from her father. "What's the surprise? I'm not sure I can handle another one."

"But this is a good one!" Jim protested. "I'm going to get married!"

His surprise did the trick of jolting her out of her depression. "You are! To whom?"

Jim's eyes twinkled. "My Egyptian lady, Lani—the woman who brought you the statuette and the chess queen. She doesn't speak much English, so you're going to have to brush up on Arabic while we teach her. Think you'll be able to like her, Alex?"

"Oh, Dad! Of course. She's a beautiful woman, and she must have taken great risks for you. I'm so happy for you!" Alex smiled and then frowned. "Dad, if you were trying to get a message to me, why didn't you just write a note?"

"Too risky," he said with a grimace. "But I figured if you didn't get my message from the statuette, you would have to figure out the chess piece eventually! I was lucky to have had it in my pocket; that's one we can thank Haman for! He insisted I keep the piece after I taught him how to play the game!"

Alex chuckled and then sobered. "Oh, Jim! I kept thinking the culprit was Haman . . . and it was Wayne!" She shuddered. "Dad, a man I lived with for a year and a half. . . ."

"Alex!" Jim chastised softly. "Don't blame yourself for Wayne! Honey, we all make mistakes. I did. Your mo—"

He broke off as quickly as he had started. Alex said quietly, "Don't bother trying to spare my feelings, Jim, really."

"She wasn't a bad person, Alex. She just couldn't handle responsibility or an infant. I wish I could tell you what has happened to her, but I really don't know anything. I haven't seen her since you were a month old. I don't even know if she is dead or alive."

"And I don't care, Jim," Alex said softly. "I suppose the in thing is to be curious about one's roots, but I'm not. I've never missed out on anything, because you made an entire world for me. Did I ever thank you for that?"

James Crosby hugged his daughter to him. A second later he heard her sob again, and he didn't even try to console her. There was nothing left to be said. She would have to fight her own mental battles of love and guilt; all he could do was stand by and pray that he hadn't made another mistake. And that D'Alesio did love his daughter. And that he did make it through.

Dan had little difficulty getting from one tomb to another and then out of the chambers that had been the final resting place of Nefertiti. The entrance was barred only by cheap wire fencing, which he was easily able to sneak through.

But then he stood within the shadows of the cliff and he could see the silhouettes of men standing guard a hundred feet or so from the entrance he was supposedly sealed into.

"Damn," he muttered softly beneath his breath. The full moon was now acting as a spotlight. The only way he was going to get off the cliff was to belly it down all the way.

Gritting his teeth, he flopped to the gravelly earth and started inching downward. How he was going to streak across the naked valley he didn't know. He would have to cross that bridge when he came to it.

Minutes—or was it eons—later he reached the valley floor. As he waited, contemplatively chewing his lower lip with his brow knit in a tight furl, he saw lights flashing across the valley. He closed his eyes. Ali's men? He couldn't be sure. Then he heard the roar of a jeep coming. He raised his head to try and get a better view.

A shot exploded into the night. The bullet whizzed by his head so close that he could feel its deadly whistle against his cheek.

The men in the jeep had to be from Ali, because the shot had come from behind him. And he couldn't sit still because he was a better target now than a sitting duck.

Dan crouched low, bunching his muscles. Then he bolted out into the open. He staggered his hell-bent run, winding a trail as he had learned to do from guerrilla fighters he had interviewed. He heard more shots, and each time he heard one, he was amazed that he didn't fall. There were feet pounding behind him, but he kept running with his zigzag motion. The jeep was in sight, and he could see Ali, Rajman and Ahman in it. Ahman was standing, aiming a rifle.

The footfalls behind Dan suddenly ceased. He couldn't stop his impetus and he careened into the jeep, desperately gasping for breath.

Ali picked him up by the shoulders. "You've been hit, my friend. A nice good graze across the temple."

Dan touched his forehead. Sticky blood came off on his fingers. "A graze," he muttered. He glanced back across the valley at the fallen man, then at Ahman, who was kneeling by the body. "Was it Randall?"

"Yes."

Dan felt a shudder ripple through him. Alex. . . .

"We've got to get the authorities—"

"Already on their way," Ali assured him.

"And Alex, and Crosby. They're in the tomb. I've got to bring you back. I've got to—"

"You've got to do nothing. You belong in a hospital."

"Not until we get Alex."

Ali sighed. "All right, my friend. But Raj and Ahman and I will do the crawling into the tomb."

Alex could have sworn that days had passed. She was so nervous that she was certain she would soon be physically sick. Her stomach churned painfully and her head was swimming. She and Jim had given up all effort to talk; they merely sat holding each other.

And then there came a noise from the corridor. She tensed with terror, wondering who it would be as she and Jim both leaped expectantly to their feet, Jim holding her protectively behind him as if he could shield her from danger with his body.

"Dr. Crosby? Alex? It is me, Ali Sur Sheriff."

"Oh, God!" Alex sobbed out with relief, feeling her head spin. A second later Ali was standing in front of her and she was embracing him. The Arab unabashedly embraced her father also, pumping his hand, telling him how glad he was that they had found him.

"Long story," Jim told Ali. "I'll explain it all later. I'd like to get out of here, and so would Alex—if it's safe."

"Yes," Ali said. "Egyptian troops, on orders from the Department of Antiquities, are outside now."

"Ali," Alex said suddenly, her throat going dry. "What happened? Where is Dan? Wayne. . . ."

"There was some shooting," Ali tried to explain. "I'm sorry, Alex, but I'm afraid Wayne is dead. And Dan—"

Alex could bear to hear no more. She let out a strangled scream that echoed in a primeval wail throughout the tomb and she fell to the floor in a dead faint.

"Oh, merciful Allah," Ali moaned.

Dan, having heard the scream from above, compressed his lips and shook off Ahman's restraining hand. He dropped down into the tomb despite the now-throbbing wound on his temple.

It was he who carried Alex from the tomb.

CHAPTER SIXTEEN

The sky overhead was cornflower-blue; the sun was a radiant orb of brilliant yellow. Alex could hear the bleat of sheep across the sparse grassland and the occasional melodious Arabic call of one of the boys tending the flock.

She closed her eyes against the sun and lay back upon a crooked elbow, feeling the heat of the ground beneath the blanket she had spread in the spidery shade of a date palm.

She had come back with Ali to the oasis in the desert to rest, and to find some kind of a peace. She had promised Jim she would return in two weeks, but he had understood when Ali had offered to bring her here and she had so quickly agreed. Strange; there had been times when she would have thought this the last place in the world she would come to be at ease. But she was comfortable here, as comfortable as she was going to be while she attempted to straighten out her tortured heart and soul.

Was it just five nights ago that she had been sealed into the tomb? It all seemed so distant. She had come to in her cot in the camp, only to discover that all hell had already broken out. Officials were swarming through the camp and the valley; members of Dan's camera crew and other press members were also arriving. Field radios were set up, and the Egyptian police were questioning everyone. It was a bedlam of jeeps and donkeys, experts and tourists. News services across the world were already broadcasting the story.

Anelokep and the circumstances surrounding the discovery of his tomb were becoming the property of the public—and history. Ironically, Wayne would have his name remembered through the centuries. He would become not a victim of his own greed but a victim of the curse of the pharaohs.

Alex had barely seen Dan. Ali had told her that he had carried her from the tomb and held her all the way back to the camp. But then he had been swarmed by the police and by his own communications team, and she hadn't been able to say a word to him.

Ali, who despised crowds and notoriety of any kind, made his decision to leave that night. He had touched Alex's pallid face and suggested that she accompany him. She had agreed; but though she had clung to Jim, she hadn't been able to find Dan. She had chewed three nails down to the quick wondering whether to leave or not, but then the feeling of humiliation over Wayne had gripped her again, and she had wanted desperately to hide, to pull herself together again before trying to face Dan.

What would he be thinking? she wondered. He knew that she loved him; she had admitted it. But if their relationship was nothing more than an uncomfortable entanglement to him, she would have to be cool and flip and convince him that she had had "tomb fever."

A cold sweat suddenly engulfed her. How could he possibly care about her? The things she had said, the things she had done. Defending Wayne. . . .

She tried to think about Wayne. She had believed she would feel pain and remorse, but nothing broke through the barrier of numbness. She didn't even hate him; if anything, she was sorry that such a bright man had been so besotted by the longing for fame.

Alex opened her eyes and then blinked again against the power of the sun. She didn't feel bad at all physically. Upon their arrival, Shahalla had given her a glass of warm wine that Ali had insisted she drink. She had slept like the dead herself until well past noon every day. And now, out here, on the oasis brink of the desert, she could almost believe that it had all been a dream.

No, not a dream. Because though her limbs felt fine, she was in pain. She wondered if she would always be in pain away from Dan. Or was the pain merely because she was just now having to accept that it was over, that both sides of the bargain had been carried out, that she no longer had any type of claim on Daniel D'Alesio.

He was bossy, she tried to tell herself. Autocratic. They would never be able to make their relationship work. He had his work; he would always be flitting around the world, breaking female hearts every time he appeared on the television screen. And she had her work. She would be able to contribute more and more to the museum; she would probably go on lecture tours with Jim . . . and eventually she would learn to forget Daniel. She was a strong person. She had proved that to herself once. She would do so again.

But it would take longer, so much longer. Wayne had never been part of her, as Dan had been; he had never had the power to make her tremble with a glance, burn at a touch, soar to rapture beyond description with the tempest of their bodies fusing.

Alex swallowed and bit her lip, her fingers clutching the fabric of the blanket convulsively.

Dan would be there during the excavation of the tomb. She would see him day after day. She wondered if he would want to continue their physical relationship until he was ready to move on. And she wondered if she would have the strength to resist him. She would have to, because she would break into a thousand pieces if she were to lie with him again, and then reach the day when he was ready to shake hands and say, "Best of luck, Alex, I'll never forget you. . . ."

She suddenly realized that the Arab boys tending the sheep were shouting more than usual. Shielding her eyes, she sat up and stared across the plain.

The boys were waving as well as shouting. She stared back in the direction from which she had come, the oasis camp of sheepskin tents and centuries-old silken elegance, of Muslim honor and the basic elements of life.

She blinked as she saw the horseman, certain, as she had been on that long-ago day when she had first seen him riding across the desert, that he had to be a mirage. But when she opened her eyes, he was still coming.

He rode the black Arabian stallion, and he was one with it.

He was dressed in black again, but not in the robes of the desert. His jeans were black, as was the loose cotton shirt he wore, with full sleeves that billowed as he rode. He had eschewed the use of a saddle, and his gallop across the sands was as smooth and sleek as the superbly muscled and toned physiques of both horse and man. His hair, as dark as the high-riding, floating tail of the stallion, was also swept back by the desert winds. And his eyes, when she met them across the distance, were as blazing and jet as the fires of the devil.

Alex stared at Dan with disbelief as the stallion performed a prancing halt just a few feet from her. She was amazed to see him slide from the stallion's back and approach her with totally unconcealed fury.

"What the hell do you think you're doing!" he bellowed, grabbing her shoulders and giving her a sturdy shake.

Stunned, Alex could do nothing but stare at him blankly for a minute. "I—I—thought I should get away."

"Without me? Worse than that, without even telling me!"

She felt the power in his arms, the wonderful heat and strength of him, and the pleasant scent that was sandalwood and musk and a little bit horse. And all man.

She wanted to kiss him. But she realized he was still yelling at her. "You're not going to waste your time or mine mourning Randall, Alex. And if you ever run out on me again, I swear I'll imprint a brand of blisters on your dimpled little rear end!"

"What! Don't you dare speak to me like that, Dan D'Alesio. You have no right—"

"I have every right in the world. You're my—" He broke off suddenly, realizing that the shepherd boys were watching their spirited argument with appreciative amusement.

"This is one discussion we're going to finish in private," he muttered, and then Alex found herself gasping with shock when he cleanly swept her into his arms and onto the stallion's back.

"Dan, I will not be carted around like this at your—" Her words were cut off with a gasp of alarm as he mounted behind her and nudged the horse into a flying canter. Dan wrapped his arms around her, and she felt the beat of his heart as she gasped for breath and prayed that he would keep her from sliding off the slick, sweaty back of the stallion. Her temper flew with the pounding of the hoofbeats, but she could do little more than utter curses at him under her breath as they rode.

Minutes later they were back at the camp. Ali was standing with Shahalla along the sand trail in front of Alex's tent. He looked up, startled, as Dan and Alex rode up and Dan irritably lifted her protesting form from the horse.

"Looks like a nice reunion." Ali laughed wryly.

"Ali, would you call him off, please."

"Oh, I never interfere!" Ali laughed, hugging his wife.

"Good," Dan said briefly, grasping Alex's hand and pulling her relentlessly toward the tent. "Never interferes!" he muttered. "Like hell that Arab doesn't interfere; he got me into this in the first place."

Alex found herself released but swung around to the center of the tent. "D'Alesio," she charged him, hands on hips, "you want out of this—you got it! The deal is over. You go ahead and do whatever it is you want to do—"

She broke off as she suddenly noticed that the massive tub in the tent was issuing steam. She glanced from the tub to Dan and started walking away from him.

"What is this? What are you doing here? How did you get here? You're supposed to be filming the discovery of the tomb—"

"We're going to get things straight once and for all. What am I doing here? I love you—and you told me that you love me. I got here by helicopter, the same as you did. And I have a talented crew filming; they can work without me. Any more questions? They can wait. I have a few things to tell you. I'll thrash you to within an inch of your life if you go walking out on me again. You're mine, Doctor, and you have been for some time. You simply aren't thoroughly convinced yet, but you will be. And you are an idiot if you feel at all foolish about Randall. I realized you still loved him—even after he tried to kill you—when you passed out as soon as you heard that he was dead—"

"What?" Alex murmured incredulously. "But I—"

"I'm sorry a man is dead; but he was living his own game of violence and he lost. And I will not let you brood over any of this; you hadn't seen him in a year, and you were not his wife when he was shot. Very shortly you're going to be my wife. You did ask me to marry you, remember? I understand that even the best of marriages have problems, which both partners have to continue to work out as they grow together. I think we can handle that. We're certainly aware of each other's faults, so we can't say we don't know what we're getting into—something very fiery but very wonderful. Now, have you got anything to say?"

"I . . ." Alex stared at him blankly for a moment, hardly able to believe all that he had managed to say in his whirlwind speech. It sank slowly through to her that he had said he loved her—wanted to marry her—that they would work out all their problems through the years.

She pursed her lips and planted her hands on her hips, but her smile broke through even as she lowered her lashes.

"Yes, you idiot. I didn't pass out because of Wayne, although I was sorry, it was terrible. I passed out because Ali said that you—oh, you fool—I thought that *you* had been shot."

His eyes became the incredulous ones, slowly filling with comprehension. "Because of me. . . ."

"Oh, you are more than an ass, D'Alesio, and please shut up because I have lots more to say!" she exclaimed. "You are the most demanding, autocratic, pain-in-the-neck man I've ever met!"

"Really?" His hands were also on his hips, and he was suddenly laughing as he stalked toward her slowly. "Well, I guess I'm glad that you're aware of all that you're getting."

He stopped before her and set his hands upon her shoulders, his eyes burning a devilish jet fire. "And right now . . ." He slipped his hands from her shoulders to her shirt buttons.

"A bath?" Alex inquired. "Oh, no, D'Alesio—" Alex suddenly broke off, noticing the jagged cut upon his temple. "Dan, you *were* shot! Are you all right? Oh, God—"

"It's a graze, Alex, nothing more. And no trying to change the conversation."

"But, Dan—"

He caught her fingers, lacing them with his. "It's nothing,

Alex, I swear it. Now where were we before you tried to wile your way out of my purpose with that sweet feminine concern? Ahh . . . the bath. Yes, I smell like a horse. And oh, yes, Alex, I'm going to join you this time. I told you that I was one devil who liked my 'price' paid with sweetly perfumed flesh and silk and satin hair."

"I think you are the devil," Alex muttered breathlessly, no longer protesting his efforts to disrobe her. "Dan, I'm not—I wasn't mourning Wayne. I was ashamed, but . . . Dan . . ." She suddenly crushed herself to him. "Dan, I do love you. So much. I've never felt anything like it. I was afraid . . . I didn't think I could stand it if you didn't love me back, and I knew that loving someone didn't necessarily make them love you too. And you kept telling me you didn't want to be shackled and that people didn't change and there are a million other women in the world half in love with you—"

"Will you hush? Alex, you must have an I.Q. close to two hundred, but there are times when I could swear you haven't an ounce of common sense! My dear doctor! You are one of the fairest beauties I have ever seen, and I am the one who is going to be guarding you as protectively as any sheikh! Alex, I was talking about *Wayne* never changing. I had simply never met the woman I could make a lifelong commitment to until I met you. And then the one woman I discovered I could love morning, noon and night for eternity seemed to thrive upon the belief that she would one day leave me for another man!"

"You are an idiot!" Alex breathed. "I fell in love with you so quickly that it was pathetic."

"We've both been fools, Alex." Dan laughed. "But I love you, and I do believe that you love me. I think we can handle everything else from there. We have lots to talk about and lots to straighten out. But right now I do want to take a bath. We're going to get married."

"Now?"

"Now. I can't chance you being a free woman a second longer. I want all the strings attached—both ways. Ali is going to have his mullah marry us. It will be a Muslim ceremony, of course. And of course, I'll be entitled to three more wives—"

"Amusing, D'Alesio, amusing."

"But it will be very legal, and very binding. I might have been slow to make a commitment, but I'm a big believer in till death do us part. Are you willing to extend your pact with the devil for a lifetime?"

Alex smiled slowly. "A dozen lifetimes," she said softly.

Dan kissed her lips briefly but tenderly. "We have to hurry then. I have a helicopter coming for us in an hour. Ali is lending us his palace in Abu Dhabi for a honeymoon week. And I intend to enjoy every minute! Servants leaving food at our door, silk sheets, the moonlight on the balcony . . . you can dress up in those little nothing silk harem outfits so that I can undress you and you can feed me grapes one by one—"

"What about you?" Alex demanded.

"Oh, I don't know. I tend to think that six-foot-three men look rather ridiculous in harem outfits!"

"No!" Alex laughed. "Aren't you going to feed me a few grapes?"

"I'll be very happy, my love, to feed you a few grapes. In fact, I intend to keep that garrulous mouth of yours very, very busy."

The moon was a disc of silver casting gentle ivory rays through the balcony window. Thousands of stars dotted the sky, and Alex delighted in them as the breeze off the Persian Gulf caressed her cheeks.

For so long it seemed she had existed in chaos; now she had found paradise. And though she appreciated each of the sensual attributes of her present location, she knew that no matter where she was, she would feel the same shivering, trembling, content excitement because Dan was with her.

He came up behind her, slipping his arms around her waist, nuzzling her neck with slow, moist kisses. She smiled, clasping the hands that held her. "This was a wonderful idea," she told him huskily.

"Yes, I think so," he murmured. He spun her around in his arms, his eyes sparkling vividly before they closed as his lips found hers. His kiss was tender and evocative, more drawing than demanding. His hands ran massaging patterns down her back, pressing her against his growing desire as they splayed over her lower back, then explored her hips and lifted her closer as they covered her buttocks.

Her breathing was jagged when he released her. "A really wonderful idea. . . ." she murmured.

He smiled, and she took a moment just to love the angled lines of his face, the nose that was just slightly crooked, the furrow in his brow, the strength of his chin, the shape of his volatile mouth. She reached out a hand to run the fingers down his cheek; he caught her hand and kissed each knuckle tenderly. Then the devil jet returned to his eyes and he began to kiss her fingers, suckling them with such guileless insinuation that she laughed while feeling the smoldering fire begin to leap to flame within her.

"You are decadent, Mr. D'Alesio," she murmured.

"I do hope so, Doctor." He lifted her high in his arms so that she stared down at him as he turned and walked across the mosaic floor to the bed with its silks and billowing canopies. She held on to his shoulders as he began to allow her to slide slowly down, her body coming into complete contact with his, feeling the friction of each nuance of his muscles, the angle of his hips, the hardness of his masculinity. He set her on the bed so that she was kneeling, and caught his breath as she reached to release the tie on his robe. She leaned against him, pressing her lips to his chest, loving the rasp of his crisp dark chest hair against her cheek as she nuzzled him. Impishly she teased his flesh with just the tip of her tongue, to be rewarded by a soft groan. His hands wound into her hair, lifting her face to his. "I love you, Alex," he told her tensely.

"I love you," she returned softly, suddenly hesitant as she studied his body with the moonlight highlighting his bronze muscles and creating the intrigue of shadows.

His hands caressed her cheeks, then followed a trail down her throat to slip beneath the silk of her robe, sliding it from her shoulders. He cupped her breasts in his hands, smiling at her intake of breath as he moved his palms over her nipples.

"I think I'm a breast man," he murmured, nudging her backward so that he could brace a knee upon the bed as he dipped his head to do homage to her breasts, kissing one while massaging the other, repeating the action to caress each swollen, aching mound with equal attention. Alex groaned at his ministrations, her fingers winding into his dark hair as she lost all strength in trembling abandon.

"Dan. . . ."

He slipped his arms around her back and lowered her to the bed, removing the remaining silk from her torso and limbs. His lips hovered over hers as he whispered softly, "You do have the most beautiful breasts . . . so firm and yet soft, delicate and yet demanding. But then I may be a leg man. I'll have to find out. . . ."

"Dan!" She gasped out his name as he suddenly left her to take her foot in his hands and kiss the toes, sending tremors shaking through her as he lightly touched between them with his tongue. His hands roamed over her calves and he followed them with his lips, biting lightly along the inside until his trail had brought him between her thighs.

"Oh, Dan . . . please . . ."

She suddenly arched high against him, abandoning herself to the delicious vortex of need. She was weak with desire and yet strong with it, responding to his lightest touch, giving, pulsing, offering her complete trust and opening to his pleasure in the sweetest of homages to his loving quest of her body. "Dan . . . oh . . . Dan . . ."

"Move, sweetheart," he whispered to her. "Don't hold back. I want it all. I love to know that it feels good."

He was beside her again, watching her again, running his fingers over her breasts, her belly, her soft femininity. "Alex, you really are so beautiful, so perfect."

She curled against him, locking her legs with his, burying her face in his shoulder, biting lightly at his neck, then passionately seeking to ignite the uncontrollable fires within him as he had in her. Her breathing was jagged, her voice husky and weak. "I think I'm a chest woman," she returned, seeking out male nipples and luxuriating in his catch of breath. "But I just may be a hip woman. I'll have to see. . . ."

"Oh, Alex."

"Here, Dan?"

"Ummm. Everywhere. . . ."

She took him at his word, touching him everywhere, sure of her love, sure of herself. And she radiated with his whispers, following his guiding commands, finding pleasure that spurred her own to greater and greater heights as she gave it.

But Dan was incapable of being still. Even as she revered his body with delicate, erotic fingers, he was seeking her again, taunting her nipples to hard rouge crests that throbbed for him, probing for the moist, welcoming intimacy he knew would be his between silken limbs that trembled and parted to his touch.

He lowered himself over her slowly, watching her eyes. They were half closed; gold in the moonlight, the lime and liquid amber dazzling with the sexuality she had learned to give so freely. He thrust into her deeply, filling her to her womb, and he loved the awe in her eyes, the way they flew open to meet his, the sweet smile that filtered onto her lips just before she gasped and encircled his back with strong, clinging arms, his hips with long, shapely legs.

There was a rightness of being within her, an embrace unlike any he had ever known. It was, and would always be, silver moonlight. And it was moonlight that exploded through him, from him and into her after the swirling magic had crested in that moment of ultimate rapture, ultimate intimacy. He was part of her; he knew she knew it, and that she loved that afterfeeling of holding part of him within her as much as she loved the ecstasy was just another thing that he adored about her.

They lay together, limbs entwined, replete.

"How do you feel about children?" he asked her after a while.

"Fine."

"Do you think a year would be too soon? I'm selfish, I want time together, but I'm also thirty-eight."

"Old man. A year sounds lovely. Boy or girl?"

"Both please—one at a time, a two-year interval. Am I being too demanding?"

"Yes, but I happen to like the demand."

"Great. Do you think I could have my grapes now?"

Alex laughed, and decided he could have his grapes. Every

man deserved his fantasy. And he was capable of making a snack of grapes into the most erotic experience, of making love again, and again.

"There are a million ways to make love," he told her solemnly, guiding her to him. "And in the next week I'd like to explore as many as possible. Am I being too demanding?"

"Yes," Alex whispered, "but I happen to like the demand."

She had never been more content, more exhausted, more replete, more comfortable within a man's arms. Consequently she slept like a baby, and the soft ringing went unheeded by her for a long time. She opened her eyes with a sweet, incredulous smile for Dan.

"I really do hear bells," she told him.

He grimaced. "No, I'm afraid not. It's the phone."

"Phone?" She had never noticed one in the room.

"Yeah, Ali keeps them, but he doesn't like them, so he hides them." He was up, delving through the Oriental nighttables. He found it in a top drawer, picked it up and then muttered, "Why am I bothering? I'm on my honeymoon."

He dived back into the bed, catching Alex around the midriff and leaving her breathless with laughter.

The phone kept ringing.

Alex struggled from beneath him. "I have this thing about phones," she murmured apologetically.

"Really?" he murmured, kissing her torso. "I have this thing about navels . . ."

He proved it by kissing hers as thoroughly as he might her mouth, making her gasp out the "hello" she finally managed to aim into the receiver.

"Alex?"

The voice was hesitant and feminine. Throaty. Incredibly sexy. It could only be one person.

"Kelly?"

"Yes! Oh, Alex! I've been trying to get you! What with the newspaper articles and all. Are you all right? I mean really all right?"

"Fine. *Fine!*" Alex gasped again as Dan lifted his weight over hers and began whispering lasciviously in her ear.

"Did you really marry D'Alesio."

"Yes, I did."

"Who is it?" Dan suddenly demanded.

Alex covered the mouthpiece as Kelly rattled on.

"Kelly."

"Who is Kelly?"

"A very good friend of mine."

"Alex!" Kelly complained. "Are you listening to me? That's so wonderful. I'm still sure the sheikh would have been more romantic."

Alex grinned, meeting Dan's eyes with a shrug. "Kelly thinks I should have gotten the sheikh."

"She does, does she?" Dan grasped the phone from her. "Hello, Kelly. Hi, Dan D'Alesio. Sorry, she gets me, not the sheikh. But hey, listen, I did my best. I abducted her across the desert on a black horse and the whole bit. And right now I'm busy trying to teach her Middle Eastern delights. She'll have to call you back. We're both kind of swept away, you know what I mean?"

"Dan!" Alex protested, laughing. His jet eyes caught hers with love and amusement and demand. He handed the phone back to her. "Say 'good-bye, Kelly,' " he commanded sternly.

Alex smiled slowly. "Good-bye, Kelly."

She replaced the receiver on its cradle and felt the sizzle of jet as he took her back into his arms. "*Definitely* too demanding," she murmured huskily, "but I *definitely* do like the demand."

EPILOGUE

UPI—May 10

CROSBY WRAPS UP EXPEDITION IN VALLEY OF THE QUEENS

A chapter within the annals of ancient Egypt was closed this afternoon when Dr. James Crosby logged in the last of the treasures from the tomb of the Pharaoh Anelokep, discovered by him last July in the Valley of the Queens.

Now that the expedition is completed, the tomb is open to the public. The vast array of gold and art taken from the tomb will first be on display in the Cairo Museum; from there it will go on loan to major cities within Europe and the United States.

It appears that the curse of the pharaohs connected with the tomb was put to rest at the beginning of the expedition; the death of Wayne Randall last August is the only loss that can be associated with the tomb of Anelokep. Randall was killed after attempting to bury alive in the tomb his ex-wife —Crosby's daughter—and broadcast journalist Daniel D'Alesio.

Apparently the tomb has brought good luck to the principal participants in its discovery. Dr. James Crosby recently married his Egyptian assistant, Lani Habu, and Daniel D'Alesio and Dr. Alexandria Crosby Randall were married in a Muslim ceremony and renewed their vows at Crosby's marriage in a Christian ceremony.

Sheikh Ali Sur Sheriff, financer of the dig, was presented with two sons by two wives during the months of the expedition. He also struck oil again on tribal land near the Persian Gulf.

With the excavation complete, Dr. James Crosby announced that he was returning to Chicago with his bride before going on the lecture circuit. The D'Alesios are planning a month's stay with Sheikh Ali Sur Sheriff, in Abu Dhabi, after which they too will return to Chicago.

Mr. D'Alesio's next documentary will be on travel down China's Yangtze River. His wife, he says, will accompany him. D'Alesio also announced, "I've recently purchased a television station within the Greater Chicago area, and we'll spend the majority of the year at home. We also plan to use our summers to film television specials and documentaries. But, my wife is an Egyptologist, and we have promised each other a trip back to Egypt every summer. We also plan to spend two weeks out of every year in the United Arab Emirates. We have a vested interest in Arabian nights."

All-new

Candlelight Newsletter

An exceptional, *free* offer awaits readers of Dell's incomparable Candlelight Ecstasy and Supreme Romances.

Subscribe to our all-new CANDLELIGHT NEWSLETTER and you will receive—at absolutely no cost to you—exciting, exclusive information about today's finest romance novels and novelists. You'll be part of a select group to receive sneak previews of upcoming Candlelight Romances, well in advance of publication.

You'll also go behind the scenes to "meet" our Ecstasy and Supreme authors, learning firsthand where they get their ideas and how they made it to the top. News of author appearances and events will be detailed, as well. And contributions from the Candlelight editor will give you the inside scoop on how she makes her decisions about what to publish—and how *you* can try your hand at writing an Ecstasy or Supreme.

You'll find all this and more in Dell's CANDLELIGHT NEWSLETTER. And best of all, *it costs you nothing*. That's right! It's Dell's way of thanking our loyal Candlelight readers and of adding another dimension to your reading enjoyment.

Just fill out the coupon below, return it to us, and look forward to receiving the first of many CANDLELIGHT NEWSLETTERS—overflowing with the kind of excitement that only enhances our romances!

Return to: DELL PUBLISHING CO., INC.   B340A
        Candlelight Newsletter • Publicity Department
        245 East 47 Street • New York, N.Y. 10017

Name_____

Address_____

City_____

State_____Zip_____